The Thousand-Year Spy

Jeff Wallace

By the same author:
The Man Who Walked Out of the Jungle
Rapidan

2024, Jeff Wallace

Historical fiction / suspense / literary fiction / World War II / espionage / military / Great Britain / Sweden / Germany

The Thousand-Year Spy / Jeff Wallace

ISBN
978-0-9983291-8-5

Glossary of Abbreviations

Allied:

COSSAC: Chief of Staff, Supreme Allied Commander, the staff entity planning OVERLORD, the invasion of continental Europe.

MI-6: The British Secret Service, Great Britain's legendary foreign espionage organization.

OSS: The Office of Strategic Services, America's wartime intelligence service that supplanted the Coordinator of Information, established in 1941 as the nation's first civilian intelligence agency. William J. Donovan directed both.

SHAEF: Supreme Headquarters, Allied Expeditionary Force, the headquarters commanding Allied forces in northwest Europe, led by General Dwight D. Eisenhower.

German:

OKW: *Oberkommando der Wehrmacht*, the headquarters of the German military during World War II. The Abwehr, Germany's military intelligence service, was subordinate to OKW.

RSHA: *Reichssicherheitshauptamt*, the Nazi umbrella organization governing the SD and the Gestapo (the secret police).

SD: *Sicherheitsdienst*. The twin sister of the Gestapo, the SD was a key intelligence organization of the Nazi party and responsible for counterespionage and rooting out perceived enemies of the Reich in Germany and in occupied countries.

SS: *Schutzstaffel*, the paramilitary wing of the Nazi party.

Swedish:

AS: *Allmänna Säkerhetstjänsten*, Sweden's General Security Service.

Part I

I therefore command that from now on all enemies on so-called commando expeditions encountered by German troops in Europe or Africa, whether these commandos are ostensibly uniformed soldiers or sabotage agents, with or without weapons, whether in battle or fleeing, are to be annihilated to the last man. It is immaterial whether they land from ships or in aircraft or by parachute. Even if these wretches upon being discovered try to surrender, mercy will be refused as a matter of principle. In every case of this kind, a detailed report will be made to the highest headquarters. Should members of these commandos, such as agents, saboteurs, or whatnot, come into military custody by other means, such as through the police in one of the occupied territories, they are to be delivered to the Sicherheitsdienst forthwith. I shall hold any commander or officer who neglects to carry out this order or to instruct the troops under his command to be answerable to a court martial.
--Adolf Hitler, October 1942

Extreme remedies are most appropriate for extreme diseases.
--Hippocrates, c. 460-357 B.C.

– 1 –

Late January 1944

With nicotine-stained fingers, General Dwight D. Eisenhower crushed out the glowing Camel, the hour's fourth cigarette, on the stone wall outside Chequers, the country house of British prime ministers. The grounds and facade preserved an evanescent glow in the misty twilight. He should head back in before the dampness wrinkled his uniform. Then again, it was damp *inside* the place. And cold.

Initially he'd declined the invitation to this evening's dinner. True to their traditions, the upper-class British hosted countless social affairs, and if he attended even a fraction of those to which he was invited, they'd nip at his precious time the way the wind made off with the dry topsoil in his native Kansas.

No house like this one in Kansas, he mused. The bronze-shaded-brick mansion overlooked the dreamy soft meadows of Buckinghamshire. He'd been here on prior occasions as Prime Minister Winston Churchill's guest. Late into the evenings the two had discussed history and especially wars the Prime Minister loved to expound upon and whose particulars Eisenhower, from his military schooling and readings, could debate with acumen. The shared appreciation had helped him secure Churchill's favor, without which he'd never have ascended to the seniormost military command among the western Allies.

His meteoric rise could segue to an abrupt plummet, he reminded himself. Aside from Churchill's embrace, what anchored him was the confidence of President Franklin D. Roosevelt and of U.S. Army Chief of Staff General George C. Marshall, his superior and mentor in Washington. Recently Marshall and the other members of the Combined Chiefs of Staff had sent him the draft of his formal mission directive, two pages that summarized his daunting task and whose contents essentially could be distilled to two words: Defeat Germany.

The directive did not specify *all* his tasks. There were critical others, the principal of which, in his mind, was reducible to almost as few words: Get along with Churchill. He considered it Unwritten Mandate Number One. As to how to carry it out, nobody could instruct him, not even the erudite Marshall. At every meeting where Churchill was present, Eisenhower wielded his mix of skills—the likeable personality, clarity of expression, honed judgment, and mental toughness—to make the relationship work and sometimes to hold his ground. He'd learned it was important to stand up to the man to gain his respect. On the other hand, Eisenhower didn't argue with him frivolously. The topic had to be imperative. Too much was at stake.

No sooner had he turned down tonight's invitation than Churchill's personal assistant phoned to say that "the PM" had something important to convey and wished to do so in person. Eisenhower accepted—see Unwritten Mandate Number One—and postponed tonight's scheduled planning meeting to a later hour. The change would disrupt the schedules of dozens of senior officers, American and British alike, not that pointing it out to Churchill would do any good. Great men, among whom the Prime Minister counted himself, did not trouble themselves with sparing the time of others.

The door creaked open, casting a yellow rhombus into the mist and framing a young aide in a dark suit. "General? He's asked that you come in, if you're not busy."

Probably these had been Churchill's verbatim words, uttered in the statesman's gruff mumble and laced with irony, as if anyone were ever too busy to respond to his direct summons. In the study, the smoky air hovered thickly amid books, austere furniture, portraits of former prime ministers, and one of Winston's attractive American mother in a black gown. The tread-worn, crimson-turned-pinkish oriental rug might have originated in Peshawar or Kabul, where Winston had served as a young lieutenant nearly half a century ago. Seated, he puffed on a red-and-gold-banded Havana. Eisenhower, never one to pass up a smoke, flicked his lighter on another Camel.

"Sherry, General?" said Churchill.

"No, thanks. I have a meeting later tonight."

"Oh?"

"At COSSAC." The cryptic reply expanded to Chief of Staff, Supreme Allied Commander, a planning entity whose nerve center resided at Norfolk

House on St. James Square, London. Tonight's deliberations would concentrate on OVERLORD, the forthcoming Allied invasion of continental Europe. The details were a closely guarded secret very few were privy to. Churchill was among the few; the young aide was not.

"Ask the gentleman in," Churchill told the aide.

A raven-haired man entered. Taller than average, probably in his late thirties, he had an athlete's build that Eisenhower, who'd played varsity football at West Point, instantly perceived. He wore a pristinely tailored three-piece suit and a striped tie from one of the prep schools or colleges whose colors wellborn British typically recognized, and Eisenhower didn't, even if over his months in England he'd come to appreciate some of the distinctions among the English classes. The term 'gentleman' differentiated a man of lineage and social standing, not necessarily of wealth, though often the case. Such status tended to confer an inalienable sangfroid, and the entrant seemed to possess it in abundance.

The young aide left, closing the door behind.

Churchill said, "Sebastian Wentworth of MI-6. One of Menzies's top men." Stewart Menzies, Eisenhower was aware, was the head of MI-6.

Eisenhower shook Wentworth's hand. The Prime Minister grumbled, "Speak."

Eisenhower had gleaned too that, among the British elites, certain standards of behavior simply were taken for granted. Toward a common citizen on the street, Churchill would have acted with gracious courtesy. To his fellow high-flier of British society, as well as to his beleaguered staff, he was brusque. No need to be otherwise.

"I'm here, sir, because we face an impasse." His crisp tone was deferential yet confident. "A rare opportunity has developed wherein we might mount a covert intelligence endeavor to improve our chances with OVERLORD. It requires the infiltration into neutral Sweden of a certain American with an uncommon mix of languages. Unfortunately, the timelines are short."

"Sounds like OSS business," said Eisenhower. He recalled that Brigadier General William J. Donovan, the Director of the Office of Strategic Services, was currently in London.

"Indeed, sir," replied Wentworth. "You see, we approached General Donovan with the proposal, and we explained…"

"Get to it!" snapped the Prime Minister.

"He declined to help. Assuredly he has his reasons, but so unusual is the chance, I doubt we shall see another like it. And without the American participation we requested, I'm afraid we lack anyone who can speak the mix of pivotal languages with a native flair."

Eisenhower saw the move. Donovan hadn't liked the proposal, whatever it entailed, and the British spymasters were jumping over his head. Churchill didn't have to weigh in. His presence made two things clear: The matter commanded extraordinary importance, and, if Churchill chose to, he could loft it over Eisenhower's head to President Roosevelt.

Eisenhower said, "When did you speak to General Donovan?"

"Yesterday, sir."

"He has the full picture?"

"Yes, we briefed him verbally."

Meaning it wasn't on paper. "All right. I'll look into it."

Wentworth was about to say more, maybe to stress the urgency or sensitivity, when he caught Churchill's glare. It meant, stop talking, you've made your pitch. The MI-6 man nodded, pivoted, and left.

Churchill puffed on his cigar. "There's another part, General. Perhaps you should sit."

Eisenhower did.

"I'm afraid I must confess to you a most distressing development," said the Prime Minister.

At COSSAC later that evening, the delayed meeting was about to begin. The OVERLORD plan, many months in draft, awaited Eisenhower's approval. To pen his signature was more than a formality. It would set in motion intensive preparations for a massive enterprise whose viability and success would depend on many things, including some he could not control, such as the industrial production of essential materiel, German force deployments, and the weather.

Eisenhower pulled aside his Chief of Staff, Lieutenant General Walter Bedell "Beetle" Smith, and spoke *sotto voce* to Smith's ear. "Have you heard of a proposal yesterday by MI-6 to Donovan at OSS?"

"No."

In 45 seconds, Eisenhower summarized the meeting with Churchill and Wentworth, leaving out only the 'distressing development' the Prime Minister had disclosed at the end. "Get Donovan's side of it, discreetly, as soon as possible."

Beetle Smith stepped out as the meeting commenced. His job was to attend to his commander's wishes, and he paid keen attention to Ike's phraseology. The word *discreetly* meant to keep the inquiry out of regular staff channels. Ike's description of the Chequers meeting was likewise telling. The British might have chosen a more conventional way to impart their complaint. Wentworth, the MI-6 man, had not been a dinner guest, and no other British officials had been present during the meeting in the study. Nothing had been handed over on paper. The nuances telegraphed that the Prime Minister did not want the matter mingled in the normal protocols that surrounded his actions. The Brits were aware too that William "Wild Bill" Donovan, an American legend, was President Roosevelt's personal appointee, and the OSS was not under Eisenhower's command, though its activities in Europe were.

Beetle penned a quick note he passed to his aide: 'General Donovan in my office, 0600 tomorrow.'

At five minutes before midnight, the call reached Donovan at his suite at London's Claridge Hotel. He listened, replied, "All right," and hung up. The caller, identifying himself as a staff officer at SHAEF—Supreme Headquarters, Allied Expeditionary Force—had stated only that the Chief of Staff wished to see Donovan at the Navy Building at 6 a.m. tomorrow. The timing suggested urgency, and Beetle Smith's involvement implied Eisenhower's. All this was obvious. The issue, whatever it might be, was not.

He returned to bed and tried to fall asleep, pulling the bedcovers to his chin. The room was chilly; not even a posh Mayfair hotel heated its rooms at night. Claridge's had been his London home away from home since his pre-war travels here in 1940. When America entered the war, the hotel became an American haunt, the fourth floor converted to a temporary military command post. Extravagant by the standards of wartime England, his room boasted a spacious sitting area and private bath. And the OSS London headquarters on Grosvenor Street was just around the corner.

Though the OSS fell under the authority of the U.S. Joint Chiefs of Staff, Donovan's personal stature, his relationship with fellow New Yorker and Columbia Law School classmate Franklin D. Roosevelt, and the civilian character of the organization had helped forge a margin of independence from the jumpy military bureaucracy. What was going on?

One possibility made him uneasy. Might the British Secret Service have brought to General Eisenhower the ill-conceived scheme they had unveiled to Donovan yesterday, and that he'd turned down? His three-plus years of dealings with MI-6, if not wholly positive, at least had been collegial. The Brits had made it their praxis to engage with him, as he had with them, in the semi-informal channels between the two intelligence services.

Unable to sleep, he padded to the sitting room and commenced to pace, cinching the belt on his silk bath robe that strained to go around his middle. In World War I, he'd not had to worry about getting fat; dodging bullets tended to keep a person lean. These days the dangers were of a different sort. When World War I ended, he returned to the United States a celebrated hero. He served as Assistant Attorney General at the U.S. Justice Department and later founded a successful New York law firm catering to wealthy people and corporations, some with worldwide business dealings. Through these connections, he gained prodigious insights into international power dynamics, and these led to his designation in 1940 as President Roosevelt's personal envoy, his mission to evaluate Britain's ability to survive what at the time seemed like a hopeless mismatch against the Nazi war machine. No question, the British used him to gain America's backing, granting him, a private citizen whose sole status was that he had the president's ear, a statesman's welcome, tour of their war zones, and the knowledge of capabilities they'd shown to no foreigner until then. To be so favored a guest of the British might lead you to believe he was an Anglophile. No, he was a pragmatist seeking his own country's vital advantage. If Britain lost the fight, the consequences for America augured dismally. He returned to Washington and briefed the president and senior cabinet members, even used his law firm's researchers to dig up a legal precedent for the lend-lease initiative FDR subsequently advocated to Congress. When in July 1941 Donovan took up his role as the chief of America's first civilian intelligence agency—initially titled the Coordinator of Information, later morphing into the military-incorporated OSS—the Brits helped him, lifting the veil on the secret methodologies they had perfected over the centuries.

The tutelage came at a price. Having championed him to head American intelligence, the British Secret Service regarded him and his service as their wards. They demanded approval authority over all U.S. intelligence activities mounted from the British Isles, colonies, and zones of influence. Beneath their patina of courtesy, they lorded their prerogatives. The war required resources—troops, ships, aircraft—and America's capacity to supply them dwarfed that of the British. In fields where the Americans lagged, and particularly in espionage, the Brits treated their former colonial subjects like stark neophytes.

Neophytes? Try running a New York law firm!

Calm down. You're not certain what they're up to.

He recalled an occasion when a senior MI-6 representative, having perhaps downed too many aperitifs, had berated him about America's "late entry" to the war. Donovan was tempted to point out that European imperialism had produced the wars of the twentieth century. Staunch allies though they were, Britain and America had their own distinctive goals in the conflict. Not that Britannia didn't favor the eradication of evil, the liberation of Europe, and chiefly her own survival, but her inveterate obsession was the continuance of her empire. Britons, particularly the upper classes, were addicted to grandeur, and nothing was grander than history's largest hegemony, encompassing five hundred million willing and not-so-willing subjects, with whom Americans, their colonial shackles thrown off but not forgotten, tended to empathize. On this crux, the sentiment of the majority of Americans who wanted to stay out of the war might have proved insuperable, had Pearl Harbor not tipped the scales. Yes, crucial U.S. interests were at stake, but having been around the same bend with the Europeans barely a quarter of a century ago, Donovan found it hard not to see them as arrogant swankpots who perpetually sowed their own catastrophes.

At the window, he wedged open the blackout curtain to look down on Brock Street. Nothing seemed to move in the quiescent British capital. An illusion. Shrouded in darkness, the city prepared, restocked, planned. Reluctantly he had to believe that MI-6 had maneuvered around him, their intent, couched in their inimitable civility, to ram their misguided caper down his throat.

The question: What should he do about it?

If he had his way, they weren't going to schoolmaster him this time.

– 2 –

Late January 1944

A jingle sounded. Alistair Bird's bony fingers dangled a bell he used to summon his analysts to his morning meeting.

Linnea Thorsell pinched together the edges of the knitted wool shawl her mother had sent her. She couldn't seem to get warm, though why that should be, she couldn't say. Russian born, the daughter of a Russian and a Swede, she had winter-hardy bloodlines, and clothes wise, she was aptly decked out in the weighty serge of a U.S. Army second lieutenant, not to mention the shawl. The fault might be with the location of her desk, in a bare-bricked corner next to a window whose panes bled the bleak chill of London's January. The view between the open blackout curtains was of chimneys receding like desolate trees toward the mist-gray slurry of the Thames River.

Don't look—it would just make her colder.

The weak light swabbed a wall tacked with maps of her topic area, Eastern Europe, currently the locus of the Russian-German front. The maps' only mark-up was a paper arrow she'd hand-lettered in Cyrillic, taped to a lower margin, and aimed at her desk. **Сибирь**, it read. Siberia.

"Your attention, please," commenced Bird. "Our morning meeting begins at nine sharp. Please try to be present and not in the loo or the reading room." A former academician and cognizant of the blandness of his innately monotoned voice, he tried perhaps too fervently to enliven it with inflections, churning a pitchy ebullience. Linnea's friend and section mate, British lieutenant Ivett Kranz, had cautioned her, "Don't listen too keenly to Alistair, it will make you dizzy."

"Everyone is reminded to fully close the blackout curtains at dusk," he went on, "and to examine the fringes for leakage. The wardens three times have cited this building; no violations from this section, I'm cheered to say. Please keep it so."

Could German bombardiers thousands of feet above spot a hairline of light? The ones who could were the home-defense auxiliaries whose logs of light transgressions brought raps to the knuckles of section heads like Bird.

"The coal keepers aren't receiving supplies in the quantities requested, and they barely suit to mete out to all the offices. A day may come when we will have to go without. Not the choice time of year, I dare say. Please be sparing with the coals."

Сибирь just got a little chillier.

"On morale topics, Saturday's dance at the Emporium will begin at seven-thirty, half an hour earlier than usual so as to accommodate a live band, quite the delight."

It was anyone's guess whether a live band would brew up a delight or a cacophony. The latter was the stronger bet. Should she subject her ears to another bashing, and herself to being hit upon by innumerable boozy officers? One admirer had stared into her cobalt-blue eyes and blurted they were luminous. She took it as a tepid compliment. She was mildly pretty, she supposed, if nonetheless a bit sturdier than she liked. The men at the dances so outnumbered the women that to be pretty to any extent, exceedingly, mildly, or hardly at all, sufficed to draw plenty of attention.

"Today's lunch dish will be Irish lamb stew," said Bird. The assembly groaned. They were too familiar with the mess hall's version of the dish.

He opened the floor to the analysts. A few raised complaints about the short deadlines of papers and the non-timely delivery of requested maps and reference books. He promised to look into their predicaments as best he could. "One more thing," he said. "The lending library asks that whoever inadvertently walked off with *Rebecca* to kindly return it. The novel is popular, and both the library's copies are missing and neither signed out." He scanned his audience as if the culprit might raise a hand. "Have a productive day."

In Bird's section, Linnea was the only American, an experiment in "intelligence interchange," so she'd been told. Why had the job gone to an OSS analyst with barely a year's experience? She'd asked her friend Ivett. "Because you're *harmless*, dear," said Ivett. "Imagine, had they foisted on us some stiff-necked Yank colonel. We'd have shunned him like the plague. You, we might take a liking to, eventually."

Her workplace was in an east-end, soot-tinted brickwork dubbed Factory House, which as the name implied had hosted industry in some bygone day. Disjointed pipework traced the ceilings, sunken metal rails bisected the floors, and stout eyelets dappled the walls. From one of the eyelets someone had hung a flowerpot that dripped water and made a slimy green circle on the floor beneath. Nobody cared, the floor was cement, just don't slip on it. The section's fifteen analysts had arranged their desks in two concentric curls around a black coal stove, its pipe an arthritic finger that vanished into the residual ironmongery overhead. The stovetop glowed cherry red—no doubt it was too profligately stuffed with coal—and currently hosted four metal cups, Linnea's among them, set to boil water for tea or Nescafe. Ivett, her saffron-shaded hair cut even shorter than Linnea's, her feet in socks—customarily she shed her shoes in the office, perhaps to lessen the effect upon others of her six-foot-plus height—sported oven mittens she wrapped around the searing stovepipe, held there for a time, then pressed to her face.

"Looks toasty," said Linnea.

"Have it here," said Ivett.

Linnea leaned in, and her friend feasted her neck and cheeks to a pair of stovepipe-heated, coal-smelling mittens. "Feels like heaven," she purred.

The OSS comprised men and women who embodied daring, sagacity, and foreign-language proficiency, the latter often amassed in immigrant households or as the children of missionaries who lived abroad. Along with training, the skills qualified the operations officers to be infiltrated into enemy-occupied countries. The organization harbored another cadre too, of analysts. Selected for their reputations in academia or industry, or at the recommendations of university professors, they mentally dissected Americas foes for the benefit of decisionmakers. Most of the analysts were based in Washington D.C., many on the wartime Mall in hastily erected buildings called 'tempos.' Only a small minority worked abroad, some in Hawaii, others at the OSS London Station's Research and Analysis Branch—to which

Linnea, though she was detailed to Factory House, technically belonged—and a handful at facilities elsewhere.

Of special interest to her was the recently lifted siege of Leningrad. Born there when the city was called Petrograd—formerly Saint Petersburg, Russia—she fuzzily recalled ornate buildings and big plazas full of gulls she'd feared would swoop down and peck at her head. Perhaps she'd witnessed such an event, and in the proximity of the gulls she kept her little hand protectively atop her hair, the other clinging to her mother's.

The family left Petrograd when she was five. Her mother, Natasha Vasilieva, would say they left everything. Enshrining the aristocratic culture that had vanished in the Soviet Union and survived elsewhere only in petite diasporas, Natasha lamented at how she missed the city's sophistication and those fabulous White Nights of summer. "I thought my Petrograd was *neizmennyj,*" she whinged. Immutable. Linnea had departed Russia too young to be sentimental about it. To pine for bygone Petrograd always struck her as akin to believing in ghosts, a whimsy of the imagination. And if you saw one? Well, you were nuts.

Her father, a vivacious Swede ten years older than her mother, was the one who brought the family out of the turbulent Soviet Union to Stockholm. Sten Thorsell's fawn hair almost matched the shade of his daughter's. An international salesman, he'd earned a certain stature in the world of business, if not yet the great wealth he craved. At home he liked to sing, and he taught his daughter the folk songs of his beloved Sweden. In 1933, when she was thirteen, he moved them again, from Stockholm to Hamburg, Germany. This time she was decidedly sentimental about it. To leave her Swedish friends dejected her, and she detested Hamburg, where at her new school the kids called her *die Ausländerin* and *die dumme Schwedin.* Though she quickly amassed German—her language talents surpassed even her father's—she longed to return to Stockholm, which in her heart was home.

She shouted at her father, "Why did you bring us here?"

"Linnea, please be patient. Time will heal everything."

"No, it won't!"

He ushered her to the window of their spacious apartment. Beyond, the River Elbe glittered like a puddle of molten silver. Here was an opportunity, he told her in Swedish, the *lingua franca* between father and daughter. Despite the economic depression clutching Europe, he would earn a fortune brokering Swedish-manufactured steel. "The Germans crave Swedish steel, and I will sell it to them!" See the elegant furniture, the stylish new clothes, the maid, the chauffeur, the fancy automobile. They would live in luxury!

To their apartment he invited businessmen, and as if she didn't despise the place enough, he insisted she dress up in her new clothes and play the cute princess. A year dragged by. Between the social hosting, he labored relentlessly, juggling timetables, licenses, berths. He should have mastered his job, inured himself to the stresses; instead, they constricted his heart. In their building's foyer one morning as he was leaving for work, he collapsed and died on the polished marble tiles.

With her father gone, what was left for them in Germany? She begged her mother to return to Stockholm. No, said Natasha Vasilieva; they must emigrate to the United States. She sat her fourteen-year-old daughter down to explain. "Linnea dear, there are things I dread to say. You must listen, so you will understand. Your father told the Germans he had great influence with the Swedish steel companies. He had no such sway. His German business counterparts found out. I believe it was his fear of what would happen that killed him."

Linnea could not imagine her father as fearful. "He was so confident."

"He pretended to be. What he was… what he was…" She buried her face in her hands. "He created his chance to make a fortune by peddling falsehoods. He borrowed great sums of money, for the license, the apartment, the automobile. He said nothing to me of the debts, I learned only after he died. I think I can sell our things and pay the debts to get us out of Germany. In Sweden are more creditors. If we return there, they will compel me to repay. I will never have enough. That is why we cannot go back."

Linnea began to cry.

Her mother said, "From a lie comes evil, always."

Through tears, Linnea growled, "Did you really not know?"

"I sensed something was wrong. I asked and he said not to worry. I should have pressed him. Blame me if you want."

Her mother fired the maid and the chauffeur and sold the car. In the years before her father's death, her mother had called her Linnea *Stenovna*, tacking on the Russian patronymic. Never again would it cross Natasha Vasilieva's lips.

The sale of their belongings commenced. Germans swarmed over the apartment, rummaging through Linnea's stylish dresses, holding them up to their Teutonic scrutiny, tugging at the buttons and lace and picking at the stitches. Her father's clothes went too, the expensive Italian-wool suits and crisp-heeled shoes into which the buyers' children thrust their feet and clopped around like midget storm troopers. Her mother haggled over the prices, only to relinquish things at a fraction of their value. The proceeds sufficed to pay off the German debts and to purchase two trans-Atlantic ship tickets, leaving just one hundred American dollars as their nest egg to renew their lives. The ship was a gargantuan passenger liner that sailed from Copenhagen. On the boarding ramp, tugged upward by her mother's hand clutching hers, Linnea could make out the hazy, unobtainable coast of Sweden across the Øresund.

Her life's experiences thus far—jerked from country to country, stripped of her Swedish friends, mocked by the Germans, left in poverty by her father—had not confected her as one trusting of her fellow man. Warily she regarded the kids who shared the steerage class. Here were Swedes, Danes, Germans, Americans. Tempting, to seek the companionship of the Swedes. On her first night, sizing up the cliques, she decided to become an American.

How do you join a group whose language you don't speak? These children had lived in America and were returning from trips to parts of Europe. Their leader was an olive-skinned boy of Italian descent named Eugenio, Gene to his friends, aggressive and streetwise. Initially he ignored her. When she took to stringing along behind him and his friends, he confronted her. "Fuck off," he said.

"Fuck off," she mimicked.

The reply might have bought her a shove, had Eudoxia not intervened. Greek American and taller and stockier than the others, Eudoxia protected her while tutoring her in the English language. Quickly she learned the names of objects you could point to: the sea and sky, the ship's accoutrements, the clothing, the food. The lessons advanced to the verbs and adjectives. Among the kids, Linnea earned some acceptance by perfectly reproducing their homey accents, of Brooklyn, Philadelphia, and Boston, most of the time having no idea what she was saying. They fed her salacious lines they bid her repeat to adults, and she played along as if the gleam in their eyes had not betrayed them. As her mischievous fixers looked on, she stepped up to a woman passenger and in a low tone said something innocent. No good; they wanted devilment, and she obliged by leading them to filch desserts from the first-class dining cart.

She disembarked in New York City bridling a weak, fragmented, no less enthusiastic English, her fourth language. By the time she enrolled at New York University four years later, her speech was without a detectable foreign accent. Weekdays she attended classes in Greenwich Village, paying her tuition by translating telegrams nights and weekends, graduating in the summer of 1942 with a degree in modern languages. What should she do with her life? She could stay at NYU and teach Russian, a job she'd been offered. Or she could translate telegrams full time. Translating paid better; her languages were in demand. Her mother meanwhile had gained fruitful employment at a paperboard factory across the Manhattan Bridge. For the first time since they arrived in America, they had the money to move from the one-room, lower-east-side hovel where they'd lived for eight years to a better apartment. Here as there they conversed predominantly in Russian, sometimes Swedish, her encouragement to her mother to practice English making only slight headway.

The summer of her college graduation, a man in a gray suit approached her at the translation service. He introduced himself as the representative of an obscure-sounding organization in Washington D.C. and interviewed her for a job, his thickset jowls double-parenthesizing a sunny smile that didn't pair with his stone-hard eyes. Of the OSS he said not a word, and she wouldn't have recognized the nomenclature anyway. No surprise that the government would court her for her languages in wartime, yet his questions had nothing to do with her translation skills he seemed already well informed about. Did she participate in sports? Most women did not; she was no exception. How about games? She played chess at the Russian chess club. Ah, the Russian chess club. Did she consort with communists? No.

True, sort of. She didn't tell the recruiter about her affair with Christopher, an assistant professor of English at NYU. Christopher had attended communist meetings. Was he a communist? She doubted it. There was a lot to doubt about Christopher. His head resembled a vanilla ice cream cone, the crown of pale-blond hair, the sides tapering to a pointy chin, his far-apart eyes lending him the semblance of an intellectual. When she told him about her anger toward her father, he asked why she nursed resentment against someone who was dead. The question was semi-rhetorical; Christopher was not empathetic by nature, nor was he as smart as he appeared. Still there were good things about him. He had money and took her out to restaurants and to movies and Broadway plays. He had a car and taught her to drive, a valuable gift. Smugly—damn, she should have known better—she contemplated what to say if he asked her to marry him. Out of the blue, he informed her of a second woman, Paula, his fiancée. But wait! He had conditioned the marriage on Paula's agreement that he could continue to see Linnea. He wanted to introduce the two of them, he said.

How about that.

"I believe you should live all you can," he said. "It's a mistake not to. It doesn't so much matter what you do in particular so long as you live your life." The line, she later discovered, was a near-verbatim quote from Henry James's novel *The Ambassadors*.

Did she love Christopher? If so, did she love him enough to share him in a bizarre triangle? To her astonishment, she had to parry the impulse to save him, this misguided man, as if she could. Her mind shouted that his self-portrayal was a fiction calculated to strum on her heart strings. He must know she'd refuse to meet Paula. The more she thought about it, the more she concluded that only an arrogant manipulator would contrive such a stunt. Her father had been a manipulator. The agonizing part was, she hadn't seen the trait in Christopher, she'd trusted him when she should have regarded him as the lump you spoon out of murky stew. How could *she* of all people have blundered so monumentally?

Because women who are not experienced with men are not wise about them. Wisdom did not come cheap. Hadn't her mother married her father when she was very young?

No more mistakes. She refused to speak to Christopher. Ignored his calls. Eventually he stopped trying.

The government recruiter offered her a position whose base salary was lower than she made translating telegrams. Forget it. Why would she switch to a lesser-paying job? He proved willing to negotiate. A higher salary was possible, he said. All she had to do was accept a commission in the Army. Language premiums would notch up the military pay. He smiled his sunny smile.

A week of testing, lectures, and filling out forms revealed she had joined America's fledgling intelligence service. A phase entitled 'military familiarization' encompassed how to stand at attention, whom to salute, and so forth. Her two weeks of barracks life were a blur, the sole memorable moment when she barged into the wrong building to face a room full of men clumsily plying needles and thread to sew patches on their uniforms. The stitches wobbled like the paths of drunken sailors, and the men stared at her as if she were their mother come to rescue them from a vexing chore.

Dream on.

Ivett restored her mittened hands to the stovepipe. "How's the paper coming?"

Linnea was in the process of drafting a forecast of likely scenarios for Poland. Practiced at its highest form, intelligence analysis aspired to be predictive. For instance, she could say with assurance that the Soviets over the coming months would seize Poland. Exactly when, how, and with what consequences were the elusive details. The analysts had watched the war's tide turn as the Germans lost at Stalingrad, Kursk, and Leningrad, where ten days ago the two-and-one-half-year siege had crumbled. If the public might cheer for the Soviet victories, the analysts didn't; they knew Josef Stalin too well. A monster who'd ordered bloody purges and intentionally starved millions in the Ukraine, he made a secret pact with Hitler in 1939 wherein each state gobbled up half of Poland, then he invaded Finland and annexed the Baltic States. Last April, the Germans announced the discovery of a mass grave in the Katyn Forest in west Russia, the dead numbering more than 4,000, all identified as Polish military officers the Soviets had executed in 1940, certainly on Stalin's orders. The Polish government in exile believed there were many more victims still unearthed. So why had America's and Britain's leaders allied their democracies with a villain? Because to lose to Hitler would be worse. *Exitus acta probat.* The outcome justifies the deed.

Linnea scoured the daily reports, the diplomatic telegrams, and the newspaper accounts. She'd been pressing to gain interviews with intelligence representatives of the Polish government-in-exile, whom she suspected held the bleakest expectations of Soviet intentions toward Poland. The British Foreign Ministry, in charge of access to the expatriate Poles, had yet to grant her permission. She guessed the diplomats welcomed no meddling in their efforts to restore relations between the Polish exile government and the Soviets, severed after the uncovering of the Katyn Forest massacre. "I'm stuck," she told Ivett. "I can't quote a single authoritative source willing to say Stalin will turn Poland into a de-facto Soviet republic, and that's just what the bastard is going to do."

"Who's getting their old country back anyway, after all this?"

Sounded like a theme, how the war would remake Europe's political landscape and by extension alter the balance of power worldwide. A speculative topic, granted. Could she write such a paper? Surely American and British leaders needed to start thinking about the postwar sooner rather than later. Maybe she should propose the idea to Bird. He'd been a professor at an English university, and he brought his pedagogic thinking to wartime intelligence work. A plodder and stickler for timely production, he assigned topics and seemed disinterested in innovation beyond. Didn't mean she couldn't sell it to him.

Now who should appear at the stove but Bird himself, his iron-gray hair a pointy wedge he slicked over a balding pate after patting a moistened sponge he kept on his desk for sealing envelopes. His tea-stained teeth were the color of the floor tiles in the women's loo. He stared at the four nearly identical metal cups on the stovetop. "I say, which is mine?"

"That one's mine," said Linnea. "I dotted the handle with nail paint." She'd borrowed the crimson veneer from the section's secretary, a British enlisted woman nicknamed Dray, reportedly short for Druscilla, whom behind her back the analysts called Dodgy Dray.

"A capital idea," said Bird. "I should mark mine too. Perhaps a loop of knitting wool around the handle. I shall ask my wife for a piece."

When he left, with a sly wink Ivett said, "Will she give him a piece, his wife?"

"If I were her, I'd need something stronger than tea first."

"A double at that."

Laughs. Bad form, to be overheard poking ribald fun at your section head. People would take note, and Bird might find out. Already he'd identified Linnea as the section's prankster. Her first prank had targeted him.

In the mornings when he arrived at his office, a cube with white-painted lower walls and the upper of glass, he always removed his coat and raised a hand without glancing up to tug the light cord that dangled over his desk. Early one morning she snuck into his office and retied the cord a foot higher than it had been. When he showed up, he reached and struck air. He flailed again. Nothing. The analysts watching nearly fell out of their chairs in suppressed laughter.

She had to credit him with a mature man's forbearance; he wasn't angry, merely nonplussed. Yet he zeroed in on her almost at once. Meant there was an informant. Dodgy Dray was a good guess. But wrong to blame her in the absence of proof. And not worth the bother.

Linnea retrieved her hot water and went back to **Сибирь.**

– 3 –

Mid-January 1944

In Berlin's pre-dawn, Willie Mauer groped at the bedside table for his thick eyeglasses. He rose gingerly, trying not to disturb his sleeping wife, fetched his uniform on its hangar, slipped into the parlor, and eased the door closed behind. Quietly he plied a soft-haired brush to remove the lint from the black fabric, twice pressing his finger under his nose to stifle a sneeze. Wretched, the city's dust these days.

Born at the turn of the century, Willie at age three had suffered an illness that left him delicate, almost wispy, his hands so finely boned they resembled a girl's. No wonder his parents kept him from sports, he whose frailty shrieked that any bump would break him like a crystal champagne glass. Another bout with germs surely would kill him. They pictured him becoming a composer or professor of mathematics, callings immaculately uncontaminated.

At age ten, he voiced his wish to join the *Wandervogel*, the German equivalent of the Boy Scouts. All that trekking through the woods would not be good for him, his parents replied. He should stick to his books. In insulating him from life's roughness, they paid insufficient attention to the fervor of his glances at the players on the athletic fields and his disgust at his too-dainty hands.

A teenager during the First World War, he achieved his *Abitur*— certificate of matriculation—at age eighteen and shocked his parents by asking their permission to enlist in the German Army. They must not have heard him correctly. Enlist? Join coarse men in a trench of mud, vermin, and death, after his father had gone to such exertions to arrange his medical deferment? Out of the question. Perhaps he had contracted an infection of the brain. They hired a doctor to examine him.

He might have enlisted anyway. He didn't, because the war ended, and not with victory. Like the fetid backwash from a clogged toilet, societal unrest spewed over Germany. Angry mobs shouted in the streets; gunshots cracked night and day as the right-wing *Freikorps* battled the communists. Berlin was anarchic. His parents deemed the southern town of Heidelberg safer. At the university there, he could study mathematics and the sciences, disciplines he excelled at. They enrolled him in 1919. When they traveled to visit him, he presented himself in clothes impeccably pressed, hair trimmed, fingernails clean. *Gott sei dank,* their son was turning out as he should, his crazy martial impulse the symptom of a tumultuous time. He graduated with honors and returned to Berlin in the spring of 1923. The economy was a wreck, jobs almost nonexistent; any that appeared, people with influence immediately snatched up. Even so, one as bright as Willie and advantaged of his father's connections had prospects to become an assistant professor at the Berlin Technical Institute. A position might avail soon, said the rumors. Was he interested?

In their apartment of oiled oak panels and oriental carpets, he asked his parents to sit. He had three things to say. First, he must thank them. They had worked so hard to raise him. Generously they had sent him to the university. He could never repay them.

His parents beamed, and his father gushed out, *"Du hast es redlich verdient, unser guter Sohn."* You've truly earned it, our good son.

Second, said Willie, he was entering the *Reichsmarine* (the German Navy, as it was called then).

Their mouths dropped open.

Third, he was marrying a baker's daughter.

"Get out," rasped his father.

Jana was the sister of a classmate who had brought her along to watch a collegiate boxing match. Willie, his parents unaware, competed in the lightweight class. The first time he heard her voice was her shout of *"Ja!"* when he landed a right hook on his opponent's chin. Her cheers rang as Willie and the other boxer traded blows. He suffered a bloody lip and bruised face and lost the match. His friend introduced Jana. She did not seem to mind the black and puffy eyes he regarded her through. "You fought spiritedly," she remarked, and it was indicative of their compatibility that he grasped at once what she meant: He should seek out a different sport. She was seven months older, less pretty than vivacious and unpretentious. She liked to shake the baking flour out of her tussock hair the way a dog might purge its fur of rainwater. Intellectually she was not in his league; few people were. Hers was a different style of erudition, yet every bit as potent. They listened to each other. When they argued, it was cogently, and through their twenty years of marriage, he trusted her with his deepest thoughts. Friends had warned him that an only child should not marry another only child. "You are too much alike," they said. The friends had been wrong. The alikeness of Willie and Jana strengthened their marriage. They needed to be strong when they learned they could have no children of their own.

Before the First World War, he would have found it impossible to gain entry to the naval officer corps as he had. Jealously the nautical peacocks guarded access to their elevated social status, demanding of prospective entrants a long and expensive apprenticeship his parents would have had to finance, and of course they wouldn't have done so. In the war's aftermath, the vice grip of the elites slackened, and so severe was the monetary inflation a wheelbarrow full of currency bought nothing anyway. And not much remained of the German Navy. The Treaty of Versailles had reduced the fleet to a handful of warships. As a junior officer, he boarded the training cruiser *Berlin* for his first sea voyage that turned out to be his one and only, his eyesight deteriorating so precipitously he could not perform his duties. The navy gave him the option to resign. He stayed and forged his career as a bespectacled staff man, the job his talents best fit. His gift was to devise orders, memoranda, policies. He spoke and wrote with a distinctive understatement that lent authenticity to his assertions. By 1936, his reputation for deft staff work had brought him to the attention of Admiral Wilhelm Canaris, head of the Abwehr, the Department for Foreign Intelligence and Defense. Mauer became an intelligence officer.

Though he'd lived most of his life in Berlin, there were days he did not recognize the capital anymore. Pulverized mortar from the aerial bombings hovered in a choking shroud. When the workmen pulled down the husks of bomb-ravaged buildings, the dust erupted as if sneezed out of a giant's nose. The explosions unearthed long-buried anaerobic bacteria which, awakened from ancient sleep, exhaled the odor of an old cow shed. Add the acridity of burnt cordite and the fumes of melted girders, and you had a noxious miasma you dared not breathe. The sole blessing: January's freezing temperatures suppressed the stench of corpses entombed beneath the rubble. To bomb a city was barbaric. Hitler had initiated the practice, bombing Warsaw, Rotterdam, Paris, London, his hubris telling him he could terrorize the populations into submission. Now, as British and American air forces heaped devastation on German cities day and night, did the damned former corporal with his Charlie Chaplin mustache register that Germany would lose the war?

Mauer had implored Jana to leave Berlin. "Please, move back to Augsburg." She had grown up on the outskirts of the old Bavarian city northwest of Munich.

"Nonsense. For two decades, I am a Berliner."

He made her privy to the bleak facts the newspapers and radio kept from the citizenry. "Joseph Goebbels and his propaganda mouthpieces say that our new *Wunderwaffen* will turn the war in our favor. People yearn for hope. It is misplaced."

"So you have told me."

"Goebbels mocks and dehumanizes our enemies. Calls them cowards. Make no mistake, the Americans, the British, and the Russians will not relent. They will overrun Germany. They are unstoppable."

"The Americans and the British are still in England, no?" Sometimes she picked apart his arguments for no better reason than she could.

"The invasion is coming. It is simply a matter of time."

"What else is new?" She meant she wasn't going anywhere. Her hair had turned gray, and when she shook it, he thought he caught a faint casting of flour in the air.

As usual, he ate nothing for breakfast. To prepare food would make a clatter and awaken her. It was still dark when he stepped onto Bayreutherstrasse, wincing at the bite of the frigid air as he strolled north. The few pedestrians he passed nodded deferentially. Perhaps they noticed the quality of his dense wool Kriegsmarine overcoat, his gloves of soft calf leather, his shoes freshly soled. The materials were of higher quality than most civilians could afford and warmer than the uniforms of German soldiers on the eastern front. In the winter seasons since Germany had invaded the Soviet Union two and one-half years ago, thousands of soldiers, lacking adequate gear, had frozen to death. In his mind's eye, he visualized them, their field coats caked in ice, torn cloths wrapped around their frostbitten hands and feet. He shook away the image.

At his spry pace, he typically took 37 minutes to traverse the three-plus kilometers to work. Not always did he follow the same route; sometimes he headed east to the Hellesches Tor U-Bahn station and there turned north.

Today he zigzagged northeast, crossing the as-yet-imaginary boulevard of Prachilee, envisioned to have become the north-south centerline of Hitler's monumental capital, Germania, as the metropolis would have been renamed. The grandiose blueprint, drafted by Hitler's esteemed architect Albert Speer, would have required the razing of numerous existing structures to clear the space for such splendors as the Adolf Hitler Platz and the adjacent Great Hall whose dome would span more than five times the diameter of St. Peter's Basilica in Rome and soar hundreds of feet higher. Hard to imagine a more immoderate motif, unless you counted the war itself. Yet if the war had done nothing to tame the Führer's illusions, at least it had put off the erection of a landmark so prominent as to be unmistakable to enemy bombardiers.

Mauer had met Albert Speer in November 1943 at a meeting of a commission charged with orchestrating the manufacture of a new U-Boat design. On the assumption that the technical discussions might yield useful intelligence background, Admiral Canaris had sent Mauer to sit in. Two months ago, Speer improbably became the Minister of Armaments and War Production. Mauer expected to find him absurdly out of his depth in the job. The architect's remarks to the gathered audience soon eradicated the preconception. Articulate in all facets of German industry, he energetically pushed measures to optimize output and reduce obstacles. He hated bureaucratic complacency. Though a senior Nazi, he parroted none of the party's rabid dogma; his mantra was excellence, a passion Mauer shared. After the meeting, Mauer introduced himself, and soon the two fell into a lively conversation about torpedo reliability. Speer not only put across his own ideas, he listened keenly to Mauer's. A miracle, that a man of such capacity had risen so high in the Nazi state. People speculated, in the event Hitler were to exit the scene precipitously—as if there were any other scenario for his departure—Speer would be the successor. If only it might happen.

The bombing last year of the Abwehr's Headquarters on Prinz Albrechtstrasse had prompted the shift of Mauer's workplace to an office in the headquarters of the Reichsverkehrsministerium, the Ministry of Transport. The three-story, statue-topped edifice stretched along Vossstrasse to the corner of Wilhelmstrasse. Not many of the windows had survived. Those that had were crisscrossed by so much tape that they mimicked problems in Euclidian geometry. In times past, the foyer had showcased paintings of historic German events. The walls were bare now, the art relocated to a safer venue. The engineers had shut down the building's elevator, judging that bomb shocks had weakened its mountings. Fortunately, the edifice had escaped more serious damage.

Mauer's secretary stood up when he entered. Forty years old, Gerta Eckhart filled out her dress as if it were a wrapper around a mound of dumpling dough. Her dresses invariably sported a Nazi pin, the petite accoutrement resembling a black widow spider; today it reposed on her left lapel. She bleached her hair to the shade of a chiffon cake. Quips he overheard suggested that some men found her cherubic-Nazi aspect alluring. He did not. In her presence, he could say nothing candid about the misbegotten warpath that was leading the nation to destruction. Sometimes he speculated that her true purpose was to spy on him, an idea not so farfetched. The Gestapo had enlisted many thousands to watch their fellow citizens. As a practical matter, however, she was useful. No matter the weather, she could be counted upon to arrive early, organize the mail, type his day's schedule, and make coffee, which though ersatz warmed and boosted him. As he had done many times when his annoyance with her soared, he reminded himself to be grateful for her diligence and overlook the rest.

"Good morning, Kommodore." She proffered a large envelope. "This arrived by courier. He said to make certain you opened it personally and to do so immediately upon your arrival."

He suppressed a frown. What had Germany come to, that a courier should levy instructions on him. "Any other demands?"

"*Nein*, Kommodore." Whether or not she'd caught the sarcasm in his tone, her expression stayed flat.

Mauer headed the Abwehr sub-section called Abteilung Eins Technik Marine, responsible for intelligence on developments in naval technology. His office was a four-meter-sided cube, the waist-level wainscoting painted Prussian blue, the upper walls a shade of parchment and decorated with a print of a sailing vessel and a framed color photograph of Adolf Hitler. Mauer had nailed up the former; the latter had come with the office. Occasionally the rumble from the bombings tilted the pictures. He straightened out the ship but let the Hitler photo hang as skewed as the man.

He examined the parcel. Commonly dispatch packets came sealed with a tie cord so you could reuse the envelope. This one the sender had taped profusely. The Führer's sapphire-blue eyes seemed to follow in haughty fascination as Mauer scissored it open and extracted a bundle of some thirty pages a pincer clip squeezed like the tenacious jaws of a Doberman. The cover-page letterhead explained the courier's imperious attitude. Headquarters of the *Geheime Staatpolizei:* the Secret State Police, or Gestapo. Top and bottom, red stamps declared *Geheime Reichssache,* the Nazi state's pinnacle secrecy classification.

A cover memo read:

```
Kommodore Mauer,
Please evaluate the contents of the attached
document and reply directly to my office. Assign
this task the highest priority. Do not share the
contents or your assessment with any third party.
Heinrich Müller
SS Gruppenführer
Generalleutnant der Geheime Staatspolizei
```

The Gestapo chief personally had scrawled his signature underneath.

From the doorway, Gerta said, "Coffee, sir?" Her eyes flicked to the papers he held. The unusual delivery had intrigued her, apparently.

"No thank you. I'll have some later."

"Very well, sir."

"Close the door, if you will."

– 4 –

Late January 1944

At 5:45 a.m., Donovan stepped out of an OSS staff Packard at 20 Grosvenor Square. Not always did he parade a military uniform; to be less conspicuous, he might sport civilian attire. Today he needed to look the part, and he wore the belted olive-brown Army dress tunic and ecru trousers custom made for him by Wetzel's of New York. Aside from the label, what set his uniform apart were the brigadier general's stars on the epaulets and the sky-blue Medal of Honor ribbon on the upper left chest.

He might have walked the two blocks from Claridge's, opted instead for the car to preserve his uniform in the steady rain. At the entrance, he returned the guard's salute. Though conveniently located, the Navy Building, like most of the London edifices assigned to SHAEF, had proven inadequate almost as soon as the burgeoning staffs poured in. SHAEF planned to move its key operations to a former British military site on London's outskirts. Stacked cartons lining the walls presaged the displacement.

He veered to the stairwell. Buffed overnight, the linoleum in the second-floor corridor gleamed. Nobody could shine floors like the military. His span with the Army had begun modestly, as a lawyer turned horse soldier in the New York National Guard. Elected troop commander, soon he found himself chasing the wily bandit Pancho Villa along the Mexican border. In World War I he led an infantry regiment and was wounded and decorated for valor. After the war, returning to the civilian world, he'd prosecuted criminals and dabbled in politics, twice running unsuccessfully for political seats. Maybe he'd try again, when the war was over.

An aide led Donovan to a chair in the Chief of Staff's suite. The space emanated the clacks of typewriters, the scuffle of footsteps, the rustle of papers. Overlay the vaguely sweet tinge of mimeograph ink, perspiration odors from the pageant of couriers—American, British, Canadian, French— the musk of damp wool, and the aroma of coffee from a steel dispenser two

Negroes in mess whites hefted in, and the space gave off the same aura as every Army headquarters he'd ever visited.

Last night he'd pondered the likely problem at hand and weighed how to make his case. His approach to negotiations was straightforward: Assert his points as cogently as possible while avoiding misstatements and digressions; the first were open to effective counterargument, the second to interruption. Sometimes it paid to have the first say, but probably not on this occasion. Among Ike's acolytes, Beetle Smith reputedly was the most ruthless, the least patient. The latter trait might tip to Donovan's advantage. Give Smith the opening forum.

There were other reasons to tread lightly. Raw though he might feel about MI-6 going over his head, he couldn't afford to be seen as disparaging of the British. Eisenhower and hence Beetle Smith were notoriously intolerant of senior officers whom they considered jaundiced toward the Alliance, and a gaffe could cost him dearly, not only here but in Washington. He'd accumulated powerful enemies, among them U.S. Army G-2 Major General George Strong and FBI Director J. Edgar Hoover. In the 1920s, then-Assistant Attorney General Donovan briefly had been Hoover's boss. The two hadn't liked each other at the time, and the passing years had fermented the sentiment into something close to detestation. That same interval had seen Hoover metamorphose from a smarter-than-average young bureaucrat to a seasoned political infighter adept at capitalizing on his one-on-one audiences with FDR.

Beetle Smith, as far as Donovan knew, was not his enemy, and he shouldn't turn him into one.

At 0600, the aide ushered him to the inner office barely larger than the walk-in closet in Donovan's New York home. The blackout curtains were closed at this hour. Donovan doubted that Beetle Smith stood up for many of his visitors. On this occasion Smith did. Of less-than-average height, lean as a cop's nightstick, he seemed to constrain his infamous ferocity by force of will as he extended his hand. "Good to see you, General Donovan. Please have a seat. I hope I haven't horned in on your schedule by asking you to come in so early."

The gracious statement did not square with Smith's reputation. Warily, Donovan said, "Not at all."

"Ike asked me to speak to you. Do you know why?"

"I don't." A fact. No point touting guesses.

"It has to do with a recent overture by British MI-6 to you. I had my staff cull the records in case you had submitted a memorandum."

"There was none."

Silence presided. Damnably, Smith savvied the advantage of saying nothing.

"The British—Sebastian Wentworth, their deputy for operations—described the matter as of extreme sensitivity, eyes only," Donovan added.

More silence.

"Two days ago, he requested my help on a scheme to mount a so-called false-flag approach. It means..."

"I know what it means."

"MI-6 wanted to borrow an OSS officer seconded to a British analytical cell here in London. Naturally, I asked why. At first, Wentworth declined to disclose details. When I insisted, he briefed me on this ploy they've cooked up. The quarry is a German admiral, secretly a communist, used to be a Soviet agent, but Moscow lost touch with him. He won't cooperate with the Brits or with us, but presumably he still will with the Soviets. He's gained a position on the German General Staff and probably has access to Nazi war plans. The British think they can reactivate him by masquerading as Soviets."

Smith seemed to cogitate all this for a minute. "Sweden is the venue?"

"Correct. The admiral is traveling there for a few days in February. The visit is the sole chance the Brits will have of getting at him. They say they need someone who is a native speaker in Swedish and Russian, and proficient in German. They don't have anybody who fits the bill. We do."

"The obstacle?"

"The plan is unsound. The Nazis have plenty of people in Sweden. The Soviets too. I believe the Soviets will learn of this shenanigan, if not immediately, then down the line, and there will be hell to pay. The president's policy is to treat the Russians as an ally. MI-6's maneuver runs sharply counter."

Smith ticked his head. He grasped the arguments.

The full story was more nuanced. Yes, FDR had ordered Donovan to keep his hands off the Soviets, seeking in part to avoid a scandal that might enrage Stalin into negotiating a separate peace with the Nazis. In 1917, at the height of the First World War, the Russians had done exactly that, giving the Huns the latitude to shift their troops to the western front. But history was not the sole consideration. Assuming the Allies won the current war, the Soviets loomed as the principal menace thereafter. Wisdom dictated preparing the intelligence groundwork. Over the past Christmas, with President Roosevelt's permission, Donovan had visited Moscow and proposed a formal U.S.-Soviet Union intelligence liaison that would entail assigning spy-service representatives to the respective capitals. It was a means of inching up on the future prey. Then word came down to freeze the initiative; FDR was having second thoughts. Donovan suspected that J. Edgar Hoover, canny to an impending encroachment on his perceived turf, had whispered dissent in the president's ear.

Smith said, "Other objections?"

"Practical ones. Even against a suitable target, false flags are tricky. The most crackerjack spymaster finds them incredibly hard to pull off. And the person the Brits have asked for is a junior analyst, a woman with no field training whatsoever."

"No one else is available with the right languages?"

"There are plenty of native Russian speakers around. Insist on native-level Swedish and good German in the same person, and you'll find the candidates thin on the ground."

"You've informed the British of your views on the practicality?"

"Wentworth claims they've thought it through and can prepare our officer in time. I'm not convinced. Even if a person has the natural aptitude, the training takes months…"

"Irrelevant."

Not many people told Donovan his judgments were irrelevant. The brusque pronouncement was closer to what he'd anticipated from Smith.

"Other impediments?"

"There's a chance our officer could be captured."

"Are you aware Churchill personally petitioned Eisenhower on this?"

"No." Though the revelation didn't surprise him. Britain's intelligence activities captivated the Prime Minister. Donovan himself had met with Churchill to discuss various topics, most recently the OSS's involvement with the partisans of Yugoslavia.

"To resolve the Soviet angle," Smith went on, "Ike probably will seek Washington's approval. As to your other points, with OVERLORD we will be mounting the most crucial military operation in history. The balance of the war and countless lives are at stake. We must succeed. If the British think they can improve our odds, and all they want from us is a single individual, the risk is acceptable. Look at it from Ike's standpoint. You're asking him to tell Churchill that he's signed onto a half-baked idea."

The ten seconds Donovan took to formulate his answer were enough to produce a cranky realignment of his interlocutor's brows. "General, that's just the kind of thing we *must* be prepared to tell our leaders. Why do you think the British were able to snag every spy the Germans infiltrated into England? Because the German Abwehr was so cowed by Hitler, they were afraid to inform him they had no meaningful espionage assets in Britain and needed a long time to prepare the right people. Hitler said, 'I want spies in England!' and the German spymasters shouted 'Sieg Heil!' and dispatched an assortment of dregs who couldn't tell the difference between a British bulldog and an umbrella."

Smith's frown had only deepened. It seemed he wasn't fond of drawn-out rebuttals, least of all that featured the Nazi salutation. "Nonetheless."

Donovan had made his case. Time to listen.

"Prepare a written summary of the MI-6 operation," said Smith. "Have it on my desk by noon today. I will contact Washington. You'll be in London for the time being?"

"Into next week."

"Can you get in touch with this MI-6 man, Wentworth?"

"Yes."

"Inform him the matter is being expedited." Smith stood up. "If you'll excuse me, I have a meeting."

Early that afternoon, SHAEF transmitted a top secret, encrypted telegram addressed eyes-only to General Marshall. It identified two action items:

1. PLEASE REVIEW AND APPROVE / DISAPPROVE US PARTICIPATION IN BRITISH INTELLIGENCE PROPOSAL OUTLINED BELOW. 2. SCHEDULE SECURE PHONECON SHAEF

COMMANDER - ARMY CHIEF OF STAFF, 1800 HRS GMT IF POSSIBLE.

The text replayed Donovan's summary of the plan and his view of the risk of inciting the Russians. Of the other objections he raised, it mentioned not a word.

Three hours brought a partial reply:

SHAEF COMMANDER PHONECON WITH ARMY CHIEF OF STAFF CONFIRMED FOR 1800 GMT.

– 5 –

Late January 1944

On the stroll back from the British military dining hall, the saffron-haired Brit towered a head over the flaxen-haired American-Russian-Swede at her side. Ivett's cigarette added to the pall from the mills, lorries, tugboats, and a rattling-by, horse-drawn cart whose nag pooped on the cobblestones. They might have avoided the choky fifteen-minute walk by taking the bus, but for Linnea's penny, the blood-pumping stroll spurred the digestion and helped loft her above the post-lunch somnambulant state she might otherwise fall into, especially when the mess hall served Irish lamb stew, whose meat component, she was pretty sure, came from spavined old goats.

Across the street strode a mother clutching the hands of her two young children. Every dozen steps or so, the mom hopped, and the children followed suit, an inventive game to keep them up without nagging them. The sight inspired Linnea to ask herself why she was an only child. Put to her own mother, the question could only rouse, "One was enough, when all we did was move," which in turn would segue to another sentimental reverie about Petrograd, so better not to bring it up.

The hopping mother's children must have had questions too, for instance, what was the object that hovered like a plump piglet in the sky? Its job, the mom would have demystified, was to keep bad airplanes away. Tethered by steel cables, the pewter barrage balloons symbolized to Linnea her life in the British capital, not so dangerous as monotonous. She hadn't expected the war to equal an excruciating sameness of the days—the section worked six and a half a week—or that the predictability she had sought—getting yanked across the world growing up will do that to you—should oppress her so. Sometimes she thought of Christopher. Would she have signed on with the OSS had things with him turned out differently?

At night, the air-raid sirens—inexplicably, many Brits referred to them as *sireens*—alerted people to the Luftwaffe air raids that had resumed after a hiatus of two and a half years. Londoners seemed inured. They had reshaped their lives around aerial bombings, substitutions for just about everything, farewells to loved ones, and wartime songs and other diversions. With Ivett she'd gone to a vaudeville show in the theater district to watch the performances of singers, dancers, magicians, and jokesters so gaudily madcap as to be enthralling. She learned about London, joining historical tours and listening to the facts, if facts they were, of kings and queens, the architect Wren, the plague, Shakespeare, the Great Fire, and so on. Twice she went to the Saturday night dances and recoiled at the raucous onslaught. Every man who spoke to her was smoking, stinking of alcohol, and shouting in her ear to be heard above the din. On both occasions, she'd fled.

You'd think she be lonely. She wasn't, aside from missing her mother. In her spare time, she put pen to the letters she mailed from the military post office where she had her own postal box, number 647, equipped with a dainty combination lock. The barracks occupants made the place livable by stringing up cloth dividers between the beds to create the semblance of privacy. Affixed to the wall was a metal bar where she hung her uniforms. A stumpy footlocker preserved her mother's letters and her second-hand books in Russian, German, and English; she'd not yet found one in Swedish. On Sundays she attended Catholic services and the follow-on social gatherings. Sometimes they trotted out biscuits or scones, and she struck up conversations with Londoners curious and a bit vexed at the brash Americans who swarmed over wartime Britain. The quip she overheard: The Americans were overpaid, oversexed, and over here. The retort she was too polite to utter: The Brits were underpaid, undersexed, and under Eisenhower.

The sidewalk tangented a cluster of market stalls where from time to time she bought chips—fried potatoes—tasty and not subject to the rationing. Ivett, prone to steer her friend of lesser height by the arm, did so to a vendor of roasted chestnuts. "A quarter pound, please," Ivett said.

"You'll get fat," Linnea warned.

"Nonsense. If I don't have nuts in the afternoon, I'll gnaw on my pencil and spread yellow flecks on my teeth. There's lead in paint, bad for you, you know."

Should Linnea point out that the remedy was not to chew on pencils? Too obvious, really.

The air raid sirens went off, the wail echoing through the market. Nobody reacted, not the vendors, the shoppers, the pedestrians, or Ivett, who fished a nut from the paper bag and peeled it with her fingers. Must be a drill.

An explosion sounded in the far distance, dully shaking the ground.

Donovan was back in Beetle Smith's anteroom. Once more it was 0600.

The prior day had bustled with OSS business. At a dinner with British generals, he discussed his recent visit to India, Burma, and China. The topic shifted to Indochina. To the generals he described the sinewy brown figures who tugged rickshaws as their sandaled feet clip-clopped along and their reed-slender wives led water buffaloes through flooded paddies. Armed with rifles, grenades, and a belief in their cause, such men and women might be able to protect Allied intelligence-gathering teams working against the Japanese. Worthy of consideration.

He contacted Sebastian Wentworth by phone and reassured him "the matter" was under consideration and would be decided quickly. What he didn't mention was his certainty Washington would reject U.S. involvement. President Roosevelt and General Marshall were acutely aware the Soviets were tying up millions of German soldiers on the Eastern Front and absorbing casualties on a scale many times heavier than were the western armies. To go ahead with the false flag risked a breach in the alliance with the Soviets, and in a U.S. election year no less, a paramount concern to the politically sagacious Roosevelt. Moreover, unlike Eisenhower and Smith in London, neither FDR nor Marshall felt the need to pander to the British. So confident was Donovan of the outcome that he'd slept like a baby last night.

The aide stirred him from his musings. "Sir, he's ready."

No sooner had he entered the Chief of Staff's office than Beetle Smith, barely glancing up from his paperwork, said, "It's a go. Please inform MI-6."

Donovan stood there—he hadn't been invited to sit—too stunned to speak.

Smith's eyes pivoted upwards. "What?"

"The rationale?"

"Washington didn't elaborate."

Donovan had not seen the outgoing message. How had the case been framed? He was about to ask when he caught the twitch of Smith's left eyebrow. What would it mean, to incur the man's wrath? Smith's pronouncements carried Eisenhower's imprimatur and were for all intents and purposes irrevocable. And he had Washington's go-ahead. To push back, Donovan might as well be Don Quixote flailing at the world's biggest windmill.

He said, "To support this project, I'd like to include my own representative alongside MI-6."

Smith's eyebrows did the Jitterbug. "You want to introduce a *condition?*"

"Not at all. Just a suggestion that an OSS man in the mix might help."

Smith's eyebrows leveled. His head was still cocked slightly askew. "Make certain the British know it's their call to accept or decline, as they see fit."

Donovan stared at the man a dozen years younger who'd been a mere Army captain at the time when he himself had been the Acting Attorney General of the United States.

"Yes sir."

In his hand-tailored Aquascutum, Sebastian Wentworth observed the busy stretch of St. James Street where it crossed Piccadilly Street. At this moment, he estimated, some 100 pedestrians verged on the intersection, their distribution 70 percent British civilians, 22 percent men and women in military uniform, and 8 percent civilians of other nationalities. He observed that the latter included a Pole, a Frenchmen, three Asians from the British colonies of India, Singapore, and Hong Kong respectively, an Arab from Palestine, and an Armenian; no doubt some were London residents, others refugees the war had prevented from returning to their native lands. If anyone were to ask him how he identified so-and-so as such-and-such, he could cite as evidence the way a man held a cigarette, the Semitic features of a woman, another's olive-tinted countenance, or the peculiar slant of an eye. He might be wrong in a few cases. That was intelligence work for you. No estimate was 100 percent certain.

You might call Wentworth the quintessential spymaster, his sole shortcoming, if you would count it as such, the lifelong hallmark to attract admiring stares. At six foot two, his athletic build honed on Cambridge's fields, he could not help but stand out in a crowd. To stay fit he swam and played tennis, sometimes volleying with professionals. In conversation he was witty and subtle, articulate on a plethora of topics, never at a loss for words. He spoke fluent French, reasonably good German, and had dabbled in Cantonese sufficiently to barter in the markets of Hong Kong. In generations past, his family had been wealthy, but as with so many legacy endowments, the annuities from the trusts had ebbed, forcing him to trim his household servants down to two and to buy fewer suits from the Savile Row haberdasher who made the finest in the land. To forgo servants entirely or to purchase his clothes off the rack, well, it simply wouldn't do.

A shiny, otherwise nondescript Packard sedan pulled to the curb, and Wentworth greeted General Donovan who stepped out. None of the nearby pedestrians paid attention. If they had, they'd have glimpsed a sexagenarian in uniform, not an uncommon sight, the hat shadowing his white hair, pallid blue eyes, and a raincoat bereft of rank, the epaulets having been temporarily alleviated of their stars. Very few would have recognized him.

Nearby was a doorway in a pinkish-stone, faux-columned façade, and Wentworth led his guest through and up a stairway to a high-ceilinged room. The tall windows shed less light with all the tape transecting the panes, nonetheless the wood and brass crafted more than a century ago gleamed gracefully, preserving the characteristic stateliness despite the proliferation of crimson fire buckets in the corners. The polished mahogany panels had felt the shadows of great men, not names Wentworth's American guest would recognize—well, maybe some of them—lions of politics, government, and the establishment, Englishmen all.

The pair shed their coats and took one of the well-separated tables. A waiter in a droopy black bow tie brought the breakfast menus. One entry, Wentworth noticed, featured ham. "Potatoes and ham?" he asked the waiter. He meant, was the ham in fact Spam, the canned product America was shipping to Britain in great quantity. In the rationing, spam had become the substitute in almost every sort of meat dish.

"Decidedly, sir," said the waiter, who knew exactly what was being asked. "I'll have that."

The American, who seemed to detect nothing remarkable in the selections, ordered a cup of black coffee. The food arrived quickly. Wentworth said, "I hope you don't mind."

"Please, eat," said Donovan.

Hovering unspoken was the impetus for this meeting--MI-6's urgent petition to the Prime Minister and the involvement of General Eisenhower. Always preferable to avoid such power plays, thought Wentworth. Invariably they left bruises on destinatary and instigator alike, not to mention, in this case, tipping Churchill and Eisenhower to the embarrassing fact that the Secret Service on its own hadn't been able to sell the endeavor. Also, how angry was Donovan, to have been dragooned so?

Across the table, the general appeared agreeably nonchalant, seemingly happy to watch Wentworth consume his breakfast. At length, Donovan said, "On the matter you raised, I'm happy to provide the person you asked for."

"Bravo," said Wentworth. The ham, though not in abundance, was quite succulent. "I'm sorry for any trouble this may have put you to."

"No trouble. If you need help in Stockholm, our office there can oblige."

Wentworth patted his lips with his napkin. The *last* thing he desired was to bring one of the OSS's stations into a sensitive operation. Though he was not familiar with OSS Stockholm per se, he had heard shocking accounts of the Americans' overseas offshoots. In Bern, Switzerland, OSS chief Allen Dulles seemed to advertise his role so blatantly he might as well hang an 'OSS: Open for Business' sign in the window. No doubt Dulles's intention was to attract a host of candidates to spy on Germany, as if espionage and industrial mass production followed the same principles. Did the Americans not comprehend that their brazen approachability lent the Nazis concordant opportunities to fling bevies of double agents at them? There were offices where the OSS people were so gallingly incompetent the local MI-6 cadre had ceased dealing with them at all.

"I appreciate the offer," replied Wentworth, smiling tolerantly. "We desire no involvement in or even knowledge of the operation by either the British or American regular complements in Stockholm."

"Your call. I do have a request."

The smile flattened. "What would that be?"

"I'd like to put a fellow in with our young officer. Better she has another American close by. That's if you don't mind, of course."

The ham had left a dissolute paste on Wentworth's teeth, and with lips shut he ran his tongue around them. "You mean during the run-up phase in Britain?"

"Yes. The run-up phase."

"I take it you have someone in mind?"

"His name is Gabriel Verrick, a deputy of mine. He accompanied me on one of my prior trips to London. I telegrammed him this morning and told him to prepare to be on his way immediately."

"Experienced, Verrick?"

"Before joining the OSS, he was a senior associate in my law firm."

Wentworth mulled over the petition. *That's if you don't mind, of course.* Well, he *did* mind, in fact the prospect annoyed him immensely. This Verrick fellow was an archon in Donovan's organization, and no doubt he would serve as his sponsor's eyes and ears, spotting the foibles and miscues every project entailed. A solicitor to boot, he'd probably make a nuisance of himself in other ways as well. Wentworth was inclined to refuse. Why complicate things?

"Do you envision Verrick as a participant in the process?"

"More like an observer."

"Are you asking us to delay until he arrives?"

"No. Just to include him when he does."

What would the consequences be, to say no? Might the venture, already elevated to the highest level, have to be raised again? Oh, the knots one had to unravel when dealing with the Americans. It would be so much easier if they put themselves under British command rather than insisting on following their own conceptions. An eternal bother, to steer them right.

"Would he observe the strictest compartmentation and not convey the details to others?"

"He'll report to me alone, using the securest channels."

"And when he learns the mission details, will he initiate independent queries or research in your archives? Hazardous, you know, if the mission specifics were to be bantered about."

"He'll mount no independent queries of any sort. I'll make that very clear."

Would the Americans abide by these stipulations? Hard to divine. The practical question: Were the complications manageable? Generally, the answer was yes. Perhaps there was a positive side. To attest that an OSS provost had been included in the run-ups might prove expedient in the event the plan, or the American woman, met with calamity.

"If those points are agreed," said Wentworth, "your deputy is welcome."

– 6 –

Late January 1944

Not far inland from the east coast of England, an olive-painted aircraft waffled in a crosswind to a jolting landing. The silhouette identified her as a B-17, the four-engine workhorse of the U.S. Eighth Air Force and the plane that filled the skies during daylight bombing raids over Germany. This particular variant was more linear than the standard model, lacking the top and bottom machine-gun turrets, the latter a so-called "ball turret" only diminutive gunners could fit into. No guns poked from her fuselage ports, either, because there were no ports, merely dinner-plate-sized windows. Her function? What else but to ferry priority passengers, dispatches, and cargo from the United States to England.

In one of the aluminum-pipe-framed canvas passenger seats, Gabriel Verrick peered through a window. They'd taken off from a base on the north shore of Long Island and landed in Iceland and Ireland to refuel. On the final leg, one of the air crew had stirred him from a fitful slumber to say the airfields around the British capital were fogged in, and they were diverting to an outlier named Snetterton Heath. How far from London was Snetterton Heath? The crewman had no idea.

Along the tarmac, a guide led the taxiing plane whose star-in-circle-dotted wingtips almost skimmed the noses of parked B-17s being mission-outfitted. The scene conjured a country carnival: the signalmen waved colorful flags; tractors tugged 500-pound, olive-and-yellow-painted bombs on linked wagons like a kids' train; scores of 20-foot-high vertical stabilizers soared like roller coasters; and jaunty artistry decorated the panels beneath the cockpits. One plane featured a snarling, cigar-chomping, fur-on-end cartoon animal outfitted in a flight jacket above the moniker, 'The Scrappy Marmot.'

After twenty hours in this plane, Verrick felt like such a creature.

The engines juddered to a halt. He rose unsteadily, levering his knees and back the way that as a child he used to wrangle the rusty handle of the well pump outside his family home. To keep from toppling over, he gripped a leather ceiling strap. He was fifty years old. Why on earth was he doing this?

"Exit the right rear," barked the crewman. "No smoking this side of the red line." To say 'please' on a military flight was apparently an alien concept.

Verrick creaked along. Damp, fuel-laced air flooded the cabin. He came to the door, where a ladder with a flimsy rope rail groped downward. He should turn around and descend backward. Like the young servicemen who bounded spryly out, he proceeded facing forward, if perhaps more staidly, a regal descent, if you will. One step and he lost his footing, twisting his knee. The Scrappy Marmot grinned derisively.

Early in the war, OSS Director Donovan had offered him a military commission. Uniform and rank proved helpful in certain circumstances, not least when interacting with enlisted personnel who had no other clue as to a person's relative importance. Verrick had opted against the idea, reasoning that he wouldn't often be dealing with those not read-in well enough to engage with him on a substance-versus-rank basis. The decision may have been shortsighted. The wartime military was all about systematization, and he was outside the system. On the tarmac, no one helped him tug his suitcase from under the pile of duffel bags where the crewmen had tossed it. A sergeant told him to wait at planeside. His knee aching, he might have sat on the duffels, had the other passengers not made off with them.

The sergeant returned. "You Verrick?"

"Yes."

"There's a car for you. Follow me."

Lugging his suitcase, he limped through a hangar to a gravel esplanade where a mud-spattered sedan waited. And here was someone he recognized, a tall, lean Negro sergeant—what was his name?—Sergeant Bowe, who had driven him around London on his first visit.

"Good to see you again, sir," said Sergeant Bowe.

They shook hands, and Sergeant Bowe took the suitcase and fitted it in the trunk. "Sorry I'm late, sir. The dispatch said to pick you up at Biggin Hill, don't take no time to get there. They changed the pickup to Snetterton Heath way up in Norfolk, three and a half hours away."

"We're *three and a half hours* from London?"

"Yes, sir. Sorry about how the car looks too. The roads are a mess this time of year. We'll be lucky not to end up behind a convoy, no telling how slow we'll go then. I got blankets in back, you can sleep, if you wanna."

Sapped from the hours aboard the aircraft, shrouded in the wool blanket, Verrick tried. The wheels thudded over bumps and holes. Military trucks belched diesel fumes, and they passed one truck only to end up behind another, reaping contemptuous sprays of muddy water across the windshield. The mud swilled from bulldozed side roads, their destinations unseen, the rimming barbed-wire fences dangling signs in bold letters: RESTRICTED AREA – DO NOT ENTER.

Military installations crammed rural England. One of them harbored Verrick's son Matt, a lieutenant in the U.S. 101st Airborne Division. Matt's regiment had sailed here six months ago in preparation for the forthcoming invasion. The letters he sent home never stated his precise whereabouts. Allude to a location or anything else militarily specific in a letter, and a vigilant censor would snip it out. How long since he'd seen his son? He pictured the boy in their apartment, which, though spacious by Manhattan standards, could barely contain him. Matt had loved the outdoors, especially the spots along the Hudson where he could pitch stones into the current. He had a lot of his New Hampshire woodsman grandfather in him, less of his career New York attorney father.

Sergeant Bowe regarded him in the rear-view mirror. "Can't sleep, sir?"

"No luck so far."

"Might help once we're clear of these noisy trucks."

"I hope so. But how are you enjoying London?"

"It's all right. Even met me a British lady on a tour of St. Paul's Cathedral. Gotta be careful where I take her, though. The Brits don't bother us none, but some GIs turn nasty when they see a black man with a white woman. I can handle myself in a fair fight, but soon as something starts, half a dozen of 'em's on me."

"My God, here we are to defeat the Nazis, and what do we confront but our own intolerance."

"Ain't it the truth, sir."

The fog shrouded them. Night fell. Verrick couldn't drop off. It bothered him to have no hint of their progress, no road signs or other markers; the British had removed them to thwart Hitler's anticipated invasion. Operation

Sea Lion hadn't come about. Neither had the restoration of the rural signs. Markers or not, Sergeant Bowe knew his way through the many turns, and they rolled into the capital at 8 p.m. local time. The first edifice Verrick recognized was Paddington Station, bustling at this hour. The tingling familiarity he'd felt on his initial visit to London recurred, as if he knew the place. Why should that be?

"We're going to Grosvenor Street?"

"Yes sir. They told me you brought 'em something."

"An envelope."

"They'll probably send you straight to the guest house after. I'll wait, give you a lift."

"I've been there. It's close by, I can walk."

"You've got a heavy suitcase. Best I take you."

Rumpled and unshaven, he pressed the front buzzer at number 70 Grosvenor Street. A remote lock clicked—if you knew what to look for, you could spot an OSS building by the special locks—and he strode to the foyer desk. The duty officer dropped his hand into a side drawer—no doubt it concealed a pistol—while Verrick produced his passport.

"How was your travel, sir?" The young man probably was a recent arrival in London, to have garnered the late duty.

"Fine, till we were diverted to Snetterton Heath."

"Where's that?"

"Somewhere three and a half hours away."

"Sorry to hear, sir."

Verrick handed over the double-sealed, file-size package he'd brought along. "For General Donovan personally," he said.

"He's already gone for the evening." The duty officer jotted a log entry, taped on a routing slip, opened an adjacent safe, and slid the envelope in. "You'll be staying at the guest house. Do you need directions?"

"No."

He extended a tagged key. "Breakfast at the guest house starts at 6 a.m. and stays open for an hour. You have a meeting with General Donovan here at ten tomorrow morning. You're to meet a Mr., uh, Khilkov in the mews behind at eleven. Bring your suitcase with you. You can leave the key in the room."

"Who is Mr. Khilkov?"

"No idea, sir."

As promised, Sergeant Bowe delivered Verrick to the guest house. During his prior stay, accompanying other senior visitors, he'd been quartered in one of the modest chambers on the second floor. Tonight he landed the so-called VIP room on the entry level. It came with a private bathroom, an almost unheard-of luxury for a wartime traveler. He spent a few minutes hanging his clothes, half-filled the tub with steaming hot water—more cause for amazement—and gingerly eased in, babying the left knee swollen from the misstep on the ladder. He leaned back and tried to relax.

As any trial lawyer could tell you, a vital synergist for success was to divine what was coming at you. No sensation was more sinking than to enter a courtroom or negotiation unprepared. Donovan had summoned him to London with no hint of the subject matter, not even what was in the envelope he'd been given pre-wrapped to carry along. And who was this Mr. Khilkov he was supposed to meet tomorrow?

He closed his eyes. Don't make it harder than it has to be. Just do whatever the hell Donovan tells you to do.

– 7 –

Late January 1944

The shortage of petrol being what it was, the messengers who delivered intelligence documents to Factory House piloted motorbikes, their motors so noisy Linnea could hear them from her desk. The messengers bore leather-trimmed canvas lock-bags chained to their wrists. Must be hard to drive that way, she thought. Known as *the traffic* from all the comings and goings, the flow comprised multiple categories of information:

– Reports from agents MI-6 or OSS had infiltrated into Nazi-occupied territories and ran from stations in neutral countries, for instance the OSS's office in Bern, Switzerland. The accounts had to be read with caution, for surely the Nazis had doubled some of the agents.

– Scoops from third-country diplomats who had traveled through the occupied lands. These tended to be observational; they could be enlightening, nonetheless.

– Summaries of press reports deemed of interest.

– Communiqués from the American and British military missions in Moscow. These conveyed more-or-less verbatim what the missions had received from the Soviets. Frequently weeks out of date, the Moscow reports tended to be propagandistic and generally so distilled of detail they essentially said nothing beyond what appeared in the press extracts.

Papers classified SECRET could be kept at the analysts' desks during the working hours, to be dropped off at the general registry at day's end. The less-common TOP SECRET or MOST SECRET echelons of intelligence did not circulate to the desks but remained in a vaulted archive called the Special Access Registry on the ground floor. To read documents of these higher classifications, you had to go—where else?—to the Reading Room. Control lists, known as bigot lists, further restricted select streams.

Linnea, a junior analyst, was not on any of the bigot lists. Rarely was she notified of anything Top Secret pertinent to her account, so it came as a surprise when Dodgy Dray, strutting her gazelle legs to Linnea's desk at 6:15 p.m., said, "There's something for you in the Reading Room."

A week ago, Linnea had gone to Alistair Bird to complain that she still hadn't received permission to talk to the intelligence wing of the Polish government in exile. "How can I finish my paper?"

He promised to make inquiries. The next day, he called her in. "I spoke to a friend at MI-6. It seems that Whitehall and your American State Department jointly have thrown a blanket over the Polish government in exile until they come round on mending their relations with the Soviets. The Poles nonetheless are still passing along their intelligence reports. My friend has offered to send you copies of the Polish pieces MI-6 has spiked."

Spiked, borrowed from journalism, meant rejected for publication, usually because the information was shy of credible. "What good will that do?"

"Some of the pieces are interesting, professedly. I'll have MI-6 dispatch the spiked ones to the Reading Room addressed to you. You can read the contents, but you won't be able to cite them without special permission. Sorry, it's the best I could do."

The spiked reports must have arrived.

Normally at this hour Linnea began to clean up, to depart at six-thirty and catch the bus to the mess hall. The mile or so walk she and Ivett took at lunchtime wasn't advisable in the blacked-out evenings. Though the dining facility stayed open until eight, experience had taught that the later in the meal period you arrived, the fewer selections availed. She'd shown up on the ebb side to find lukewarm soup and crusty bread the sole fare.

What to do? If her tricks on Bird had branded her the section's mischief maker, they'd made her no less the diligent analyst. To leave pertinent intelligence material unread till tomorrow was a sin, in her view. She decided to have a look at the spiked reports before she left.

She collected her notes, separating them from the numbered reports, stuffing the former into an accordion file she deposited into the section's four-drawer safe, dropped off the latter at the registry window where fortunately she didn't have to wait in line, checked her desk to make sure she'd left no papers behind—a security violation might result in a reprimand, forfeiture of pay, or worse—and hurried downstairs to the Special Access Registry. She showed her identification and signed the roster under the vigilant eye of the

Control Officer, who was ensconced behind a window that resembled the ticket booth at a train station. Here she received a clipped sheaf of documents, and at a table in plain sight of the Control Officer, she began to flip through them. Although note-taking was allowed, the notes couldn't leave the Reading Room and had to be remanded with the documents. She took no notes, planning merely to scan the reports and, if warranted, come back tomorrow for a closer reading. There were sixteen pages of single-spaced text, the first ten mustering skimpy details, none illuminating; it was obvious why MI-6 had decided not to circulate them.

The final report, six pages long, was different.

The subject line read: WEHRMACHT BELIEF THAT THE SOVIETS PLAN TO LET THE GERMANS ANNIHILATE THE POLISH RESISTANCE. Meant to be précis-like, intelligence subject lines might maunder into gnarled thickets of interwoven clauses. This one made two points: first, that the information presented the German perspective; second, that it expressed a supposition. The text began, "In the assessment of officers of the German Army…" Someone working for the Polish resistance must have overheard some drunken Wehrmacht officers bloviating. It went on to say the Red Army would hurl an onslaught at the German defenses in Poland sometime in the spring of this year. The Germans expected the Soviets to lay the groundwork by pressing the Polish resistance to mount softening-up attacks behind the German lines. Once the Red Army broke through, however, they would slide the freedom fighters, a potential hindrance to Soviet plans to subjugate Poland, to the opposite side of the friends-versus-foes scale. The unnamed Germans posited that the Red Army would pause in its advance on Warsaw long enough for the Wehrmacht to wipe out the resistance.

She saw why MI-6 had spiked the report. The predictions came across more as Nazi propaganda than objective intelligence. Could the Soviets be so diabolical that they would manipulate the scenario to obliterate their Polish allies?

The report went on. The Wehrmacht officers had based their assessment on military interrogations of captured Red Army soldiers and an evaluation of the weaponry the Soviets had been supplying to the Poles, small arms and ammunition apportioned in such dribs and drabs the partisans would not be tempted to stockpile them. The revelations seemed too detailed to have been randomly overheard. Had the Poles recruited a genuine source within the German military? The more she digested the contents, the more plausible they seemed.

She could use this to finish her paper!

She went through a second time, committing sections to memory. The subject matter, she knew, would roil like stormy wave-tops in her mind, perhaps to keep her awake tonight. Alistair Bird had said she wouldn't be able to cite the spiked materials without special permission. In the evidentiary indices to the intelligence assessments she had authored to date, she'd never cited or even considered citing a spiked report. She would have to ask Bird, the same Bird she had made flail at the up-tied light cord, to press a reluctant MI-6 for permission.

"Excuse me, Lieutenant Thorsell?" said the Control Officer. "Your section head wants you upstairs."

What time was it? Seven-thirty! She'd be lucky to get to the mess hall before it closed. She returned the documents and hurried up the staircase. The lights in the section were out, the solitary glow emanating through the half-glass walls of Bird's office.

"Oh, hello," he said, batting bloodshot eyes. He'd not bothered to slick down his hair, and the light from the hanging bulb glared off the bald pate. "I thought you had left. I called the mess hall and asked them to make an announcement to summon you to the phone, only to learn you were in the Reading Room. I suppose you can hardly be blamed for staying late to do your work, eh?"

"The spiked reports arrived. I need to talk to you about…"

"Grosvenor Street called. They want you there at once. They've sent a car."

She blinked. "Did they say why?"

"Of course not. They never tell us anything, those people."

Those people. As if she were not an American.

"You had better go. The driver has been waiting half an hour."

The OSS must have an important document to translate. Twice before she'd been summoned to the OSS building on Grosvenor Street to elucidate Russian-language documents. This was the first time they'd sent a car. As for dinner, well, she supposed she'd have to go to an eatery, costing her money. Dammit.

The driver of the military sedan, a woman corporal in an olive skirt and blouse, stepped out to open the door.

Linnea said, "Sorry to have kept you waiting, I was in the Reading Room..."

"No need to explain, ma'am."

Cigarette smoke saturated the car. In the prolonged wait, the driver must have chain-smoked half a pack. They crossed the Thames at the Westminster Bridge, Linnea gripping the door handle so she wouldn't slide across the vinyl seat in the turns. Beneath the streetlamps turned off and the blackout curtains in the overlooking buildings pulled shut, the headlight-hooded car plodded along like a mole sniffing the ground. Past Hyde Park the driver weaved into Mayfair, stopping at the mouth of Grosvenor Street, which along with the adjacent, eponymous square represented the American epicenter in Britain. A soldier at a checkpoint shone a flashlight in, making sure, Linnea supposed, that the back seat was not full of Nazi marauders. He waved them through. The driver segued along the street, turned right at an intersection, and swerved abruptly into the maw of a garage. Someone closed the doors behind. It was 8 p.m.

OSS London kept one of its offices at number 70 Grosvenor Street perpetually available for General Donovan, who on his frequent overseas travels commonly stopped in the British capital. As fitted a military workplace in wartime, the furniture was plain and functional: a desk, three straight-backed chairs, and a coat rack. The windows faced the street, the open blackout curtains admitting the somber daylight, the dull wax of the floorboards obscuring the scratches and wood knots the way a meteor shower might look through a lens-fogged telescope. The walls were bare except for a photograph, slightly askew, of President Roosevelt.

His knee still aching, Verrick limped in. His exhaustion from the long flight had enfeebled his sleep. Things gnawed at him: the unknown rationale for his presence; the impending invasion that would deliver his son into the war's deadly vortex; and Sergeant Bowe's disquieting tale of being accosted by white soldiers for having an English girlfriend.

Donovan smiled. "Gabe, good to see you. Coffee?"

"Yes, please."

The OSS Director set out cups and poured from a Thermos. Their friendship stretched over more than 25 years, originating in France in 1918. Verrick had joined the 165th Infantry Regiment, an outfit that from its New York National Guard origins was sometimes touted as the 69th Infantry or 'The Fighting Irish.' Donovan, then the regiment's Chief of Staff, had assigned him to tactical planning. After the war, when Donovan accepted an appointment to the U.S. Justice Department, heading the Anti-Trust Division, he invited Verrick to sign on as one of his attorneys. Despite the abysmal salary—DOJ faced severe budget problems at the time—Verrick moved to Washington. The pay improved when Donovan later brought him to the law firm he founded in New York City, and Verrick rose to become one of the firm's senior associates. Across that span, Donovan became nationally famous. Twice he ran for political office, and his story even made it to Hollywood, actor George Brent portraying the wartime hero in the film *The Fighting 69th*.

Six months in advance of America's entry to the Second World War, President Roosevelt created America's first civilian intelligence agency, naming Donovan as its director. No one, no matter how talented, could have forged an organization with the requisite capacity in so brief a time. Donovan did the next-best thing. Wielding his celebrity as a prominent New York Republican, former U.S. Assistant Attorney General, Medal of Honor winner, and person they made movies about, he attracted bright and talented people, initially from his own circle of contacts. Verrick and several other lawyers from the firm were early picks. As the American war effort expanded, so did the OSS's roster, into the thousands.

"You got here fast," said Donovan.

"Less than 12 hours after I received your message, they had me in the air." He took a sip of coffee, waiting for Donovan to reveal the reason for all the urgency.

"I've got a sticky situation, and I could think of no one better able to handle it than you." The OSS Director summarized the British plan, recounting his initial refusal and how the Secret Service had harnessed Prime

Minister Churchill to press General Eisenhower. "MI-6 pulled out all the stops. I haven't seen them do that before. Or to put forward so reckless a gimmick."

Donovan's attitude toward the venture would have surprised most of the people who worked with him day to day. True, to approach a German admiral under a Soviet false flag sounded like the plot of a bad movie. Yet Donovan had gained the reputation of one willing to lend his endorsement and his organization's resources to eccentric ideas. Verrick, who'd been around him longer than any, read the boss's objections from the correct angle. If the gambit came to the attention of the Soviets, Stalin would blow his top. That the Soviets were sons of bitches counted less than their continuing participation in the war. For every casualty the Germans inflicted on the British and Americans, the Soviets suffered ten. The grim arithmetic hadn't escaped FDR. Churchill, likewise aware of the unequal burden the Soviets bore, had to know that Stalin would hold him personally responsible for hijacking their agent. The Prime Minister had backed MI-6's ploy anyway. Why?

"The strangest part of all is that they need our help," said Donovan. Indeed, the premise flew in the face of precedent. The British had a long tradition of teaching foreign languages to the university students who became the bureaucrats, diplomats, and intelligence professionals of their vast, multi-lingual Empire. "The requirement is for a person who speaks native Russian and Swedish, as well as passable German, and we seem to have the only ticket in town. Linnea Thorsell is one of our analysts. She was born in Russia and lived for nearly a decade in Sweden."

"What else do we know about her?"

"Let's have a look." Donovan scissored open the package Verrick had carried across the ocean, extracting a folder he opened on his desk. As he'd commonly done at the law firm, Verrick came around to read over his boss's shoulder. "She's been working the past seven months in London in an interchange with analysts of the British Joint Intelligence Committee at a facility called Factory House. That's probably how MI-6 became aware of her."

"Her training?"

Like a two-headed hydra, Donovan and Verrick leaned over the file. Sometimes the latter stopped the former from turning the page, occasionally

Verrick turned it himself. Linnea's IQ scores were in the top percentages. A high intellect was a fluky thing; the pattern it took in an individual might or might not endear him or her to the OSS. Donovan flipped to the forms that Linnea's recruiter and the OSS evaluations staff had prepared. One, titled 'Operational Training Recommendation,' featured decision spaces. DO NOT RECOMMEND was checked. In the comments section, the evaluator had scrawled, 'Subject insists she has no interest in operational training.'

Her background investigation sheets summarized her academic transcripts, the mid-1942 balance of her bank account ($108.63), and her salary from her job translating telegrams. Appended were copies of the lease she and her mother had signed on an apartment at East 28th Street, Manhattan, and an older lease for a place on East 6th. The war having stretched thin the resources of the FBI, the Bureau had contracted with retired agents to perform security-clearance investigations. The investigator who'd done Linnea's must have come from the Bureau's cadre of gritty former cops and Texas Rangers who'd gone toe-to-toe against the nation's most vicious gangsters in the 1930s and to whom J. Edgar Hoover's archetype of college-educated, polite, clean-cut, and sober FBI agents stuck to about as well as whitewash to a bristly wild boar. In hand-printed words peppered with the occasional misspelling, he recapped his interviews with Linnea's employer, college professors, and known acquaintances. Her only security blemish, he wrote, was her association with 'shady Rasputin types' at the Russian chess club.

OSS inductees were asked to fill out an elaborate personal statement, the form cueing, 'Tell us about yourself. What special talents do you possess? How do you feel about foreign travel and adventure? Use the back of the sheet if necessary.' People generally penned self-descriptions so anodyne they lent scant insights to readers who sought to get past the basics. Linnea's said she was a college graduate and unmarried. She noted her girlhood in Russia, Sweden, and Germany, her arrival in the United States at age fourteen, and her academic studies. Her talents were her languages. At the end, she stated, 'I have experienced all the adventure I care to, and I would much prefer to live a stable and predictable life. In 'Crime and Punishment,' Fyodor Dostoyevsky wrote, 'From a hundred rabbits you can't make a horse.' I am a rabbit, as I wish to be.'

"Unique in two respects," remarked Verrick. "Hers is the sole file I've seen that quotes Dostoyevsky, and the first that says, 'I am a rabbit.'"

"She sounds completely unsuitable," said Donovan. "If I've learned anything since I put together this organization, the first requirement to deploy a person operationally is their honest desire to participate. A second is rigorous training, both general and specific to the mission."

The file contained a copy of both the order posting Linnea to OSS London's Research and Analysis Section and the later amendment embedding her in the JIC analysis group, but as was so often the case in the precinct of file-reviews, nothing explained how either designation had come about.

Verrick said, "Is there an evaluation from her British section head?"

"Apparently. I've asked for copies. They haven't arrived yet. No matter, it's your direct opinion of her that will drive my decision."

"Drive it how?"

"I'll be in London until Friday afternoon. Probe the situation and report to me in person before then. If you perceive this to be as big a can of worms as I think it is, I can still try to pull us out. I'll talk to the president if I have to."

Suitcase in hand, Verrick exited to Grosvenor Mews behind the headquarters. A ruddy-faced, stalwart-built fellow in his mid-to-late thirties with curly, possibly ungovernable black hair took the luggage to load it in the boot of a sedan. At first Verrick thought he was simply the driver. Not until he was behind the wheel, and Verrick in the passenger seat, did the fellow extend his hand and in a tuneful Scottish accent say, "Avry Khilkov, MI-6."

"Gabriel Verrick, OSS," he managed, just as a coughing fit seized him. He lifted his arm to cover his mouth.

"Catch something on the flight?"

"I'm fine. Must be the air."

"That's London for you. Like dwelling in a coal mine. If it's not the soot, it's the lorry fumes. Luckily you'll be outside the city the next couple of weeks.

Staying with us is the only practical way to imbed you in the revelry, not so far you won't be able to pop back when you have to."

They headed northeast, or so Verrick guessed from the angle of the sun, visible this morning through a skimpy overcast. Rows of houses betrayed gaps like missing teeth. The Germans had been reenacting the 1940 Blitz with a 1944 version people were calling the 'Baby Blitz.' Baby or not, it was wreaking destruction.

"How was the travel over?"

Airplane engines still thrumming in his head, Verrick related the journey, leaving out only his knee-wrenching stumble on the ladder.

At the mention of Snetterton Heath, Avry said, "Where's that?"

"Damned if I know."

The dense neighborhoods receded, and they wended through residential and industrial suburbs divided by meadows widening to fields. Cows and horses flashed up and dissolved. Another fifteen minutes brought them to a gravel track. "We've got a house and several hectares technically co-located with RAF Hornchurch. Affords us privacy and the liberty to practice with firearms without attracting a lot of attention. By the way, do you have one?"

"A gun? No."

"Good. The RAF regulations mavens insist that any firearms at our site be kept under the watchful control of the designated armorer, the position falling unfortunately to me for the time being."

A quarter mile along they nosed to a drop bar by a white-painted guard shack, currently vacant. Avry climbed out and lifted the bar. "We don't bother to man the gate. The locals are respectful of the fences and warning signs. Also, Bags keeps watch."

"Bags?"

"You'll see."

The tires crunched up a curving driveway to a three-story, white stucco house. Avry pulled into the slim lot alongside. When Verrick got out, a cream and gray German shepherd in a wire-fenced kennel barked furiously. The Scot raised his hand. The dog quieted.

"Good thing he's behind the fence," said Verrick.

"She. Meet our watchdog, Baguette. Bags for short. A friend to those she protects."

"I'm sure."

Avry gave him a tour of the campus he called the Hornchurch Lodge, introducing Verrick as 'Gabriel'—first names only, a house rule—to the housekeeper, Mrs. Edda, and to the cook, Mrs. Tatum. Upstairs were eight bedrooms. Verrick's window faced the front grounds, where visible to the left were a patch of the RAF airfield, and Bags, who stared up at him in the window as if she'd never taken her eyes off. At the house's rear was a single-level extension with two classrooms and a gymnasium that vaunted canvas mats, barbells, and a hanging punching bag. "We just added this wing," said Avry. "An indoor shooting range in the works will make us an all-weather, fully equipped training site."

"Is Linnea here?"

"Not yet. Sebastian Wentworth's bringing her personally this evening. Marks her with a white stone, to merit the escort of one of Menzies's high priests."

"May I ask, has anyone involved in this enterprise met her?"

"I haven't. I've read the appraisal from her supervisor at Factory House. He says she's uncommonly astute."

"Ah."

Seeming to guess his thoughts, Avry added, "Whether his opinion is worth a wink to a blind horse, I've yet to ravel out."

– 8 –

Late January 1944

A lean, fortyish American woman with a stony air led Linnea from the garage through a courtyard, into a house, and up the stairs to a bedroom. "You'll find everything you need for the night. Someone will be along soon with your instructions." The doyenne did not introduce herself, and on her way out, she pulled the door shut. A mechanism clicked, Linnea waited a minute and tested it. Locked from without.

Soon came and went. She supposed she'd have to wait until morning to be told her purpose here. The room had a sink, a glass bottle of drinking water, a tumbler, a writing table with an assortment of books atop it between marble ends, and a toilet behind a corner half-wall. On the bed, a heavy wool blanket overlay crisp sheets. What the room didn't offer was food. No doubt they assumed she'd already eaten dinner.

She perused the books. Pass the time reading? Better to assess her situation. Had she committed some terrible security violation she was unaware of? Was she under arrest and confined to this room? No, the surroundings were too cozy. More likely they had summoned her either for an interview with a Russian speaker, a document requiring translation, or to brief someone on her analytic specialty. Knowing which one would be helpful to organize her thoughts.

And why the hell had they locked her in?

The room chilled. At 10 p.m., she stripped to her underwear, climbed under the bedding, and pulled up the wool blanket. Damn, she was hungry. She should have told the woman she hadn't eaten.

She slept more soundly than she expected. Not until 6 a.m., her Timex wristwatch ticking in her ear, did she stir. She dressed, made the bed, and drank the last of the water in the glass bottle. At the desk she flipped open one of the books, a volume of essays. At once she smelled hotcakes, as if the pages harbored the aroma; somebody must be cooking breakfast downstairs.

The woman soon showed up with a tray she carried to the writing table. "Good morning," she said, her expression no more fathomable than it had been last evening. "I hope you slept well."

"Yes. Can you tell me…"

"Someone will be by to explain." Without another word, the woman left, pulling the door shut. Would she lock it again? Linnea counted to three, and the telltale ratchet sounded.

The meal boasted the hotcakes she'd smelled, a cup of coffee, glass of orange juice from powder, eggs that amazingly were not, and—what was this?—six slices of bacon! The British mess hall reserved bacon for Sundays and rationed the slices to two per person. She wolfed down every morsel.

Afterward, from the table drawer, she ferreted a cardboard box with a new wooden toothbrush and packet of tooth powder. She was brushing her teeth when a tap came at the door. "Come in," she said, blotting her mouth.

The lock clicked. The visitor was a fellow in his early thirties in a civilian suit and wire-rimmed glasses. He flashed big teeth. "Hello, Linnea. I'm Bill. I hope I'm not interrupting your breakfast."

"No," she replied, as if this were her apartment and she were the host to a traveling salesman. She indicated the chair. "Please."

He sat, crossing his legs. She perched on the corner of the bed.

"I'm sorry not to have stopped by last night. I was tied up with another matter. By the time I got back, it was so late, I thought it better not to disturb you." He had a New York borough accent—Queens?—and sometimes his voice trailed off in a mumble, a pattern she'd encountered before among sundry New Yorkers. "I trust you found the accommodations comfortable enough."

"Yes."

"You've eaten?"

"I did." He seemed friendly. She must not be in trouble.

"Sorry too you were locked in. We didn't want anyone to see you."

As if that made sense.

"There's very little I can say about why you're here, because I know only that you have been identified for an important project. You should regard what you learn from this moment onward to be bigoted at the highest level. Whatever other caveats may apply, you will be briefed by the parties involved." From his coat he extracted three documents that he laid out on the tabletop along with a fountain pen. "Sign, if you don't mind."

The first document declared her acknowledgment that she was henceforth under the command of (blank line) and would obey (blank line's) orders, the second that she understood her duty could be hazardous and she would receive an additional $55.00 per month pay, pro-rated as appropriate, between the dates of (blank) and (blank). Third, she agreed to the special security provisions of (blank) and pledged to disclose no information to any unauthorized party, to preserve no written notes, and to take no photographs, subject to criminal penalties. The blanks and extra pay aside, the documents were no different from forms she had signed upon her induction into the OSS. She scratched her signatures.

"Do you know how long I'll be with the, uh…?"

"I don't. At 3 p.m. you'll leave here by car. We don't have the destination yet. In the meantime, Mrs. Wolters will help you pick out a set of civilian clothes. We can have them tailored on short notice, if need be. Please leave your uniform, shoes, and any belongings, including your underclothes, wristwatch, wallet, military ID, and meal card, in this room. We will keep them for you. Bring along nothing of your own, not even money. Speak to no one other than Mrs. Wolters or me."

"What about my work at Factory House?"

"Your section head will be notified that you've been posted on temporary duty." He collected the forms, grinned, and said, "That's it for me. Good luck." The door shut behind him, and again the lock clicked.

When Mrs. Wolters stopped by to fetch the tray, Linnea asked for a second cup of coffee.

Mrs. Wolters took her to an upstairs room where against a wall posed a rack of clothes on wooden hangers. "Pick out anything you like."

She didn't like anything. The selection was dreary, scratchy, blah. The OSS had the resources to purchase the best garments in London, outfits from Selfridges, Harrods, even the so-called bespoke dressmakers. The arrayed clothes smacked of second-hand shops, whiffs of an old-lady's closet. After fussing through, she settled on a pleated gray skirt, a white cotton blouse with collar laces she tied in a bow, and a hip-length wooly coat. The items fit reasonably well. From a bin of thick-heeled shoes, she extracted a few pairs, plowed her feet in, and chose the least ugly. Alongside the shoe bin was one of accoutrements—belts, pins, scarves, hats—from which she plucked a black, narrow-brimmed cloche hat and a plain white handkerchief, both of which she inspected for cleanliness. Whoever had put the selection together possessed a shrewd eye for what Linnea thought of as British drab, the purpose, she assumed, to exhibit a woman so bland that no one would give her a second glance.

Reluctantly she surrendered her uniform and the small billfold that held her military ID and a few pounds in cash. She had no stockings; military women rarely wore them, though a few—Dodgy Dray came to mind—penciled vertical lines down the backs of their legs to imitate seams. On her bed lay muslin underwear and woolen socks. At least they were new.

Mrs. Wolters brought lunch. More nervous than hungry, Linnea ate the fish sandwich, chips, and a pickle. Just before three—so she guessed, being no longer in possession of a watch—Mrs. Wolters led her outside and to the garage. The uniformed woman who'd driven her to the house last evening sat at the wheel of the sedan. Mrs. Wolters slid into the back seat beside Linnea. For a while the driver meandered through Mayfair. Linnea might have asked their destination, had the countenance of her chaperone invited questions. They threaded into adjoining Soho, purring up behind people who strolled blithely in the roadway. The rationing of petrol had severely thinned the motor traffic.

On Great Pulteney Street, they halted in front of a pub. "Head straight through to the alley in back," said Mrs. Wolters. "The rear door should be open. Don't interact with anyone in the pub. A car will be waiting on the other side."

Any hint who might be in the car? No.

She crossed the sidewalk to the pub, tugged open the heavy door. The dimly lit interior stank of rum and beer. What would her taciturn escort say, if she were to drop onto a barstool and order a pint? She shook off the whimsical idea; having no money ruled it out anyway. She tapped through. A walkway sluiced to the alley where awaited a black sedan, the rear door ajar.

She climbed in, and a spindly gent garbed in the male equivalent of British drab sprang from behind the steering wheel to thump her door shut.

Opposite her sat a trim, onyx-haired man who looked to be in his late thirties. In an upper-class British accent, he intoned, "Hello. My name is Sebastian. You shouldn't say anything for the time being." He stretched an arm across her and snapped shut the window curtain. The interior darkened.

The curtains didn't keep her from looking through the front window. The car took a series of turns, she supposed to make sure no one was following. The cityscape retreated, and in the fading daylight they jostled along a country road through dim hamlets whose residents had already drawn their blackout curtains. She smelled farms. The olfactory tinge must have goaded the piquancy of the half-digested fish sandwich to gurgle up from her stomach. The collar laces pinched at her neck. She untied them.

The ride smoothed. Good, the jolting was over. She'd feel better in a minute, and the sensation she was going to vomit would lapse.

It didn't. She clasped her hand over her mouth. "You'd better pull over," she trumpeted through her fingers.

"Beg your pardon, mum?" said the driver.

"Pull over. I have to throw up."

He swerved to the side, and she leapt out and upchucked over a roadside hawthorn hedge fronting a redbrick house. Half-digested fish remnants hung like desiccated petals.

She breathed. Done?

No. She heaved again.

Impressive. Whatever they had in mind for her, surely they'd re-think it. She wiped her mouth with the back of her hand, returned to the car. "Do you mind if we keep the window open?" It occurred to her that Sebastian had asked her not to speak, probably so the driver wouldn't glean she was an American.

"That would be fine," said Sebastian with a sigh.

– 9 –

Late January 1944

Dusk shrouded the Lodge's south-sloping lawn. From his window on the second floor the English would have called the first, Verrick peered between the blackout curtains. A car, its headlights hooded, crunched along the driveway to halt in front.

By comparison with most American lawyers entering their quinary decade, he was in good shape physically. He watched his diet, didn't smoke, and played squash in the winter and tennis in summer. Even so, the last forty-eight hours had wrecked him. One of the surprise revelations of intercontinental air travel was the debilitating fatigue it imposed. Throw in his patchy sleep last night and the difference in time zones—London's clock at Greenwich Mean Time plus an hour, five hours earlier than Washington's on U.S. War Time—and it was all he could do to keep his concentration. War was better left to the young. Sounded like a famous quote, by whom he had no idea.

He had little to gripe about. Not long ago, having shuttled by train from Washington to New York City as he frequently did, he'd been home to celebrate his twenty-third wedding anniversary. He and his wife Grace lived in a spacious three-bedroom apartment on Riverside Drive, the windows featuring a prize view of the Hudson. He could afford the place because his job at Donovan's law firm had paid him what he judged to be a king's ransom, and even if his OSS salary didn't keep up, he'd still come far from the circumstances of his youth. The family cabin in Sullivan County, New Hampshire had edged dense, hilly woods full of wild game. They ate what his father shot or trapped or his mother grew in their small garden. If the gunsights, traps, and garden came up empty, as often happened in winter, they subsisted on oats fried in lard with scraps of sun-dried deer jerky thrown in for flavor. Rain or cold, the children walked a mile to the one-room schoolhouse. It was how people lived, and most of them stoically shrouded the distress from their deprivations.

Less so behind closed doors. His father's anger pivoted like a weathervane from shouting tantrums to stewing silence. A few drinks greased a resigned, sardonic humor. At least he didn't gamble, curse, or hit. He had expected his life to turn out differently. It should have. The newspapers and books he read might have lofted him to a respectable employment. He preferred to hunt, chop wood, and brood. Their half-acre of land was ill-suited for a farm, and he wasn't one who'd have thrived in the pursuit; farmers had to grit. His indolence and aversion to doing other people's bidding forced his wife to take low-paying jobs. One was as an attendant at an old folk's home. Summers she brought young Gabe to help ease the old timers in or out of their chairs and play the boy crutch. When he wasn't bearing their gnarly hands on his shoulders, he read aloud to them. At home he kept reading in a corner where the light fell from the hanging bulb. His mother had decreed it could stay on as late as anyone chose to read. His father didn't argue, not about the light, anyway.

Was there an unspoken conspiracy between mother and her first-born that his readings would strengthen him to bear the knobby hands of his parents in their old age? Maybe, but he wasn't able to help her much. She died young, in her late forties, when he was fresh out of law school and penniless. His father he did support later on, sending him monthly stipends until the man's death in early 1940 at age 85. The passing occasioned a reunion with his two brothers and sister in New Hampshire. Their humble origins considered, they'd all done well; they had jobs and families. The siblings saw each other from time to time, less of him. That he had money was hard to hide. He offered to pay the funeral expenses, arousing resentments: Thank you, big shot from New York. The offer stood, and they accepted. The goodbyes were awkward. It would have been nice to have stayed in closer touch. He hadn't seen them since.

New York's prewar law scene was a seething *ignis fatuus* of money, power, and stress. Temptations offered, yet in marriage as in his profession, he was as faithful, predictable, and, yes, as boring as he appeared to be. He worked exhausting hours, often seven days a week. Any book he endowed with his precious time had to be pertinent to some dimension of his job. Rarely did he bother with fiction, which struck him as trivial. Occasionally he attended movies and stage productions with Grace, who enjoyed them immensely. He couldn't help spotting the artifice that spoiled the show. The exceptions were the dramas of Shakespeare whose insights into humanity's subterfuges tantalized him.

Then Donovan inveigled him in the domain of espionage, where the intrigues seemed to coalesce out of thin air. Spycraft was said to be mankind's second-oldest profession and far dirtier than the first. The comparison was inept. A deeper look revealed a duality: To trick one's enemies and those who would abet them was essential. No less so was to be exactingly honest with one's colleagues. An intelligence officer must embody an infrangible integrity alongside the aptitude to dissimulate, qualities that shouldn't easily coexist in a person. They required one who grasped that truth embodied in absolutism equaled fanaticism, and deception might be as virtuous as it was villainous.

Trust played a role in relationships with foreign allies too, as long as you fathomed the nuances. Foreign intelligence officers could be friends and collaborators, but they were also sharks who in the perceived furtherance of their national interests might take a bite out of yours. Knowing when to be candid or opaque or to lie outright, and to glean the circumstances when you might be lied *to*, were forms of art. No doubt Donovan had summoned Verrick here for the latter's skillfulness at navigating the tricky waters.

The hazard: The Brits were the Great Whites of the trade.

Two passengers alighted from the car's backseat. From her kennel, Bags barked, startling the young woman. The porch bulb illuminated her pale skin, not uncommon in winter, yet hers was nearly as white as his bleached shirt. The visage made him think the so-called Factory House must be a cave-like cloister.

He descended the stairs. In the foyer, a tall man in an elegant suit and overcoat looked up and said, "You must be Gabriel. I'm Sebastian." They shook hands. The Englishman turned, apparently to introduce the young woman. She had vanished somewhere. Nonplused, he said, "I take it Avry has given you the shilling tour?"

"Yes. I even fed Bags her dinner."

Sebastian laughed. "You have a friend for life. We'll have to afford Linnea the same privilege."

"Where is she?"

"Probably the loo. I'm afraid the turns along the road did her no favor."

Which explained her paleness. Verrick mentally crossed out his speculation about Factory House.

"So you're to keep the good general informed of our preparations?"

"Yes, him and him alone," said Verrick.

A nod. Must be the answer the Englishman wished to hear. "You're one of his deputies?"

"That's right."

"May I ask the title of your position?"

"They keep changing it. I think the latest is so-and-so for émigré affairs. Bottom line, I do whatever the boss tells me."

"Ah. A shared propensity. I bring it up out of protocol. You and I are of the same official rank, apparently."

The same rank in organizations of unequal standing, Verrick construed. Not equal at all.

Linnea emerged, veering first in the wrong direction along the adjoining hallway, spurring Sebastian to call, "We're this way." Roughly five-foot seven, she posed straight without appearing stiff, her fawn hair cut just above her shoulders accentuating her pallor and the depth of her cobalt-blue eyes. The file had spotlighted her gift for languages, her scores in Swedish and Russian the highest possible, and fluent-plus in German. He expected a foreign accent to infuse her speech and was surprised to hear pure American. "Sorry to keep you waiting," she said. "I got sick during the ride and had to compose myself." Her unfortunate car sickness must have embarrassed her. It hadn't shaken her poise. Looking him straight in the eye, she proffered her hand.

"Gabriel Verrick," he blurted.

"Are you with Grosvenor, sir?" From the five syllables, she must have picked out his American accent.

"Yes and no. I represent our organization. I traveled yesterday from the States."

"And this is Avry," said Sebastian, "your head of training."

She shook Avry's hand. "Might I fetch you a glass of water?" he said in his rich brogue.

"Yes, please."

"While he brings that, let's get started," said Sebastian. He led them to a room with a door sign that said Classroom 1 in the gymnasium wing. A long table on one end mushroomed a photo projector aimed down the length at a collapsible screen. "Sit here, please, Linnea. Gabriel, this side."

Avry arrived, situated the water glass in front of her, and fitted a slide strip into the projector.

The lights dimmed.

On shaky legs, Linnea stepped from the car. At least she'd avoided spattering herself with vomit; the front of her coat and skirt looked clean. She retied the blouse laces at the neck, faced what appeared to be a large country house, and jumped when a massive, oddly colored German Shepherd commenced to bark menacingly from within the confines of its kennel.

"Please follow me," said Sebastian.

If America contrasted with European countries in a fundamental respect, it was that the former lacked an aristocracy. What substituted was the possession of money, bestowing a kind of nobility on anyone who had enough of it. Unlike her father's strategy to earn money, Linnea's took no account of luck or trickery; hers was an alertness for opportunities and the earnest application of her talents. To protect herself from employers who might exploit her, she'd joined a labor union. Her stronger protection, her in-demand languages, gave her some negotiating power. The key was to know how far she could push, and cognizant of the prewar job market, she appraised her alternatives. If the translation service treated her unfairly, she'd quit and go elsewhere.

A different kettle of fish, the OSS. She did well in elevating her salary signing up. The downside? She was in the Army, compelled to obey orders, and beyond the safety of unions or the option of going elsewhere. People in the military went to war. Bombs fell on them, their planes crashed, torpedoes struck their ships. Did the hazards pertain to her? Complacently she thought they didn't. She signed on with the government on the calculation that doing so might segue to a better job at war's end. When asked if she was interested in operational deployment, without hesitation she replied no. To be yanked as a child from country to country might infuse one with an enduring travel lust. In her case it had done the opposite, scraping away any inclination to pursue adventure, and with the Russian literature she'd studied at NYU still running around in her head, on the personal statement the OSS asked her to compose she penned in a line from *Crime and Punishment:* 'From a hundred rabbits you can't make a horse,' adding, 'I am a rabbit, as I wish to be.' Later she'd pondered the wisdom of revealing herself so openly on a form likely to become a part of her permanent file.

Another quote from Dostoyevsky: 'The more cunning a man is, the simpler the trap he must be caught in.'

At the table, the man who'd introduced himself as Gabriel Verrick took the chair opposite. He had winced slightly upon saying his surname; she supposed he shouldn't have. Here was a man who wanted to do the right thing. His kindly expression seemed to correspond. Above his pewter moustache, the heather eyes regarded her empathetically. He must see the ghostly pale, frumpily dressed young woman she'd faced in the loo mirror. At least she knew something she hadn't before: how readily she could get car sick. Like everyone else aboard the troopship that had delivered her to Great Britain, she'd been seasick, but until today she hadn't thrown up from riding in a car.

What if they put her in an airplane?

Avry switched on the projector, filling the screen with a smoky blur. A German naval officer took grainy shape, the uniform black, the gray hair framing an imperial face. He appeared to be in his fifties. The rough margins suggested the photo had been torn from some publication. "Meet Admiral Constantine Diefenbach of the German Kriegsmarine," said Sebastian. "Six months ago, he was transferred from the Kiel naval base to the General Staff in Berlin. He's 56 years old and a member of the Nazi party. Almost certainly he knows the details of German plans to repel the Allied invasion of the European coast. Hitler has commanded that the invasion be hurled back into the sea. Obviously, no Allied intelligence goal ranks higher than to penetrate German intentions toward the event."

The projector ratcheted to a new slide. A multicolor map of northern Europe flashed up, Sweden and Germany highlighted in a mustardy yellow.

"Strategic bombing has set back Germany's military industries. More than ever, the Nazis need the high-quality ball bearings that Sweden manufactures. The Allies are exerting immense diplomatic pressure on the Swedes to sever their exports. I assume you're aware of this, Linnea, from your analytical studies."

Was she being asked to comment? She decided not to.

"It used to be that Germany could intimidate the European neutrals into compliance without much strain on the part of her diplomats. The Wehrmacht's collapses on the Russian front have reshaped the scenario. The Nazis now must deal with the neutrals according to the same rules as everyone else, through negotiation. Two and one-half weeks from now, Admiral Diefenbach will lead a delegation to Stockholm to arrange terms for the further purchases of Swedish steel and other materials valuable to the German war effort. Why is a naval officer leading a diplomatic mission? Formerly a military attaché, he knows the protocols and is intelligent and charming, qualities that pay dividends at the negotiating table. On top of all that, pillars of the Nazi regime like Foreign Minister von Ribbentrop and SS leader Himmler hold him in esteem."

A third slide showed a photo of a walled structure, unmistakably the Kremlin in Moscow.

"The most remarkable thing about Diefenbach is the one he's gone to the greatest lengths to conceal: He's a communist. Once in power, the Nazis thoroughly gutted the communists from the German establishment. He lasted because he was in the hands of professionals. The Soviet NKVD secretly recruited, trained, and ran him beginning in the 1930s. Founded as the Cheka—the Extraordinary Commission to Fight Counterrevolution and Sabotage—by Feliks Dzerzhinsky in 1917, the NKVD is among the world's most capable espionage services."

Her mother would have called them the *Okhrana*, thought Linnea, a holdover from the Czarist days when whispered tales of the shadowy, reputedly omnipotent organization abounded.

"In the late 30s, the NKVD like the rest of the Soviet apparatus fell victim to Stalin's boundless paranoia. Many Soviet intelligence officers were summoned to Moscow and ruthlessly purged, and the same fate probably befell the poor fellow who handled Diefenbach, who went dormant until 1940. It was then that the NKVD, resuming its activities under fresh management, reactivated him. A woman named Maria Toft became his cutout. She met with him in Berlin, received the intelligence he collected, and passed it to a radioman who transmitted it to Moscow."

The screen displayed what appeared to be the passport photo of a middle-aged woman with grayish hair curling at the shoulders. The bitter twist of her lips hinted she comprehended the risk she was taking. "In July of 1941, the Nazi counterintelligence watchdogs sniffed out Maria Toft. We don't know for certain how they caught up with her. Their radio-triangulation capabilities had advanced far by then. Or perhaps a lowly neighborhood informant noticed something amiss; sometimes all it takes is the smallest trifle to compromise a spy. The authorities stormed the residence and were seconds from seizing her when she killed herself with a pistol. In their consummate way, they searched the place, tearing up the floorboards, dismantling the furniture, and ripping open the walls, fireplace, and ceilings to the studs. Their efforts uncovered the remnants of a notebook written in a simple code, which when broken revealed the existence but not the identity of the agent she was the cutout for. The Nazis thereupon codenamed the mysterious spy GALILEO. For a while, the hunt for him intrigued Hitler personally, but like most others, the Führer came to assume that GALILEO had escaped eastward. Only a few German counterintelligence diehards believed he remained in place, dormant and awaiting the chance to reactivate. Which is precisely the status he occupies."

Verrick said, "You know for certain that Diefenbach is GALILEO?"

"Yes."

"How?"

"I'm afraid I can't go into that."

Linnea said, "May I ask a question?"

"By all means."

"How reliable is your source?" She thought of the sketchy, often flawed intelligence that crossed her desk, and the intriguing 'spiked' report she had read last evening.

"Right that you should ask. Very established and reliable, I'd say."

Clearly Sebastian didn't wish to discuss the sourcing.

"Which brings us to the reason we are here. In Berlin, GALILEO is unapproachable. His trip to Sweden introduces a singular opportunity. We surmise that, if he believes he is being recontacted by the Soviet NKVD, the service that ran him while he was active and whose communist creed he holds dear, he will agree to resume spying. We plan to warm him with his own kindling, so to speak. If we succeed, he will think he's gone back to work for the Russians. In reality, he will be responding to our requirements."

She caught the slight furrow of Verrick's brow.

"It won't be easy to get to GALILEO, even in Stockholm," resumed Sebastian. "Whoever comes near him will first have to pass as one who belongs there. To the spy himself, the approach must be utterly convincing, or he'll balk." Sebastian looked at her and said what she dreaded he would say: "Linnea, with your native Swedish and Russian, we think you can gain access to him and carry it off."

She choked out, "He speaks Russian?"

"Fluently. In the 1930s he was posted as a military attaché in Moscow, probably the venue where the Soviets recruited him. Even if his Russian has worn a bit rusty since, he'll be able to detect a native versus a non-native speaker. As to how he will react, having had no contact with his controllers for two and one-half years, certainly he will be taken aback. He'll pull himself together soon enough. We have brainstormed the four main possibilities. Initially he might play dumb until he trusts your bona fides; acknowledge his past role but insist that it's too dangerous to resume; agree to reactivate conditionally, perhaps introducing a delay; or consent to resume immediately and unconditionally."

Or a fifth, that he pulls out a pistol and starts shooting. She stole a glance to Verrick, who from the tweak of his mouth seemed to be thinking the same thing.

"We'll walk you through the variations. The more authentic you are, the more reassured he'll be. Keep in mind, a significant boost to his motives will be his comprehension that Germany is losing the war, and the Soviets winning. It's a bounty he'd be unwise to pass up, to be in Stalin's good graces when the dust settles. GALILEO has survived this long; he's no fool. Odds are he's been anticipating an NKVD attempt to reactivate him, and it gives us a fair chance of success."

Verrick said, "Any chance the real Soviets will have a go at him while he's in Stockholm?"

"The NKVD has a large residency there. The Swedes don't like the Soviets and keep a close watch on. For the NKVD to attempt to contact their man in Stockholm would risk compromising him. We don't think they'll try."

Verrick's expression had gone flat. What was he thinking? That the plan seemed founded on conjecture?

No one asked her if she accepted the role Sebastian had in mind. Perhaps they assumed she'd already committed to it, or that joining the OSS embodied sufficient consent, or that signing the hazardous duty agreement equaled volunteering.

Who cared what they *assumed*? At no point had she agreed to this.

She resolved to speak to Verrick in private.

– 10 –

Late January 1944

The four moved to the dining room that opened beyond the hallway off the front entrance. Unsettled from the car ride, she'd have eaten little in any case. The main dish, mutton stew, cinched it. She downed a few of the vegetables, avoiding the meat, and declined the red wine, of which Sebastian had a glass, Avry two, and Verrick none.

Avry's craggy face made him look older than his lively Scottish brogue let on. He entertained them with tales of his encounters with the locals at the Hornchurch pub. "'So yer one of the lads from the base,'" he mimicked, parodying the east-of-London accent. "To which I give a grunt, and they likewise, grunts all around. They're too polite to ask why I'm not in uniform. Perhaps they guess I'm a flier on holiday, as if any flier in his right mind would spend his holiday in Hornchurch."

He sipped his wine, and she caught the tick lines around the russet-of-fallen-leaf eyes that flashed amusement, discernment, discretion. "The ones who scare me are the kids who blurt out what they're really thinking. A boy scutters up and says, 'Are you the one with the giant dog at the Chatham House?'—that's what they call the Lodge in town—and I say, 'Wah dah'r ye tokin' a-boat?' One day he and his chums wandered up the lane, he tells me, paying no heed to the signs, and gained the fierce beast's personal acquaintance. Scared them straight out of their bones. Big as a horse, the lad bursts."

"She *is* as big as a horse," said Verrick. Everyone laughed.

The dinner over, Verrick and Sebastian stepped off to chat. She hoped to adjourn to the bedroom Avry had pointed out—top of the stairs and 'round to the right—but she hadn't yet entered. She folded her napkin.

Avry said, "Up for a walk?"

"At night?"

"There's a path. Come on."

…*your head of training.* It wasn't a request.

Adequate on pavements, her thick heels were ill suited for the soft ground; the edges dug in and threatened to tip her. Fitfully she balanced to the kennel, where Avry clipped a leash onto Bags's collar and handed it to Linnea. "From tonight on, she'll glean you're one of us." He aimed a flashlight, illuminating a path descending into skeletal woods. The dog, massive enough to have dashed off dragging her newly appointed leash-holder behind, gently led.

She said, "Your name, is it Russian?"

"Avrelian Maksimovich Khilkov in full, of Russian aristocratic lineage, or so it's been touted."

"My mother would approve. She believes in such things."

"The English, too. They're inescapably enamored with royal blood. Personally, I have my doubts about how much I possess; I suspect a few mutts may have jumped the fence along the way. Of course, I don't advertise the suspicion, among them especially."

Curious, that an officer of the British Secret Service would differentiate himself from the English. Was the sentiment genuine, or a technique he trotted out to build rapport with her, *us* against the ruling establishment? She pictured the kids on the ship who'd tried to trick her into jabbering bad words to adults.

She said, "Do you speak Russian?"

"I score as fluent in grammar and comprehension, though nowhere near passing for the real article. My parents are. They tried to immerse me as a lad. Typical brat, I wanted to talk like my Edinburgh pals. It's a wonder I learned any Russian at all."

They passed along a chain-link fence topped with barbed wire. A mile or so off, a tower and the roofs of hangars phosphoresced in the glow of a half moon. Flashlights blinked on and off like fireflies around the ghostly outlines of twin-engine planes. "Night-fighter Mosquitoes, radar equipped," he said. "Fastest kites in the sky."

He'd been with MI-6 for six years, recruited out of Oxford University where he taught Russian and served as the assistant rugby coach. In the 1930s, he'd traveled to the Continent and picked up fair French and some German. "The languages were my ticket to the corridors of intelligence. If I'd been a mere professor of English, the spooks would have paid me no mind, and I'd happily have spent the war in the quietude of academe."

Another rapport-building device? As to whether he was married or had children, he disclosed nothing.

"Have you been to the Continent since the war started?"

"On three occasions. To France twice, by parachute and boat, and to Norway."

"How's your Norwegian?"

"I'm able to ask for directions. I relied on my other languages and the odd interpreter to get my meaning across. A nerve-wracking place, Norway. Every minute felt like it was borrowed at exorbitant interest, each move a toss of the dice. And the place is jeelit as hell."

"Jeelit?"

"Bone-piercing cold."

"Will you go back? To the Continent, I mean."

He didn't immediately answer. The flashlight glimmered off the austere trees and filmy pools and Bags padding contentedly ahead. When the outline of the Lodge backdropped the trees, he said, "Let's stop here for a minute."

She tugged the leash. Obediently Bags sat.

"You must be wondering to yourself just how daft a caper this is. I thought so myself when I first heard it—a cold approach and a false flag to boot? Yet the more I mull it over, the more rightful it strikes me, to have a go, I mean. We haven't a single agent worth a bawbee in the German military, least of all a penetration of the General Staff. Shameful, with the invasion looming.

"You asked if I'll go back to the occupied Continent. Honestly, I won't relish it, the odds tend to catch up. Now, Sweden's a separate case, a neutral country. Not that you don't have to keep your wits intact, but the worst that can happen, if the Swedes arrest you, is you're interned for the duration, feasting on reindeer stew."

Reflexively she grimaced, recalling the gamey meat.

He laughed. 'We'll just have to spice it up, won't we?"

"You're going too?"

"How could I pass?"

Most decidedly she needed to talk to Mr. Verrick.

Avry showed her the dogfood cabinet, and she heaped three scoops into Bags's dish. When she unclipped the leash, the animal brushed by, the big tail swishing against her knees.

Between the Lodge's dining room and the kitchen ran a galley with a nicely stocked bar. The entry level was dark; everyone else seemed to have retired to their rooms. Verrick located the galley's light switch, flipped it on, poured himself a Scotch, and in the same seat he'd filled for dinner regarded the inch of roan-tinted fluid. Donovan didn't drink liquor. Verrick permitted himself one drink daily. Helped him to reflect.

He'd been in his room when he caught the door to Linnea's open and shut across the hall. She'd gone somewhere with Avry, apparently, and come back. He deliberated whether he should knock and inquire how she was doing. No doubt she was tired. Better to let her rest.

What must she think of all this?

Wentworth's false-flag plan had an undeniable allure. To acquire a penetration of the German General Staff would be invaluable. Certainly Linnea comprehended. More than that, she had raised the cardinal point underpinning the project's feasibility, the question Verrick himself had been about to: How reliable was the British source who'd revealed that Admiral Diefenbach was a communist and former Soviet spy?

Right that you should ask. Very established and reliable, I'd say.

'Established,' common in law and many other fields, in intelligence terminology meant *vintage*. The process of vetting a live agent was at best painstaking and oft-times impossible, and intelligence services rightly balked at unshackling a source from the misgivings that pervaded. To achieve the imprimatur 'established and reliable,' his or her information must have been corroborated repeatedly and on critical points. Rare was the source who met the standard, yet by his choice of words, Wentworth had awarded him or her a blue-ribbon standing.

Maybe the source wasn't a person at all. Verrick was among the few Americans read into ULTRA, the codename for the product from Bletchley Park, the phenomenal British unit that had cracked Germany's machine-coded communications. Bletchley's wizards might have deciphered the Nazi GALILEO file, meaning that these were the enemy's own secrets. It would explain Wentworth's faith in the sourcing, up to a point: If the Germans themselves didn't know GALILEO's identity, how could the Brits have intercepted and broken it?

The ones who had the real goods on the spy were the Soviets; they'd recruited and run him. Yet to assume the source of MI-6's information was a Soviet seemed to kick the legs out from its unconditional reliability. No sane intelligence service would withdraw the fire blanket of skepticism that fitted a Soviet source.

Here was a proper mystery.

The briefing had not touched on other key facets: How did the Brits plan to put Linnea in front of GALILEO? And if the spy did agree to reactivate, how would they handle him when he returned to Germany?

In Berlin, he's unapproachable.

Not trivial challenges. But the legendary spymasters must have thought it all through, and no doubt they would elaborate in due course.

He finished his drink and headed upstairs to bed.

– 11 –

Mid-January 1944

Gott im Himmel, was the sun out? Through the spaces between the tape convoluting his office window, the sunbeams scattered breadcrumbs of light across Mauer's desktop and the Gestapo packet. If only the crumbs led somewhere. They didn't. The damned document was incomprehensible.

Like the confines of a prison cell, his office dispirited him. Bleakly prosaic, the photo of Hitler, the desk and chairs, the metal safe. Early in the war, he had volunteered for combat duty and astonishingly been granted a position aboard the auxiliary cruiser *Komet,* based with the fleet at the Kiel naval base. More than twenty years ago, his parents had forbidden him from going to war. Now at last he would! He had durable eyeglasses with an elastic strap to hold them on in rough seas. The terrible eyesight that had plagued his first sea voyage would not hinder him from performing his duties.

An officer at sea does not require many possessions. Authorized to bring only two regulation-sized trunks aboard *Komet,* Mauer had been at home packing them when he received notification that his orders had been rescinded. Why and by whom? No explanation was forthcoming. To his surprise Admiral Canaris personally took up his cause, demanding to know why the assignment had been revoked and one of his officers treated so dismissively. In the First World War, Canaris had served aboard the German warship *Dresden* and commanded a U-Boat. He understood the lure of combat duty.

A week passed. Canaris summoned him. In the corner behind the desk, two dachshunds lay supine on their blankets. If the admiral left the office, the pampered pets would pad along, their bodies wriggling like tubular accordions on stunted legs. "I'm sorry to say I cannot budge the fleet," said Canaris. "They won't change their minds or discuss why."

Mauer knew why. At forty, he was old for combat duty, soft from deskwork, rounded at the middle. He wore thick glasses and had almost no experience at sea. Why the hell *would* the fleet want him?

The rationale didn't stem the ache of rejection. He went to see his friend Gels Belk, who other than Jana was the sole person with whom he could share his candid opinions. They'd met eight years before by way of their wives, members of a reading club at a time when readers could choose books that weren't Nazi approved. Gels's fellow officers had nicknamed him *der Zauberer,* the sorcerer, for his prematurely white hair and almost freakish sapience. Assigned then to the Abwehr's land intelligence section, he listened to the sad tale of the lost assignment, pondered for a minute, and blurted, "You're truly out of your mind, you know that? To have applied for sea duty at your doddering age? An absurdity. And you're *mournful* they turned you down?"

"I'm crushed."

Gels scoffed. "How could it have come as a surprise? You're as fat as me."

"I am *not* as fat as you."

"Well, almost. And you're a bigger fool. Resentment is like a rotten egg that when you break it leaves a terrible mess over you and everyone else."

"That comparison makes no sense."

"You should be thanking the heavens, my friend. Do you realize how many combat officers at this minute are wishing they worked for the Abwehr in Berlin? Damned near all of them."

Perhaps Gels had been right. The British sank the *Komet* in 1942.

Last November, British bombs had destroyed the Abwehr's original headquarters of stately old mansions at 76-78 Tirpitzüfer Strasse, striking at night. Though the event brought the war somewhat closer, it failed to break the fearsome monotony of Mauer's duties. Sometimes he thought he would have been happier aboard the *Komet,* even if it meant to have met his fate. Yet whether his work was tiresome or not, never had it reeked of dishonor. The Abwehr was an entity of the German military, subordinate to the Oberkommando der Wehrmacht, or OKW, and supportive of those who fought the war. The Gestapo, by contrast, was a creature of the Nazi Party and servile to its political interests. Until recently, he might have objected to being ordered to examine this packet of nonsense the Gestapo had sent him, arguing that the directive originated outside his military chain of command and therefore had no validity. Alas, the situation had become fragile. Heinrich Himmler, Hitler's henchman and head of the SS, hated the notion that a German intelligence organization could exist outside his control, and he had petitioned the Führer to subsume the Abwehr under the Reich Security Main Office, the Reichssicherheitshauptamt, or RSHA, the umbrella board governing the Gestapo and the Sicherheitsdienst. Perhaps reluctant to annoy the Wehrmacht, Hitler so far had refused. But rumors had it that Admiral Canaris and his senior assistants were suspected of disloyalty. Sooner or later, said the rumors, Himmler would pull the Abwehr under his dark cloak alongside the other Nazi slime worms. To the officers of the service, the change portended evisceration. Hadn't Himmler declared that the first demand of German intelligence bodies was not truth but loyalty to the Führer? And heading the RSHA was a Nazi ideologue named Ernst Kaltenbrunner whose scarred face evoked the monster he was reputed to be.

All this considered, nothing had happened so far; the Abwehr still remained aloof from Himmler's clutches. The calm before the storm? No matter. To refuse the Gestapo would be foolhardy.

He paged through the document again. What the hell was he looking at? An interrogation transcript, that much was obvious. It opened with the questions, "Are you a spy? What was your mission? Who are your contacts?" The replies were no more than a gallimaufry of disassociated words. There must have been preliminary questions about the subject's identity, but these portions had been excised. Why? And why had they sent *him* the repulsive thing?

He picked up the phone and listened for the dial tone. Six weeks ago, a massive air raid had destroyed Berlin's central telephone exchange. Repairs had left the connections spotty. Today the line sounded functional, and the automatic switching must be too, for no operator interposed. He dialed the number on the letterhead.

"Front office," a woman said curtly.

"Good morning. Might I be connected to Gruppenführer Heinrich Müller?"

"And you are?"

"Kommodore Wilhelm Mauer of the Abwehr."

"Wait."

In the background clacked typewriters, probably transcribing whispers from the thousands of snitches the Gestapo employed. A male voice snapped, "This is SS Standartenführer Bernhardt Stabl, adjutant to Gruppenführer Müller. What can I do for you, Kommodore?"

"This morning I received a document by courier…"

"I'm familiar with it."

"I think it may have been sent to me by mistake. The Abwehr is not an analytical organization."

"I am aware of the functions of the Abwehr. There was no mistake."

"Have you read this mishmash? What am I to do with it?"

"Extract the essence. Tell us what it means."

It meant nothing. He caught himself. Stabl radiated the tone of one speaking to a muddled teenager. To defy a Gestapo prelate would be unwise, especially when the status of the Abwehr bobbed in uncertainty.

Mauer said, "Have you given it to others?"

"Not your concern."

"Perhaps I could pose follow-on questions to the subject."

"Not possible."

Meaning the subject was dead. "Might you tell me more about him?"

"He was a British naval officer."

"His name?"

"How is that pertinent?"

"I can research it. Perhaps we have him in our files."

"He isn't there. We looked."

"May I speak to the interrogator?"

"Not practical. An SS unit in France was responsible."

"When was this?"

"The first days of January."

So, ten days or so ago, Mauer inferred, the SS had interrogated a British naval officer and killed him in the process, a violation of the Geneva Convention and the principles of correct treatment of military prisoners of war. To mind came Hitler's grotesque order of 1942 ordering the execution of those deemed to be commandos.

Stabl said, "Please give the document the highest priority."

"I understood the cover letter."

"Listen, Mauer, we sent it to you because you are said to be proficient in such things."

As if he'd spent his career elucidating gibberish.

Stabl added, "Your favorable reputation is not one that describes the Abwehr in general. I hope you will not disappoint us."

"I'll lend it my complete attention."

He didn't; he had more sensible matters to attend to. As evening darkened the windows, Gerta pulled the blackout curtains shut, flattening the seams against leakage. Perhaps because he had promised Stabl, he pulled the document once more under his nose and paged through, percolating the same incoherent mishmash as before: random numbers and words, like far, heavy, deep, viscosity.

He stared. Viscosity was not a random word.

The German *Viskosität* was a derivative of the Latin *viscositas* and a near cognate in English. Had the subject really said viscosity, or had he been misunderstood?

He picked up the phone and again dialed the letterhead number. Two minutes later, Stabl was on the line. "What is it, Mauer?"

"May I ask, is there another, more complete version of the report?"

"Why would there be?"

"You said the subject was a British naval officer. He must have been questioned in English, and the responses translated into German."

"This is pertinent for what reason?"

Evasive as hell, this bastard. If Stabl had been a regular staff man, Mauer would have reamed his ears. As it was, he kept his tone explanatory. "Some terminology, if not translated by an expert, can suffer a degradation of meaning."

A pause. "I will let you know."

Half an hour later, the phone rang. Gerta answered. From the doorway, she said, "A call, Kommodore."

He picked up. *"Ja?"*

Without preamble, Stabl said, "How is your English, Mauer?"

"I read it well enough." He had studied English at the university, and it had advantaged him at the Abwehr to keep up the skill.

"A courier will bring you the full copy and reclaim the one you have."

The courier arrived. Mauer handed over the original, already dog-eared from his paging through. "Is it all here?" said the courier, his deep-brown leather jacket glistening from the rain.

"Except for the cover letter addressed to me. I removed it."

The courier stuffed the papers in his lock bag and gave Mauer a taped bundle. He clicked his heels, spraying droplets on the floor, and departed.

In the open doorway, Gerta said, "Shall I stay, Kommodore?"

"No. Go home to your family. I'll lock up."

She seemed uncertain. Generally, she was the one who opened and closed the office.

He'd already scissored open the package. "You should go."

– 12 –

Late January 1944

A tap at her door prefaced Avry's muffled voice: "Breakfast in ten minutes. I'm leaving here the clothes you should wear and a Swedish newspaper. Be sure to lock the newspaper in your drawer anytime you're not reading it. The same goes for items you may have that bear your name, such as letters."

What letters? She'd been ordered to leave everything behind.

"Oh, and loop the key cord around your neck."

She rubbed her stomach still sore from yesterday's vomiting. Avry had warned her they'd be off to an early start. She clicked on the bedside lamp to view the wind-up alarm clock. 4:30 a.m.!

Why hadn't she spoken to Mr. Verrick last night? Was it uncertainty, or exhaustion?

Half asleep, she staggered to the door, creaked it open, and collected the clothes that rose in a gray cairn. Here were two pairs of rubber-soled boat shoes and two sets of dense-cotton RAF sweats. Grimacing, she pulled the cold fabric over her bare legs and examined herself in the mirror. Baggy and sexless.

The newspaper was a week-old copy of the *Stockholms-Tidningen*. Too sleepy to browse the front page, she plopped it in the top dresser drawer equipped with a lock, turned the key fitted with a cord, and looped the cord over her head. The room door had no lock.

"In here," Avry called through the double doorway to the new wing that hosted the gymnasium and the two classrooms. In the foreground, a folding table featured a breakfast of porridge, fruit, and bread rolls. No bacon, but coffee, thank God. "From this morning on, you'll eat your meals here with me. Now is the last time you'll speak English in training; it's strictly Russian after, with Swedish and German occasionally. We'll bring in a native Swede and German for you to practice. The exceptions are when you speak to Gabriel, or in the event Sebastian wishes to have a word."

She picked up a bread roll, still warm, and commenced to slather butter on.

"Oh, and we're expecting the clothier today. She'll size you for the Continent. Garments are a way either to blend in or attract unwanted attention. Sport the wrong stitching or materials, and you might as well wrap yourself in the Union Jack. We buy up articles from émigrés who've arrived recently from the Continent. Don't worry, we've washed out the lice."

"*Khorosho,*" she replied in Russian. Good. She couldn't think of what else to say.

Breakfast over, he led her to Classroom 2, skirting the canvas exercise mats on the gym floor. He spoke in grammatically proper Russian: "Gym rules: never step on the mats in shoes, it grits them up." She thought his Russian was a bit gritty too, his Scottish accent staining it like the feet of someone who'd trodden through coal dust. All her life she'd spoken Russian with her mother, and she'd studied the literature in college. Now she was hearing from him words she hadn't encountered before, like *kovrik,* mat, a derivative of *kovr,* carpet.

The windowless space smelled of paint. A dozen small tables and their accompanying chairs marched front to back in three rows. He said, "As perhaps you already know, women can be as adept as men at espionage, sometimes more so. In western society, preconceptions about women are nearly universal. A woman is presumed to be physically weaker than a man, hence unthreatening. If she goes about as if she knows what she's doing, she's given the benefit of the doubt. When she speaks, in the absence of other indicators, her statements are accepted as truthful. Your native speech and self-presentation lend you the ability to become effectively invisible in Sweden. Between now and the day you approach GALILEO, we will emphasize your deportment, cover identities, the infiltration, the operational setting, and all else we can foresee to boost your confidence. The inverse of the woman who knows what she's doing is the one who plainly doesn't. She garners scrutiny."

He brought out a detailed map of the Stockholm archipelago. She hadn't known the city by way of a map, and it took her a minute to orient herself to the place names. She and her parents had lived in a spacious apartment on Karlavägen Street near Villagatan, and she'd attended a private school close by on Styrmansgatan. On many occasions, in the company of her parents or friends, she'd traversed the downtown streets and plazas.

"The German delegation will stay at the Delfin Hotel." He tapped his finger on a plaza near the city center. A multi-page floor plan he handed her delineated each of the building's eight stories, the fourth housing the hotel's choicest rooms. "They'll probably host GALILEO in this posh corner suite that fronts the square. We have brochures and photos to familiarize you. Bear in mind, they're dated and the details may have changed. Just as outwardly you must show assurance, inwardly it behooves you to hang onto your mental reservations."

As if she were about to relinquish them.

His fingertip ranged southward to the district called Gamla Stan. "The safehouse will be here. Memorize the streets between the safehouse and the Delfin Hotel and devise how to wend from one to the other, so you'll comprehend the ground as if you've been walking it every day of your life. The plan is to get us to Stockholm a few days in advance of the German delegation, giving us time to adjust *in situ.*"

Had she been to Gamla Stan? She couldn't remember.

He handed her a plain white blouse, told her to put it on, and posed her against an unpatterned backdrop. Here he snapped photos with a Leica camera, adjusting her face-on and in profile, smiling and deadpanned, for perhaps twenty shots.

"Redon your sweats top," he said. He tipped up the watch he wore on the underside of his left wrist. "Half an hour's long enough for the digestion. Let's go."

Dark and drizzle obscured the airfield tower and hangars. He fetched Bags, and they descended at a jog into the woods thick with droopy clouds his flashlight beam seemed to embarrass in furtive acts. The leashed dog padded ahead, following the path whose circumference, she guessed from the stroll last night, measured half a mile or so. Already she was gasping for breath. As a young girl, she'd been able to run like the rabbit she later declared herself to be. No more. Like most women, she rarely exercised beyond walking. Not ladylike, society declared.

Avry said, "We'll do two circuits today. If you get tired, slow down, don't stop. Make it your goal never to quit."

If you get tired… She wheezed. Tripped and fell. Pushed to her feet and lolloped on, threading the puddles and leafy spinneys, her boat shoes slurping. At length he said, "Far enough."

Spent, she slumped to the ground. Bags trotted up and licked her face.

"Up, up! Never sit down after exercising, your muscles will cramp. Keep moving. Learn to ignore the pain."

The woods behind the Lodge concealed an airplane mockup with an open door three feet above a sawdust pit hemmed by old railroad ties. There was also a line of tall wooden posts that metal bars connected at the top. Beside the mockup, he handed her the flashlight and Bags's leash. "I doubt we'll be parachuting in. We'll use this just for fitness training. Tuck your arms in tight, otherwise the propwash will spin you like a top."

"The propwash?"

"Always practice as if for the real thing."

He demonstrated the jump exercise, exiting the door with a compact leg spring, landing, and falling sideward. "Press your feet and legs together, knees bent and spongy, or you'll sprain them on impact."

Twice she leapt from the mockup, landing in the soft sawdust and rising caked head to toe in the stuff. They proceeded to one of the overhead bars whose vertical sides featured stubby ladder rungs spiking out. "Let's see your hands. Soft. Any Russian woman would have hands tougher than this. Climb up, bar to your chin, hold for five seconds, legs dangling, then lower yourself on the same count." He demonstrated. "You'll develop calluses and grip strength. Useful, a grip. It affords you the capacity to hang on."

She ascended to the bar, counted to five, lowered herself slowly, and repeated. Her arms ached. On her third hold, Bags ran up and planted herself directly underneath, staring upward. Gently Avry tugged her back. "Nay, Bagsy girl," he muttered in English. "There are times I wonder how clever you really are."

At the Lodge she clumped upstairs to change, pulling off the damp sawdust-caked shoes and sweats. She smelled of sod. Dirt rimmed her nails, and her palms glowed red, the skin torn.

Any Russian woman would have hands tougher than this.

Upon their arrival in Manhattan, her mother had rented a room in a lower-east-side tenement. It accommodated a single bed where they slept at night, a table, two chairs, a diminutive icebox, and a chipped sink that butted from the wall. You wouldn't think one room would demand much cleaning, yet her mother scrubbed incessantly, preserving her child from the plagues the shabby oubliette surely must encase. To cross the room was to delve through a rain forest of white rags hanging from the crisscrossed clotheslines. The skin of her mother's hands dried to the roughness of flint. Linnea called her the Cossack of Clean. Her mother didn't take offense. She didn't laugh, either.

Every second evening, the Cossack insisted, Linnea must bathe in the floor's tub. Other residents used it, and sometimes she had to wait in line. Her mother waited too, to scour the porcelain before her daughter entered. She didn't ask her to join in the cleansing. What she must scrub were her hands, to present them for inspection before she left for school in the morning. "Never go out with dirty nails, people will think you're a peasant."

At the sink in her room, she lathered her hands and nails, spuming away the grime.

Though Verrick had license to speak to Linnea at any time during the day, he kept his distance, watching from the sidelines, comprehending not a word of the discourses in Russian that lasted through dinner. Not until afterward did he tap at the door of her room. When she opened, he said, "Do you have a minute?"

"Please come in, sir. I was about to come see you." She indicated the single chair and perched on the corner of the bed, hands in her lap. He noticed that she didn't fidget, and her uncombed fawn hair seemed to prevail in a state of natural order. The wan skin he'd observed last night had taken on a bit of color, her cheeks flush. The interval had done nothing to dim the intensity of her eyes. A keen mind underlay, he thought. Keen minds were not so rare. Poise under pressure was, and trickier to discern. Did she possess it? Her file hadn't answered the question. No file captured a subject's true persona, least of all hers.

"How are you, sir?"

"Good." Her statement she'd been about to come see him seemed like the logical place to start; she must have something to say. His lawyerly grounding cautioned him to put her at ease first. "They've given me complete run of the Lodge," he said. "I've been exploring."

"Oh?"

"Did you notice the bedrooms have names painted on?"

"I didn't."

"From outside the doors, look at the frames above. There are eight bedrooms altogether, five on this floor, and three of lesser size on the third. At first, I thought the names were of persons, perhaps esteemed former occupants: Amber, Ginger, and so on. I opened a few—none are locked—and discovered they refer to the wall colors. Amber's are a shade of reddish-orange, Ginger's a diluted brown. My room, Nile, is blue, yours, Lily, white."

"You peeked into all of them?"

"I had to, how else could I satisfy my curiosity? Avry has the room at the top of the stairs. Impossible to let Carmine go unconfirmed."

"And?"

"Faded closer to pink now."

She laughed. No doubt she intuited the silly preamble was meant to lighten the mood.

She was not beautiful, yet there was an Apollonian aspect about her, a calm repose that imparted in him the serenity of a soft breeze. He noted the impression, set it aside. "I thought we should have the chance to speak in private and as candidly as possible. What's said between us will remain in our own channels." He thought it best not to define the channels more explicitly or to evoke Donovan's name. Time to hear her out.

"There seems to be an assumption I agreed to do this thing," she said. "I wasn't asked, merely informed."

"Ah."

"To go on with it, I would have to believe I *can* do it. I don't."

So much for the calm repose. She was telling him she was quitting.

Rationality was his foundation, and on it he planted his feet. This woman was an officer of an intelligence service at war, crucial to a project British MI-6 thought could help win. Lives were at stake, his son's among them. In World War I, Verrick had witnessed the effect of machine guns. It was the first conflict in which armies had used the weapon *en masse*. As with all innovations, the practitioners had become virtuoso, learning how to interlock fires and arch the bullets in predictable patterns called 'cones of fire' that landed in ovals blandly called 'beaten zones.' The flight of bullets, exactingly plottable on the dispatch side, slaughtered men on the receiving end. Soon the Allies would invade the Continent, and his son would tread across the deadly beaten zones.

Also, how would the Brits react if the sole person they believed could bring off this scheme of theirs opted out?

I'll be in London until Friday afternoon. Probe the situation and report to me in person before then. If you perceive this to be as big a can of worms as I think it is, I can still try to pull us out. I'll talk to the president if I have to.

In the military, as in other professions, the recipient of instructions must interpret them. Whereas some directives were so straightforward that no ambiguities could exist, 'probe the situation' brimmed with nuance. True, the OSS Director hadn't liked having had the mission shoved down his throat, but to raise it with the president? Churchill had involved himself, and the American decision-making had encompassed Generals Eisenhower and Marshall. Donovan expected Verrick to do more than simply observe. He was to intercede as he saw fit.

He evaluated her demeanor. Here was the young woman who had written, 'I am a rabbit, as I wish to be.' Where was her center of gravity? A person unafraid to appear weak often wasn't. Yet it was too soon to know for certain. He was a lawyer. Good lawyers sought clarity. They asked noncommittal, open-ended questions and steadied their clients.

He said, "How did they identify you for the mission?"

She said she had no idea. Informed at Factory House that a car was waiting outside, she'd been driven to a residence behind Grosvenor Street and locked in her room overnight. The next day her minders had put in front of her forms to sign, taken away her uniform and possessions in favor of bland clothes, and relegated her to Sebastian without a word of explanation. The episode would not have ruffled a seasoned intelligence officer. Her, a novice, it had.

"I'm as caught out as you are," he said. "Just like you, I was summoned blind. On the flight, I kept asking myself, why the hell was I heading to London? We've both heard the reason now. Still, I'm not at the center of things, whereas you are, and you're faced with a considerable challenge. A lot to have thrown at you."

She didn't comment.

"In the First World War, I traveled to France with the Army. It took a long time to get to the front, first by crowded ship, then in the back of a truck on rutted roads, only to arrive by night and to march seemingly endlessly over terrain whose features I couldn't make out. I had no clue where I was, no control over anything. Until then I hadn't understood the sheer *gall* of war, and I deeply regretted my decision to join up. Days went by before I regained my equilibrium. Even if it's not a close parallel to your situation, can you relate?"

For the first time her gaze swept over the white walls, as if they were papered in her life's history. "I think so."

"I wish I could tell you I grew comfortable in my surroundings, but I never did. What transpired was a kind of curing process, and it led to my being able to contribute."

"You were trained, though."

"Military classrooms had versed me in tactics and battle planning. I knew what the map symbols meant. The training that truly mattered commenced once I got there."

She didn't appear to buy any of it.

He said, "What I mean is, to feel the ground shake underfoot, and that it troubles you, is normal at the beginning."

"Time will heal everything, you're saying."

"My goodness no. I wouldn't say that, and I don't believe it. What time does is to lend perspective."

Perhaps she was pairing his stated experiences against her own. Whatever she thought, her expression didn't give it away.

He wasn't swaying her. Try something else. "What do you think of them? The British Secret Service men."

"They seem very adroit."

In the silence, he turned the word over. "Too much so, you mean."

She nodded slightly.

"What gives you the impression?"

"At Sebastian's briefing last evening, and the talk with Avry afterward, there was this… slickness."

"As in manipulation."

"A form of it."

"And it troubles you, to be the target."

"Yes."

They sat in silence for a minute. At length he said, "They are our friends, but fundamentally they do represent a foreign intelligence service. It's like letting a tame shark into your swimming pond. If you go into the water, you must always bear in mind that the shark regards you as a potential meal."

"Tame sharks exist?"

"They don't. That's my point, I suppose."

He wasn't getting anywhere. What else might he try? She was perspicacious as hell. Throwing encouragement at her wouldn't work; she'd see through it. He had to speak from the heart. "Listen, I'm not a spymaster by profession. In the civilian world, I'm an attorney. Nonetheless I think I understand the principles of the secret world. To have done my lawyer's job these many years, I couldn't help but to have learned something of the gradations of truth."

She stared at him.

"Bear with me, please. In espionage, as in the practice of law, when dealing with self-interested parties, we must assume that a percentage of what they tell us may be disingenuous. It's not that we become comfortable with falsehoods, but we do learn to tolerate ambiguity. Sometimes the best we can achieve is a reasonable notion of what's true. Imperfect? Certainly. It happens that no one has devised a better approach."

"Just accept it, you mean."

"I wouldn't put it that way. I'd say give our friends a chance, and some more time. If you can do that, I'll try to ferret out what's at the heart of these proceedings. Isn't it preferable, if you can, to make a more informed decision?"

She seemed to ponder this, her eyes roving the wallpaper again. Meanwhile Verrick took stock of his statements. Yes, they'd been from the heart, but no less were they faithful to his duty. Her quitting would detract from the war effort. He'd tell her so, if he had to.

She said, "You'll be here?"

"I intend to be."

"All right."

He asked for no further commitment, and she gave him none.

Alone again in the dining room, he poured himself a Scotch. The silent house enshrouded him like a gray robe. Clearly Linnea hated to be manipulated. He had done exactly that, or attempted to, and she must know it.

Hell, what was leadership, if not a form of manipulation, to give people the confidence that their leaders knew what they were doing.

Bullshit.

You didn't lie to her.

Avry came in. "A Scotch man too, I see." He beelined to the liquor cabinet, hefted the bottle to the table, and poured himself a shot. "So, how do you like our little chateau?"

Verrick half smiled, grateful the Scot had derailed him from his ruminations. "The seclusion is pleasant. Seems like we're far enough from the airfield to be insulated from the noise."

"Wait till the wind shifts and they rev up the Merlins. You'll barely be able to hear yourself think."

As if the decibel level of airplane engines demanded much contemplation, neither man spoke for a spell. The room had a fireplace, unlit, topped by a mantle where a curvy, wood-embedded captain's clock pointedly ticked. The hands pointed to 3:30, wrong by hours.

Avry said, "I should thank you for keeping yourself at an unobtrusive distance. I hardly know you're there. Makes me guess you've done this type of thing before."

"I haven't. What good would it do me to be close up? I don't understand Russian."

"Ah. Just practical, then."

"Have you trained many women?"

"Depends on what you mean. In matters of service tradecraft, no. In life, I've tried. I have a wife and three daughters. Guess who ends up jumping through the hoop? There must be an adage for it."

"What do you think of Linnea?"

"Too early to say. Her Russian, as advertised, is pristine. Here I am, a former professor of Russian, and she's corrected me on points of speech. With other topics, she's quick to grasp the governing concepts, and she seems able to detect the difference between when I'm speaking from theory or personal experience. So far, she's kept her concentration. Again, it's early on."

"Her weaknesses?"

"Physical endurance, plainly. Her legs are hardy enough, she can walk along forever. She soon gets winded running. Her arms need a lot of work too. Good thing we're not infiltrating her anywhere the Jerries occupy."

"How much time do you have?"

"Twelve days, give or take." Avry didn't have to point out that the timeframe was absurdly short. "I'll fix what I can. Other things, we'll have to live with. Those eyes of hers light up her face like a bloody Very gun. To be striking can have its advantages. In our situation, the opposite is recommended."

"Her poise under pressure?"

"Yet to be ascertained."

Verrick finished his Scotch.

"Another?" said Avry.

"Thanks, but no."

"A disciplined man. A rare thing, when the drinks are free."

"Do you agree with Sebastian that the false-flag ruse has a chance of success?"

"I do. He's my boss, isn't he." He seemed to re-think the reply. "Unless we put the ball in play, we achieve nothing. The gain outweighs the risk. As for offending the Russians, I don't think they're all that enchanted with us in any event."

"What about running GALILEO in Berlin? How will you?"

"I'm not privy to that bit. You'll have to ask Sebastian." The Scot gazed at the two-dimensional coating at the base of his glass. Apparently disfavoring low-dimensional things, he poured a second drink. "Do you mind if I ask how you ended up with this assignment?"

Verrick explained his background with Donovan in the Great War, the Justice Department, the law firm, and the OSS, stuffing more than twenty-five years into less than two minutes. On his role in the project, he wasn't sure how much Avry knew of the top-level brouhaha that had surrounded the Americans' deliberations on the proposal, so he abstracted. "Donovan asked me to keep an eye on things."

"Sounds altogether prudent."

"It's what we call an unstructured job. The danger is, I might end up contributing very little, or nothing."

"If so, it means we're doing *our* jobs properly. Why not seize the opportunity to relax?"

"Perhaps I will."

Avry lifted his glass. "To unstructured jobs."

They clinked glasses. Verrick said, "Do you expect Sebastian will drop by in the next day or so?" The MI-6 deputy had gone back to London last night and had not appeared today.

"I cannot say. Men of his ascendance don't always keep the wee working level informed. Was there something you wanted passed along?"

"Yes, I'd like to have a look at the file on GALILEO."

"I'll see the word gets communicated, sir."

– 13 –

Mid-January 1944

Mauer stared at the interrogation report on his desk. To each page were clipped his notes, lending the stack the aspect of a harried animal that if touched would bite.

Be patient, he told himself. Insights sometimes came slowly, like the smoke of a candle that burned in the basement of a house and whose smell after a time grew faintly detectable on the upper floors.

Not a musing he could share with Standartenführer Bernhardt Stabl.

He had re-read the damned thing more times than he could count. This version included the identity of the English officer, Royal Navy Lieutenant Benedict Callahan, whose name Mauer had searched for in the Abwehr's files to confirm it wasn't there. The questions and replies were in English, the German translations in parentheses alongside. A few of the English terms had been mistranslated. He scratched out the entries and penned in replacements.

The results made no better sense.

A career naval officer, Mauer took as a given that, if captured, he must divulge nothing of use to the enemy. The Geneva Convention of 1929, to which Germany was a signatory, required a prisoner of war to supply to his captors only his true name, rank, and service number. The interrogators could compel nothing further. The convention did not pertain to spies. Hitler's Commando Order of 1942 branded commandos, whether in uniform or not, the equivalent of spies, stripping them of the protections afforded to captured soldiers and mandating they be executed. Perhaps the subject had been a commando given over to the claws of the SS. The report didn't say.

The questions, many times repeated, were straightforward: What was your mission? Who were you to meet in France? Where and when was your meeting to take place? The replies, when they happened, invariably were a single word or number with no apparent relevance to what had been asked. The interrogator then said, 'What is the significance of this word?' or, if the reply was a number, 'What is the significance of this number?'

The report did not reveal how long the poor fellow had lasted. Mauer guessed he tried to resist and was crudely tortured, obliterating his coherence. In the hands of an expert interrogator, no individual, no matter how determined, could hold out indefinitely. Yet technical artistry and ineptitude existed in the same proportions among inquisitors as they did in other fields. Through miscalibration of the techniques of the trade, bunglers might kill their subjects, severing the opportunity to extract what they knew. The death of Lieutenant Callahan seemed to leave the meaning of his replies forever lost.

The phone rang. Gerta in the doorway said, "For you, Kommodore."

The background clack of typewriters heralded that the call originated from Gestapo headquarters. What did he look like, wondered Mauer, this Stabl fellow whose voice twitched as if insects were running up and down his back? "What is your progress, Mauer? You've had the full copy for some time, *ja*?"

"Four days."

"Long enough. We are curious as to when your conclusions will be ready."

"I don't know. I haven't been able to conclude anything."

"Not very efficient."

"Don't tell me about efficiency! The report was ten days old when it reached me. It reeks of a botched job!"

The silence on the line screamed he'd gone too far. His terrible eyesight wouldn't save him from a transfer to some far-flung hellhole. A complaint from the head of the Gestapo could precipitate his reassignment, perhaps to the main body of the Abwehr at the bunker complex called Maybach II at Zossen, 30 kilometers south of Berlin, to work in the same Spartan conditions as the rest of the staff. Jana could not accompany him there. Yet as dismal as the prospect seemed, it might at least prod her to leave Berlin.

Why not just say he was done with the damned thing?

To mind came Albert Speer, who in the months since they'd met had posed as a role model for excellence. Speer wouldn't have put up with this absurd task. On the other hand, Speer was one of Hitler's favorites. Mauer wasn't. Foolish, to provoke the Gestapo. Why not at least wait a few more days, then tell the bastards he'd wracked his brain and achieved nothing?

He said, "I am giving it the highest priority. Sometimes these things take time."

The line clicked. He rested the receiver in the cradle.

There was something else. When he peered at the document, a fascination seized him. *Viscosity was not a random word.* A secret hid in the pages. The right inspiration might reveal it.

He deposited the report in his safe, clanged shut the door, spun the dial, and seized his overcoat. At her desk, Gerta stood up when he passed through the outer office. How many times had he told her not to jump to her feet in his presence? The Nervous Nellie couldn't help herself, and he'd given up remarking on it. "I'm heading over to Bendlerstrasse," he said over his shoulder. "I shouldn't be gone longer than an hour or so." Bendlerstrasse could only mean the massive OKW headquarters complex, Bendlerblock, they called it.

He might have requested a staff car. He chose instead to walk. At the exit, he stepped into a snowfall of mammoth flakes. As a boy, he would have stretched out his tongue to catch them, not of course within sight of his parents, who'd judged snow to be as unclean and liable to sicken him as the rest of the outdoors. They never reconciled themselves to the notion that the persona they superimposed on him did not fit. In later life, it must have shocked them, to grasp that they'd never really known their son.

He plodded along, the snowfall slowing his stride. At Leipziger Platz, he circuited the bomb-damaged remnants of Wertheim's Department Store. His mother had taken him once to Wertheim's, Europe's grandest shopping venue at the time and flaunting fabulous wares and décor. Afterward the Nazis had stolen the store from the Jewish owners and imposed a different name. Now he traversed Potsdamer Platz, at whose center the picturesque electric traffic-signal tower used to reside. Erected in the 1920s to control what had been Europe's busiest intersection, the tower, like the Weimar Republic in which it had stood, had become a kind-of chimera, invisible except as a ghostly blur out of the corner of your eye. The traffic too. The war shortages had made petrol as unobtainable for ordinary people as genuine coffee.

At the architectural ogre that was OKW, he showed his identification, wiped his feet on the straw mat, and trudged up the stairs to the third floor. Here he located the door to Gels Belk's office, rapped twice, and pushed inside. At the desk, his friend looked up. The belly bulged as prominently as ever, and the hair that had inspired the nickname *der Zauberer* shone as vivid white. Gels had eluded the Abwehr's relocation to the bunkers at Zossen by taking a liaison job at OKW. With mock sternness, he said, "What's this? You didn't make an appointment?"

"Are you busy?"

"Oh, yes. Terribly." Gels's voice fell an octave. "Never have I been so bored. OKW doesn't care a sausage about the Abwehr's information. Come in, sit down."

Mauer took the seat alongside the desk and with his handkerchief wiped the melted snow from his glasses. "How is Alicia?"

"Fine, or so I gather from her letters. She's with relatives in Garmisch, safe from the *dicke Autos.*" 'Fat cars' was Luftwaffe fighter-pilot slang for enemy bombers. Somehow the term had parachuted from the cockpits to the stuffy pigeonholes of the German military headquarters. "And Jana?"

"Stubbornly she refuses to go to her cousin's home in Augsburg."

Gels chuckled at what was not a laughing matter. To forego decorum long had been a facet of their friendship. He said, "Do you mind if I smoke?"

"Yes, I mind."

"Fuck you, this isn't your office." *Der Zauberer* lit a cigarette, black Ukrainian *makhorka* tobacco from the grotty smell.

"Those will make you blind."

"You would know."

Mauer sighed. He should see Gels more. It lifted his spirits.

"What brings the head of Eins Technik Marine to the Bendlerblock?"

"I'm afraid the Gestapo have put their hooks in me."

"Is that so?" Gels glanced to a side door, no doubt to make sure it was closed.

Mauer said, "I recall you mentioning that you interrogated prisoners of war when you were in North Africa with Rommel."

"Soldiers of the British Eighth Army. The job fell to me because I speak English."

"Did you ever… that is, were the prisoners ever forced to speak?"

"Enticed, cajoled, tricked. Not forced. I wouldn't do that sort of thing or tolerate it under my authority. Against the Geneva Convention, you know."

"What were the results?"

"Not bad. Early on, the war was going poorly for the Tommies, and many of the prisoners thought it inevitable we would win. We were polite to them, gave them tea and strudels. Some of them provided us with useful information."

"Did you participate in SS interrogations?"

"Never. Oh, from time to time, the SS called on me to review what they had extracted from some poor wretch. I was happy to keep my distance. If they got their clutches on someone they deemed a spy... well, you can imagine."

A minute passed while Mauer waited for his friend to elaborate. Apparently he wasn't going to. "Were their methods reliable, the SS?"

"Reliable? What are you talking about? Spit it out. You're acting like the cat that circles the bowl of milk."

"I mean... Here is the situation. The Gestapo have given me an interrogation report to make sense of. The SS were the ones who prepared it. The subject seems to have died in the process."

"Umm. Frequently the fate of those the SS interrogated. What do you expect from chicken farmers?"

The reference was to SS leader Heinrich Himmler, whose father had been a chicken farmer. Purportedly the father had urged his son to take up the occupation. Dangerous, quips about Himmler. How thick were these walls?

"The subject's replies are nothing but disassociated words and a few numbers. I'm trying to discern if they're just babble or might contain hidden truths."

"May I see the transcript?"

"No. Believe me, you don't want to."

"I get your drift, a sticky thing like that. As to your question, I have always assumed a tortured man will say anything to stop the pain. Or, under the combined influence of drugs and duress, he might lose his mind and rant incoherently."

"How does an interrogator deal with such responses?"

"You ask as if I would know. Are you serious, Willie?"

Mauer didn't reply.

Der Zauberer dragged deeply on his cigarette. "Where did the sessions take place?"

"In France, or so I was told. The report doesn't say."

"Who carried out the questioning, a headquarters or a field unit?"

"I don't know. What's the difference?"

"The SS headquarters units are better equipped. They might have a Magnetophon, for instance, and make a recording."

"Do they take notes too?"

"Always. The interrogator generally has an assistant, sometimes a regular stenographer. A translator as well. These helpers or their notes may amplify what is in the official transcript. You should ask the Gestapo."

"I will. Other ideas?"

"The team prepares methodically. They transcribe the daily notes or recordings and assemble fresh questions for the next session. That's at headquarters. In the field, things may be more ad hoc."

"How so?"

"Rushed. No Magnetophon; the damn things always break in the field. Perhaps no assistant either, sometimes the interrogator must do everything himself: devise the questions, take notes, report the results. Conditions may be difficult. In North Africa, we were in tents, and we couldn't keep the sand from blowing in. Have you ever tried to write on paper covered with sand?"

"I can't say that I have."

"The SS are never so far from civilization that they don't have a car battery close by, and drugs. You have to be skilled to use such methods, and the SS thugs quite often aren't. The more haphazard the proceedings, the shoddier the results."

"What would you do, if you were me?"

"Who was the subject of the interrogation?"

"All I have is his name, and that he was a British naval officer, rank of lieutenant."

"His duties and other background?"

"The Gestapo won't say. The name is not in our records."

"The first rule of interrogation: Know whom you're talking to. If the sons of bitches won't tell you, they are doing you a disservice. Throw the report back at them."

"I've considered that."

Gels stared. "It intrigues you, doesn't it?"

"Perhaps." Having polished the lenses of his eyeglasses, Mauer shifted his efforts to the frame. "There is another reason. What worse time to be branded inept, as the RSHA prepares to devour the Abwehr."

Gels puckered his lips and blew out a lungful of smoke. "Be that as it may, do you really wish to gain the reputation as the one who unriddled this matter for the Gestapo? You know as well as I do there are dark things going on, people arrested upon a whisper of dissent who are never heard from again. The so-called deportation of Jews who might as well have been erased from existence. SS murder-units rove over the eastern lands. Canaris himself has decried these despicable acts. A reckoning will come at the end. I believe I have acted honorably so far. So have you. Why tarnish yourself now?"

Mauer didn't reply. In unmistakable terms, his friend had declared Germany was going to lose the war. But even in private with Gels, it was wiser not to agree outright.

"Of course, I am speaking hypothetically," Gels added.

"So I gathered." Mauer pushed to his feet. "It was good to see you. By the way, you're fatter than ever."

Gels laughed. His eyes didn't. "Pay heed, old friend."

Outside the snow had turned to rain, leaving slushy puddles too wide to leap across. Why had he dashed out without his overshoes? By the time he returned to his desk, the soles of his shoes were saturated. He took them off, leaned them against the radiator to dry, laid his wet socks atop, and in bare feet dialed the Gestapo Headquarters and asked for Stabl.

"Yes, Mauer."

"Did the interrogators make Magnetophon recordings of their sessions?"

"There were no recordings."

"What about notes?"

"No."

"Was there a translator, or a stenographer, who participated, with whom I can speak?"

"No."

The phone line clicked.

Mauer squeezed the dead receiver as if it were a neck he could strangle.

– 14 –

Early February 1944

Linnea awoke in an otherworldly light, a dusky bluish hue serrated with red, as if someone had painted blue a rusty bucket and scraped a chisel over. She rose, padded across floorboards not as cold as you'd expect, and tugged aside the curtain. The window looked out at a skeletal tree, the branches in ghostly silhouette against the marsh and the airfield. She traced the dim curves of the hangars. The peculiar ambiance must stem from moonbeams piercing the clouds and sheening off the marsh water. Maybe the odd luminance had inspired whoever had painted the color names on the doors. She should tease Avry that his room should be renamed *Pink*.

She returned to bed, pulled the comforter to her chin, settling her gaze on the chair where Verrick had reposed. The Lodge's first-name rule aside, 'Gabriel' didn't match her mental construct of the man. 'Mister Verrick' worked better. What to make of him? The last man she wholly trusted had been her father. He'd told lies and died, leaving her and her mother stranded in debt. To trust Verrick, whom she had met less than two days ago, was out of the question. Her father had been gregarious and brimming with enthusiasm. Verrick was the opposite: diffident, contemplative, and somehow effete and durable at the same time. Why then her odd sense of kinship with him? Was it that they were both Americans? He gave the impression of listening in a concentrated, empathetic way, and he seemed to detest artifice as much as she did.

I'd say give our friends a chance, and some more time. If you can do that, I'll try to ferret out what's at the heart of these proceedings. Isn't it preferable, if you can, to make a more informed decision?

Preferable to what? She would be stringing people along, playacting a horse when she was inexorably a rabbit. To speak the languages was one thing, to pass for a lifelong Russian quite another. Her father had been a pretender. To follow in his footsteps didn't square with her life's plan.

Did Verrick genuinely mean to help her decide, or was he manipulating her?

Much to think about.

The day commenced with physical training. In the beam of Avry's flashlight, he and Bags following, she ran along the path to the airplane mock-up. Here she sprang, landed, and rolled, then ascended the bar and lowered herself, ripping the skin on her hands.

Yesterday she had muddied up her room's sink rinsing off her boat shoes, probably not the first person to have made the mistake. A wicker laundry basket later materialized in the corner, and on the dresser a tented card with neatly hand-printed housekeeping rules:

-- Kindly wash your soiled shoes at the outside faucet, not in the sink.
-- Your dirty clothes go in the bin, not on the floor, if you please.
-- If you would re-use your towels for two days or three, we'd be most grateful.
-- Before you leave the room in the morning, be mindful to lock your top dresser drawer.
The Housekeeping Staff

The tight schedule didn't afford the luxury of a morning bath. She rinsed her shoes and socks at the hose bib on the side of the house and traipsed barefoot upstairs, finding her bed made and yesterday's sweats washed and folded atop the covers. She doffed the ones she was wearing, washed her hands, forearms, and face at the little sink, and redressed. Avry sat at the folding table in the gym, the breakfast of sausages, real eggs, toast, and berry jam already laid out.

In Russian, he said, "Eat hearty. From here on, we'll shift to the diet we anticipate in Sweden. Because meat is rationed there, people eat more fish. So shall we."

Great.

In Classroom 2, he introduced a middle-aged woman named Mrs. Johansson. In Sweden the surname was like Jones; reasonable to presume it was an alias. Tall with straight, swept-back gray hair, she had a deeply lined face, non-condescending eyes, and exceptionally long fingers. Avry, adopting the superintendent's posture that became his standard for the language sessions, took a seat off to the side.

In Swedish, Mrs. Johansson asked Linnea about herself. Her replies emerged so syrupy she might have been sucking on a wad of honeycomb. "That's why we're practicing, dear," said Mrs. Johansson, "to bring back your natural speech-flow, and to acquaint you with Sweden as it exists today."

At Mrs. Johansson's request, she recounted the Stockholm of her memories, summoning details she'd not thought of in ages: locations, friends, their elegant, six-room apartment, her paternal grandfather's house they had visited from time to time on the city's outskirts, and her attendance at his funeral when she was ten years old.

"It seems you were materially well off," said Mrs. Johansson.

"We were, for a time."

"What happened?"

"My father died. He put us in debt. But we had left Sweden by then."

Mrs. Johansson related the changes Linnea hadn't been present to witness. Early in the war, the German blitzkrieg had rolled over Poland, and in April 1940, the threat veered northward, the Wehrmacht suddenly invading Denmark and Norway, Sweden's neighbors. To the east, Finland had become Germany's ally. Sweden was surrounded. Nothing seemed more fated than that Germany would win the war and dominate Europe. For some Swedes, this wasn't so troublesome. Didn't Germany and Sweden share cultural, linguistic, and economic affinities? The Swedish Nazis urged their countrymen to seize the opportunity and join the Axis.

The Swedish people didn't buy it. Overwhelmingly they desired to remain neutral. The government leaders were more pusillanimous. Fearful of offending Hitler, they tiptoed, leaving to their own devices the Swedish Nazis who threw their weight around as if it were inevitable that their country would become Germany's sidekick. "They used to strut about in their brown shirts and leather cross straps. They don't anymore, but they remain willing to intimidate people, even with violence. The Delfin Hotel is their lair, an odious place."

"You've been inside?"

"Many times. The lobby used to be charming. People would rendezvous there amid the flower vases and the polite servers. You could order coffee and pastries. That was before the Nazis purchased it. Who could have foreseen swastika banners hanging from the upper balcony, pictures of Hitler on the walls, and copies of the propaganda rag *Dagsposten* all around? Lately they have been using the Delfin to put up visiting German dignitaries."

Linnea nodded.

"The hotel employees are all Nazis who wear identification badges with photos pasted on. The head of security takes orders from the German embassy. He carries a loaded pistol and has detained people against their will. And worse."

"Worse?"

"I'm sure Avry will explain, if you ask him."

Mrs. Johansson tutored her on how to comport herself so as not to stand out. She must avoid nail paint, lipstick, and other prissy adornments the rationing had rendered extravagant. For formal business and social settings, she should don silk stockings that commonly would have been mended time and again. The hem of her shirt or dress should level just below the knee. In snow, shoes were a quandary. If she had to walk a far piece, she should wear sturdy boots and take along her shoes in a bag.

When she was out, she must carry at least one and preferably several ration-ticket booklets. There were tickets for meat, eggs, butter, flour, sugar, and other rationed commodities. "No woman leaves her ration tickets behind. Be aware of your surroundings. Pretend to look at the stalls and shop windows. We try to appear aloof and unaffected, we Swedes, yet we are forever on the hunt for lucky purchases. Stops to peruse are expected and can help you determine if someone is following you. If you spot a tail, memorize as much as you can about them without calling attention to your awareness."

"If I buy something, do I haggle over the price?"

"You won't know what's fair. Act like you're in a hurry. The vendor will be less surprised when you pay what he or she asks."

"Okay."

"That's enough for today. Can you recapitulate the lesson?"

"I'm unadorned, aloof, and unaffected in public, dressier in business settings. I always carry my ration tickets, hunt for goods in a hurry, and pay the full price so I can peg who's following me but give nothing away."

Mrs. Johansson tipped her head. "Concisely put."

In Classroom 1, Avry resumed in Russian. "For your entry to the Delfin Hotel, you'll be Hamfrid Matisson. She's a real person, a hotel employee. We're going to borrow her identity temporarily. You'll have a hotel badge in her name but with your photo."

How could she get away with impersonating a woman the other employees knew?

Already he'd moved on. "On the street you'll be Thorgun Lindstrom, a near inverse of your true name, easy to remember. You'll have papers in her identity. If someone asks, you're the receptionist for a steel trader, like your father's business. Our concept for Thorgun Lindstrom is two layered. Openly she lives her receptionist's life. She hides the other. She's a criminal, a thief."

"Why the hidden side?"

"In the event you're detained in the hotel, they'll soon realize you're not Hamfrid Matisson. Larceny is a plausible explanation for why you're impersonating Hamfrid. You'll offer a reluctant confession and apologia, and they'll either turn you over to the police or throw you out on your ear. Either way, you'll be out of their hands."

Sounded complicated.

"With GALILEO, and with him alone, you'll become Vena Nadovska of the *Narodnyy Komissariat Vnutrennikh Del*, the Soviet NKVD. No need to say so to GALILEO. He'll grasp immediately who you represent."

Vena Nadovska was twenty-eight, four years older than Linnea, he explained. Most NKVD selectees had established themselves in some other occupation before entering the service, and her prior experience was as an accountant in the Soviet bureau that redistributed lands. In the NKVD, she graduated from the *Shkola Osobogo Naznacheniya*, the service's training center east of Moscow, gaining an education not only in spycraft but in the foreign customs nearly unimaginable to ordinary Russians.

"Is Vena a real person?"

"She's a character we've created. To GALILEO, she has to be as real as a slap across the face. Verisimilitude is the key to *lozhnym flagom* (the false flag). To succeed, you must manifest her persona so convincingly that you bridge your mark's doubts. It's less important that you behave like a real NKVD controller than how GALILEO *thinks* such a person would."

"How can anyone know what he thinks?"

"We have a fair idea."

No surprise, he didn't say how they'd come by it.

"Won't he be expecting me to say some secret phrase or password to verify I'm legit?"

Avry smiled. "Precisely so. He'll want to hear the name *Sophia;* it tells him you're his long-lost *podruga* from the NKVD. Bear in mind, the name won't cinch your bona fides unless you are credible to him in every other respect. He's aware that the NKVD fields women for their utility to pass where men cannot. You must typify what he expects: competency, acumen, and Stalin's unbending resolve."

In Russian, Stalin meant *of steel.* Her mother had told her how the communists had pressed their harsh thumb on the Petrograd elites, confiscating houses and apartments too extravagant for a single family. Doctors, lawyers, musicians, and others of the bourgeois were compelled to labor with shovels. Linnea retained the image of a Soviet female commissar who yowled at people she deemed revolutionarily deficient. Like a sharp stick, the woman's harshness had jabbed into the soft tissues of Linnea's memory.

The session became an acting class. "Stand with your feet shoulder-width apart, level your chin, and stare your interlocutor in the eye. No matter how he reacts, don't look away."

She stared.

"We haven't got the scripts yet, so we'll improvise. Say, 'I have a message for you, comrade. It concerns Sophia.' Then you'll hand him a letter from Sophia."

She repeated the line, extending an imaginary letter. "I feel like I'm in a bad movie."

"You'll get over it with practice. Don't blink so much."

"Is it smart to carry a letter into the hotel? Shouldn't I memorize whatever it says and relay it verbally?"

"Good, you're thinking as a field hand thinks. There are reasons we're doing it this way."

He didn't say what the reasons were.

For lunch they ate grilled turnips, mushrooms, and slivers of herring she pushed around with her fork. "Mrs. Johansson said the Delfin Hotel has detained people, and worse. What did she mean?"

"According to rumor—there are no dates or names—two individuals who entered the Delfin vanished without a trace. The good citizens of Stockholm have made the story into folklore."

"What do the good citizens say happened?"

"That the Nazis whisked the poor sods off at night via the delivery entrance at the rear of the hotel. German merchant vessels dock at Stockholm. It's not hard to imagine the Nazis jostling the captives into a car with German diplomatic plates and spiriting them past the dockyard security and aboard a ship."

They ate in silence for a few minutes. Mrs. Tatum had overdone the meal's Swedish authenticity. Linnea didn't recall the herring in Stockholm being quite this fishy. "The two who vanished, were they Swedes?"

"Supposedly Russians."

"Russians."

He waved dismissively. "Listen, the neutral capitals of Europe are awash in every form of intrigue you can imagine. Stockholm's no different. It's a market where cash is traded for information, most of it gossip or pure bilge. Peddlers of all varieties abound: embellishers, fabricators, paper mills, sophists. Part of what's put out is disinformation. I wouldn't be surprised to learn that the Swedish Nazis concocted the rumor of the disappearances to frighten the public, so they'll steer wide of the Delfin."

Many of the reports that had crossed her desk at Factory House purportedly conveyed secrets from foreign spies. Some beamed authenticity, others were wispily sourced, a few were clearly gimcrack. Details ranged from ample to fragmentary to nonexistent. The analyst's art was to extract truth from the boundless realm of what was not. You had to avoid intellectual traps whereby you stamped as valid that which matched your preconceptions and brushed off what contrasted. Like Venus Flytraps, hidden assumptions enticed the unwary to fall in. Humility was an analyst's friend. What was that quote of Dostoyevsky's? 'The cleverest of all, in my opinion, is the man who calls himself a fool at least once a month.'

The story about the disappearances at the Delfin sounded apocryphal. To mind came Mrs. Johansson's description of the hotel: Nazi flags, Swedes who wanted to be Germans, a security manager who carried a gun.

No, this was one fish she wasn't going to eat.

– 15 –

Mid-January 1944

The damned interrogation document was laughing at him.

After Gerta closed the blackout curtains for the evening, Mauer sent her home. In her absence, he could pace his office, pondering the details, stretching out his arms as if he were holding a gossamer net to snare its secrets from the air.

All he caught were sore shoulders.

To hell with it. He sealed it in his safe, locked the outer office, and headed out to walk home.

The afternoon had pulled him into mundane administration. He sifted through writeups from subordinates, acquiesced to or resisted the transfers of select personnel, and presided over a promotion ceremony for two of his sergeants. Aligned stiffly in the slushy courtyard, they saluted as the new insignia were clipped on. One, having suffered a wound that left him unable to straighten his maimed fingers, had perched a sad, downward-facing claw at his eyebrow.

Mauer crossed the bridge over the Landwehr Canal and turned southwest toward Schöneberg. The sleet had turned back to snow, and the wind shook the bare tree branches like a jealous miser. Forecast to last through the night, the precipitation augured a hiatus from the bombing raids. It also swept the sidewalks of the usual passers-by. He was almost to Bayreutherstrasse when he spotted a lone woman hurrying toward him. Half running, she flashed the kind of apologetic smile Berliners gave when they thought their behavior might appear unseemly.

Before the war, the marble tiles of the foyer floor of his apartment house had sheened, buffed daily to perfection. The war years had left the floor dusty and scratched up, nonetheless the tiles were still reflective enough to catch the image of Mrs. Emmit, the building's *Portierfrau*, as she sat knitting at her little table. Fair guess she was among the nearly half million German citizens the Gestapo had enlisted as informants. Like mice infesting a kitchen, the unpaid watchers fed on dropped crumbs. What did it say about the German people, that they should be embarrassed to be seen to run along the sidewalk, yet willingly tattle on their neighbors?

"*Guten abend,* Frau Emmit," he said, his tone genial but not chirpy, which would sound unseemly in this weather.

"*Guten abend,* Kommodore."

He headed up the staircase that wound upward around a hollow core. Glancing over the rail down to the wool-knitting informant, mentally he pictured a dud bomb smashing through the roof and plunging down the open stairwell to squash her.

He shook away the image. Not like him, to entertain meanspirited thoughts.

On the second level, a floor-to-ceiling crack a few millimeters wide evinced actual bomb damage. The explosions that thus far had rattled the building had left it essentially intact on its foundation. Survive a few air raids, and you might succumb to a fool's inertia. Why scuttle underground, to shoehorn oneself among the fearful skulkers gasping to breathe the diminishing oxygen, the blue lights eerily illuminating the condensation dripping from the ceiling, when you could wait it out in the comfort of home? The air wardens were supposed to account for everyone; they couldn't possibly. In bombed apartment buildings, you found the bodies of people who had died from laziness.

He hung up his uniform and donned his nightclothes. Like his wife, he wore three layers to fend off the chill if they had to rush out. Not lazy, he and Jana. If an air raid destroyed their belongings, they would have the clothes on their backs and the small case of prepacked essentials all Berlin families were required to carry to the air-raid shelter. Tonight they kept on the three layers, even if the cloud cover meant they would not have to worry about bombs or the whumps of the 88-millimeter anti-aircraft cannons testifying that the killers were overhead. *Fitzerei,* people called the strange, pervasive angst. The strangest part? You could get used to it.

She had prepared a modest dinner. Dismal, the food supplies these days. Jana spent much of her time standing in lines to buy vegetables, all rationed, even potatoes, and the even scarcer meat. They ate at the table by the window where in summer you might look at the heart-shaped linden leaves. Not tonight. The trees were leafless. The blackout paper covering the panes kept you from seeing out anyway.

"What did Gerta do today?" Jana never tired of hearing of his secretary's eccentricities. "Is she still trying to catch a glimpse of your Gestapo dossier?"

"She can't restrain herself. Nor can she forego wearing that ugly Nazi pin of hers. If she didn't have it on, it would be as if she had gone out naked."

"Perhaps that would entertain you, a naked hellcat in your office."

"You conjure the truly frightful."

"Have you found the hidden secret?"

He'd told her no specifics of the highly classified report, merely his frustration at trying to sift meaning from the jumble. "I'm starting to think I never will." He related his meeting with Gels, not failing to embed that his friend's wife had gone to stay in Garmisch. "He said he hopes Alicia remains there, safe."

If Jana caught his implication that she should decamp too, she gave no hint. To bait her was no easier than it had ever been. "Did Gels help you?"

"He tried. I was hopeful, but in the end, no."

He cleaned the dishes, a chore that integrated with his longing for order, while in the parlor Jana paged through a dog-eared magazine he had brought home. After he dried his hands and sat down, from beneath the armchair he retrieved *Professor Unrat*, Heinrich Mann's 1905 novel about a teacher who, trying to impose his moralistic will on his students, falls under the charms of a nightclub dancer and to his ruination. In 1930, the book had been made into a film, *Der Blaue Engel*. Later the Nazis banned film and book alike. Mauer had kept his copy. He couldn't bear to read the Nazi-era publications awash in circumlocutions and outright lies.

Before their radio stopped working, they had listened to music in the evenings and occasionally tuned in illegally to the BBC's German-language news broadcasts. The radio console posed on a carved umber sideboard inherited from his parents that occupied the parlor wall like a coffin at a wake. Atop lay screws and the back panel he'd removed to identify the defect. When the Nazis had come to power, they subsidized radio sets to drive down the prices so they could spread their propaganda to a wider audience. The war economy had made the parts expensive again. He hoped to barter with a junk man for a used vacuum tube he could install himself. So far, he hadn't had the time.

The book slipped from his fingers. Too tired to plow through a single paragraph, he slid it back under the chair. Sleep beckoned. His great pleasure was to snuggle to his wife under their prize down comforter, a wedding present from long ago, the warmth especially sweet knowing the sirens would stay quiet tonight. Millions of his countrymen were spending the night on the winter fronts or on submarines far from their families. He was lucky, so very lucky.

He checked the base of the age-tarnished, triangular-base brass lamp on the bedside table. One of the angles harbored his 9-millimeter Luger automatic pistol; another a pouch of important documents, money, jewelry, keys; the third his billfold with his military identification. In the event of an air raid, he would snatch up the Luger and the billfold, and Jana would grab the pouch and the little suitcase posed at the foot of the bed. The pouch and billfold contained photographs of him and her. If they became separated, they could show the photos around. Have you seen this person?

Please, God, don't let it happen to us.

The lamp's base sprouted a frayed, fabric-sheathed wire. His mind flashed the image of a car battery, the wires running to a captive belted to a chair. *I am electricity, and you have used me to shameful ends!*

Not me. I'm merely the one who searches for the truth.

Liar! Self-deluder! Do you think the sin is greater in the one who throws the switch, than in he who lurks behind the scenes?

Face pressed to Jana's hair, he squeezed his eyes to shunt the noxious voice from his head. The interrogation document was driving him mad. Tomorrow he would send the vile thing back to the Gestapo. He'd done the best he could with it.

The dying Britisher had done his best too, hadn't he?

Commonly the subjects of Gestapo and SS interrogations were simple halfwits who'd been overheard to spout some disloyal remark. Predictably they knew nothing worthwhile and served only as examples, to be tossed beaten senseless in a gutter or sent off to a concentration camp. Real enemies required more finesse. Some possessed an ancillary value to the Reich and must be handled with velvet gloves. Then there were those whom the interrogators could roast like bratwurst on a stick, spies or commandos Hitler's standing order already had condemned to death.

The inquisitors initiated their procedures perfunctorily. If they had plenty of time, they commenced with silence or innocuous queries, no need to utter threats, the subject already had built his or her own mental castle of terror. If time were short, the interrogators might proceed straight to torture. They assumed the subject would lie. What if the subject answered honestly straightaway? No difference, the technique must be played through, only unbearable agony could certify they had extracted the truth. What was the proof that it had become unbearable? Death was a convenient metric.

With the British naval officer, they'd taken their devilish formula to the end, yet his answers had remained jumbled and impenetrable. Why the result? Had he consciously tried to confuse his interrogators, or was he braying out whatever words his drug-addled mind sparked? A man's brain was nothing if not thousands of synapses that electrical impulses leapt across, usually like perfectly choreographed ballerinas. Under the influence of chemicals, they might more resemble staggering drunks. The SS bastards had botched the job. Like every military man, Mauer hated incompetence, no matter the endeavor. *You have to be skilled to use such methods, and the SS thugs quite often aren't.*

He had to go to the bathroom. He extricated himself from the bed's cozy warmth and padded to the toilet. One of the drawbacks three layers of clothes imposed was the difficulty relieving oneself. He fussed open the garments and began to pee. From the toilet evanesced a wispy steam, the product of the infusion of a warm liquid into the cold. At the university he had studied chemistry, a subject that always had fascinated him. Throughout history, chemists had mimicked magic, deconstructing compounds to reveal their mysteries. Astonishing discoveries emerged, some purely by accident. In the mid-1600s, German alchemist Hennig Brand, chasing the passion of the era, tried to convert substances into gold. One day Brand boiled urine, and after some additional refinements out precipitated a fiery metal he named phosphorus.

Mauer stared at the bubbly toilet water. Could the document's contents be boiled, so to speak, to extract the hidden element within?

A whimsical thought. He dismissed it and went back to bed.

16

Early February 1944

Verrick had the autonomy to roam about the Lodge and its grounds as he pleased, as long as he adhered to a handful of security restrictions. He was not permitted to leave the perimeter on foot. In the unlikely instance he happened upon Hornchurch locals or someone from the RAF base, he mustn't speak to them. Nor could he consort with the Swedish woman, the soon-to-arrive German linguist, or the occasional messengers who delivered papers to Avry. On the premises, he must refer to everyone by their first names only. There was a phone in the parlor he could use. If he had to phone Wentworth at MI-6, he should ask for Pearlman, Wentworth's work name. Verrick was welcome, Avry said, to take his meals at the folding table with him and Linnea, as long as he heeded that the sessions were part of her foreign-language immersion. Clearly joining them would prove awkward, so he chose to eat alone in the dining room and to speak with her one-on-one in the evenings. Discussion of classified matters was forbidden in the presence of the Lodge's domestic staff—the cook, Mrs. Tatum, and the housekeeper, Mrs. Edda—though he could converse with them about the food or laundry or whatnot. Out of politeness or house custom, they called him Mr. Gabriel.

You might expect Mrs. Tatum to be stout and Mrs. Edda spindly. The inverse held true, and it was the latter who, on the morning of day three, having hefted her corpulence up the stairs, tapped at his door, panting out, "Mr. Gabriel, sir?"

He opened the door. "Good morning, Mrs. Edda. Are you all right?"

Her face was flushed, her chest heaving. "Quite all right, sir. I'm up and down the stairs countless times each day."

"Ah."

"There's a call for you in the den from Mr. Sebastian."

He descended to the parlor to the right of the front door and picked up the phone. "Hello?"

"How are things going?" said Wentworth.

"Smoothly, as far as I can tell."

"I'm told you wish to see a certain file. Would you be up for a jaunt in the country?"

"Sure."

"Splendid. I'll be by at eleven to pick you up."

When he informed Avry of Wentworth's impending arrival, he caught a glimpse of Linnea in earnest dialog with the dove-haired Swedish woman. She looked to be in her late forties, her lively inflections calling to mind gifted teachers from Verrick's youth, her sing-song voice no doubt pouring out a fascinating story. Of the words in Swedish he caught through the open doorway, he comprehended none. Did the woman speak English? Irrelevant. He wasn't allowed to interact with her.

Wentworth showed up in a sedan he drove himself. With Verrick ensconced in the passenger seat, he steered northwest, threading towns and hamlets that thinned the further they receded from outer London. Clouds shrouded the low hills. Patchy snow pocked the fields. When road spray grimed the windshield, Wentworth switched on the stubby wipers, the view constricting to what could be discerned through the diminutive parabolas they carved out. Luckily none of the mud-flinging military convoys Verrick had encountered on his first day were evident. The few lorries they passed bore RAF roundels on the bumpers, suggesting the presence of airbases nearby.

Ninety minutes delivered them to a paved lane between high fences topped with barbed wire. Wentworth nosed the car to a closed gate featuring a guard house, military policemen, and alert-looking soldiers who steadied a loaded Bren gun atop sandbags. Nobody was getting through here who didn't belong.

Without being told, Verrick gleaned he was at Bletchley Park.

One of the military policemen stepped through a pedestrian opening. "Pull to the side there, sir, while we verify your authorization."

A prolonged wait commenced. Wentworth smoked a cigarette, and Verrick rolled down the window. Beyond the adjoining fence, a footpath wended through snow-dabbed woods. In summer, he supposed, the vegetation would have screened everything. Today the leafless shrubs revealed figures apparently out for a lunchtime stroll, some in uniform, others in civilian attire, at least half of them women. Occasionally one swiveled his or her head to gawk at the car stopped by the gate, and it struck him that their

undoubtedly saved the life of the spy she handled. She did leave something behind, though, torn-up pieces of a coded notebook the searchers discovered. The code was weak, and the SD broke it. We've not seen the whole of the contents, only what the Germans described in their communications, nonetheless there was enough to indicate that the spy they were chasing had four sub-agents. The Germans codenamed them EUROPA, GANYMEDE, IO, and CALLISTRO, and the principal spy GALILEO."

"After the great scientist and the moons of Jupiter he discovered," said Verrick.

"Precisely, sir."

"The revelation about the sub-agents must have sent the Nazis into a frenzy."

"Indeed, sir. One that has lasted years. Here at Bletchley Park, we've followed the saga, and it has opened an invaluable window into the SD and their methodologies."

"Proficient, the SD?"

"The department hunting GALILEO is the counterintelligence wing headed by Rudolf Fenzl. He's capable and respected, but the real dynamo is his deputy, Elena Rolke. We think she's the one who christened GALILEO and the Moons. If I were a spy in Germany, the last thing I'd want is that foxhound on my tail." The quip provoked a brief round of laughter from the indexers and lent a glimpse into Lieutenant Rahilly's ebullient personality. Behind her glasses, her blue eyes beamed. "Rolke's track record is near flawless. What makes it *near* is that she's never tracked down GALILEO or his Moons. The blemish doesn't charm her. Senior Nazis on the security side have referred to GALILEO as the 'thousand-year spy,' whose meaning we're not altogether certain of but which seems to be a play of sorts on the Thousand-Year Reich and may be a sardonic jab at Elena Rolke for continuing to chase after him, though he's long gone quiet. She's not very popular, we surmise, fiery perfectionist that she is."

"Abundantly the shrew, it seems," Pell tossed in, provoking more laughter.

"As recently as three weeks ago," Rahilly went on, "we saw indications the SD still were sifting through their list of suspects, a list that includes Admiral Diefenbach, whom we know to be GALILEO. Probably he attracted their scrutiny because he served prior in his career as a military attaché in

Moscow and speaks fluent Russian. Lately, though, they seem to have taken a step back in their suspicions, for he's been posted to the General Staff in Berlin."

Verrick said, "Have you discovered the identities of any of the sub-agents, the Moons?"

"No, sir. The SD haven't either."

"Surprising, that they've eluded the Germans?"

"Very."

Rahilly delved into GALILEO's education, family, and military record, segueing to the secrets the Nazis believed the spy had betrayed to the Soviets. "He tipped them well in advance to the timing of the German invasion of the Soviet Union, code-named BARBAROSSA, a warning Stalin unwisely chose to disregard."

"How did the Nazis ferret out what GALILEO had passed to the Soviets?"

"Analysis of interrogations of Soviet officers they captured after they invaded."

"Why are you certain that Diefenbach and GALILEO are one and the same?"

Rahilly seemed momentarily at a loss for words. Pell spoke up. "We're assured so, sir. You won't be surprised to hear Bletchley Park compartments counterintelligence information. Our section doesn't have access to that particular piece, a highly bigoted one, I would think. It's also possible that the knowledge originated from a different source than encrypted signals, isn't that right, Mr. Wentworth?"

From behind the indexers, Wentworth said, "Quite so."

The briefing concluded. Wentworth excused himself to make a phone call, and Verrick asked directions to the latrine. The captain escorted him to the hall's end and posted himself outside the door in the wait, probably to make sure the American didn't wander off where he wasn't supposed to. When he returned to the indexers' sanctum, he spotted Wentworth in the adjunct office, phone receiver to his ear.

Lieutenant Rahilly was at her desk. Verrick walked over. "Informative briefing."

"Thank you, sir."

"I thought of another question. I hope you don't mind."

"Not at all."

"In the intercepts, were there indications why the SD relinquished their suspicions of Admiral Diefenbach?"

"It's not conclusive that they *have* relinquished them, not entirely. The SD aren't the types to let go, once they've sunk their teeth in. As to why they've eased up on him a bit, we've seen no explanation. Bear in mind, the Germans don't send all their communications over the air. Some pieces go by wire, others by courier. And, as Captain Pell said, not every piece makes it to this sub-section."

"You probably know the SD as well as anyone. Do you have a hunch?"

"You're asking me to speculate, sir. I prefer to keep to what's in the indices."

"Understood."

She hesitated. Here was an American bidding her to show off the mind whose agility no one outside this file-cabinet-stuffed room normally perceived. She said, "It's fair to assume they had a reason, though. The SD doesn't go thrashing about without one. As German services go, they're extraordinary."

"Better than the Gestapo?"

"The Gestapo are policemen. Assiduous they are, coppers nonetheless. They're like the lion tamers at a circus who flourish their whips quite skillfully. By contrast, the SD are the acrobats soaring overhead."

He visualized her two archetypes, the one controlling and menacing, the other nimble, volant. "So what might be a reason the SD would take the spotlight off Diefenbach?"

"For one thing, to accuse a high-ranker like him, they'd require permission, meaning convincing someone very powerful, like RSHA boss Ernst Kaltenbrunner, or SS head Himmler. To do that, they'd have to show evidence more than he's not Caesar's wife." The metaphors seemed to fly from Rahilly's lips.

"I'd have thought the evidentiary bar was low in Germany."

"Generally it is, sir. Regarding those in powerful positions, senior Nazis especially, it tends to rise. The bastards go about stabbing each other in the back so much, if they didn't heed to some standard of proof, they'd have exterminated themselves by now."

"If only."

"The admiral has societal perceptions on his side too. He's from a prominent business family, people who traditionally scorn the communists. Not that there isn't precedent to the contrary. One of the legendary Admiral Tirpitz's great nephews became a member of the Red Orchestra. The SD has to be careful how they proceed, knowing they'll be second guessed. Hard proof would suit them, the more ironclad, the better."

He was about to ask her what might constitute ironclad proof, when he saw Wentworth hang up the phone.

"That's very helpful, Lieutenant. Thank you."

For the third time today, he withdrew from people whose cross-section with his life was all too flitting. An irony of the intelligence business, that the details he'd amassed about GALILEO were more than he knew about most of the individuals he met in person. Probably Lieutenant Rahilly could make the same assertion of the names that populated her indices.

He and Wentworth followed Captain Pell outside.

17

Early February 1944

At the briefing on her first evening at the Lodge, the projector had spewed a gritty image of Admiral Diefenbach's face, the uniform hat brim shadowing his eyes. Sharper was the black-and-white photo Avry now showed her. It captured the admiral at a social gathering of some kind, seated among people whose attention seemed to be wholly on him. He wore no hat, and beneath graying hair trimmed in a military style, the tick lines around his eyes and mouth hinted at a wry amusement.

"Born in 1888 in Köln to a well-off family," Avry biographed, "he achieved his *Abitur*—his secondary school matriculation certificate—at age 18 and gained a prized naval cadetship. In those days, German naval officers ranked among society's elites, and none entered their fold even as a lowly cadet who hadn't the proper provenance. His family name and wealth met the standard. During the Great War, he served at sea, and reportedly he was well regarded by one and all. And why not? He's handsome, intelligent, and rumored to be charming."

Linnea stared at the saucy, half-bent smile in the photo. "What color are his eyes?"

"Hazel, according to the file."

"He doesn't look like the type to be a spy."

"To look like a spy is the last thing a spy wants; it gets him killed. But you raise a good point. Why did he become one, this scion of the establishment? A privileged upbringing isn't always the bed of roses you think. In espionage as in life, relationships drive motivations. His father was a successful industrialist. The two older brothers entered the profitable family business making fabric dyes. He chose the military. I'd wager the father was a browbeater who stirred rebellion in his youngest son."

Maybe GALILEO's father was a liar too, she thought.

"It may have been animus toward his father, or a hidden sympathy with the naval mutineers who in 1918 precipitated a socialist uprising across Germany, or something else entirely that sparked his communist epiphany.

Karl Marx never envisioned that the first country to embrace communism would be Russia; he theorized England or Germany would take the epic honor, but in the terrible conditions that prevailed after the Great War, Germany looked to be running a close second. Communists abounded. We surmise that GALILEO's inner seed already had sprouted when in the late 1920s he joined the military attaché corps and learned Russian. Quite often the choice agent is the fish that flirts with the hook. The NKVD were the fishermen, and probably they didn't have to work all that hard, they simply played to his existing passions and brought them under control. In return, they promised him the proletarian utopia.

"He returned from his four years at the German embassy in Moscow just as the Nazis were ascending to power. The German military traditionally has kept aloof from politics, and his sudden and hearty enthusiasm for the Nazi brand almost certainly came at the NKVD's urging. They'd trained him thoroughly in spycraft, and in Hitler's Germany, he needed the skills. A military officer who betrays the Fatherland commits the worst of all crimes— *Hochverat,* they call it—and if he's caught, he pays his coin to the hangman. He married a Berlin woman of social standing, and she boosted his rise. One of his triumphs as a spy was to tip off the Russians to the impending German invasion. It wasn't his fault that Stalin dismissed the warnings, as he did others.

"The SD and Gestapo knew they had rats in the straw. By 1941 they were hard on his heels. They pinpointed Maria Toft and showed up to arrest her, and if she'd have hesitated an instant to do herself the coup, they'd have wrung his identity out of her and nailed him in short order."

"The NKVD hasn't been in touch with him since?"

"We don't think so. The Toft episode coincided with an ardent German counterintelligence campaign they mounted soon after they invaded the Soviet Union. Over the year that followed, they closed down all the Soviet spy networks, including the infamous Red Orchestra. In foreign espionage, the Germans are run of the mill. In counterintelligence, on their home turf, they're as ravening as it gets. The NKVD dared not try to recontact their man. Another factor was that he spent two of the war years at the Kiel naval base on the Baltic. Even if he'd been able to slip secrets to the Soviets, he didn't have the access they were after, to eastern-front war plans. Better to save him for later."

"Like when he's on the General Staff? If you noticed the opportunity and figured out how to get to him in Stockholm, why won't they?"

"As you heard at the slide briefing, the Swedes aren't fond of the Soviets and keep them under heavy surveillance. The Swedish security services have relations with the Germans, and the Soviets know that if the Swedes catch them sniffing around the admiral, the Germans will hear of it, and that'll be the end of him. Bear in mind, the difference between the Soviets and us is, when we make a mess of things, we don't get stood up against a wall. Dicey innovation isn't something your typical NKVD *kulak* likes to trifle with."

Her job at Factory House had familiarized her with the NKVD. They were aggressive and formidable. Wasn't it equally possible that the risk for them lay in *not* seizing the opportunity to contact their agent? Would a Russian spymaster want to tell Stalin he'd let slip the chance?

Bad idea, it seemed to her.

If leaving Bletchley Park proved less time-consuming than entering, neither was it quick. They waited seven minutes at the gate while the guards fussed over their rosters. "Do you visit here regularly?" said Verrick.

"About once a month," said Wentworth. "I've wasted more of my life at this gate than I care to think about."

At last the sentries waved them through. The tires thudded over bumps set in the road, presumably so vehicles couldn't hold the speed to ram through the gate. More security exemplars to note.

Verrick said, "I was surprised to hear the briefers refer to GALILEO by that name. Is it the common practice for British intelligence personnel to use the same codename the Germans have assigned to an agent?"

"On the contrary, it's an anomaly."

"How did it come about?"

"What can I say? The smarter they are, the more people like to rattle the mental cages we put them in. In this case, they rather liked the Germans' codename and kept on using it."

Bletchley Park had offered them neither food nor drink. Wentworth stopped at a country pub in the nearby village of Shenley Brook End. The edifice might have emerged from the age of Shakespeare; the ceiling beams drooped, the floor sagged, the rough-hewn tabletop three inches thick bit into its legs with ancient iron nails. The table adjoined a window whose panes rippled under the gravity of centuries. Wentworth said, "The rationing taken into account, I think you'll find the fare here palatable."

The fireplace wasn't putting out much heat. The locals kept their coats on, so the two out-of-towners did likewise. Verrick said, "This far along in the war, are people faring better?"

"By baby steps, you might say. They grow vegetables in whatever plots of ground they can carve out. And they've adapted to the shortages by devising ingenious recipes to spice up what you'd think would be the blandest of dishes."

As if to test the assertion, both men ordered the single menu item, potato soup. Neither broached the ISOS-ISK briefing until Wentworth, glancing around to make sure no one was within earshot, said, "I'll ask you to repeat nothing of today's show to Linnea or Avry. Any knowledge whatsoever of the Park's exploits would preclude their work on the Continent. Linnea has read some of the special products embedded in order-of-battle estimates, but their true origins were concealed amid information from other sources."

The soup came. Steam purling from the surface conjured a perpetually bubbling cauldron in the kitchen, the boilover gumming the rim; no doubt Verrick had collected too many Shakespearean images. In any event, the thick broth went down rich and tasty.

At length the MI-6 man said, "I know you'd like an answer to your question about how we pegged our man. To ask is entirely reasonable, yet I'm afraid there are things I cannot discuss, at least not at present."

"If the ploy works, how will you run him in Berlin?"

"I can't speak to that either. I'm sure you understand."

GALILEO was, or had been, a spy for the Soviets. Had the British garnered his identity from a Soviet source? In vain Verrick listened for any hint to this effect. He'd asked to see the GALILEO file, and Wentworth had acquiesced with a visit to Bletchley Park and a briefing by the ISOS-ISK indexers that shed an incomplete light. Unsurprising. No foreign spy organization was going to lay all its cards on the table. The need-to-know principle applied, and he'd had his share of experience with it from both ends.

Among the consumers of intelligence, few were more insatiable than military leaders and their staffs. Lives depended. The spymaster walked a shaky rope, to enlighten while protecting the identities of vulnerable sources. The term 'need to know' conveyed an intrinsic hubris—I know better than you—not to mention that to withhold access could be awkward in the extreme. Verrick had witnessed pufferies of indignation: Who's this clerky fellow to tell me what I *don't* need to know? Not everyone complained. No louder modus existed to broadcast your unimportance than to declare you'd been denied information because you lacked the need to be told.

In Washington some months ago, Verrick had been called upon to brief a senior official of the Roosevelt administration. At one point, the recipient pressed him for the identity of the source of a piece of intelligence. Verrick replied with an aggrandized restatement of the banal source description.

"I asked *who* the source is," snapped the official.

"I'm afraid I can't reveal names, sir."

"You *do* understand who I am."

"Yes, sir." Verrick politely declined to divulge the source's identity, thinking it sad that a man erudite enough to have risen so high in government wouldn't know better than to insist. But you didn't brush off such a personage unless you had top-cover, which in this case Verrick did, from Donovan, who in turn had it from President Roosevelt. Nonetheless he could almost hear the sharpening of the bureaucratic knives. The official or one of the others he'd stonewalled along the line would plunge one in his back, if they got the chance.

Wentworth probably could relate stories of his own.

Verrick said, "Do you think the cloud of suspicion over our friend really has been lifted?"

Wentworth might have deflected the question. Perhaps he thought it better not to overplay his hand. "We believe so. Why else would they permit him to travel to Sweden? The Nazis harbor suspicions about a great many people. They can't afford to throw them all to the wolves, and with a powerful man like him, they dare not attempt it without evidence."

"Might he still be under surveillance by the SD?"

"We can't rule it out, which is why we need Linnea's unique language talents. They lend her the wherewithal to slip past the watchers."

"If he remains under suspicion, he's probably sentient of the fact. Won't he be jumpy, to be contacted out of the blue?"

"Likewise conjectural."

The rule of thumb, in law as in espionage, was to study the matter as thoroughly as possible. Awareness, even if conjectural, lent one an advantage. More information was always better. Seeming to read his thoughts, Wentworth said. "If you're worried about her being attuned to the risks, don't be. Avry will cover every bit of ground, I assure you."

The last mouthful of soup had hidden a chunk of gristle. Verrick might have spit it into his napkin. Instead, he chewed and chewed.

– 18 –

Early February 1944

Write nothing down. A rule of the Lodge, Avry said. Her memory was strong. By no means was it faultless. Why couldn't she at least jot down the Swedish words she wasn't accustomed to? She asked him.

"Notes are a crutch. In the field, they can jeopardize you. People catch sight of you writing or examining them, and they think it odd. You might drop or misplace them. If you're captured with notes, there's no talking your way out. Make yourself remember what you read, see, and hear."

The camaraderie he'd tried to forge with his us-against-the-English act had fallen flat. True, he was a Scot of Russian ancestry, his nature feisty and rebellious. The characteristics made him no less *them*. Apparently intuiting her verdict, he relinquished the pretense. She liked him better without it. His face she classified as swarthy, the florid skin and aslant lips under the shambles of black hair. She basked in the beams of his russet eyes that studied her every movement and gesture.

Someone else was observing too: Verrick from the sidelines. Sometimes he was there, sometimes not. In contrast to Avry's critical gaze, Verrick gave off the benign interest of a parent watching his daughter skate around an ice rink. In the evenings he always asked her what they'd been talking about in Russian, and she explained. The scrutiny of the two men might have annoyed her. She found it comforting. When had anyone paid her so much attention?

The training day concluded. She ate dinner, and in her room she donned her second set of sweats to wear to bed. It saved time, to rise already dressed for exercise. Mrs. Edda had tipped up her other set of boat shoes to dry. Very thoughtful.

A knock at her door. She opened to Verrick.

"Do you have a minute?" The question was his customary opener, though their evening discussions always took half an hour or longer.

"Please come in, sir." She offered him the chair and took her habitual seat on the bed corner.

He said, "I'm awestruck how you can switch languages as smoothly as a singer moves from one song to the next. I wish I could do that."

"Just an accident of my upbringing."

The look in Verrick's eyes said he knew there was more to it, a rare talent she possessed.

"Listen, I'm heading to London tomorrow, just for the day. I wanted to get your update on the training regime."

As with her prior narrations, she lapsed into the present tense. "I'm still not used to the early exercises, and I'm half asleep when I begin running. It helps that Bags is excited to see me and loves to go on the wooded path. She jumps up and down when I do the parachutist exercises."

"Parachutist?"

"Avry says they're strictly for fitness." She showed him the torn calluses on her hands.

"My goodness."

"In the mornings they've been bringing in a woman who calls herself Mrs. Johansson. We converse in Swedish."

"The lady with the straight gray hair."

"Yes. Soon they'll add a German speaker. I've translated plenty of German, but I haven't spoken it since college, and I'm sure to be rusty."

"The topics of your discussions with Mrs. Johansson?"

"All things Swedish, and how to blend in when I get there."

"And in the afternoons?"

"Avry steeps me in GALILEO's history and psychology and coaches me on how to portray Vena Nadovska."

"The NKVD officer."

"I'll be in the role for no more than ten minutes, says Avry. We've rehearsed versions that have gone just six. That's if GALILEO agrees immediately."

"What do you say to him?"

"The scripts, as Avry calls them, haven't arrived. The rehearsals so far have concentrated on my deportment." She suppressed a smile. Avry's word conjured a child made to stand in a corner for unruly conduct. "I'm to enter the hotel between midnight and 1 a.m., the exact day to be determined. The lateness has advantages. The delegation's business—the last-minute clarifications and the messages to Berlin—will be finished by then."

"What if GALILEO is in the hotel's bar?"

"He's a teetotaler and should be in his room."

"What if he brings his wife to Stockholm with him?"

"He won't, supposedly."

"And if he's asleep?"

"The knocks should wake him up. He doesn't take sleeping pills."

"How do they know he's a teetotaler and doesn't take sleeping medications, and that he won't bring his wife?"

"I don't get answers to those kind of questions."

He smirked. "Nor do I."

"Anyway, I'll give my spiel and hand him a letter. I haven't seen it, but Avry says it's in German and from Sophia, a name GALILEO will be listening for, to affirm the bona fides of the one who recontacts him."

Verrick seemed to ruminate for a minute. At length he said, "Does it all make sense to you?"

"Not entirely." She related her skepticism at MI-6's premise that the Soviets, assuming they hadn't already contacted GALILEO in Berlin, wouldn't try to do so in Stockholm.

"You've said so to Avry?"

"He says we should trust the opinion of his service."

"Ah."

"Something else too. What's with the letter? I'm not allowed to write anything down, so I'll get used to remembering and won't get caught with notes, and yet I'm to carry a piece of paper into the hotel? Isn't that a bad idea? What can the letter possibly say that I can't tell him face to face?"

Verrick's gaze drifted, as if he were trying to sieve the letter's contents out of thin air. "You've mentioned this as well?"

"Same answer."

"Perhaps I can speak to Avry on the subject."

"No, I'll raise it again."

He nodded slightly. She took it that he approved of her inclination to handle the matter herself.

She retold Avry's analogy that GALILEO was like the fish that flirted with the hook, and the NKVD were the fishermen.

"Does that mean he volunteered to the NKVD?" He raised his hand. "Never mind. So he's like a fish, is he?"

She laughed. "My mother used to take me to a spot on the lower East River to fish. Free food, right? There were always hobos around. My mother was wary of them, and she never let me talk to them or go fishing by myself. We must have been a weird sight, this uppity Russian woman and her teenage daughter casting our lines in the water. The hobos were friendly, though."

"Catch much?"

"Little fish, mostly, but once I caught a pretty big one. I held it up for the hobos to see. They applauded. My mother was appalled."

"Do you feel as if you're far from home? New York, I mean."

She didn't think of New York as home. For a long time, Stockholm had held the distinction. "Sometimes."

He stayed quiet for a minute. He seemed to be giving her the opportunity to revisit her earlier declaration that she was not cut out for the mission. She'd decided to let it drift. Why, she wasn't sure, but her map studies and the Swedish language sessions had resurrected the city she left eleven years ago. The place tugged at her. Sounded like a reason, anyway.

"Is your mother still in New York?"

"Yes. We write often. Reminds me, can you have someone check if I have mail?" She told him of the military post office near her barracks and gave him the combination for her mailbox, number 647.

He wrote it down. The rule about not making notes didn't apply to him, apparently. "If you have mail, I'll arrange for it to be picked up."

"Thank you."

"Other concerns or difficulties?"

"No sir."

"I'd ask what I could bring you from London, other than your mail, but I don't think you're allowed to have anything that's not from the Continent."

"Just you, sir. You're the exception to the rule."

He left. Why had she uttered the stupid quip at the end? Not the kind of thing she commonly said, least of all to a senior officer. Was it trust she felt? If so, why? He wasn't her friend or her mentor.

Or was he some sort of guardian angel?

She reminded herself she didn't believe in such things.

19

Early February 1944

From time to time, Verrick had noticed around the Lodge a gentleman perhaps sixty years old, his legs bowed, his back curled like a question mark, who seemed perpetually to contemplate the ground as if in search of lost items. In his coat of sourwood brown, he solemnly tended to the shrubs, fed Bags, and effectuated outside repairs. Occasionally he fired up the brick-walled incinerator where Avry burned papers. His name, or perhaps his nickname, was Lenny, and he was the one who chauffeured Verrick into London the next morning.

Along the way Verrick's mind drifted to a longer trip he had taken, with Donovan in 1932, from New York City to Albany by train. Donovan was on the cusp of announcing his candidacy for governor, and Verrick feared he would be asked to join, or worse, to manage the campaign. Their military service together in World War I had rooted their relationship, and their shared work at the Justice Department and the law firm had fused it. Plainly Donovan trusted him as he did few others. The rewards for Verrick had been many. Practicing with the prestigious firm, he earned more money than his poor parents could have dreamed of, and his lucky—he would not go so far as to say wise—investments had endured despite the depression. He had the latitude to handle his cases as he liked, briefing Donovan occasionally. But to jump into politics? He detested the political arena, New York's especially. And Donovan was a figure of immense energy. To shepherd his campaign would be to chase the horse that always bolted from the stall.

For three hours they clacked alongside the scenic Hudson. Donovan, studying his notes for his speech to the Albany Law School's soon-to-graduate class, said little. Presentations to schools and organizations were his common fare. The one today had a special purpose: publicity. The word was out that he would enter the governor's race. Reporters would be present, and they'd ask the war hero for his views. What did he think about incumbent governor Franklin D. Roosevelt's candidacy for president? Across the state, people would read his replies in tomorrow's newspapers.

Donovan's speech unfolded to enthusiastic applause. He was popular. Maybe he'd win. To play a role in the campaign might earn Verrick an appointment to the state government or judiciary, prizes men spent their careers pursuing. So why did he dread the prospect of being asked?

The speech segued to a reception in one of the school's original spaces dating back to the 1850s, or so he was informed. The attendees, the capital's elites whose financial and political backing would be requisite to a successful gubernatorial bid, had gathered to have a look at the guest of honor. Off to the side, Verrick was content to converse with the invited law students. He sipped a glass of grape juice. Prohibition remained in effect. Not that private gatherings didn't serve alcohol, but it would have been *faux pas* to do so at one where Donovan was the featured attraction. In his days at the Justice Department, he'd made a reputation for vigorously enforcing the law, prohibition included.

Verrick heard his name called out. "Gabe, come up here, please." Donovan was gesturing.

Reluctantly he approached. "Ladies and gentlemen," announced the boss, "I'd like to present one of the attorneys at my firm, Gabriel Verrick. We've been together since the war. Gabe is the fellow I rely on when tempers become frayed. Whether hunched over a map in France with the bullets flying, or across the table during heated negotiations, when he speaks, people simply relax. It's like magic. There are attorneys and there are great attorneys, but Gabe is the rarest of the breed, the one who calms everybody down."

The guests clapped. Was it true, what Donovan said? The bit about calming people down while the bullets were flying was nonsense. As for the rest, most people were quick to mirror the attitudes they perceived; rudeness they reciprocated in kind, the same with peremptory treatment. Verrick didn't. Disapproving of his father, he'd learned the hard way that to show it was unwise. Better to rein in his emotions, be purposeful, non-distractable, and speak in a dispassionate tone. He brought the discipline to Donovan's firm, where he was the boss's friend, answerable to no one else. The status might have drawn sneers from the other lawyers behind his back. Tirelessly he built his own reputation, founding his cases on research and well-structured argumentation. One of the reasons he calmed people down was he knew his business to a T. Worth a mention? Apparently not.

On the journey back to New York City that night, Donovan asked him to head his campaign. Verrick took a minute as if to digest the offer. Then he respectfully declined.

The ensuing political contest lasted months. The boss was rarely in the office. Verrick's non-participation in the campaign was obvious to the other attorneys. They guessed he was on the outs. Perhaps the split was inevitable. Very different they were, Donovan and he, a surfeit of ambition in the one, a cautionary restraint in the other. He would be wise to weigh his alternatives. Should he circulate his name to other firms? To do so in the middle of the campaign would look like he was stabbing Donovan in the back, unthinkable. What about setting up an independent law practice? The country languished in the depression. At thirty-eight years old, he would be venturing onto thin ice. The notion still enticed him. He'd have to forgo his stylish Manhattan apartment and the fat paychecks that paid the rent. Did it matter? Not to Grace, who'd always considered the place excessive, or to his son Matt. Himself? Hell, he'd grown up in a cabin in the New Hampshire woods.

He'd just about made up his mind when Donovan lost the election. Two days later, reappearing at the firm, he summoned Verrick. "Shut the door, please," said Donovan.

Verrick guessed he would be asked to resign. Mentally he was prepared; he even knew what to say: To serve with Donovan had been an honor, and he was and forever would be grateful.

The campaign had taken its toll. Donovan's normally fastidiously combed hair was askew, his skin blanched. At his desk he fiddled with papers. Verrick stood. He had not been asked to sit.

"You were smart to have stayed away from the campaign," Donovan said.

"Smart had nothing to do with it. I don't like politics."

"You who could have the world in your hand, and you don't like politics. Be that as it may, thanks for keeping an eye on things while I was gone." Donovan handed him a bonus check, the largest he'd ever received. It was as if the refusal never had transpired. Verrick went back to being the one called in to ameliorate rancorous scenes, the lawyer who calmed people down. When America entered World War II, Donovan brought him to the OSS, where the topics were different, the role the same. The boss's man.

Maybe he was like one of the Galilean moons, a body so inextricably bound to the larger planet that his existence could not be independently defined.

Lenny swerved into Piccadilly Circus in central London. "Sir, might I drop you a couple of blocks from Grosvenor? Mr. Sebastian doesn't like me motoring too close to the Americans."

"That's fine."

At Oxford Street, he stepped out. The Mayfair sidewalks were dry, the air below freezing, the thoroughfare no less thick with people whose breaths plumed like the steam of locomotives. As if to certify the impression, specks of soot tasting of coal seemed to collect on his teeth. He veered into a sidestreet that for some reason was crammed with British soldiers. "Where's yer 'at, lad?" gruffed a sergeant to a hatless private who cowered under his glare. Verrick detoured around them. On the next block, he passed a grocery, where from the bed of a horse cart a boy tossed potatoes to his mate at a storefront. The boys wore short pants, and their shivering knees no doubt marred the accuracy of the pitches; Verrick barely ducked a sailing spud. At a crosswalk he had begun to step off the curb when an approaching bicyclist dinged a warning. For the benefit of the Yanks, the municipal authorities had posted signs: DRIVE LEFT, LOOK RIGHT!

Today was Donovan's last in town; he was departing this evening to Washington. He'd asked William Casey of OSS London to find them a discreet venue to meet. In his early thirties, Casey was brainy and articulate despite a mumbling vocalization style. His dark eyes behind wire-rimmed glasses were shrewd. Like Donovan and Verrick, he had been a New York lawyer, and in Washington he'd served on Donovan's front-office staff. The OSS Director appeared to have enormous confidence in him.

Like many of the buildings in central London, the OSS headquarters at 70 Grosvenor was more than one hundred years old, and the floors hosted spaces that didn't pair with their present-day purpose. According to legend, the edifice once had been the workplace of one of London's eminent dressmakers. Inlaid mirrors and platforms seemed to corroborate the tale. Casey led Donovan and Verrick up the inner stairwell to a fourth-floor storage room at the hallway's end. Within were gathered mannequins that in their time might have draped the resplendent gowns of princesses. Now the mannequins exhaled the aura of a surrounding audience.

"I promised Wentworth I wouldn't tell our London staff about GALILEO," said Donovan, "but Bill has to be in the loop. He'll be your contact here when I leave."

Verrick confirmed that Casey had been read into Bletchley Park's ULTRA product. "Do you know Sebastian Wentworth?"

"I've met him," said Casey. "Wealthy family, Eton man, elected to 'Pop,' a society for the *crème de la crème*, champion athlete for Cambridge, 1928 or so, I forget the college, maybe Caius…" Casey halted. No doubt he could have gone on in this vein. Taking stock of his interlocutors' puzzled stares and gleaning that what for the Brits might scintillate with nuance meant exactly doodle to his fellow Americans, he resumed with the cogent facts. "He's Menzies's go-to man for clandestine operations. Reportedly he's brilliant at it."

Verrick regurgitated the briefing that Wentworth had presented at the dining table. When he trotted out Wentworth's assertion that GALILEO recognized the end was coming and would be wise to be on the Soviets' good side, Donovan interrupted, "So the wisdom is, GALILEO is a smart cookie, and smart cookies go with the winner?"

"Yup."

To the three lawyers, the syllogism sounded like a bad day in court.

Verrick outlined the mystery of how the Brits had pegged Admiral Diefenbach as GALILEO and that Wentworth had refused to elucidate and the Bletchley Park's ISOS-ISK indexers did not seem to know.

"Might the indexers have known and been purposefully withholding it from you?" said Casey.

Verrick thought of Lieutenant Rahilly. "I don't think so. My guess is that MI-6 has a mole in Soviet intelligence. The NKVD were the ones running GALILEO. The Brits know he volunteered to work for the Russians and he's a teetotaler who doesn't take sleeping medication. You don't dig up those particulars except from deep in an agent's file."

Casey said, "Why did the Brits reveal the details to Linnea?"

"No idea."

"If it's true they're running a Russian mole," said Casey, "they'll want to keep us out. There are those in MI-6 who think the Soviets have us penetrated."

"We think the Soviets have *them* penetrated," said Donovan. No one doubted that at war's end, the Soviet Union, a dictatorship, police state, and nemesis to the world, would be America's leading intelligence objective. "A source like that would be invaluable. Look for the chance to press them for access."

"How big an annoyance should I be?"

The mannequins seemed to lean forward to hear the OSS Director's reply. "Keep asking questions. Stay within the bounds of courtesy. You're an annoyance to them just by your presence."

How did that fit with being the one who calmed everybody down? Did Donovan think the Brits were going to let something slip simply because Verrick was *there*? He was as likely to elicit an unintended response from Wentworth as he was from the mannequins.

Casey said, "When Linnea walks in on GALILEO, what makes the Brits think he'll buy that she's NKVD?"

Verrick related the deportment training reminiscent of preparing an actress for a role, one predicted to last no longer than ten minutes. He mentioned the letter she was to deliver, the contents kept from her so far. "Sophia is a codename GALILEO will prick up his ears for. The letter probably gives him contact instructions to use in Berlin."

"How will the Brits run him there?"

"Wentworth wouldn't say."

"Do they think the Soviets will go after him in Stockholm?"

"Wentworth doesn't seem worried. He says the Swedes watch the Russians so closely they dare not take the risk."

Casey's and Donovan's stares gave away their doubts.

Verrick said. "How do you want me to report?"

"Via Bill, once a week, eyes only for me, no copies, no files."

Descending the stairs, it occurred to Verrick he had mentioned nothing about Linnea's initial inclination to quit the mission and his cajoling her to be patient. The omission wasn't deliberate, the topic simply hadn't come up.

Verrick gave Casey the number of and combination to Linnea's post office box at the military compound. Casey promised to check. "Are you heading back to Hornchurch today?"

"This afternoon."

"Too bad. There's a bash at the Navy Building at seven. I go to these affairs so I can rub elbows with the SHAEF staff. I've made some useful contacts."

"Thanks. Some other time."

To fill the four hours before his scheduled rendezvous with Lenny, Verrick stopped by the file room. At the half door, he asked to enter and to select personally the files he wanted to read. The clerk frowned. His job was to confirm clearances, pull the dossiers requested, and sign them out across the barrier. No one else breached the sanctum sanctorum.

The clerk made a phone call. A minute later he opened the door and said, "Make yourself at home, sir."

Verrick did. At the clerk's desk, he went through the accordion folders on Sweden, one for each calendar year since 1941. There were intelligence reports from the U.S. Military Attaché's office and the OSS in Stockholm, classified analytical assessments, newspaper clippings, and a copy, filed in the 1941 folder, of a 1940 National Geographic Magazine with an article on rural Sweden. The country counted itself among the five major European neutrals; the others were Portugal, Spain, Switzerland, and Turkey. The distance across the Baltic Sea from the port city of Malmö to Rostock, Germany was roughly 90 nautical miles. If you peered from the Swedish coast, across the Øresund you could trace the silhouette of Nazi-occupied Denmark. A maritime climate in the south became sub-arctic in the north. Some years sidestepped summer altogether, eliding from spring to autumn like a leaping reindeer.

The economic and political climates interested him more. Since the mid-1930s, the Swedish Nazi party had gained a limited popularity. The party's rant that the Swedes were Aryans too was meant to stir racial pride, and their contention that Sweden should become Germany's ally had sounded simply pragmatic early on. Neither argument persuaded the Swedish public. The

Nazis hadn't won a single seat in the Riksdag, the national parliament. They *did* achieve a foothold in the security apparatus. According to an assessment by OSS Stockholm, Germany's clandestine services acted much as they pleased in Sweden, flourishing in the hands-off status the internal security organs granted to them but not to their British, American, or Russian counterparts.

More potent than the Swedish Nazis' sway or lack thereof had been the political calculus among the country's leaders that, in dealing with Hitler, they must tread on eggshells. So as not to provoke Germany and reap a complaint from her vigilant embassy in Stockholm, they discouraged press reporting of Nazi policies and even war crimes, going so far as to confiscate newspapers that contained critical articles. And they had acceded to the regular rail transit of Wehrmacht soldiers—euphemistically called 'leave traffic'—to and from Norway across Swedish territory, a gross departure from the principle of neutrality.

You might say, what alternative did the Swedish leaders have? Look at their borders. To the east, Finland had sided with the Germans. Norway and Denmark to the west were German occupied, and the Germans controlled access from the North Sea along the Skagerrak Strait, their anti-aircraft guns menacing the air corridors from the adjacent shores of south Norway and the Jutland Peninsula. Vital imports via so-called 'safe-conduct' ships could proceed only with German permission. Other precious goods came from Germany herself. And don't forget the damned Swedish Nazis still chanting their approval of Hitler and his noxious anti-Semitic creed. Styling themselves after Germany's Nazi Brownshirts, the Swedish sympathizers had infiltrated certain bureaucracies and establishments. One of their domains was the Delfin Hotel in Stockholm.

Yet over the years the balance had shifted. In early 1943, Germany suffered a crushing defeat at Stalingrad, and the Nazi juggernaut that had blitzed over Poland, the Baltic states, and large portions of the Soviet Union began to reel backwards. The western Allies unleashed massive strategic bombing of German industries. And the Germans weren't the only ones who could interfere with the 'safe-conduct' ships delivering the bulk of Sweden's fuel oil. Faced with Allied threats to sever the critical supplies, the Swedes began to walk back their acquiescence to German demands. Last August they terminated the deplorable 'leave traffic,' and they began to train exiled

Norwegians and Danes in 'police procedures,' a veil so thin the Germans couldn't help but glean that the true intent was to help consolidate anticipated post-Nazi regimes in the neighboring nations. And in October 1943, the Swedes truly surpassed the shoddy benchmarks of the European neutrals. At the request of Danish physicist Niels Bohr, they came to the aid of Danish Jews the Nazis had begun to arrest. The Swedish government broadcast its condemnation of the roundup and announced a policy of open asylum for the Jews, and with the Coast Guard assisting, more than seven thousand crossed the Øresund to safety. Sweden at last had shown boldness, defiance.

And yet not undone were her trade ties to Germany, to which war-essential materials continued to flow.

In the 1942 folder, Verrick came upon a reference to a document not in the files, and he asked the clerk if it was available. He had to sign a log to net a double-enveloped statement from OSS Stockholm addressed 'Eyes Only' to General Donovan, with an info copy to the London station chief. The prose related the obstacles imposed by none other than the U.S. Minister Plenipotentiary to Sweden, essentially the ambassador. Convinced that espionage was the business of the devil, the Minister Plenipotentiary had constrained the espionage prerogatives of the OSS men in Stockholm to what they could elicit at social gatherings or pry from the tight lips of Swedish government officials. Moreover, he'd insisted that the U.S. State Department stamp the passports of assigned OSS personnel with 'OSS,' declaring their intelligence affiliation not only to the Swedish security services, but to every meddler who might have cause to examine their documents. Outrageous, the policy, yet not far out of step with the mentality of many American consuls who held that OSS officers under diplomatic cover were deleterious to statecraft abroad. The document revealed nothing of how the matter ultimately played out, but there must have been some resolution; later chronicles showed that the OSS station in Stockholm had taken up its charter role in a capital full of spies.

Among them were the Soviets. Wentworth predicted the Soviets in Stockholm would leave GALILEO alone. Donovan and Casey rightly harbored doubts. Verrick too. If the Brits could get to GALILEO, why couldn't the Soviets? The NKVD was cunning and resourceful, and the barest nod from Moscow would set them in motion. Had Wentworth cavalierly dismissed the danger, or did he possess deeper insights into the NKVD's intentions?

Before Verrick finished his review of the files, he had a look in the Germany holdings, scanning for any mention of the SD's spyhunt of July 1941. He found nothing.

Donovan had left to board his flight to the United States. Casey handed Verrick the two letters he'd fetched from Linnea's mailbox. He provided something else too, a copy of the efficiency report prepared by her section head at Factory House, Alistair Bird. 'Miss Thorsell works tirelessly,' wrote Bird. 'She is innovative... goes beyond what is expected... has great stores of mental energy and unmatched linguistic talents and cultural astuteness.' To unravel personnel evaluations, you had to sift through the positivistic logorrhea in hopes the writer would at some point concede to candor. In the third paragraph, Verrick found what he was looking for: 'Miss Thorsell's ingenuity matches or surpasses that of people markedly more experienced than she is. In terms of discipline, she is less mature. An improvement in this facet is called for. A natural leader, she will head up her own section one of these days, if she can quell her prankish penchants.'

Prankish penchants? Whatever pranks she'd carried out, they'd nettled Bird enough that he had alluded to them on the record. MI-6 must have read the evaluation. The trait wouldn't have troubled them. Mischief makers themselves, they'd have adjudged her as of their same stripe.

A block at the bottom of the efficiency report afforded the subject the option to affix his or her statement, a resort rarely taken except in cases where he or she considered the evaluation unjust. Linnea had checked the box 'I do not wish to make a statement' and signed her name.

He handed the evaluation back to Casey. "Thanks."

"How long will the training phase last?"

"Another ten days or so."

Casey penned a number on a card. "If you need anything, call me, day or night. The number's clean."

20

Early February 1944

At the Oxford Street corner where Lenny had dropped him this morning, he re-boarded the black sedan. The afternoon was bright, the sun flickering like a movie projector through the intermittent clouds. By the time they reached the Lodge, it had plunged to a jaundiced puddle on the horizon. Bags in her kennel stared at him.

"She could use a walk, sir," said Lenny. "Care to take her out?"

His knee still hurt from the slip on the plane ladder. Maybe a walk would help. "Why not?"

The wind blew from the direction of the airfield. As Avry had warned, the plane engines roared so fiercely they might have been a few yards beyond the trees. The aircraft soon took off, and the woods quieted except for his and Bags's shuffles in the leaves. The dog must have apprehended in Verrick a laissez-faire attitude; soon she drifted well off the path, sniffing at the ground and guiding around the wet spots. In minutes they were at the fence. Beyond stretched a flooded expanse hundreds of yards across, the curved silhouettes of hangars and fighter aircraft beyond. Disconcerting, to think these same planes would scythe over the German-occupied Continent, each pilot cognizant that today could be his last. For some, maybe not from this airfield, it would be.

"God watch over you," he said aloud.

It was dark when he restored Bags to the kennel. He dumped two scoops of dry dog food into her bowl. The Lodge's protocols and people had become familiar. The sole car in the lot was the one Lenny drove. A second would have manifested the presence of the Swedish woman, or that a courier was here, or that Wentworth was visiting. He entered and at once detected the aroma of mutton, often on the menu in various of Mrs. Tatum's recipes. Upstairs he tapped at Linnea's door, and reaping no answer he slipped the two letters underneath. In his room he changed his shirt—the sooted one went in the wicker basket; tomorrow it would return cleaned and pressed—and swapped his necktie for the spare he'd brought along. As he shut the dresser drawer, he neglected to ease his thumb out of the way, and the hard edge smashed against his nail. He swore under his breath. The thumb throbbed. Ice might help. They'd have some in the kitchen.

Mrs. Tatum examined his thumb. "Goodness, sir, what have you done? Oh, I fear you'll lose your nail." She rooted out a rubber bag, stuffed it with ice, and shaped it around his thumb. The cold numbed the pain, not his sense of stupidity. First his knee, now this. He had come away from the Great War with a few scratches and a minor loss of hearing from German shells exploding nearby. Donovan, by contrast, had been hit three times, the third by a bullet through his knee. Heroes rarely egressed from war unscarred. Verrick's thumbnail and sprained knee hardly classed him alongside.

He was wasting his time here.

Keep asking questions. Stay within the bounds of courtesy. You're an annoyance to them just by your presence.

Over the years, Donovan had handed him many tasks. By far this was the most pointless. He understood not a word of Russian or Swedish and couldn't even pretend to be contributing. The premise that the Brits might reveal their Soviet source, if one even existed, was illusory. At the law firm, his salary had been on par with the top lawyers in New York, his time exorbitantly priced. What was it worth here? Yes, he'd promised Linnea he would stick around. Did she need him anymore?

Unlikely.

His mind leapt to his son Matt, quartered at some tentscape in rural England and about to be dropped into the war. Maybe he could ask to see Matt. Why shouldn't he? Casey had said he'd made contacts at SHAEF. Perhaps one of them could pass a message to the 101st Airborne Division that Matt's father was in England. Good bet the Army administrators would grant a brief furlough. Yes, to make the request was taking advantage of a connection others didn't have. Was it unethical? Not really. And if he didn't try, he might regret it for the rest of his life.

The prospect rejuvenated him. He stayed in the kitchen for dinner, cradling the ice bag around his throbbing thumb and listening to Mrs. Tatum go on about how she prepared the foreign menus for Linnea and Avry. A chore, to collect the right ingredients, which the market in Hornchurch did not always have, requiring Lenny to drive her to Romford. The petrol, imagine. Verrick nodded sympathetically.

He headed to the phone in the parlor. The radiance from the lit fireplace made the ice bag drip condensation. He shook his hand dry, spun Casey's number, and halted on the penultimate digit. Casey had said he'd be going to a bash this evening. Better to wait until tomorrow. He hung up.

A wooden case proffered books on British history and statecraft. He examined a few, one with a price in smudged pencil, 10s—10 shillings, half a pound—implying someone had purchased it from a second-hand shop. The pages smelled musty. Stiff and dry, they broke like crackers when bent. His grammar school had served a poor community, and the teachers, their textbook budget as sparse as palm trees in rural New Hampshire, had set aside class time to repair the old textbooks. They gave the students glue, wax paper, and a stack of books to page through in search of rips. If the children encountered a tear, they applied glue and sleeved it in a scrap of wax paper so the glue would dry without adhering to the other pages. Most of the girls took diligently to the task, the boys indifferently, except for Verrick. Like a hawk hunting prey, he scanned for rips, fixing each, handing in books blossoming petals of wax paper. If he found no rips, he introduced some of his own to mend. What did it say about him, that he would create flaws to demonstrate he'd fixed them? Did he enjoy the project's craftsmanship, or was he willing to manipulate things as it suited him? Whichever it had been, he could no more decipher his motives forty years ago as a schoolboy than he could the raw emittances of the German Enigma machine.

On the shelf was a three-volume set that looked somewhat newer than the other books: *Mr. Secretary Walsingham and the Policy of Queen Elizabeth*, by Conyers Read. He bunched the trio under his left arm and trundled to his room.

– 21 –

Mid-January 1944

To distill meaning from a dying man's gibberish.

To toady to the Gestapo.

To swear the Hitler Oath. Mauer and his contemporaries all had sworn the damn thing; he knew no one who had refused. Not many believed in Hitler's Aryan hokum. They consoled themselves that the Nazi leader promised the restoration of national greatness, the German birthright that the Versailles Treaty had robbed away. You might think Hitler's way was imprudent and debased and still pledge your life to it.

You had no choice anyway.

A bright dawn edgelit the bedroom window's blackout paper. Before the war, a sunny winter morning would have been cause for gladness. Today it meant the bombs would rain, if not on Berlin, on another German city.

As he walked, he passed a block the police had cordoned off. Within sawhorse barriers, men surrounded a dud bomb half-buried in the pavement. The air raids scattered duds, sometimes by the dozens. Though preferable to the ones that exploded, they begat a tremendous nuisance, embedding themselves in buildings, streets, parks. In the city center, specialized teams had to defuse them. The less-populated outskirts might see Russian prisoners of war, promised cigarettes, plying their luck. Sometimes the bombs detonated when shifted by a millimeter, and even if they never went off, a 225-kilogram deadweight crashing through the ceiling wasn't an event that left a house intact, or its occupants.

He must convince Jana to move away. The argument would have been easier if they had children or living parents. It didn't help that she and her closest blood relative, her cousin Mara who lived outside Augsburg, could tolerate each other's company no more than a few minutes before they began to snarl like rival wolverines. You don't have to live with Mara, he mentally rehearsed. Take a room in a boarding house or hostel.

At the office, Gerta looked paler than usual. Where was the little Nazi brooch she habitually pinned to her dress? Better not to rummage his eyes over her. What did he care if she wore the damned thing?

He opened his safe and retrieved the Gestapo document. Last night's idea, to boil urine, as Hennig Brand had done toward his discovery of phosphorus, had stayed with him. Tabulation was his instinct. Thus far he had not counted the repetitions, merely eyed their approximation to each other. He began to sum them, ticking off each reiteration. The most common response the interrogator had recorded was none—*Der Befragte gibt keine Antwort*, the subject doesn't answer—with 72 repetitions. The next commonest was *unentschlüsselbar*, indecipherable, with 58. Of the comprehensible replies, the vast majority were single words. He listed the handful he construed as having a technical or military association, parenthetically tacking on the number of times they appeared:

Far (3)

Pressure (3)

Flow (2)

Range (2)

Viscosity (2)

Heavy (2)

Current (2)

Clearance (1)

Deep (1)

Depth (1)

Depth and deep obviously were identical in concept, as probably were far and range, and flow and current. The latter referred to fluids. Pressure likewise. Water was the ubiquitous fluid. Two themes echoed, water and distance, evoking the idea of ships.

He hunted the words that pointed to tangible objects or substances:

Smokestack (4)

Tin can (2)

Ramp (2)

Mud (2)

Exit (2)

Steel (1)

Leaf (1)

There were terms with navigational connotations:

Lane (3)

Eastern (2)

Turn (2)

Western (2)

Rising (1)

Shallow (1)

Narrow (1)

Transport (1)

Laager (1)

A handful were common pronouns: You (3): Them (3); They (2) What (3). No question marks. Had the subject meant it as a question? Unknowable.

A name: Tom (1). A friend? A codeword? A fragment of Tommy, slang for an English soldier? Mentally he rustled up the extensions of 'tom' he could think of in English: tomorrow, tomato, tomboy, tomb, tomahawk. They illuminated nothing.

Importance (1). What had the subject meant? The word didn't seem to attach to any other.

There were cardinal numbers, nine in total, all multiples of ten he arranged in descending order: 170 (1); 140 (1); 120 (1); 110 (1); 80 (1); 70(1); 50 (1); 40 (1); 30 (1). Each utterance prompted the interrogator's reflexive 'What is the significance of this number?' The next line unfailingly read, 'The subject makes no answer,' or 'indecipherable.' Did the numbers have meaning, or had the Britisher simply been dirging on, his brain misfiring?

Some retorts expressed rage or pain: Please; stop; God; mother, each appearing only once. The subject had been a British naval officer. For centuries, the British had been the undisputed lords of the sea. It was impossible not to admire them for their accomplishments, their legendary élan in adversity.

The SS had murdered him.

Flatten your emotions!

He breathed, closed his eyes. When he opened them, he was calm. Down the lists he roved. Clearly the words spoke to a nautical theme. Smokestack, the most repeated, might relate to the funnel of a ship. Transport, used as a noun, similarly conjured sea vessels. So did tin can, American Navy slang, he recalled, for destroyers, the small, agile fighting ships commonly assigned escort and anti-submarine missions. From a Royal Navy officer's mouth, tin can made less sense, unless the officer had assimilated American naval jargon.

He revisited viscosity, the word that initially had snagged his attention. Water had viscosity, as did denser liquids like oil and mud. Mud appeared twice. The more viscous the ground, the more men and vehicles tended to mire in its transit. He pictured the eastern front as it had been described to him—he'd never been there—Wehrmacht trucks sunken to their axles in mud while Soviet artillery shells rained. The same could happen during an amphibious landing as men and vehicles unloaded from vessels and trudged through the wet sand. Sand—had he missed the word? Maybe it had disappeared among the 58 indecipherable responses. What would it sound like, tumbling from a tortured man's lips? He tested it: "Sand, sand, sand."

From the doorway, Gerta said, "Were you speaking to me, Kommodore?"

She must have ears like radar. "No, I wasn't."

When he looked again, the space was vacant.

Another word missing was tide. Ocean beaches experienced tides. Their timing was a critical factor in planning amphibious landings. Might the lesser numbers indicate tidal shifts measured in feet?

By that afternoon he had acquired a handbook of tide tables for the English Channel. The shores of Brittany in northern France witnessed phenomenal spring tides, as high as 50 feet. "Tide, tide, tide," he muttered, this time under his breath. Why not assume the subject had said sand and tide, and the interrogator had not picked them up.

Ramp too fit the premise. Landing ships had ramps. In a large-scale landing, destroyers—tin cans—would protect the landing ships. Clearance might apply as well, a reference to the separation the bottoms of landing craft needed from the obstacles the German defenders had embedded on potential landing beaches.

Interesting, not particularly helpful. Everyone knew the invasion was coming. It would involve thousands of ships and planes and tens of thousands of men. Initially the invaders would be vulnerable to counterattack, especially by armored forces. Driving them back into the sea offered the best chance for Germany to create a stalemate on the western front and negotiate an end to the war. To fail to defeat the invasion amounted to a death sentence. Of the Abwehr's intelligence objectives, none was more consequential than to glean in advance when and where the invasion was coming. General Gerd von Rundstedt, overall commander in the west, predicted it would strike at the Pas de Calais, where the distance across the English Channel was shortest.

Army Group B Commander General Erwin Rommel, nicknamed *der Wüstenfuchs*—the Desert Fox—in charge of defending the coastline, argued that Normandy would be the site. Hitler had yet to choose between them.

Mauer reexamined the registered words. Why should the dying man have gibbered smokestack four times? Modern ships had smokestacks. To a sailor, the feature was no more significant than any other on a ship: the bow, the deck, the bridge, the anchor. Or did smokestack refer to something else, perhaps a soaring chimney, a landmark visible from afar?

In the Abwehr were officers who had served at sea and were knowledgeable of the manmade prominences along the English Channel. By mid-afternoon, he had phoned three, asking each if the sea passage featured a land-based flue that sailors looked to as a navigational marker. None recalled such, although there were prominent lighthouses, they said, among them the Île Vierge and Héaux de Bréhat in Brittany and the Phare de Gatteville on the Normandy coast. As he listened he sketched a smokestack, shading it in black, a distinctive white stripe across the middle, turning the pencil on its side to stroke wavy lines of smoke billowing out.

The air raid sirens commenced to wail, warning of a daylight raid, either on Berlin or one of the outlying areas. He pictured strings of 225 kilogram bombs spilling from the planes' bellies. Two-twenty-five, there was a number for you. His thoughts flew to Jana. "God protect her," he whispered. Mindlessly he kept rubbing the pencil. He looked down. Leaden smirches obliterated the sketch.

He threw it away.

– 22 –

Mid-February 1944

Role-play was today's gig, Linnea as Vena Nadovska of the NKVD, Avry as GALILEO. She knuckled the doorframe of Classroom 2 that mimicked GALILEO's room at the Delfin Hotel, entered at his word *"Ja?"* and squared off to the man.

"Stop!" said Avry. "Listen, you're not a chambermaid here to change out the dirty ashtray, you're a bloody Chekist professional. To you, I'm not a German admiral, I'm an agent, and you're the one who controls me. From the instant you step in, you dominate the scene."

He showed her how. The straightness of her back, her uptilted chin, and her locked stare would define her before she said a word. Agent controllers, he said, were like the parents of brat children. Give the brats too much leeway, they took advantage. Crack the whip too hard, they sulked or ran away from home. A good controller anticipated his or her agent's legitimate needs and held the line against outrageous demands. To listen was the *sine qua non.* Agents were prone to circumlocution. Sometimes they withheld information they perceived not to their benefit to divulge. Controllers must press them, always exuding forbearance and empathy toward those they were asking to risk their lives. The agents did not have to like their controllers. They had to obey them.

"Don't let GALILEO fool you, he'll have expected this encounter for a very long time. He knows damn well you'll be ordering him to do something that can get him killed. The business boils down to this: You're sending your agent out to risk his life, and it imposes on you the rigorous burden of responsibility. As you levy orders, you're always willing to listen to his reservations and to answer them."

All this sounded contradictory. "How, if he knows better than I do what can get him killed?"

"It doesn't mean you let him drive the mission. That's *your* job. If his first reaction is to balk, reason with him on how he can accomplish it."

"What do I say?"

"First, tell him to read the letter. If he still demurs, beguile him, always pushing in the direction of accomplishment."

She'd heard that English was the language that best suited masters to speak to their underlings. Avry's Scottish-accented Russian, possessed of an almost operatic resonance, worked fine. He could be the cajoling coach. When she imitated Hamfrid Matisson, the hotel employee in whose identity she would enter the Delfin, he said, "She poses with her feet primly together. When she speaks, her voice is the classic Swedish singsong. Let's see that winning smile of yours, Hamfrid darling."

She smiled.

"You've got to shed all that when you go from Hamfrid to Vena. Spread your feet to shoulder width, a fighter's stance. Make your voice authoritative and compelling. When you show your teeth, it's not to smile. The first words out of your mouth are, "Listen to me, comrade!"

"Listen to me, comrade!"

Sometimes his criticism stung. Concluding five repetitions of the bar-hang exercise, she showed him her hands, the baby calluses in shreds, a symptom too of her frequent washings. "What's this, your ouch-oh-it-hurts face? Is it a hurt-free life you're after? Do you think the Chekists would commiserate?"

He gave her a roll of white medical tape.

If the NKVD was not a sympathetic culture, the OSS by contrast seemed to be. During his visits to her room, Mr. Verrick unfailingly asked how she was doing. Was the concern in his voice real, or was he an agent controller doing his job? So what? The controller's empathy was not fake, at least according to what Avry kept telling her. By the time she came face to face with GALILEO, she really would give a damn about him, she had to, because he'd sense her genuineness, the same as she could read Verrick's.

The business boils down to this: You're sending your agent out to risk his life, and it imposes on you the rigorous burden of responsibility.

Along the running path, with each footfall, the words thudded like weights tied on.

Today was buzz-the-spooks day at Hornchurch RAF. The Typhoons blasted over at 300 miles per hour, rattling the windows and chasing Bags inside her shelter. Mrs. Tatum and Mrs. Edda stuffed cotton in their ears. Avry shook his head. "The sheep-necked bastards think it's right hilarious!" He referred to the fluffy wool collars on the RAF pilots' flying jackets.

The so-called scripts arrived. The text was in Russian, the pages stitched together with thread at the corners, each copy sporting a sky-blue cover reminiscent of a legal document. Avry regarded them curiously, as if he'd never before seen scripts. Indeed, as he admitted to Verrick, he hadn't. "They're not used for normal missions, or any other than this one, to be perfectly unvarnished about it."

The opener turned out as Avry had introduced: "Listen to me, comrade!" The next dozen or so lines comprised an oration on how GALILEO must perform his sacred duty and obey the instructions in the letter from Sophia. Variations followed, stemming from what he might say. If he balked, he got a stern diatribe. His questions reaped replies, most equating to, "You will find your answer in the letter, comrade."

From the sidelines, far enough away so he didn't impinge, Verrick observed. He had to credit the Scotsman with a flair for his job. Avry took her through her lines as if she were the lead actress in a stage production, honing her performance to a fine edge, adjusting her emphasis on certain words. He tapped her lightly under the chin to lift it, pressed at her lower back to straighten her stance. The OSS could not have pulled off the transformation of one of its officers in so short a time. True, Linnea was naturally talented. To bring it out in a practical way was testament to MI-6's finesse.

Last night Verrick had speed-read through the biographical volumes on Sir Francis Walsingham he'd taken from the parlor bookshelf. Like Verrick, Sir Francis had been a lawyer whom the exigencies of his era beckoned into spycraft, and like the latter-day British intelligence professionals, he was adept at intercepting communications and using the information to protect his monarch's reign. In the nearly four hundred years since, the spymasters had learned every trick to uncover secrets and thwart their enemies, an unequaled heritage.

Reading about Walsingham might have given Verrick hope that his stay at the Lodge would teach him a thing or two about the profession. What it accomplished was to reinforce to him beyond doubt that he was wasting his time. He was the voyeur to foreign-language exchanges he didn't understand until they were later explained, a prod for access he wouldn't be granted, and his boss's revenge on the Brits, his presence an affront Donovan knew he wouldn't take too far. How could the Director have assigned *him*, critical cog that he was in the OSS's war effort, to this frivolous role?

The question seemed to answer itself.

In the parlor, a sign above the phone proclaimed, SAY NOTHING YOU DON'T WISH THE HUN TO HEAR! He dialed and gave the operator Casey's 'clean' number. In three minutes, Casey was on the line. "Anything new?"

"Not really. I'm calling to ask a personal favor."

"Shoot."

"My son Matt is a lieutenant in the 101st Airborne Division. He's at a camp somewhere in England. Can one of your contacts at SHAEF get in touch with the division adjutant and pass the message that I'm in town and would love to see him? It wouldn't have to be for more than a few hours."

A fighter aircraft roared overhead. Casey said, "What the hell was that?"

"Typhoon. Nothing to worry about."

"The timeline?"

"My guess is I'll be finished here in a week or so. I assume I'll be sticking around in London for a short while after."

"Consider it done."

Military organizations traditionally went to some lengths to offer their personnel the option to attend religious services on Sunday or Shabbat. After exercises Sunday morning, Avry told her that to go would take up the time the service lasted plus the drive to and back. They'd have to make up the lost training that evening.

She declined. An unencumbered evening was worth more than a shot of theology.

He briefed her on the sequences of the infiltration plan. First, they'd journey to eastern Scotland, where an aircraft equipped with snow skis would lift off, cross the North Sea, thread the Skagerrak Strait, and enter Sweden, a flight of nearly 800 miles. A team of Swedish "friends" had picked out a frozen lake where the plane would set down. The friends would collect Linnea and Avry, shelter them as necessary, and transport them to Stockholm, where they'd make their way to the safehouse approximately a kilometer from the Delfin Hotel.

Why travel to Sweden in this complex way? Aircraft chartered to a commercial firm made regular runs to Stockholm to deliver and retrieve the British diplomatic pouch. The flights also carried individuals with diplomatic credentials. The Swedish government, Avry explained, kept an eye on the diplomats of the warring nations, especially the British, whose apartments the Swedish internal security service—the Allmänna Säkerhetstjänsten, or AS— was said to have bugged. When a British diplomat arrived in Sweden, the immigration authorities copied his or her passport. New arrivals could expect to come under surveillance, and any anomalous behavior or failure to adopt a customary routine would attract even closer AS scrutiny. If the goal was to remain invisible, diplomatic cover would have the opposite effect.

Over breakfast of fried leeks, fish, and dense, grainy bread, Avry said, "We have another week or so, which affords us the chance to fine tune your identities and brush up on your German, in case you'll need it with GALILEO. We'll have Mr. Grün, a native German speaker, coming over this morning."

So badly grooved and warped were the fingernails on Avry's left hand, they mirrored the surface of a phonograph record left too long on a hot stove. By contrast, those on his right appeared normal. Was this how nails grew back from a pulling-out with pliers? Had he been tortured? If so, why had his tormentors ripped out the nails only from his left?

Breakfast seemed a bad time to ask.

Mr. Grün—probably another fake name, *grün* meant green in German— wore a forest-jade suit as if to match his moniker. His brown eyes did not accord, nor did the parchment-pale skin of his face. Avry introduced them in German and took a chair behind her in Classroom 1.

"*Guten morgen,*" said Mr. Grün. "*Wiederholen sie, bitte.*" She was to repeat.

"*Guten morgen.*"

"*Ich habe gehört, dass sie in Hamburg geleben haben.*" He'd heard she'd lived in Hamburg.

"*Ja, ein Jahr.*" Yes, a year.

"*Sprechen Sie bitte in vollständigen Sätzen.*" She was to speak in complete sentences.

"*Ja, ich habe ein Jahr lang in Hamburg gelebt.*" Took her a minute to growl it out. As she'd feared, her spoken German was appallingly out of practice.

"Your Hamburg accent is quite prominent," he went on in German. "If you're going to have an accent, Berlin's is preferable, even if people think it's snooty. Can you speak in *Hochdeutsch?*"

At school in Hamburg, she'd learned the so-called high German and spoken it later with her language professors at New York University. She said, "*Ja, ich glaube schon.*" Yes, she thought so.

"Please speak *Hochdeutsch* exclusively from now on. Germans are very attuned to accents. There is no advantage to giving away that you lived in Hamburg, *ja?*" He looked to Avry for affirmation.

"*Du hast recht,*" said Avry in the German familiar. She guessed Herr Grün was an MI-6 employee whom Avry had dealt with on prior occasions.

Grün cracked the whip when her phrases lapsed into the colloquial. An hour on common subjects segued to military terminology: ranks, units, tactical appellations. From her analytical work, she grasped the meanings; she only had to memorize the vocabulary. The tedious session lasted three hours, and she left Classroom 1 straight to Mrs. Johansson in Classroom 2.

"Two hours in Swedish," said Avry.

Good God.

At lunch, which was later than usual, her head spun from the three languages. A phone call summoned Avry at the beginning of the meal, and she was grateful for the silence, less so for the oily fish and boiled potatoes. She ate a few bites and went to the dessert, a tasty slice of *Ostkaka,* Swedish cheesecake topped with a dollop of currant jam.

Training ended at six. Exhausted, she picked at her dinner. On the way to her room, she detoured outside to the porch to breathe the fresh air. Snow blanketed the yard and mounded an inch deep on the porch rails. Through the giant flakes she could barely make out Bags's kennel. Snow would be the everyday landscape in Sweden. For the first time since she had arrived at the Lodge, her anticipation surged.

Avry must have noticed her from the window. He came out. "See? We've arranged this spectacle to prepare you for Stockholm." His arm swept over the snowscape.

"Very accommodating."

"We try, we really do."

"The Swedes who are meeting us on the ground, are they trustworthy?"

"They're Mrs. Johansson's husband and sons, dedicated and thoroughly tested. They despise the Nazis. But you shouldn't speak about them with her, or of her with them."

"I take it their name is not really Johansson."

"Correct. You won't know their true surname, in case something goes wrong."

"What if it does?"

"Oh, a plenitude of scenarios, take your pick. The main one is that the Swedish government catches you and interns you for some length of time. They'll confine you to a camp, and you'll feast on reindeer, as we spoke of."

"The other scenarios?"

"One is falling into the hands of the Swedish Nazis, unlikely if we do our jobs properly."

"The worst case?"

"That the Swedish Nazis toss you over to the Germans, who'll try to spirit you out of Sweden and into Germany. They'll interrogate you. The rule of thumb: Stall for twenty-four hours, to afford us the time to get the others safe and you out."

She almost asked him what had happened to his fingernails. "How would you get me out?"

"Probably we'd fall on the mercy of the Swedish AS and admit with a plenteous show of contrition that we've broken the rules and infiltrated you into Sweden, and, terribly sorry, but the Germans have captured you, and could the Swedes kindly recoup you? The compulsory diplomatic tantrum will ensue, and the accompanying slaps on the wrist. Maybe they'll expel some of our people. Still, we don't doubt they'll acquiesce."

The plan struck her as elaborate and slow. "Have you done it before? Asked the Swedes to rescue someone from the Nazis?"

"I don't think so. We haven't had to."

"Will I be armed?"

"London gave it some consideration. Also, whether to provide you with a suicide capsule. The verdict was we didn't have time to train you properly with firearms, and it would chagrin us deeply were you to kill yourself prematurely, or by accident. On top of that, to carry either one risks painting you in your true colors. Not the brightest dobbers, the Swedish Nazis, but neither are they so thick that they won't sort out a professional if they've got their mitts on someone with a gun or an L-pill. I'll have a sidearm, so don't worry."

The snowfall suddenly didn't look so pretty. Hard as hell to run in the stuff.

He said, "I suppose the weather precludes the out-of-doors routine in the morning. Expect a late wakeup and maybe calisthenics in the gym."

"Bags will be disappointed."

"You should have seen her when she was a puppy, romping in the powder. That was four and a half years ago. She's become inured."

Four and a half years backtracked to September 1939. The Brits had been at war for some 1,600 days, more than twice as long as the Americans. Multiply her fatigue today by 1,600, and it was how the British people must feel.

She went inside.

– 23 –

Mid-January 1944

Mauer phoned the Gestapo Headquarters and asked for Stabl. In the wait, he sipped from the cup of ersatz coffee Gerta had brought.

Stabl said, "Please tell me you have finished."

"Not yet. I need your permission to bring the report to an expert on amphibious landings."

"Who?"

"Admiral Erich Raeder, the former Commander-in-Chief of the Kriegsmarine."

"Wait." The phone piped clacks, murmurs, and rustles of paper. Stabl came back. "You may not show the document to Raeder. You are permitted to discuss the contents with him in general terms, with no allusion to their origins."

"May I show him a list of the key words?"

"All right."

"And mention that my mission is from the Gestapo?"

"As long as you reveal no other details."

Brilliant.

Gerta spent the day attempting to make an urgent appointment with Admiralinspektor Raeder, having no success until Mauer suggested she impart that the request was on behalf of the Gestapo. "Seven p.m.," she said from the doorway, "at the admiral's villa in Charlottenburg."

He requested a staff car. You never knew what kind of banger the motor pool would cough up these days, and what appeared was a canvas-topped, open-sided Kübelwagen that must have failed its road-test for the eastern front. The Wehrmacht driver likewise. Sheathed in a *feldgrau* overcoat whose torso and back were stuffed with blankets, his face wrapped in a scarf, he resembled one of the plump Blutwurst sausages that long ago had ceased to hang in the windows of Berlin butcher shops. He rattled westward toward the suburb, circumventing blocked avenues and cutting so many U-turns that Mauer feared he would get carsick and throw up over the windowless door.

Raeder's modest home hunched on a quiet residential street that wintry linden trees watched over like ancient Goths. "Stay here," he told the driver. "I probably won't be more than thirty minutes."

The driver folded his arms and seemed to submerge into his blanket-stuffed overcoat.

From Gerta's Gestapo name-drop, the admiral had taken the hint that the topic was sensitive. Once they were inside his study, he locked the door. He had led the Kriegsmarine until forced to resign a year ago, reportedly for refusing to endorse Hitler's plan to scrap Germany's big warships. If you'd have expected a profusion of naval bric-a-brac in his den, you'd have been wrong; the place was as Spartan as the man, the sole artifact a tabletop model of a sailing yacht. He showed his guest to a chair and circled behind the oak desk, where, the lenses of his eyeglasses like the windows on the bridge of a naval vessel, the eyes behind as chill as its crow's nest, he dourly gave the younger man the stage.

"Sir, I have been assigned to evaluate information that may relate to the forthcoming enemy invasion of the Continent. Unfortunately the references are so vague they tell me very little. I come here in the hope you can make something of them." Across the desk, he proffered the list of the words and numbers distilled from the interrogation report.

Raeder scanned them. "This is all you have?"

"I'm afraid so."

"And I suppose you are not permitted to say where the information came from."

"That is correct, sir."

"And yet you bring it to me. Why?"

"You planned Operation Sea Lion."

Raeder ticked his head. "I have trouble believing you are serious, Mauer."

"I am."

The admiral adjusted his glasses. His squeezed face could have doubled for a leather chart folder soaked in sea brine and dried out. "Some of the words perhaps hint at the ingredients of an amphibious campaign. The word 'rising' is an example. During the planning for _Seelöwe_, we debated the landing's start-time. My planners argued we should put to shore on a rising tide, so as not to risk stranding our landing barges until the next cycle. My decision was to land as the ebb commenced. 'Narrow' could suggest the width of the attack, 'exit' perhaps a beach exit, an essential element in the site selection, 'ramp' the ramp of a landing craft, 'viscosity' the quality of the sediment. It is critical to know if the keels will slide on packed sand or stick in mud."

"I wondered if those might be the meanings."

"Why then is there no mention of tides, cross currents, sandbars, sea mines, defenses, obstacles, seaports, logistics, or preparatory bombardment? Why are there no place names, military units, nomenclatures of sea vessels, or names of commanding officers? The numbers are rounded to the tens, not very precise. They could be azimuths or distances in miles or kilometers. As shown here, they could represent anything."

"I believe the list is incomplete."

Raeder smiled wanly. "Incomplete. A gross understatement, wouldn't you agree?"

After a pause, Mauer said, "I would."

"Let me ask you, do you think the secret of the invasion might lurk in these words?"

"I was hoping you could tell me, sir."

"Let me show you something." The admiral stepped to the wall, where he flipped through a leaning selection of what Mauer guessed were pasteboard-mounted charts. He chose one, wiped off an accumulation of dust, and brought it to the desk, laying it face up. Mauer gazed at a colorful rendering of the English Channel and southern Britain opposite the shores of France, Belgium, and the Netherlands. A black-rimmed oval lassoed the coastal region of England from Dover to Portsmouth. Slender lines of scarlet tape, each annotated with numbers and classes of ships, fed into it from across the water. Within the oval, symbols resembling toy tops labeled the zones for parachute landings. "This was an early-stage planning map," said Raeder. "The components were amended many times thereafter. I bring it out because it sketches the broad concept. What are your impressions?"

"Complex, sir."

"Profoundly so. An amphibious invasion is the most intricate of all military endeavors. It involves the coordination of sea, land, and air elements in exacting sequences. Unlike land-based attacks, the setting changes based on the tides. The risks are immense. For the forces that make the landing, retreat is exceptionally difficult, if not impossible. May I be candid with you, Mauer? I mean, you won't parrot what I say to the Gestapo?"

"I will not, unless it bears directly on the meaning behind the words."

"In the spring of 1940, I told the Führer that if we were to invade England, we must prepare. He viewed the invasion as a last resort—he thought the British would sue for peace—and so he waited until the middle of July to order us to begin. I had hoped we would have until the following spring. He wanted us poised to go in *twelve weeks*. The timespan was beyond our capacity. We had minimal maritime resources, inadequate intelligence on British countermeasures, and no meaningful experience in amphibious landings.

"When I briefed these limitations to the Führer, he waved his hand as if they were inconsequential. Here I must give him his due. If we had succeeded in putting ashore a sizable and correctly supplied expedition, we might well have defeated the British. But indispensable to our success was air superiority. Without it, the channel would have become a death zone for our flotilla. The Luftwaffe's failure to destroy the Royal Air Force gave the Führer no choice but to relent. We never rekindled the pursuit." The statement prompted an expression of bitterness so transient it was gone almost before Mauer caught it.

"The Führer has named me Admiralinspektor of the Navy. The title is meaningless; I am in all practical ways retired. My former colleagues nonetheless keep me apprised of the military situation. The enemy calls their plan to invade the Continent OVERLORD. The name is a high secret, one of our spies obtained it, the name, not the plan, unfortunately. Still, certain hallmarks can be assumed. For Seelöwe, we amassed approximately two thousand barges to cross the channel in calm conditions. The Americans and the British have probably twice that number of landing vessels, many specially designed to assault a hostile coast. Compared to our dearth of experience, they have carried out amphibious landings in North Africa, Sicily, Italy, and the Pacific, giving them a wealth of lessons to draw upon. We had twelve weeks to prepare. The British have spent more than four years, and the Americans two, devising their attack. You may be sure they have examined every iota imaginable and that their scheme will count among the masterpieces of military planning, rivaling God's blueprint for the creation of the universe. Do you see what I am driving at? You bring me this list of isolated words and ask me to draw inferences, as if I might puzzle out the secret of the invasion. It is absurd."

Leveling a cold stare, Raeder handed back the papers.

"I apologize, sir."

"I have heard of you, Mauer. They say you are erudite, of sound instincts, an officer with potential. So I must point out, as perhaps you know, the Gestapo has done you no favors assigning you this farce. Jettison it as soon as you can. That is my advice."

– 24 –

Early February 1944

The night of the snowfall, she dreamed she was a child again, and she ran barefoot over the luscious grass of a meadow. It was summer at dusk, and the encircling trees, deep loam against the indigo sky, swished like giant dog tails. Her parents were there, and her friends, and the children chased each other in the rapturous serenity only children can feel. The meadow seemed familiar. Had it existed in reality? Perhaps only sleep could stir the memory. The vivid dream's tranquility stayed with her as she padded down to breakfast at the civilized hour of 6 a.m.

Avry said, "Training will be in English this morning."

"What's the occasion? A visit by the Prime Minister?"

He smiled wanly.

"What's the reason?"

"You'll see. Don't eat too much."

After breakfast, he led her to the gym mats. A woman arrived. She evinced an earthy aspect, her short hair mussed, her cotton sweats sheathing thickset legs and shoulders. A guard at a women's prison? In a Scottish accent even more pronounced than Avry's, she bayed, "I'm Ailith. You won't need my full name. Shoes off."

Linnea unlaced her boat shoes and kicked them aside.

"Hold your head still."

Ailith fitted a padded leather helmet snugly over Linnea's head and buckled the strap snugly under her chin. Next came a pair of leather boxing gloves. Thus weighted, her arms resembled long-stemmed mushrooms.

"Open up, then."

"Open up?"

"Your mouth."

Ailith pushed in a rubbery mouth guard that bulged Linnea's lips. Boxing training. What genius had thought this up? She glanced to Avry and Verrick on the sidelines, the latter wearing a quizzical expression.

Ailith donned boxing gloves. "Please step out on the mat."

Please? Well, she'd have to, wouldn't she?

"Hold up your arms to protect yourself. Higher. The key is to keep moving and stay on your feet. In a real fight, your best chance is to get away from your opponent as swiftly as possible. Most importantly, avoid falling down. Sidestep to your left, keep your balance. Arms up! Higher."

Linnea raised them, not high enough, and Ailith promptly punched her in the face. Her head snapped, and she fell down.

"Up, up! You'll need to be quicker than that. Stay on your feet. Did I not say it was important?"

You did, come to think. She tasted blood in her mouth.

"Another go."

This time Linnea jounced forward to strike, and the woman clobbered her with a right cross. Down she went.

"What was that, a roundhouse? Worst punch you can throw. Slip left. Mind your balance. Eyes up!"

Blood dripped from her nose. The herky-jerky movements were exhausting; already she was wheezing and frothing around the mouth guard. Nonetheless she was getting the idea, preserving her distance and fending off the jabs.

"A fight saps the strength out of you faster than a rip flattens a bike tire. The longer the bout, the worse it gets. Soon you'll barely have the strength to lift your arms. That's why you've got to stay on your feet. Fall down and it drains you all the more to get back up."

Warily she shuffled leftward, staying out of reach. In the second round, she took a couple of glancing hits but managed to bound away. Ailith didn't land any blows in the third, and she called a halt, resting a glove on Linnea's shoulder. "You did well for your first try. The purpose was to familiarize you with what it's like to get hit. Men know the sensation, most women don't. Hit a woman, she falls down and becomes all the more vulnerable. Remember, stay on your feet and KEEP MOVING! If you're cowped, don't lay there, get up *fast*! Let's take your gloves off. You can pull your mouthpiece out."

With her sweaty, leather-smelling fingers, Linnea extracted the rubbery, slobber-and-blood-streaked chunk through her misshapen lips. Her jaw ached.

"If you're trapped and can't get away, you're not going to hit a man hard enough with your bare hands to incapacitate him, you'll just break your bones trying. Best to strike him with a heavy object when he's not looking. Lamps are good. If you hit him, he'll be stunned momentarily. That's when to clobber him again! What do you see here that can hurt someone?"

She gazed around. No lamps handy. She shrugged.

"Use what you've got. There's an ashtray on the table. Bash the hard edge against your opponent's eye. Isn't that a teacup beside it? Use it." Ailith picked up the cup's saucer and jabbed it edgewise into Linnea's midsection. *Oof.* The blow made the case better than words.

"Keep in mind, your first goal always is to get away. Don't hesitate; you mightn't have to run far, but you must be quick!"

Avry sent her to her room to wash up and change out of the blood-speckled sweats. She splashed water on her face, staining the towel red. In the mirror, she examined her fat lip and the swollen skin below her right eye.

The punches had knocked the dream of the childhood meadow straight out of her head.

The next morning and for the remainder of her mornings at the Lodge, she descended the stairs bracing for "the training will be in English," and another pummeling. It didn't happen. Ailith must have gone back to whatever dungeon she'd come from. Linnea had to concede that the unpleasant ordeal had imprinted a cognizance she could be hurt, spring-loading her to run away. On the wooded path with Bags, she jogged faster. *Don't hesitate; you mightn't have to run far, but you must be quick!* At the drop bar, she lowered herself, visualizing doing so from a cliff. Her fingers accrued layers of hospital tape. The exertions fueled a mental alacrity. To her lips sprang her languages. The scripts grew so familiar she didn't have to look at the pages anymore.

Portraying GALILEO, Avry invented variations he threw at her. In one, he became confrontational: "Who are you, and why the hell are you in my room?" In another, he shied back. "I think you've got the wrong room, miss."

Pragmatic: "Do you realize how dangerous it is, your being here?" Pensive: Initially he said nothing, then pleaded with her to leave him alone. Defiant: Glaring at her with an expression between reproach and fury, he told her to get out. In each iteration, she voiced her lines and handed him the letter—"From Sophia, Comrade. You must read it!"—that he thereupon pretended to read with mock consternation, incredulity, trepidation.

"When do I learn what's in the letter?" she said.

"In Stockholm. The infiltration phase is ticklish. Best not to fill your head with details too soon."

A messenger delivered her authentic Swedish clothes, used but in good condition. She tried them on and was surprised at their correct fit and stylish flair, counting a richly knit white sweater, a gray silk dress, two blouses, two skirts, socks, underclothes, and silk stockings, the latter showing mending stitches. For footwear came practical shoes, dress shoes, snow boots, and a pair of galoshes, and for outerwear heavy corduroy trousers and a loden wool coat with a fur-lined hood. A strapped leather handbag graced her shoulder and a Suveran man's watch her wrist; apparently Swedish women commonly wore the model. All had been purchased in Stockholm, flown to London in the diplomatic bag, and the garments tailored to her size by a seamstress who used Swedish-style stitches and Stockholm-bought thread.

In her memory, her evening sessions with Verrick blurred together. Always she related to him what she'd learned that day, for instance the sequences if she were to be captured: First, she'd say she was Hamfrid Matisson, the hotel employee. When that cover collapsed, as surely it would if put under a spotlight, she'd fall back to Thorgun Lindstrom, a petty thief whose intentions to pilfer valuables theoretically would prompt her captors to toss her out. Only under unbearable pressure was she to admit she was Vena Nadovska of the NKVD. Stalling would buy time for the British to recover her from the Swedish Nazis, or from the Germans.

"Did Avry say how they'll recover you?"

"They'll fall on the mercy of the Swedish internal security service, the Allmänna Säkerhetstjänsten."

His expression darkened. "Let's hope it doesn't get to that."

"I don't like it either. What if the Swedes ask, who *is* this person you want us to rescue, who uses a Swedish name?" She almost told him about her long-lived distress at the debts her father had accumulated and the falsehoods he'd perpetrated. Though Verrick seemed to sense something was on her mind, he didn't prod.

Sometimes the training was so repetitive she had nothing new to report. They conversed anyway. She relaxed in his company, lapsing into her Manhattan argot or just listening as he regaled her with funny or cautionary tales of his life as a New York lawyer. He'd handled the cases of millionaires, the heads of big companies, famous actors. He described the spacious, Hudson-view apartment where he and his family lived on Riverside Drive. To Linnea, veteran of a lower-east-side tenement, the place sounded so grand it might be a movie set. "Don't be impressed," he said. "We keep it to entertain, otherwise it's just where we hang our hats. Grace is completely down to earth, and I'm a New Hampshire backwoodsman at heart."

Uh-huh.

He and Grace had met in Ithaca, New York, when he was a law student at Cornell, and her practical nature counterpoised his propensity to go about with his head in the clouds, or so he said. Their first encounter was on a frigid winter morning as he slogged the snowy route between his boarding house and the law campus. "She'd noticed me along the stretch—it was over two miles—as I lugged my heavy book bag to classes. She took pity."

"Love at first sight?"

"Well, she was eye catching, then as now. I must say my initial love was for her car. My feet were frozen near solid that day."

Linnea laughed.

He hoped soon to see his son, who was with the 101st Airborne Division somewhere in England. At the mention, his smile flared, reminding her of her father's visage when he'd sung Swedish folk songs.

She said, "When this is over, you'll go back to the States?"

"I expect so. I'll go wherever they send me."

Who were *they*, specifically? She didn't ask. Some bigwigs, what did she care?

He related his childhood, his father's stewing silences staring at a bottle, their poverty, his helper's job at the old folk's home. His openness spurred her to reveal her animus toward *her* father, a man of falsehoods and bad decisions. He had not wanted to die. It didn't excuse him for risking his family and ruining their lives. Verrick disported a wordless empathy. Should she ask him what he thought? Like Christopher, would he scold her for the futility of nursing anger toward a dead person? Or would he agree that her father had done the unforgivable?

She didn't ask. Instead, she shifted to her mother. From bygone Petrograd, she'd embodied a city of charm, culture, and intellect, only to emigrate to America and become the Cossack of Clean. She wrote to her daughter in Russian, the sole tongue in which she genuinely could express herself. Lest the censors balk, Linnea wrote back in English. For some reason, it bothered her immensely that she wouldn't be able to write to her mother from Sweden. But wasn't it silly, her angst, when she'd be there so short a time?

He nodded his agreement.

In bed after their meetings, she mused over what she'd confided to him. Always it struck her that to unveil so much about her life was out of character and that her basis to trust him was by no means firm.

So why did she?

Unusual indeed.

"The military says no war plan survives the first shot," said Avry. "In espionage, your plan might not survive the first word. You must be ready for the unexpected." In this second week of training, his critiques had grown fewer. His commentaries still inclined toward the pedantic.

She was gussied up in her smart Swedish clothes portraying Vena Nadovska and again going through the always-varied shtick with Avery as GALILEO. When the iteration ended, she said, "Vena's too harsh."

He blinked. "Harsh? She's NKVD."

"I mean, 'Listen to me, comrade,' and the rest of this rant. For years, GALILEO risked his life for the Soviets, and what do they do when they show up? Harangue him and shove a letter in his face. If I were him, I'd be aghast."

"You don't think London has thought it through?"

"Maybe they thought it through wrong."

"Ah. What would you propose?"

"Didn't you say agent controllers have to show empathy?"

"Within boundaries."

"Let me try something."

"Be my guest."

At first she stumbled. Three tries and she firmed up the character she had in mind, a version of Vena who was respectful and engaging, her tone mellifluous. Avry let her innovate, accepting the letter she extended. "Yes, comrade," he said without sarcasm. "I will do my duty."

She said, "What do you think?"

"Quite charming. I'll ask London."

She ate dinner, took a bath in the tub at hall's end where the water was hot, and changed into her next-day's sweats. Mr. Verrick, somehow able to intuit when she was finished with the end-of-day rudiments, stopped by to hear her latest update. He'd hurt his left thumb; the nail was an eggplant color. As with Avry's misshapen nails, she didn't ask.

She told him of her idea to revise Vena Nadovska's spiel.

"How did Avry react?"

"He was patient while I acted it out. He's asking London."

"What inspired you to suggest the change?"

What *was* the reason? A disdain for artifice? Empathy for GALILEO? She didn't feel any. Perhaps she didn't like to be stage-managed. When she and her mother had reached Manhattan after the sea journey and immigration processing, her mother pulled her by the hand as they inquired street to street for a place to stay. Linnea jerked away. 'I can walk on my own!' The outburst drew stares from the other pedestrians. Never again had she allowed her mother to take her hand.

"The character they've scripted is too theatrical. I mean *bad* theatrics. Her lines are bombastic."

"It seems to me, if you don't find your performance credible, how can you expect GALILEO to?"

Did he mean it, or was he just telling her what she wanted to hear?

The next day, Avry brought her the verdict: "London says to stick to the scripts."

"Why doesn't that surprise me?"

"Kindly lend an ear. Your idea had merit. London gave it proper deliberation. But we have just the one try at GALILEO. Better to insult him than to let him doubt who you are. The harshness, as you call it, blunts his anxiety. Politeness sets his wheels spinning too fast."

Her expression must have told him she wasn't buying it.

"Reflect on this," he went on. "If we *were* the NKVD sizing up our man for the first contact in two and a half years, we'd want to put in front of him someone he's met previously, straightaway to get past any doubts about our bona fides. That's the ideal. But what if such a player's not at hand, or the situation in Stockholm makes it impossible to slip our first choice into GALILEO's presence? We'd have to use an alternative. Were Vena real, she'd face the same challenge as you do, to persuade GALILEO in short order she's who she says she is. You see, it's not nearly as big a Vaudeville show as you think."

Right.

The roleplay was too preposterous, her image of the trenchant Soviet too superficial. That evening she told Verrick, "How can I stand there and *yammer* at GALILEO? You said it yourself. If I don't find myself credible, how will he?"

"I really thought London would accept your reasoning."

"They say a gentler version of Vena will make him think too much. Which is nonsense. He'll think, who's this vitriolic bitch who shows up in my room, rails at me, and rudely shoves a letter in my face? He'll be furious."

"You may antagonize him, I agree. On the other hand, do you want to invite a dialog that could unravel the false flag? Maybe it's what London wants to avoid."

There must be a version of Vena who would neither infuriate GALILEO nor stimulate a prolonged conversation and risk shredding her credibility. In bed that night, she invented Vena's history, starting with her childhood on a peasant farm southeast of Petrograd. The one-room hovel where she and her family lived had no plumbing. Her fingernails were gritted from the soil in which she thrust her hands to claw up turnips. If she harvested none, her brothers and sisters went hungry. Every time she glimpsed the hated landlord riding by, she cursed the man's soul, hissing *"mudak"* under her breath. She cursed her father too. Either he was breaking his back tilling their bleak patch to pay the landlord, or he was drinking cheap Vodka, the alcohol-tinged sweat seeping from his pores. A few drinks summoned the wrath he vented at his family. The sound of weeping women enraged him more. She learned not to cry. Warily she watched him until he passed out, then she crept over to steal sips of the throat-warming Vodka from his bottle. Life's harshness tried to stunt her intellect and impose the mental set of deprivation, her fate had she continued to plod down the peasant's path.

By a stroke of fortune, her mother was able to enroll her at the village school at age 11. Years behind the other students, she couldn't read. The other kids laughed at her mistakes. She flew at them, shrilling her father's raw temper. Every day she forced herself to thrash away the shame, plying a willpower made sinewy from gouging in the soil for edibles.

Year by year, episode by episode, Vena's life coalesced. In the chaos of the post-revolution, she gained a job as a bookkeeper in the government bureaucracy. She was hawk eyed, impossible to trick, her favorite targets the *mudaks* who tried to cloak their wealth from the revolutionary tax authorities. Her qualities came to the attention of an official who arranged her introduction to the Chekists, and through the sinister gates of the NKVD she passed. The imaginings helped untangle how Vena came to be as she was. Some pieces stayed knotted. For instance, could a peasant girl have risen so far in the NKVD that the apparatchiks would trust their prized German agent to her hands? Few women became full-fledged agent controllers.

The shortcomings might be why Linnea didn't share her paradigm with Avry or Verrick.

– 25 –

Mid-January 1944

The time had come to throw the cursed interrogation report back where it had come from. Mauer had done all he reasonably could with it. More: He'd reaped Admiral Raeder's scorn, playing the Gestapo's pathetic jester in front of the celebrated officer, a profound humiliation.

What would Albert Speer do under the circumstances? A pointless musing. Speer was a visionary, technocrat, designer, methodologist. A military strategist he was not. How would Speer be able to make any more sense of the jumble than Mauer could?

"Kommodore?"

He looked up. Gerta was standing in the doorway.

"What?" he said.

"I thought you had called for me."

"No."

She retreated.

My God, had he been talking to himself?

He picked up the phone and dialed the Gestapo headquarters, his mind whirring in the clickety-clack-ridden wait.

Stabl said, "Yes, Mauer."

"I would like to show the words and numbers to one more person."

"Admiral Canaris, you mean. Out of the question."

"Not Canaris. Albert Speer, under the same stipulations that applied to Admiral Raeder."

Stabl laughed, regained his composure, and burst out again. "Really, you are a hoot. You must explain."

"I want to ask Speer how he would go about solving the problem. He may suggest a way I haven't thought of."

"Why him?"

"He's an architect. He thinks in multiple dimensions."

The line went silent for a minute. Mauer pictured his interlocutor rolling his eyes.

Stabl said, "I'll call you back."

To Mauer's great surprise, the Gestapo assented.

He phoned the Ministry of Armaments and War Production and asked for an immediate appointment with Minister Speer, explaining to the secretary that he was the naval officer who had spoken with the minister several months ago about torpedo reliability. Two hours passed. He was about to make a second call and name-drop the Gestapo when the secretary rang back. The minister would see him at four this afternoon.

To prepare, he assembled another list of responses from the interrogation report—out of frustration, he'd crumpled the first—and rehearsed how he would present the problem. Then he removed his tunic and painstakingly picked off the lint.

He might have saved himself the trouble. The two hours he spent in a holding room with a dozen others, each let in to see the Reichsminister before he was, harvested so much lint he might have worn his uniform to bed. The pace of the shuffling in and out testified to the daunting burden Speer faced, to sustain Germany's wherewithal to fight the war while her enemies pulverized her industrial infrastructure. Adding to the havoc, less than two months ago, an RAF raid had destroyed the ministry's headquarters, requiring a relocation to new offices.

It was almost 6 p.m. when the secretary said, "Kommodore Mauer? You may go in. Please make it quick, the minister must leave shortly."

Speer offered his hand. Thirty-eight years old, his umber hair receding, he was tall and striking. By some miracle, his ascension to one of the Reich's highest offices had not corrupted him. His work had taken a toll nonetheless; his skin was pallid, the eyes bloodshot. "You know, Mauer, I enjoyed our prior conversation immensely. Your comments on torpedo performance spurred me to rethink our quality-assurance process. Changes resulted. I must thank you."

"Not necessary, minister."

"You presented your ideas thoughtfully and without the time-wasting prattle I hear from so many others. Clearly you have a technologist's mind, which is why I agreed to see you on short notice. Unfortunately, the day has run away from me. Can you hurriedly summarize the reason for your visit?"

Mauer did, introducing the topic as he had with Admiral Raeder, explaining that the listed words seemed to point vaguely to the forthcoming invasion of the Continent. He held out the lists. "I know this isn't the kind of subject matter you normally examine."

Speer scanned the pages, frowning slightly, flipping from one to the next. He looked up. "What am I to make of it, that you would bring me such a thing?"

"I meant no offense. I hoped you could suggest a method I haven't already used."

"This was your idea, and yours alone?"

"I assure you."

"With anyone else, Mauer, I would be suspicious. You wouldn't believe the intrigues afoot these days. These words are important?"

"I believe so."

"Hmm. You are correct that intelligence analysis isn't my field. On the other hand, as you are no doubt aware, industrial analysis can be every bit as daunting. I see you've tabulated the repetitions. Have you done a second-order derivation, pairing the close synonyms of these terms with one another?" Like Mauer, Speer had been a math whiz in his youth.

"Repeatedly."

"May I keep this copy?"

"As long as you show it to no one and destroy it when you're finished. I'm afraid those are the restrictions I'm under."

"All right. If I come up with anything, I'll call. Make sure my secretary has your phone number. I must go." Speer stood up slowly, wincing, pressing his hands to the desktop. "Damned knee. I hurt it recently, and it doesn't seem to be getting any better."

Having witnessed the hectic goings-on at the ministry, Mauer didn't dare hope that Speer would revisit the lists or call him back. Nonetheless, the next morning, Gerta tapped at the doorframe of his office with an unusual urgency. "Kommodore, the Minister of Armaments and War Production is on the phone!" A publicity campaign to reduce the waste of materials had posted Speer's photo everywhere, on billboards and in the press, making him one of the most recognizable figures in Germany, a celebrity.

He snatched up the receiver. "Mauer here."

"Listen, sorry to have been in a rush yesterday. You know, I ended up giving more attention than I intended to this project of yours. Maddening, how these words and numbers go round in your mind, once you put them there."

"You are right about that."

"I thought at first I might try the equivalent of a strength analysis. If you know the load-bearing requirements for each of the pillars in a structure, you can configure your design along certain symmetries. So I played with the idea. Then it struck me that you have almost as many unknowns as knowns, 58 of these so-called indecipherables. Is there a means by which you might deduce what they refer to?"

"I'm afraid not."

"The indecipherables could be anything, don't you agree? What they represent must change the count of extant repetitions and add new words. Unless they are revealed, they render it impossible to affix values to the strengths. No method can bridge a gap so wide in the data. I know this isn't the breakthrough you were seeking. Perhaps you will find it useful nonetheless."

"I think your conclusion may be decisive. I am grateful."

"I'll destroy the list as you asked. Take care, Mauer."

The line clicked.

Early February 1944

Half in shadow, Verrick relaxed at the dining room table, his drink of Scotch in front. The galley light threw triangular shadows off the ceiling beams, sketching out what mimicked a black and gray Backgammon board overhead.

Avry came in. "Mind if I join you?"

"Please do."

As before, the Scot fetched the bottle.

Verrick said, "You must be nearing the finish."

"Another day or so. London's making the flight arrangements."

"Has London given you a say in the planning?"

Avry poured whisky into his glass, seeming to ponder how to answer. "Not enough. A field man always wants to call the shots, doesn't he?"

"What about for this proposal of Linnea's, as to her role-play of the Soviet, Vena Nadovska?"

"I'm the classic middleman, able to see both sides. I know it upset her, London's decision. She seems to have kenned it out, though. When the time comes, she'll be the only one in the room with GALILEO, to play it as she sees fit."

"I suppose that's true."

"While all this was shaping out, I half thought you might intervene on her behalf. That you didn't bespeaks a sage professional reserve. It hasn't gone unnoticed." Avry lifted his glass.

"I do have a question."

The Scot laughed. "I spoke too soon, perhaps?"

"No, something else. A perceived contradiction. Why have you given so much emphasis to training her as an agent controller, when you've scripted everything she's going to say? She's there to deliver a written message. Wouldn't it be simpler to avoid all the complications and just slip a letter under GALILEO's door?"

"You're a barrister, Mr. Verrick. To you, I suspect, a piece of paper can be a grand and mighty thing. To an agent risking his life, it's got a flimsy aspect. A human face makes all the difference. GALILEO expects an NKVD emissary to pitch up at his doorstep sooner or later. To give a man what he awaits is a potent step toward convincing him. It doesn't mean he won't treat Linnea to a withering circumspection. The more we imbue her with the agent-controller's persona, the better chance she's got of withstanding his scrutiny, and thus of swaying him."

"Well, maybe I do put too much weight on the written word."

"Have I resolved your contradiction?"

Verrick's turn to lift his glass. "You couldn't have done better had you been my own witness on the stand."

"Well, sir, I'm pleased to hear it, even if you phrase it in such an unnerving way as that."

The final morning, she exercised at the usual hour. Skeins of fog like white worms curled around the beam of Avry's flashlight. She didn't need the illumination; by now she knew the path by heart. Over puddles and fallen branches she leapt, and at the bar she performed ten perfect lower-downs. Still panting from the exertions, she fed Bags. The roar of planes from the airbase drowned out the patter as she washed the mud off her shoes.

Training lasted till noon. Avry for the umpteenth time went over the map of Stockholm and the Delfin Hotel's floor plans, rousing her impatience. She thought she detected in him the same sentiment, that the recapitulation amounted to busywork. He ran through it nonetheless, quizzing her on locations, exits, times. "You're in the lobby facing the elevator. Which way's the security office?"

"To my left rear and down the little hallway."

"How many paces?"

"About twenty."

"You're on the fourth floor leaving GALILEO's room. Get to the nearest exit other than the main. Don't use the elevator."

"Down the stairs to the ground floor, right and along the corridor, left past the laundry room to the fire exit on the side."

"You're at the back door. Paces and times to the respective street corners, at a flat run."

"To the right, thirty, about six seconds. Left is more like forty, and nine seconds."

"You're outside at the mouth of the alley to the right of the hotel facing the plaza. How far across to the far side at a crisp walk?"

"Seventy paces, thirty-five seconds."

"Good. Off to pack your things."

Elegant, her Swedish ensemble. The exception was the straw-and-ammonia-acrid, rope-and-toggle-battened canvas valise that apparently had spent its life tumbling in baggage cars. As neatly as she could, she folded and packed in her clothes. She bundled up the Swedish newspapers and hefted them as Avry had instructed to a lock-cabinet in Classroom 2. On the way back, she broke the rules and said her goodbyes in English to Mrs. Edda and Mrs. Tatum. Accustomed to the comings and goings of Secret Service trainees, neither asked where she was headed. Mrs. Tatum gave her a jam-filled scone that Linnea balanced on her palm to eat. Upstairs, she took a bath. Steamy bathwater might be in short supply in Sweden.

She was in her travel outfit when Mr. Verrick stopped by. He took the chair while she stuffed into the valise the clothes fresh from Mrs. Edda's laundry basket. Oddly proud her hands were free of the hospital tape that had decorated them for almost two weeks, she wanted to hold them up to show him.

He asked her the launch point.

"Somewhere in Scotland. We leave early this afternoon and fly north. The hope is to get ahead of a storm that's forecast. It will be my first time in a plane."

"Try to get a seat with a window," he said. "I've always been fascinated at the sight of the landscape from above."

She updated him on her training, citing Avry's repeated emphasis on her agent-handling skills, the importance of listening and empathy, and how agents were like brat children to whom discipline was anathema.

"I guess that's one way to look at agents," he said.

"I never thought it would be so complicated. Like being a new parent, I suppose."

"Do you feel prepared?"

"I'm surprised to say that I do."

"A credit to you and to your virtuosity with languages."

"I must not have told you about my first few German lessons. I was awful. It came back, though. Probably no need to speak German anyway, only in the event GALILEO has lost some of his Russian."

"The NKVD handled him in Russian?"

"Yes." Another tidbit Avry had shared without elaborating how he knew.

"And running him afterward?"

"The letter from Sophia will say. I won't see the contents until we get to Sweden. Avry says I shouldn't fill my head with too many details in advance of the infiltration."

Verrick said nothing for a minute. She guessed he didn't accept the explanation any more than she did.

"Did he let on when you might return?"

"Depends on how things go. If there are no flaps, in ten days or so."

She gave him the letters she'd received from her mother and one ready to post. "Mail this and hang onto the old ones for me?"

"Of course." In the doorway, he added, "You'll keep your wits about you?"

She nodded. "Will I see you when I get back?"

"Count on it."

You'll keep your wits about you? A fatuous thing to have said.

In his room, he packed his suitcase, lightly layering the shirts and trousers to keep them from wrinkling. *I'll try to ferret out what's at the heart of these proceedings. Isn't it preferable, if you can, to make a more informed decision?* He'd been tempted to apologize to her, because he hadn't ferreted out a damn thing except that the Brits seemed to be up to something they hadn't disclosed to the Americans. To mention it would be unwise. The revelation might kick the legs from under her newfound confidence.

Between the open drapes of his room, the sun cast on the floor a shape like a miniature of the Lodge, the roof a simple triangle. The passing minutes narrowed the transcendent image to a trapezoid. Soon it would collapse to a single line, the sides indistinguishable. His own sides were more distinct, at least to him: On the one, he was a paragon of truth and integrity, on the other, a slick manipulator. All rolled into one.

He carried his suitcase to the foyer, where Lenny was waiting to drive him to London. His last act at the Lodge was to say goodbye to Avry and wish him luck. The Scot was on the phone, apparently on hold. Verrick slipped in, "Do you think she's ready?"

"Aye, she is." He switched the hand holding the receiver and shook Verrick's. The call resumed. "Excuse me, please."

Lenny veered onto Oxford Street at 3 p.m., dropping Verrick, as he had last time, half a kilometer from 70 Grosvenor. Mist rose from the pavements a brief rain had doused. The February afternoon was warmer than usual, the streets crowded. No one seemed worried that the Luftwaffe would stage an air raid. His trepidation had a different source. Had the Brits devised their plan as perfectly as they could? In war, people waded into peril, sometimes to their deaths. A leader had to come to terms. If Donovan hadn't assigned him this mission, Linnea would be nothing to him but a name on a dossier. As it was, they'd fused a bond, a kind of transference. To trust people was not easy for her. She'd come to trust him, intuiting—knowing—he genuinely cared. Not only that, she knew he could read her. Despite her deep misgivings about the mission, she'd stayed with it because of *him*.

She was talented. She was prepared. Over and over, he told it to himself.

Through the puddles he strode, a man carrying a suitcase, a common sight. What was uncommon was the sky of pale pastel colors that dabbed the streets, buildings, pedestrians. Linnea had alluded to a storm; perhaps the weird illumination was a preamble. Would the city ever again look so unworldly as it did this minute?

Like the other questions that assailed him, it was unanswerable.

He had phoned ahead to alert OSS London to his return. Across the foyer desk, the duty officer passed him a folded note that read, 'I'll stop by your room at 8 p.m.—Bill,' and the key to the same VIP guest room where he'd overnighted two weeks ago. He walked there and deposited his suitcase. He might have hung around the guest house until his meeting with Casey at eight, but still a little stir-crazy from his stay at the Lodge, he decided to venture out to a restaurant. He headed eastward toward Regent Street. At the first eatery he came to, people queued half a block. Nothing flattered the quality of an establishment more than the length of the wait to get in, but to stand in line just to eat alone struck him as lamentable. He kept walking. The fuel rationing had thinned the number of motorcars, and like the other pedestrians he was content to wander down the center of sidestreets. For over an hour he strode, passing posted menus whose meat selections were spam and rabbit and a vegetable dish called Woolton Pie. In the end he bought a bag of salted chips and ate them in King's Square on a bench facing the sandbagged statue of King Charles II. Here was a king known for his jolly vacuity, his great accomplishment to restore the English monarchy and so-called normality, which, if Verrick remembered his history, the preceding Cromwell era had plunged into such dire supply that the people were happy to reinstate kings and queens.

Pigeons warbled up in hopes of crumbs. He finished the chips. Too bad, pigeons.

He might have stayed a while longer, but it was getting cold. He creaked to his feet and plodded back to Grosvenor Street.

Casey said, "I made a few calls about getting your son to London on furlough. I expect an answer back soon."

"Thanks."

"What happened to your thumb?"

"Smashed it in a drawer."

"Should I get a doctor to look at it?"

"Not worth the trouble."

The younger man pressed on his hat. "Let's go for a walk."

On weary legs, Verrick accompanied Casey westward toward Hyde Park. The blackout had extinguished the pole lamps, and their shadowy posts seemed to pantomime the pillars in a coal-mine whose miners maundered through the dust.

"Anything new on the Soviet source?" said Casey.

"Only that GALILEO was handled in Russian. The Brits knowing that is a further indication they have access to a Soviet file."

"What's in the letter Linnea is to give him?"

"Avry told her she shouldn't know the contents before they get to Sweden, in the event she's captured during infiltration."

"Or is it to keep *us* from knowing?"

"Your guess is as good as mine."

They turned left at the snaking pond called the Serpentine. To tread the shore in the blackout seemed perilous; he couldn't make out where he was putting his feet. Blind-stepping as if atop a cliff, he divined that as long as he didn't look straight at the water, he could perceive the vague shimmer at the edge. To stay safe was to stare at the dark.

Casey said, "Donovan wants you to stay in London through the duration of the GALILEO mission, and maybe beyond, to probe for insights on MI-6's Soviet source."

"I thought he might." No point commenting on the nonexistent chance that he might gain further insights. When a notion seized Donovan, as this one had, a prodigious effort was generally required to see it through to the end.

They curled around to Park Lane. A taxi, its blackout lights like the slit eyes of a cat, purred past. "Take your time about coming in tomorrow morning," said Casey. "Ten o'clock, say? I'll try to find you a place to hang your hat by then. No need for a secretary, I wouldn't think."

"No need at all," Verrick muttered.

– 27 –

Mid-January 1944

Mauer rose from bed. Gently he pulled the quilt over his sleeping wife. In the parlor, he commenced to pace.

Where did it hide, the secret of the interrogation report? What had he overlooked?

He had tabulated the Britisher's responses. How about the *questions?* What was the most common? Even without the document in front of him, he had the answer at once: 'What is the significance of this word?' The next commonest: 'What is the significance of this number?' Each time the subject had burbled out a word or number, his inquisitor spewed one of the two questions, as if the naval officer, drugged and in immense pain, would have been able to expound.

Mauer halted in his tracks.

What if the Britisher *had* answered?

Perhaps his replies had been out of direct sequence with the questions. By then, the poor devil had lost all sense of order.

What had he said?

Smokestack.

Four times the Britisher had uttered the word.

Suddenly an image jumped into Mauer's head. He stopped in his tracks, mesmerized.

Could it be so simple?

He took a deep breath. He was quivering, not from cold, from the sheer ardor of his thoughts.

Perhaps he should speak to someone before he drafted the concept. Not long ago, he would not have hesitated to bring his idea to Admiral Canaris, who backed his subordinates even when their views ran afoul of the Nazi hierarchy. In 1941, Canaris had assigned him to a commission investigating the British Navy's puzzling sinking of an entire group of German resupply ships in the Atlantic Ocean north of the Azores. The ships' separation by many miles should have safeguarded at least some of them. The commission members studied the evidence and concluded that simple bad luck had prevailed. They acknowledged the slim possibility that a British spy had infiltrated the Kriegsmarine and divulged the vessels' coordinates. Mauer was the sole participant to speculate that the British had cracked the wireless communications. Impossible, the others declaimed. The Enigma device, completely infallible, had encrypted the messages reporting the ships' locations. When he argued they should raise the possibility in their report, they scoffed. One member even insinuated Mauer must be trying to protect the presumed spy.

Canaris shielded him. "Listen, Mauer," the admiral counseled, head tilted, bushy brows squeezed together, blue eyes weary. "You cannot go about proclaiming that the Enigma codes can be broken. Look at the mathematics. Take one million and cube it, and the result still won't equal the permutations Enigma creates for just one line of a message."

"The mathematics are strong, clearly, sir. What I'm saying is, the device may be used in a way that makes it vulnerable."

Over the past year, Canaris's gray-white hair had turned mostly white, no doubt from the stresses that ceaselessly embroiled him: the tussles with Hitler and the General Staff who demanded the impossible, with commanders who complained that the Abwehr's intelligence was neither as accurate nor as timely as it should be, and with subordinates who insisted on hypothecating the most farfetched notions. "Write your thoughts in a memorandum. I'll pass it discreetly to Admiral Dönitz. He is open-minded. In the meantime, for God's sake, discontinue your conjectures with the commission."

"Yes, admiral."

Where was Canaris now? Reportedly traveling, as he frequently did. The time was surely coming when Himmler would take over the Abwehr and install his own adjuncts, and no one would protect officers who spoke the truth. Himmler respected only what suited his purposes.

Fucking chicken farmer.

From the map department, Mauer acquired the nautical charts he needed. Now the .85-by-1.2-meter papers lay all about. He leaned over his desk, adjusting his protractor, measuring distances, and tracing lines on semi-transparent paper overlays. The Gestapo report, a grotesquery of markers resembling an uprooted shrubbery, hulked to the side. No longer did he consult the contents. He knew them word for word.

"Coffee, Kommodore?" From the doorway, Gerta's eyes roved over the strewn charts. A day ago, he had been tempted to show her the Gestapo report, his mischievous, perhaps cruel impulse to witness her bafflement. Now that he grasped what it signified, out of the question.

"Yes, please. First bring me the typewriter."

"The typewriter, Kommodore?"

"Yes."

He planned to deliver his conclusions to Stabl in person. Better to face the bastard than to send them by courier and wait for a reaction certain to be skeptical. Mauer's judgments ran against the prevailing wisdom. No doubt Müller and Stabl would feel compelled to try to pick them apart; the Gestapo were nothing if not creatures who preyed on the weakness of others. And his supposition *was* weak, he had to admit, built on extrapolations founded on assumptions. Wisps of guesswork. Boiled piss.

Why should he open himself to criticism? Why not say he had discerned no meaning from the report?

Because to do so would be an abnegation of his duty, he told himself, and contrary to his principles. He was not the Führer's favorite architect, no, but he could uphold Albert Speer's example for professional rectitude.

Gerta lugged in the bulky typewriter weighing ten kilos. He had no worries she could cope; commonly she shifted the machine from place to place when she dusted the outer office, her daily chore to wipe up the seeped residue from the bombings and fires. No sooner had he said "Thank you" than he required her help to change the damned ribbon. When she leaned over to thread the reel, he stole a glimpse for the Nazi pin. Still absent. Perhaps she'd lost it.

"No visitors or calls," he said.

He commenced slowly, not solely because his manner of typing was to peck at the keys. He must express himself with faultless clarity. After an hour, his back aching, he pushed to his feet and rolled his shoulders, only to arch again over the typewriter. Immersed in the black type, he lost his mindfulness of the discomfort, the cloudy day beyond the window, the throaty growl of trucks, and the phone Gerta never let ring more than once. Daylight faded.

He prepared the title page last. When he pulled it from the typewriter and added it to the seven other pages, they consummated the most speculative and most crucial document he'd ever written. He appended the endnotes with cross-references to the report and clipped on his pen-and-ink overlays and a folded chart. The product made a stack whose physical depth seemed to lend substance to an ephemeral hypothesis. His eyes stung. What was the time? Seven p.m. He should dismiss Gerta.

In a normal speaking tone, knowing she would hear him, he said, "You may reclaim your machine."

"Yes, Kommodore." She came in, lifted the typewriter, and lugged it out. Why hadn't he brought it to her? Was it protocol that ruled him, or arrogance?

Unbidden, she returned to pose at the front of his desk. He looked up, puzzled.

"Kommodore, if I might ask… I know you are busy with something very important. I hate to bother you…" Her voice broke.

More than three years they had worked together. Had her voice ever shattered so? No, he'd have remembered. "To ask what, Gerta?"

"My brother was killed in Italy. They sent his body home. Tomorrow is the funeral."

The news shocked him. He'd never had a brother. To lose one must be terrible. "I'm very sorry. You should have told me sooner."

"Yes, Kommodore." Tears streaked her face. Had she shed the black-widow pin because she'd lost faith in the Nazis? Their misbegotten cause had cost Germany millions of lives, and now it had taken her brother. For the first time in their association, he stepped around to hug her, just as the phone rang. Perhaps Jana was calling. He lifted the receiver.

"Dare I ask if you've made progress, Mauer?" Stabl's voice sounded even more pinched than usual.

"Yes. I am prepared to deliver my conclusions."

"Which are?"

"Significant, I think."

"You should have notified me."

"I finished my report this very minute."

The line went silent. The reply must have stupefied the Gestapo man. Or perhaps he was conferring with Müller.

Stabl said, "A car will be outside your building in ten minutes."

Gerta had heard the exchange. "Will you be coming back tonight, Kommodore?"

To his surprise, he laughed. She stared at him.

"I'm sorry," he said. "What I mean is... never mind. When I leave, please lock up, go home, and take as many days as you need with your family."

"Thank you, Kommodore. You are very kind."

No, he wasn't. He might have done more to know her, his meticulous secretary. He had acted distantly toward her, mocked her to his wife. When he'd bothered even to glance at Gerta, he'd barely looked past the Nazi pin.

He slotted the assembled documents into his briefcase and headed to the street. The car was late, and he waited under the falling snow that whitened his shoulders. No bombs tonight. The precipitation hazed the Reich Chancery building across Vossstrasse, depicting it like the vague backdrop in a pointillist painting wherein your mind supplies the details. Out of morbid amusement, he tried to project Stabl's face onto the canvas. To what profession had the Gestapo man belonged before he'd risen to SS Standartenführer? Mauer pictured a butterfly catcher flailing his net, his eyes straining for the flutter of colorful wings. Or had he been a shopkeeper or baker like Jana's father, his mug streaked with flour? Evil men did not necessarily look evil.

The dots shaped Mauer too, as an innocent boy, as fragile and pale as the snow, clutching his mother's hand on the paths in the Tiergarten where she'd taken him to enjoy the scenery. The park's designers had envisioned it to depict a primordial forest full of mysterious recesses and paths. Perhaps he'd been trembling, for she said, "Don't worry, Willie. I won't let anything hurt you."

Had she been alive to this day, she couldn't have protected him from himself. Even as he had railed at the Gestapo's tyranny, he'd imagined showing off in front of them, astonishing them with his cleverness. No one had expected him to squeeze meaning from the interrogation report. How they reacted would depend on how they viewed his findings, as a masterstroke of analysis or an outlandish fantasy. They'd either laud him or laugh him out of the room. If the former, they might insist he brief the Führer. Canaris's tenure as the Abwehr chief was nearly extinguished, or so the rumors went. Hitler would designate someone to replace him. Mauer imagined himself promoted to Admiral and his name circulated to all the luminaries of Berlin. The next time he made an appointment to see Albert Speer, he wouldn't have to cool his heels in the Reichminister's holding room.

A fool's daydream. He shook it from his head.

Out of the snowfall a black Opel sedan materialized and shushed to the curbside. He was reaching for the door handle when the driver leapt out, ran around, and opened the back door for him.

Most unexpected.

– 28 –

Mid-January 1944

On his way back from the Gestapo headquarters at Prinz Albrechtstrasse, Mauer had the driver drop him at the Nollendorfplatz. He might have asked to be driven home, not unreasonable on a snowy night. Averse to showing the Gestapo man where he lived—as if the secret police didn't already know his address and everything else about him—he opted to walk the better part of a kilometer to his apartment on Bayreutherstrasse.

The snow lay white and pure, five centimeters deep, the solitary footprints his. It was past 10 p.m. when he arrived home. He inserted the key in the apartment door as quietly as he could, hoping Jana had not stayed up, but here she stood in her three layers of nightclothes. "Have you eaten?" she said.

"No."

"Sit." She went about retrieving the plate she'd covered and put away.

More tired than hungry, he obeyed, dropping into the chair. "I delivered my report on the Gestapo project tonight."

"Thank God you're done with it."

"I went to their den. It's like a smokehouse, everyone puffing on cigarettes. The Gestapo aren't subject to the tobacco rationing, I suppose. They kept me two hours. I had to explain my conclusions to two officials, then to Heinrich Müller himself. I hadn't met him before tonight. Hard to believe that this stumpy little man is the one whose name frightens people so."

The food in his mouth kindled his hunger. She seemed pleased to see him eat. "Were you frightened?"

"Terrified. I snapped the Hitler salute so sharply I nearly tore my shoulder from the socket. Then it struck me how humdrum they were, just bureaucrats going about their business. Stabl, the one who has been phoning to nettle me, looks like a clerk in a shoe store."

"Were they unkind to you?"

"Not at all. They were courteous, Müller especially. He congratulated me, extolled my work—he has the most suffocating Bavarian accent—and said my findings would go to the Führer. I thought he said it to humor me. Then he passed my report to a secretary and directed her to retype it on the special typewriter. It seems our great leader's eyesight is as bad as mine. He hates to wear glasses, and documents given him must be typed in a gigantic font." He went back to his food, chuckling while he chewed, thinking he must sound discomposed.

His mouth slowed, stopped half open.

Jana shook his shoulder. "Wake up, Willie. You'll choke on your food."

He stirred. "Yes, thank you. Perhaps it is a fitting time to break out the Steinhäger."

She fetched the German gin, the sole alcohol in the apartment. So far the distinctive earthenware bottle had survived the bomb shocks. She poured him a small glass, and one for herself.

"Prost!" He tossed back the shot, wiped his mouth with the back of his hand. "Have you ever asked yourself why the man you married has not been more successful?"

"What are you talking about? Certainly you are successful."

"I mean like Albert Speer. Look at him. At thirty-eight years old, he is the Minister of Armaments and War Production. I am just as good with calculations as he is, yet he became Hitler's favorite architect."

"Hitler's favorite sycophant, you mean."

"You are being unkind."

"Am I?" she said. "Do you think Albert Speer is a good man?"

"I do."

"Isn't he one of them, a top Nazi, devoted to their plan to make war on everyone? If the Nazis are bad, how can he be good?"

She had bested him again. True by definition, what she said about Speer.

Was he himself any different? He obeyed the Nazis' orders, danced in step to their sinister tune, and consequently wore the shame of all who applauded Hitler's sophistries or mocked Jews or wrapped a copper wire around the balls of a prisoner strapped to a chair. What could be more proof than tonight?

His head bobbed again.

She plucked the fork from his fingers. "Enough," she said. "Time for bed."

Part II

A truth that's told with bad intent
Beats all the lies you can invent.
--William Blake, *Auguries of Innocence*

All warfare is based on deception.
--Sun Tzu, *The Art of War*

- 29 -

Mid-February 1944

Mrs. Tatum knelt by Bags, who lay on her side.

"What happened?" said Linnea, lowering her valise to the porch.

"Oh, she ate something she shouldn't, I'll wager. Not the first time she's made herself sick. You'd think she'd learn."

"Will she be all right?"

"I'm sure, dear. You go on."

Bags gazed mournfully up at Linnea. No more would they see each other, she and the giant dog who'd been her spirited exercise companion. "Get better," she said. "I'll miss you."

An RAF lorry honked at the gate. Avry gave a thumbs up, and the driver lifted the bar and drove through. The two travelers climbed in the back, closed the canvas flaps, and perched on the wooden benches. Centrifugal forces tugged as they looped the driveway, rumbled down the gravel road, and swerved left on the main. Ten minutes of jerky stops and starts delivered them to a distant corner of RAF Hornchurch and the tail of a twin-engine airplane painted in a camouflage pattern. The main hangars mounded at least a kilometer off.

One of the airmen said, "If we don't get aloft, we won't stay ahead of her." The storm, he must mean.

They boarded. Recalling Verrick's suggestion, she claimed a window, but fearing she'd become airsick, she hardly looked out once they'd taken off. After thirty minutes, not yet having thrown up or even felt the urge to, she began to steal glances at the scenery. The brown and tan patchwork blanched whiter the northward they flew. In two hours, they touched down at an airbase somewhere north of Aberdeen. Avry descended the ladder and strode to the tarmac's edge to consult with a fellow she couldn't make out in the dusk.

He came back. "Bad news. They'd hoped to get us out with enough time for the plane to return ahead of the storm. She's come in too fast. We're stuck for the time being."

The RAF billeted them in an isolated, half-cylindrical Nissen hut. The blizzard rolled in, and against the white swirl, the scene might have been on a Hollywood movie set whose decorators had forgotten to paint the backdrop. Blown ice crystals tapped the metal sides like a saltshaker in the grip of a mad salt enthusiast. The place had been left unheated, and the stove at center seemed to take forever to chafe up. Outside, a fence prevented them from venturing further than the latrine twenty paces off, the snow-sheathed ground wearing the same ambiance night and day.

The storm worsened; the saltshaker became castanets. Anticipating that they might be weathered-in, Avry had brought along an assortment of Swedish newspapers she proceeded to read cover to cover. An RAF sergeant in a cocked cap delivered boxed rations. He spoke in a gravelly Welsh accent she strained to comprehend. Had he been put on light duties for diarrhea, or gonorrhea? Best not to listen.

She and Avry fitted the hut to their comfort, its center diagonal the unspoken divide between her domain and his, and they communicated as if across an international boundary. The exceptions were during the meals eaten from olive-painted tin cans she regarded with the same perplexity as she did the sergeant who brought them. The stove eventually warmed the cans set atop. She cut her finger fiddling with the jagged lid of a can of peanut butter. More hospital tape.

Avry reverted to his trainer's role. He showed her how to disassemble and assemble the Finnish Lahti L-35 9-millimeter automatic pistol he passed across the territorial line so she could practice. As she fitted the gun parts together, his accent rang so lyrically she expected the lines to rhyme. "The life of a field man infiltrated into the occupied countries is a lamentable monotony. Everything moves at a crawl save for your fretful mind. You hunker in a barn or an attic awaiting the hour to meet your agents, constantly thrashing at what might go wrong. Night or day, you're never at ease. A car door slamming could be the SS pitching up to arrest you. Unnerving, how sounds mimic each other. The wind murmurs in the trees, and you'd swear it's the hushed voices of raiders. A branch breaks, and it's the bolt-snap of a Schmeisser. You're conscious that anyone who sees you can betray you. You might play cards to pass the hours. If you ask me, you're better off keeping your Argus eye on the situation. In France, I stayed in a house that featured a hideaway in the ceiling in case the Nazis made a random check. It had a ladder I could pull up. Out of the hide, I counted my footsteps to the ladder, never permitting myself more than half a dozen, and always I reminded the family that sheltered me to efface the smudges the ladder's feet left on the floorboards. Smudges or no, the setup would have endured only a cursory inspection. If the Nazis surmise a dwelling to be a spy's den, they'll rip it down to the bare studs."

"Were you ever caught?"

"By the Nazis, no, thank God. In France, a competing group of partisans barged in and made my life uncomfortable for a spell."

"Is that what happened to the fingernails on your left hand?"

"Sometimes it transpires, when their leader's elsewhere, that the underlings in such a band will give run to their enthusiasms. These were on the hunt for informants; the same were picking them apart. My French groupmates stayed tightlipped about who I was, and their reticence only made the interlopers more paranoiac. I'm grateful they went after my fingernails and not my teeth."

"Did you tell them who you were?"

"Those halfwits? Not a chance. The leader showed up, and none too soon. He apologized profusely and poured Benedictine on my fingers. Hurt like hell. Preferable to have drunk the stuff."

Avry and the sergeant mounted a Scottish-Welsh conspiracy of some kind wherein the former acquired a bottle of rum. He offered her a splash, tipping the neck toward her metal canteen cup. She declined. At night the stove went out. They slept on the floor. The RAF sergeant had given them an ample supply of blankets, and she laid one underneath her to blunt the cold and arranged the rest atop, hoping she could wait till morning to don her boots and plod to the outhouse.

The faint glow from the snowfall seeped through the window, catching her exhalations that pirouetted into ephemeral silver nebulae. Wasn't life so, an ever-so-brief vibrancy and then gone? How was it that men could devote what little time they had to waging wars and enacting cruelties and deceptions on each other?

In her readings of Fyodor Dostoyevsky, she'd come across two quotes that dealt with deception. She couldn't remember the precise wording. One had to do with the secrets a man is afraid to tell others, versus the ones he fears to tell even himself. The second excoriated the man who lies to himself until he can no longer distinguish truth from falsehood. Her letters from London reassured her mother she was safe and comfortable, true except for her last letter, written at the Lodge, whose lines rang like the concoctions one tells a stranger at a bus stop. To protect her mother seemed right and normal. She wasn't allowed to reveal the truth anyway.

Was she lying to herself too?

Once she learned not to put the stirrup piece in backwards, disassembling and assembling the Lahti was child's play. She reread the Swedish newspapers. Mentally she perambulated the streets of Stockholm and the corridors of the Delfin Hotel. At dusk on the second day, she was about to start again on the newspapers, when Avry announced their flight was a go.

They gathered their things and tromped outside. Fat clouds jumbled in the sky, poor girls' necklaces of wan stars between. The RAF sergeant loaded their bags and the mission gear into the rear of an open truck, and they balanced atop like riders on a camel's hump across a snowy field. The aircraft, Avry explained, was a German Heinkel He-111 that had been forced down intact in Britain and refitted for infiltration missions. The fuselage bore no insignia. "They've replaced her interior bomb racks with extra fuel tanks so she can venture deep into Europe and back without the need to refuel. The Luftwaffe based in Denmark and south Norway prowls the skies over the Skagerrak. If they spot her, good chance they'll assume she's one of their own."

Snow skids had replaced the plane's wheels. A hatch accommodated their entry, and her nostrils flooded with the odors of oil, canvas, rubber. She squeezed between the extra fuel tanks that resembled jumbo coin dispensers. A crewman with bulging eyes pointed her to a mesh seat. "We're a crew of three," he said, paying no heed to Avry coming up behind. "The pilot, navigator, and me. I'm Graham."

"Hello." Avry had instructed her to reveal no names to the crew.

"She's a hale rig," said Graham.

"I've heard."

"Tricky to fly, though. The engines' torque keeps trying to flip her over."

"Umm."

"You'll notice me watching from the bathtub in the belly for planes that might sneak up from behind. Don't be alarmed. Standard procedure."

If anything was alarming, it was his pop-eyed fixation on her.

The co-pilot came back to brief them on the flight duration—roughly three hours—the location of the airsick bags, and what to do if they went down on land or at sea. He gestured to the stowed raft. When the pilot left, Avry leaned over and bared in his trilled-r-hearty brogue, "He has to haver on like that. The safety regulations. At this latitude, the North Sea is freezing this time of year. If we have to ditch, a raft is just self-delusion."

The pilot doused the cabin lights. The engines thundered. She squeezed in the rubber ear plugs. Her mesh seat adjoined a window, and she watched the ground recede and the snow-carpeted landscape meld with the wave caps. When clouds intruded, she huddled under the blanket Graham had doled out with the earplugs. Now he pulled up a metal grate to expose the so-called bathtub in the belly, and, as he had foretold, took up a prone position to watch through rows of low windows.

"Make yourself comfortable," shouted Avry from the side opposite, barely an arm's reach off.

The aircraft bucked, yawed, and pitched. The prior flight had been smooth by comparison. She clutched the airsick bag in the expectation she'd soon have to barf. In the wait, she propped her feet on a parachute, closed her eyes, and drifted off in fits and starts. She hosted mental quirks she'd not revealed to anyone, even her mother. One was a lifelong, irrational phobia of being rendered upside-down that the crewman's snippet about the engine torque flipping the plane had reinterpreted as rational. She thought the fear might trace to the gulls of Petrograd, swooping fiends eager to snatch away children they dangled by the feet. Another eccentricity no less illogical was her unease toward clouds. She guessed this too might derive from the white gulls lurking against the opalescence. Her father, unaware of her distrust of clouds, had played a game with her, the object to build a story around a cloud's semblance. One day in Hamburg, he pointed to a puffy cumulous. "What do you see?"

"A fox eating a lamb who is smiling," she said.

"Smiling, the lamb? Why, if he's being eaten by the fox?"

"She. The lamb is a she. The fox is a he."

"And she's smiling because…?"

"She knows something the fox doesn't."

"What does she know, the lamb who finds amusement at her own death?"

"She will be reborn as an eagle, and she will kill him."

Her father's grin flattened. "The fox doesn't sense this?"

"He knows only the taste of blood in his mouth."

"So he's to be punished for his nature. Is that fair? He is just doing what foxes do."

"The fox's nature doesn't mean he should get away with it."

She didn't tell her father that she was the lamb, or that the fox wore his face, he who'd ripped her out of Stockholm and brought her to this dismal city. The blood he tasted was money.

Not long afterward, he died. She did not get her revenge. None was possible. All she could do was silently rage at him whose nature had stranded his family in a raft on the wintery North Sea.

The airsick bag had slipped from her fingers. She woke up, and half in a panic she searched all around until she found it by the parachute. No, she didn't have to throw up, not yet, but she wasn't going to be caught without.

Across the fuselage, Avry read a paperback novel with the same blasé detachment as when he monitored her language lessons. If he'd noticed her scramble for the bag, he gave no sign. The crewman Graham, apparently having relinquished his watch for trailing aircraft, clambered up and down the length of the cylinder checking the seals on the auxiliary fuel-line fittings and the snugness of straps and buckles. He brought them coffee in aluminum cups with covers that kept the liquid from sloshing out when the aircraft bucked in the turbulence. "Inventive, the Jerries are," Avry shouted. "The cups came with the plane."

In the tail section, a metal toilet bulked from a fuselage beam. Without her asking, Graham had rigged a curtain so she might have a modicum of privacy. She gritted her teeth when she descended to the lip the temperature of ice. When she returned, Avry shouted, "We're crossing the Swedish coast."

She chanced a look. Through the window, fractures in the clouds revealed a fleecy gray surface, sea or land—maybe an infinity of snow-covered fir trees—she couldn't tell. The plane descended and the view sharpened. Snowy meadows, streams, and woods scrolled under. She discerned a few farmhouses, some at the rims of white expanses that must be frozen lakes.

On the bulkhead, a red eye flared. Avry butted his fists together. Strap in. Graham clambered forward, shouting, "When we touch down, keep your safety strap buckled. If the pilot spies something he doesn't like, he'll hotfoot out, and it's the wildest ride you were ever on."

Thanks.

Past the window, whiteness blotted everything. The skids touched and the pilot reversed engines until they glided to a halt. Graham unfitted the belly hatch, and she dropped the airsick bag to help Avry and the co-pilot toss bundles through the opening. Avry deftly slipped through, lowered himself to the ground, and slapped an arm around one of the figures outside.

"Your turn," yelled Graham. "Good luck to you."

The hands of three men caught her as she dropped, and she joined them in hefting the bundles out of the way. One hundred yards off hulked a sleigh hitched to a thick-legged nag a boy kept calm in the blast from the Heinkel's engines.

The hatch thumped shut. Avry pulled her away some paces. "Brace yourself," he shouted.

She aped him kneeling in the snow, head down, as the plane whipped its tail around, revved furiously, and sprinted off in a snowstorm of its own making.

– 30 –

Mid-February 1944

At the Berlin headquarters of the <u>Sicherheitsdienst,</u> Kriminalkommissar Elena Rolke studied the intelligence report that had landed on her desk. She pouted the thin lips that shrouded her prominent teeth. Here lay an opportunity, if only she could present it convincingly enough.

She was thirty-three years old, her jutting chin hinting at a certain imperiousness, her eyes in their shadowy sockets floating like hard-boiled eggs dropped into a jar of black paint. In keeping with her duties as a counterintelligence officer in the SD, normally she wore civilian attire. Today, beset by paperwork, she showed off her uniform of steel-gray wool, the skirt hugging her trim waist and hips, the jacket fanning to wider-than-normal shoulders and sprouting her head with its severely angled face. Strictly speaking, no SS uniform for women existed, a fact no one dared mention in her presence. Within the Nazi security services, few women achieved high stature; Nazi policy barred them from the requisite roles. She wasn't deterred; she knew enough men in high places to circumvent the vituperators who stuffed the party's middle echelons. Her ambition was to become the highest-ranking woman in Berlin, and her colleagues and subordinates knew better than to get in her way.

The mission of the SD's counterintelligence wing was to hunt down enemy spies, and Elena had labored tirelessly to achieve her present position as the wing's deputy. Most people could not comprehend her passion to catch spies; the pursuit seemed unwomanly. She thought the trait must be in her blood. Her great uncle, Graf Alfred von Schlieffen, had been Chief of Staff of the German Army and the author of the famous offensive plan that bore his name and the army had wielded—some would say botched—at the onset of the First World War. Her grandfather and father too had been notable soldiers. Her martial heritage was like the tinge of black elderberries crushed into a wooden floor, indelible whether you tried to scrub it out or not. To her it was a mark of honor, and she didn't give a damn who noticed.

At the age of twenty-six, she had married a Prussian baron in hopes the union would prove advantageous. A fumbling, doting sort he was, nonetheless proud. The pride made him plead with her to abandon her job with the Nazi security organ and stay home as a good German *Ehefrau* was supposed to, producing offspring like a hearty cow. She refused. Two years along, utterly bored with the marriage, she divorced him. Her life was austere—wartime, *ja?*—not that she didn't entertain lovers. They soon disinterested her. The notion that another person might be emotionally vital to her never had taken root. You either possessed *Zweckmässigkeit*—usefulness—to her or you did not.

Report in hand, she strutted along the carpeted corridor whose fibers glittered from miniscule grains of glass. Weeks ago, a British aerial bomb had struck nearby, shattering the adjacent windows. She'd been in the building when it happened, and she waded through the choking dust to make sure no one was injured. The panes had been replaced with plywood and everything cleaned up, the employees of the SD preserving a businesslike collectedness through it all. *Nur richtig.* As it should be.

At the hallway's end she entered the office of her department head, Kriminaldirektor Rudolf Fenzl, on the phone at the moment. Twenty years older than her, he had wizened, bloodshot eyes that descanted the strains of his job. Fenzl personified two arguably contradictory traits, a profound cynicism and an equally deep integrity. She approved of both. Rare, a senior Nazi who made it a point not to lie, so she was loyal to him, if not the slightest bit deferential. Habitually she barged into his office without knocking, beaming her impatience if he happened to be busy with something or someone else.

To the phone he was saying, "Is there any chance, my dear fellow, that this matter is not as trivial as it sounds?" Who was his interlocutor? Probably one of the haughty Reich-crats who thought they merited a favor from the SD and who if called upon later would prove unable or unwilling to reciprocate.

Fenzl hung up and faced her. He'd once described her as "the Reich's best spycatcher, possessed of the instincts of a champion hunting dog," ruefully adding, "one that must be kept on a short leash." To say so and to do so were altogether different. A frown creased his lips. "What woes do you bring me, Elena?"

She set the report in front of him. "Have you seen it?"

He picked it up, seeming to weigh the two pages in his fingers. "No. What does it say?"

"That British commandos plan to attack our delegation in Stockholm."

"What delegation?"

"Admiral Diefenbach's. Next week, he is traveling there to talk the Swedes into continuing their steel exports to Germany. His stronger motive, I believe, is to secretly rendezvous with the Soviets, to receive instructions, or perhaps to defect."

The counterintelligence wing had kept Diefenbach's name on the list of suspects who might be the elusive Soviet spy codenamed GALILEO. The absence of solid evidence and his stature as a senior military officer and Nazi had shielded him from the pressure they'd have applied to a common suspect. Not that the SD's suspicions hadn't had an effect. For almost two years, they'd succeeded in bottling him up in Kiel, where he could do less harm. But now he was back in Berlin, on the General Staff.

Fenzl said, "You know as well as I do that Diefenbach has been declared trustworthy."

"He isn't trustworthy, Rudolf. Merely dormant."

"Tell that to Kaltenbrunner." Ernst Kaltenbrunner was the head of the Reich Main Security Office, or RSHA, the SD's parent organization.

"A drunken lunatic."

"Keep your voice down, for God's sake!" No doubt he was thinking her leash should be tightened.

Neither of them brought up Walter Schellenberg, the SD's Director. Elena's same age and branded a *wunderkind*, he was politically shrewd enough to have kept his distance from the controversy surrounding Admiral Diefenbach.

Fenzl read the report, his eyes flicking up now and then as if to reassure himself she was doing nothing threatening. She had lit up one of the Gauloises Bleues cigarettes an acquaintance had brought her from Paris. At length he said, "This is utter nonsense. The British would never mount a commando attack in a neutral capital. Where is it from?"

"Constantinople."

"A city so full of information peddlers they trip over each other. Fabricated rubbish."

"How would a fabricator know our delegation is traveling to Stockholm? The trip has not been publicized."

"So, disinformation."

"From whom? The Russians? The British? Neither would benefit from its spread." She didn't mention the Americans, not from a preconception that the OSS was incompetent, rather that she considered the American intelligence service to be the hand puppet of the British.

He pushed the report to the edge of his desk as if to move it as far away from him as possible. "Where are you going with this?"

"Diefenbach should not be allowed to travel to Sweden."

"We have no say in the matter, and this drivel certainly will not change anything."

She blew out a mouthful of smoke. "Then I can use the information to control the delegation."

"Control them *how*? If you raise a stink about this silly threat, they will simply stay at the German Embassy. You could control them there only with the ambassador's consent. The ambassador is Hans Thomsen, one of von Ribbentrop's bright stars, and he will grant you nothing without the Foreign Minister's direct approval."

"We won't have to involve him. The Embassy's guest quarters are under repair, and Stockholm's Grand Hotel has become such a nest of foreigners that the delegation plans to avoid it. They have reserved rooms at the Delfin, a smaller hotel the Swedish Nazis operate."

"So?"

Fenzl's good traits, she thought, did not stop him from being as stubborn as a nail in oak. She said, "With the help of the Swedish Nazis, I'll guard the hotel so he won't be able to meet with his Russian handlers."

"He'll just slip out the back door."

"We'll seal the exits."

"Hmm. You would still require the help of the SD's attaché in Stockholm. How reliable is he?"

"His name is Gutermuth. I don't know him, and from his file, he seems unimpressive. I'll take charge of him when I get there."

Elena had come close to catching the mysterious spy in July 1941, three weeks or so after Hitler invaded the Soviet Union. By then, the only Soviet intelligence officers still in Germany were the so-called illegals, men and women shrouded in innocuous occupations and identifying themselves as third-country nationals—Hungarians, Romanians, Swiss—or in rare cases as Germans. Cognizant of the prowess of Nazi radio-signal triangulation teams, the Soviet radiomen had grown facile at sending quick messages using mobile rigs, never broadcasting twice from the same location. Elena personally led the combined SD-Gestapo spy hunt. For months, the radio-triangulators had intercepted signals originating from west Pomerania, all broadcast under the same 'fist,' the sender's distinctive style of tapping out Morse code. She theorized that the spy or his cutout encrypted the messages using one-time pads—unbreakable—and delivered them to the radio operator, who traveled to far-flung locations, set up his antenna, transmitted the message twice, and fled. The signals arose every two weeks or so from the outskirts of small villages and towns that collectively spanned a huge area. By the time the triangulators arrived at the transmission sites, the radioman was long gone. She guessed a Soviet submarine in the Baltic Sea crept within range to receive the signals.

She needed manpower. To gain a meeting with the general who commanded the region's Wehrmacht reserve division, she had to drop the name of her famous great uncle. The division commander, a typical Prussian cocooned in the elite cape of stupidity that bade him believe he was smarter than everyone else, set their meeting for the evening at the handsome villa where he resided. Over dinner, in a dress of ebony taffeta, sipping the French Moselle she had brought along, she asked him for two hundred soldiers, explaining in detail how she planned to deploy them at a dozen or so checkpoints. Military men tended to disassociate women from military thinking. To encounter one who articulated a cogent tactical plan using the proper terminology seemed to enthrall him. She heightened the effect by listening in mock absorption to his theories of war while seductively fingering the rim of her glass, showing off her nails she had painted crimson for the occasion.

He lent her two companies of soldiers to use for a month.

Her analysis of the broadcast sites indicated that the radio operator avoided patterns, occasionally ranging far, at other times transmitting a mere kilometer from a site he had used previously. She posted half of her borrowed soldiers at checkpoints on the main roads. Guessing her quarry would use the side roads to elude them, she dispersed the others in flying squads she relocated every few hours. In the second week, one of the flying squads stopped a car. As the soldiers commenced to search it, the driver bolted into the woods. He proved slower than the young men who gave chase. In a compartment under the automobile's back seat, they found the radio set and wire antenna.

Elena brought him to Berlin where, no doubt hoping to avoid torture, he confessed immediately. An illegal documented as a Danish salesman who traveled the countryside, he was a trained NKVD technician specializing in clandestine radio signals. As to the messages he sent, he received them via impersonal contact and already pre-encoded for transmission. Their purveyor, he divulged while smoking a cigarette Elena had given him, was a waifish, middle-aged, castor-haired woman in a brown herringbone coat. She deposited small rolls of paper inside crushed cigarette packs under a boxwood shrub behind a cement bench near the Old Market Square in Potsdam. By rights he never should have caught a glimpse of her. One day he arrived early to collect the package and spotted her at a distance. He wasn't close enough to see her face, and he knew nothing of her identity or where she came from. He transmitted the messages at prearranged times using a directional antenna aimed northeast.

In the interrogation room, Elena regarded him across the desk. "What did the messages say?"

"I have no idea." He smiled slightly, a feeble attempt at insouciance. Fear paled his forty-year-old, as-yet-unharmed skin. Like bare branches dripping melting snow, his thinning hair collected sweat that then trickled down his forehead.

"How often did you unload the drop?"

"Two weeks apart, always on a Thursday or Friday."

"How long since the last time?"

"Four days."

"What was the safe signal?"

"What do you mean?"

"You know precisely what I mean. A chalk mark on a wall, a ribbon looped over a tree branch, a flowerpot set on a windowsill, that communicated to her it was safe to load the drop."

"We don't use such rudimentary practices."

"How did she know it was safe?"

"She didn't." He shrugged as if to say, it's a tough business, you take your chances.

"So, we may assume the woman will show up again at the bench in ten days."

"Yes. Watch the spot and you will catch her."

He was lying. The safe signal, Elena guessed, was the nugget the NKVD had adjured him to withhold at all costs. In its absence, not only would the woman avoid the drop site, she'd glean that the radioman had been taken. Then she would warn the spy and flee.

"Tell me the safe signal, or it will go poorly for you."

"Do you wish that I invent something? As I said, we don't use such signals."

"Fine. Have it your way."

The Gestapo men on her team dragged him away. How long would he hold out? A day? A week? In the meantime, not knowing how the signal system worked, she couldn't estimate how long she might have to identify the woman. Already it might be too late. At most she had ten days.

"Keep him alive," she told the interrogators. The SD's policy was to 'turn' captured radiomen so they could be used to feed false information to their Soviet masters.

Her team interviewed the Deutsche Reichsbahn employees who administered the trains between Berlin and Potsdam. The inquiry seemed to go nowhere; the woman's description was imprecise, and the line counted among greater Berlin's busiest, the challenge confounded by the Reichsbahn's penchant of shuffling its attendants among the many routes. The radioman, meanwhile, had tried to kill himself by biting through his tongue in hopes he would bleed out. His minders stopped the bleeding, stitched his tongue to resemble bird tracks on wet clay, and sleeved it in a prophylactic wire mesh flexible enough to permit him to slabber out intelligible syllables. The questioning ran around the clock, still he held out, a tougher nut than he looked.

At last, an old ticket puncher—anyone's guess how his trembly, bowed legs negotiated the train's length—nodded his grizzled head. Yes, he had perforated the ticket of a woman whose granite-gray hair brushed at the collar of a brown herringbone coat. He guessed her to be in her early fifties. Once he even chatted with her, asking why she traveled every two weeks from

Berlin to Potsdam. She was visiting her elderly mother, she'd replied. Would the ticket puncher recognize her if he saw her again? *"Bestimmt."* Certainly.

Elena borrowed him. The spy hunters questioned the platform masters and ticket vendors. One of the latter recalled a woman of like description who purchased round trips to Potsdam. Could the vendor pick her out of a crowd? She thought so. Elena conscripted her too.

The expanding canvas required the marshalling of Gestapo and local police. Elena poured her precious time into negotiations with the organizational suzerains to assemble the resources. The spy hunters brought suspects before the ancient train attendant and the ticket vendor. They squinted. *Nein.*

On the eighth day, in a neighborhood in southwest Berlin, a paunchy mail carrier remembered a woman who wore a herringbone coat and otherwise matched the description. She was Maria Toft, resident of an upstairs apartment in a row house. Discreetly the mail carrier showed Elena the facade. He'd been delivering mail to her for five years, he said, and they'd chatted from time to time. In her odd accent—no, he'd never asked where she came from—she'd told him she took in sewing for her neighbors and had a son in the Wehrmacht. *Sehr bewundernswert,* he added. Very admirable.

Elena said, "Has the boy ever been seen to visit her?"

"Nein."

A fictitious son, she thought. The city register showed the woman to be fifty-one years old, listing no relatives.

The true prize was the spy himself. Was Maria Toft's apartment the meeting site, or did they rendezvous elsewhere? The tightly squeezed streets afforded nowhere to post surveillance, and worse still, the neighborhood was a *Kietz,* Berlin slang for an insular ward whose residents instantly would spot lingering outsiders. If Maria Toft caught the faintest whiff she was under suspicion, she'd slip into the adjoining alleys that zigzagged like swastikas. The only option was to arrest her without delay.

Elena disguised her team in utility overalls and sent them door to door to ask if anyone was experiencing electrical problems. When the burly duo came to the house's street door, they rapped and waited. If Maria Toft was the one to open it, they would yank her out. If someone else answered, they'd play it through as utility men, going door to door inside, seemingly harmless, the goal to take the woman alive.

In an unmarked car on the kietz's periphery, Elena chain-smoked Gauloises. The SD had kept the campaign as discreet as possible, nonetheless it had been necessary to mobilize hundreds of men. She had reported the radio operator's capture to the RSHA's leadership, who in turn notified OKW. If the spy had penetrated the upper echelons of the military or security services, he might have learned of the radioman's arrest and the hunt for the gray-haired woman and tipped off Maria Toft.

The team came back. No one had responded to their knocks at the house's front door. In other circumstances, Elena might have contacted the landlord for a pass key or sent one of her men to tickle the lock. No time. "Force your way in," she said. "Get to her as quickly as you can."

The street door of seasoned birch took two shoulder-thuds to dislodge. The men had not even mounted the stairs when they heard the sharp crack of a gunshot.

Elena knew what she would find. Upstairs, burnt cordite suffused the hallway outside the apartment whose door had been kicked open. In a maroon velvet-upholstered armchair, Maria Toft slumped as if from an exhausting day, the barrel of the 6.35mm Model 9 Walther in her lap still smoking. The shot fired upward through the mouth had blown through the back of her head. Elena pried the pistol from the woman's fingers and with her flashlight checked the teeth. Good, the bullet had not destroyed the back molars; a dentist could examine them for microfilm that might nuzzle inside a hollowed-out crown. She searched the clothes. The pockets were empty, not even a pfennig.

In the disapproving glare of the corpse's open eyes, the searchers commenced in hopes of finding one-time pads still intact. The shelf harbored books, and on the chance the bindings concealed pads, they cut them open. They interviewed the neighbors. Everyone admitted to having encountered Maria Toft at one time or another, always just in passing. No one had paid much attention to the retiring dowager.

The team dislodged the dead woman from the stuffed chair and slashed the upholstery. They crowbarred up the floorboards and disassembled the furniture. With sledgehammers they bashed open the walls and dismantled the fireplace, breaking apart each brick looking for concealments. Elena lent her attention to the linen tablecloth whose ironing stains mimeoed the tracks of a meandering hoofed animal; spies had been known to bury microfilm in the seams of fabrics. She found nothing. The apartment's antiseptic quality suggested that Maria Toft had been warned. A miracle she had not already bolted.

A second miracle. The pried-out base wall of a closet coughed out the torn-up scraps of a notebook. Like children around a jigsaw puzzle, the team spread them on the tabletop and reassembled several pages of encrypted handwriting. These were brought to cryptologists, who recognized the Russian-origin cipher. Broken, it revealed Maria Toft's mission, to collect and forward intelligence from a primary agent and four sub-agents. Their identities would have been too much to hope for, even so, it was a spectacular windfall. The story of Galileo Galilei's discovery of the illustrious *vier Monde des Jupiters* had captivated Elena in her childhood, and she codenamed the principal agent GALILEO and the sub-agents CALLISTRO, EUROPA, GANYMEDE, and IO. Reinhard Heydrich, the RSHA director at the time, briefed the case to Hitler.

In late 1941, the authorities began to wrap-up the profuse Soviet spy ring dubbed *die Rote Kapelle*—the Red Orchestra—eclipsing the search for GALILEO. More than one hundred eventually were arrested and put on trial. The spy-hunting hierarchy assumed that Maria Toft's spy had been part of the larger ring but had escaped. Elena never believed it. Suspicions burgeoned too that the discovery of the torn-up notebook pages in the otherwise sanitized apartment had been improbable; why hadn't Maria Toft destroyed the scraps? The Soviets must have planted them to throw the scent off the Red Orchestra. Elena disagreed. Why was it so hard to accept that Maria Toft simply had made a mistake?

Relentlessly Elena continued the hunt.

"Your obsession with Diefenbach has become unhealthy, Elena."

Fenzl had said so before. She guessed he was the one who'd come up with the annoying sobriquet *der Tausendjähriges Spion*—the 'thousand-year spy'— that seemed to mock her endless pursuit of the case.

"Relax, Rudolf. I won't arrest him without fresh evidence."

"Fresh, *strong* evidence." In German, strong was *stark*, a word you could clench your fist to. Hitler was fond of such dramatisms. Fortunately, Fenzl wasn't.

"Of course."

"How long will the delegation be in Stockholm?"

"Three days. They arrive on the afternoon of the first day, have all-day meetings on the second, and gather for a final session the morning of the third. I will get there a day early and leave with the delegation."

"You will require too many people. The authorities in Stockholm will raise a stink."

"My team will consist of four only: myself and three others. The Swedish Nazis will supply the additional manpower. With their help, I'll do what is necessary in a discreet way."

His lips tightened to a slash across his face. The relentlessness with which she pursued her intentions never ceased to put him on edge. "However discreet you may try to be, if Diefenbach truly *is* GALILEO, he will see through it and outmaneuver you."

She met his stare.

His composure broke first, a smile breaking over his stained teeth. "Please do keep me informed, Elena."

– 31 –

Mid-February 1944

The brain-juddering caterwaul of the aircraft engines faded to the gentle hiss of sleigh runners over snow. It might have soothed Linnea to sleep if the cold hadn't clenched her in its stiff grip. In the back atop the parcels, she pinched the fur-rimmed hood around her face.

The driver steered the sleigh off the frozen lake into evergreen woods along the same tracks he'd carved coming in. The forest around lay virgin and mysterious, the land flat; only a few times did the nag have to strain up a rise, exhaling a vaporous moustache as she went. Linnea observed no roads, buildings, or lights, though occasionally she glimpsed the white sweeps of frozen lakes. Now the sleigh angled off the path and halted, and the two boys riding in the back jumped down to drag a fallen spruce across the cut. When they climbed back on, the nag broke a new trail, scuffing eastward toward the dawn's salmon-shaded penumbra.

Avry introduced Lars and his sons Marcus and Runi. He didn't say their last name or repeat that they were the husband and sons of Mrs. Johansson. In his late forties, his anorak, hair, gloves, and eyes of mottled gray, Lars seemed to emulate a wolf. He spoke to Avry in English and to Linnea in Swedish. "You grew up in Stockholm, Thorgun?"

She deadened a frown. It was the first time anyone had called her by that name. "Yes, we were here eight years or so."

"When did you leave?"

"In 1933."

"So you are not originally from the capital?"

"No." Avry had warned her to reveal no details of her life outside of Sweden.

Lars seemed to know better than to pry. His attempt at conversation with her having gone nowhere, he shifted to monolog. "Sweden has become the land of shortages, rationing, and military conscription. We perform drills for air raids that never happen. We can't do much about those things. With those that we can, we are far too pragmatic. Nobody likes the Swedish Nazis, who are stupid and obnoxious. The government should simply round the devils up, but our leaders remain reluctant to take any step that might provoke Hitler. To me it feels wrong."

"Sweden did save the Jews of Denmark," she said.

"Yes, that was something, but not enough. We need to be stronger, take a real stand. If you ask me why I'm here with you today, I think that is the reason."

If Lars was the crafty canine, son Marcus was the brawny bear. Chestnut hair capped a colossal head he swiveled to scan the woods, occasionally fixing on something. He cradled a rifle he looked quite capable of using.

"How old are you?" said Linnea.

"Eighteen. He's thirteen."

He referred to straw-haired Runi, who opposite his taciturn brother proceeded to play the magpie. Without respite he gabbled on, the paucity of her responses having no effect other than to lend him more time to expound on the family's every detail. They lived in a farmhouse, owned three horses, a truck, sixty hectares of land, utterly despised the Nazis, secretly were friends with the British—as if Runi wouldn't blurt out any secret—and, oh yes, his mother had been abroad this past year, he wasn't sure where, but he supposed in England. Linnea spoke only in Swedish, leaving him to conclude that, like his mother, she must be a Swede in league with the Allies.

At the edge of a clearing, Lars stopped and Runi immediately quieted. Distant vehicles gnarred. Had the Swedish Army detected the plane's intrusion last night? The sounds faded. Lars waited five minutes and flapped the reins. She relaxed.

In the afternoon, they came to a rough timber farmhouse. Runi trotted ahead to open the doors of the adjoining barn while Marcus circumambulated the buildings, scouring for tire or foot tracks or other signs someone had encroached while the family had been gone. The sleigh zithered to the barn, where they unloaded the parcels through a trap door into a cavity beneath, its walls lined with shelves. Items soon filled them: a radio with antenna and parts, two submachineguns of a type she didn't recognize, four Lathi pistols, ammunition, six lights attached to wooden panels she supposed had been used to mark the landing area for the plane, several large flashlights, and a bundle of paper money in several currencies, the bills creased and floppy from use. By the time they finished, the daylight had fled.

The farmhouse's overhanging, snow-packed roof lent the illusion of amplitude to a space severely cramped within. Lars decided that Linnea should take the ceiling nook where Runi normally slept. Accessed via a vertical ladder through a hatch, it proved too small to stand up in, and to stow her coat and valise barely left room to lie down. A wrong move and she'd fall through the hatch, which made her think of the ceiling hideaway in France Avry had described, except that nobody was counting footsteps.

She descended the ladder. In the kitchen, Lars was making dinner, a fish stew. On the table lay vegetables. He pointed to a knife and some potatoes and carrots.

"Where do I wash them?" she said.

"Not needed. Chop."

She did and almost chopped off her index finger, inflicting a cut luckily not too deep. Without a word, Lars plucked the knife from her hand and gave it to Runi.

"Do we go to Stockholm tomorrow?" asked Linnea, mistress of finger-taping, applying a strip to the cut.

Lars flicked his eyes toward Runi. There were topics not to be discussed in front of him, apparently. She made herself useful doing nothing.

Marcus clicked on a Bakelite-console radio and tuned in the scratchy voice of the TT News Agency on Radiotjänst. In the world beyond, battles were underway. The Allied beachhead at Anzio on Italy's west coast was under relentless siege by German forces, and in the Ukraine, the Soviets had pushed the Germans back across the Dnieper River. When the radio fell victim to static, Marcus, cross-legged on the bare floorboards, restored the reception. The news ended and a swing jazz program commenced. Runi sidled back and forth as he chopped vegetables.

Lars brought out a bottle labeled Brännvin—Swedish brandy—poured everyone a shot, and raised his glass. "*Skål!*" The stuff was bitter, unlike any brandy she'd tasted, the foreignness making her wonder how Swedish she really was. She set aside the alcohol and drank ice-cold water Lars said had been drawn from the well. Maybe it would wake her up.

It didn't. Halfway through the meal, her head began to droop.

"You should sleep," said Lars.

"Is there a bathroom?"

"An outhouse. The path is to the right. No lights, I'm afraid."

She donned her coat and tromped along the path sunken in the snow. Though the sky was moonless, the ambience proved sufficient to define the way; she even sighted a fox skulking in a clump of deadfall, watching her.

She muttered, "If you're so clever, why can I see you?"

A courier delivered to 70 Grosvenor Street an envelope addressed to Mr. Gabriel Verrick. He tore it open, extracting a folded slip of vellum handwritten:

Let your pledged word ever be sacred. Never promise to do a thing without performing it with the most rigid promptness. Phineas Taylor Barnum
   Pearlman.

Wentworth had a gift for elegant nuance, thought Verrick. P.T. Barnum was an American.

Linnea and Avry had arrived safely in Sweden.

In a telegram to Donovan, Verrick reported the event. 'Our officer was fully prepared. She demonstrated her language skills to a high proficiency.' Briefly he pondered saying something about her initial reluctance. No, why complicate things? He added the latest snippets that further implied the British had access to a Soviet NKVD file, and to the final paragraph he tacked on the kind of pseudo-optimistic statement that often gilded such messages, that he'd stay alert for opportunities to press for access.

He carried the text to the communication window for transmission. Before he passed it through, he flattened the paper against the wall and crossed out the last line.

Through SHAEF channels, Casey's message had reached the 101st Airborne Division that First Lieutenant Matthew Verrick's father was in town and would like to see his son, if possible. Matt's chain of command granted him a furlough lasting from sunrise to dusk this coming Sunday, the time window encasing the drive from his military base to London of two hours and forty minutes each way. Left was an interval barely exceeding three hours, far too short, thought Verrick. Still, it was more than most fathers with sons in the military got these days.

On Sunday morning, he curled out of bed like the edge of freshly scissored bond paper, tidied his jacket with a lint brush he borrowed from the cleaning closet, daubed his shoes with brown Shinola polish, and buffed them to a luster, not too shiny. Just before noon he legged to the designated military drop-off point at the Marble Arch.

An olive-green truck with white stars on the doors growled up, and from the back leapt U.S. Army paratroopers, their bloused jump boots gleaming. "Form up," one of them barked. They made two ranks. "Atten-shun!" Boot heels clicked in unison. "Be back here no later than fifteen hundred. Don't be late. Stick, dis-missed!" The men dispersed, and the confident young officer who'd given the commands stepped toward Verrick.

Matt was twenty-three. From Fordham University he'd gone straight to the Army, and his year with the paratroops had filled him out from a lanky boy to an easy-flowing six-footer. Silver airborne wings adorned the space above the left chest pocket of his wool tunic, a slim garrison cap with a sewn-on parachute-glider patch arching his head. Like the other men of the Verrick family, he'd never been much for hugging. He gave his father a rugged handshake.

Along Bayswater Road they hooked into Hyde Park, each adjusting his pace to the other's. "Are you hungry?" said Verrick. "There are restaurants within a few blocks. Some aren't bad."

"I know. I've been to London to gawk at the monuments."

A father, Verrick couldn't suppress the compulsion to repeat himself. "You're not hungry?"

"Not yet. Let's walk for a while."

They crossed Hyde Park, emerging into Westminster residential neighborhoods of stately apartment houses and ordinary brick rows. Some sported elegant wrought-iron fences, others lovely blue or yellow window planters. Here too were a few grim reminders of the blitz, the husks of bomb-struck houses waiting to be rebuilt.

"How's training?"

"It gets old," said Matt. "We're like a bunch of thoroughbreds running around the practice track over and over, waiting for the real race to start."

The real race was the invasion everyone knew was coming, the timing a secret few were privy to. Verrick was not among them. Worry for his son doused him. He shook it off. In minutes they were as lost as you could be in central London. He didn't mind. Matt was here, relating the foibles of his battalion commander and the miserable ship voyage the soldiers had braved across the Atlantic. He was lucky to have sixteen practice jumps under his belt. The parachute jumps were being cut back because the jumpers were incurring too many injuries. He went on about the dreaded 'Mae West,' the salacious metaphor depicting when a parachute's suspension line—he called it a 'shroud line'—looped over the silk canopy, fashioning two bumps and cutting down on the lift area. Jumpers had suffered broken ankles, legs, backs. Other training entailed fifteen-mile marches under weighted packs, maneuvers in soaking rains, hand-to-hand combat in the sawdust pits, and hours on small-arms and grenade ranges. Matt ran the battalion's grenade range, his role to face the thrower, command "pull" and "throw," and hope like hell the SOB would not drop the live grenade. If he did, Matt hurriedly must snatch up and toss the 'damned pineapple,' or kick it into the sump and dive away before it exploded.

"Have men dropped live grenades?"

"A few. Nobody's been hurt on my range, though."

Verrick gulped. "Good to hear."

Of his own job, he said nothing, and Matt, aware that his father's law-firm boss and old friend William Donovan commanded the OSS, probably figured it better not to ask. They came to a tall, coalsmoke-blackened stone wall stretching out of view in both directions. "I recognize this wall," said Matt. "It encloses the grounds of Buckingham Palace." In minutes, his son leading, they curved around to the grand plaza facing the many-windowed residence of King George VI. "I'll bet the King is gazing out at us this very minute." said Verrick. Matt shrugged.

They guided along the offshoot called The Mall and through the Admiralty Arch to Trafalgar Square. Verrick's knee ached from ninety minutes afoot. Matt looked like he could keep going forever. Maybe he could have.

"You must be hungry by now."

"If you're twisting my arm, why not?"

The expression wasn't one Matt would have used before the war. His acquired repertoire no doubt included phrases he was too polite to utter to his father. Along Fleet Street they found an eatery Matt approved of. The entrée he selected and that Verrick seconded—baked salmon noodles— proved tasty despite the meager salmon portions and the likelihood the noodles had come pre-cooked out of a can from America. The white wine that accompanied, though blasé, was restorative after the long stroll.

"Do you think you'll parachute in with the invasion?"

"I hope so. We're training with gliders too. I'd sure hate to ride one of those rattletraps into combat." He described an accident he'd witnessed in which a section of a glider's flimsy tube-metal skeleton had broken off and impaled one of the soldiers through the abdomen.

Verrick grimaced. "Did the poor fellow survive?"

"Yeah, but for him, the war's over." He said it so offhandedly he might have been remarking on someone who had run out of cigarettes. It occurred to Verrick that Matt had been nonchalant about everything: the parachute jumps, the grenade range, the palace, the meal, and spending time with his father. In front of him stretched momentous events. By contrast, today was trivial.

Not to Verrick. As they sauntered to the pick-up site, the three hours having gone by with heartless rapidity, the impending farewell brought him to silence. My God, was this the last he would see of his son? To preserve his composure, he bit his lip. The covered Army truck that with any luck might have been delayed was waiting at the Marble Arch, the paratroopers gathered at curbside.

"Gotta go, dad."

"Take care of yourself."

"You bet." He shook Verrick's hand, stepped toward the truck, and spun around. "Don't hang around watching till we leave, okay?"

"Sure."

To turn away was almost impossible, but he kept his promise, the tears flooding. Walk, don't stare over your shoulder; he's a tough young man in the company of fine soldiers who know what they're doing. They'll look out for each other. He caught his son's voice calling out the roster of paratroopers, a dozen names.

By the time he had crossed into Hyde Park and glanced back, the truck was gone.

– 32 –

Mid-February 1944

They entered Stockholm from the west, Lars's Volvo truck lumbering through neighborhoods erected by the scores in the 1930s, some still in progress. Construction workers swarmed over blocks where Linnea recalled tenements and shanties. They'd been torn down, leaving the churches the sole facades that looked old. More consistent with her memories were the wood-masted fishing boats bobbing along the Norr Mälarstrand quay, and the massive Stockholm City Hall with its arched windows and infinity of rose-hued bricks.

Oddly sedate, the city center. Lars attributed the stillness to the rationing of fuel and the regulations the government had enacted some years ago forbidding drivers from blowing their horns. "Beware of the cars," he cautioned. "The drivers are so law abiding they will run you over without honking first."

He let them off at a sidestreet near Drottninggatan. Traffic was heavier here, the air clotted with diesel, the windows staring down like relatives she hadn't seen in a long time and who were less charming than she remembered. No snow today; the sidewalks were free of ice. At a vendor's stall, she purchased cigarettes for Avry, using one of her ration coupons and paying with some of the öre coins Lars had given her. The other customers ignored them, this mismatched couple bundled against the February cold, he who gawped like a fisherman after a grueling day on a boat, she altogether ordinary unless you looked into her eyes. You couldn't, because she lowered them. Avry had cautioned her to avoid eye contact with strangers, nature having bestowed her gaze with what he called "a startling radiance." Flashing them would invite attention the way a lit window at night attracted enemy bombers.

Overdramatic, she thought. She averted her eyes nonetheless.

Southward they rounded Gustav Adolfs torg and its dominating statue of the eponymous king and horseman silhouetted against the overcast. She'd been here before, on some bright holiday with her friends amid crowds and cheering. Where was the joy at her return? The Swedes afoot paid no heed to the place; their lines to it were unbroken. Among them she was a ghost popped out of the trap door of her memory.

Across the bridge they gadded into Gamla Stan. Oldness wafted like mildew from the peculiar nooks and squeezed lanes, the sidewalks so narrow a pedestrian walked a tightrope to stay on. At the square above the alley where the safehouse skulked, Avry lit a cigarette and gazed with no discernable interest at the people, parked and passing automobiles, doorways, and window curtains. Apparently sighting nothing perturbing, he sauntered to a cast iron gate he opened with the key Lars had given him. Inward it swung with a prolonged creak, and he threaded a stunted alley and hooked rightward up wooden stairs whose surface someone thoughtfully had scraped free of ice. With a second key he opened the apartment door, and inside he loped at once to the window and tugged shut the Venetian blind. She trailed him, peering past the edges of the still-jiggling blind slats to the alley twelve feet below. Her arms retained their strength from her many lower-downs from the practice bar; probably she could do the same here, if she had to.

Stuffy, the warren. A faint perfume scent lingered. She toured the two rooms, the bare floorboards groaning underfoot. Painted a gaudy raspberry, the rear bedroom was barely wider than the droopy bed within. The main room doubled as bedroom and kitchen, the dusky yellow wallpaper seeming to ooze like spattered mustard. A ceramic sink cowered under the brow of varnished cabinets that stowed chipped plates, glasses, a dinged-up pot, a cast-iron skillet, and an electric cooking ring. The bed opposite, if bed it was, was so short it might have been designed for a legless person. Between posed a spindly table, two chairs, and a blocky ottoman upholstered in paisley cretonne on which the telephone stuck up like a midget's head on shoulders. The only matching items were half a dozen liter-size glass water bottles and four big jars of pickled herring Lars must have supplied. Against the wall, he'd erected an ironing board so ostentatiously it might as well have sported a placard with her name printed on. The sole wall décor was a black-and-white poster of Greta Garbo in an exotic hat, her head tilted, a hand curled suggestively under her jaw.

It took Linnea a minute to find the water closet behind the wallpapered door. The space was claustrophobic—she had to wedge herself alongside the toilet to shut the door—no less a refinement over Lars's outhouse. A loose wallboard surrendered to her prying, exposing a concealment cavity Lars had installed. Before she reclosed it, she stashed in Hamfrid Matisson's hotel badge, the map, a stack of Swedish kronor, Avry's Lahti, and the spare ammunition.

In the front room, Avry was opening the radiator valve.

"What do you think?" she said.

"What do I think? Well, as safehouses go, it's so lamentable that a recruit choosing it would be drummed out of the service. Boxed in, no secondary exit, and if you somehow get out, what do you encounter but an alley that ends in a bloody locked gate!"

She'd been about to comment on how cozy the place seemed.

"There's an excuse, mind you," he went on. "In a housing-short city, Lars was able to acquire the place without a lot of questions. The alternative would have been to poach from the resources of our residency, and knowing how closely the Swedes watch the buggers, they'd probably have blown the gig from the start."

At 3 p.m., as the daylight through the window began to wane, Avry said, "Good time for you to stroll to the Delfin Plaza. Don't get too close to the hotel. On the way back, pick us up some fresh food. Make sure you've got your ration tickets."

Lars had examined the forged Swedish ration-ticket booklets they'd brought from London bearing Thorgun Lindstrom's name and declared address. "These are good," he pronounced. "We have no national identification system here in Sweden, except of course for passports, which not everyone possesses and nobody uses except to travel abroad. Sometimes, if the police stop you for some reason, and they don't know you, they'll ask to see a ration booklet. Keep it handy."

He'd examined the hotel badge too. It was of powder blue cardstock, the fancy black letters of 'Hotel Delfin' debossed, her photograph glued on, the front stamped with a red authentication seal, and the back signed by the hotel security manager, all encased in celluloid with an attached clip. The danger was that the hotel might have changed the badge's pattern since MI-6 somehow had come up with an exemplar. Linnea would clip it to the chest pocket of her white blouse over a gray skirt, the uniform for supervisors.

"I'm fairly certain this is correct," Lars had said. "I'll confirm it before you go in."

She descended to Skeppsbron by the waterfront, narrowly dodging a streetcar piloted by a uniformed woman who apparently adhered to the same horn-blow-averse rectitude as the automobile drivers. She crossed the Norrbro bridge, passed the Riksdag House, and threaded into the city center. Now and then she glanced back, the confident Swedish woman appraising her surroundings. No one was paying her undue attention.

In bed at the Lodge, mentally she'd prowled the map routes between the safehouse and the hotel plaza. To tread the live streets was like being in the audience on the premier night of a much-anticipated theatrical play. She encountered marvels the stage-setters of Stockholm must have put out for her entertainment: a bottle-green door sporting a polished brass knocker with the face of a goddess; a nook from which snouted a black Citroën limousine, the hood the tableau for a bouquet of flowers perhaps flung there by a spurned suitor; a chained dog who bayed out in a multi-pitched yowl a cat must have taught him; and an outdoor urinal where a man peed, not an uncommon sight on the Continent and one her mother years ago had reproved her not to stare at. She hooked into what she thought was a through-street and halted abruptly at a dead end. Someone rudely had erected a building here, blocking the way. The map was out of date; she'd have to mark the change. Retreating, she noticed on the adjacent wall a glued-on poster with the words EN SVENSK TIGER and a drawing of a tiger with vertical blue and yellow stripes, the colors of the Swedish flag. She had read about the posters, the equivalent of the American 'Loose Lips Sink Ships' campaign, the caption dual-meaning, 'A Swede Keeps Silent' and 'Swedish Tiger.'

Mrs. Johansson's photos of the Delfin Plaza, snapped in sunlight, had made it look more impressive than the evening's twilight was willing to grant. The hotel constituted the sole striking feature, its granite cornices alternating with redbrick bands like the cherry layers in a Black Forest tart, the open or closed blackout curtains like knowing winks. People tilted into the wind off the estuary. Two policemen clopped past on horseback. Amid the faint musk of burning coal, buildings scaled the florid sky; a bronze dolphin leapt from a waterless fountain. This must be what ordinary looked like.

Had she been here before? Yes, her father had given her a coin to toss into the pool at the base of the then-gushing fountain, prodding her to make a wish. "Ask for happiness, and you will have it," he'd said, so typical a statement from him. He was the broken fingernail she could not stop running her thumb over.

She'd been staring at the fountain too long. She skirted the plaza counterclockwise to the exit. The blackout here was not very black. A string of electric bulbs limned the path to a stretch of open-air grocery bins crowded with bundled women toting cloth shopping bags. Avry had handed her such a bag—more of the impedimenta from Lars—and asked her to pick up food. Some of the bins were empty, the vegetables sold out; others had been thoroughly picked over. At one, she noticed the blue hem of a maid's dress jutting from under the coat of a woman scrabbling through potatoes. Clipped to her coat, not well seen because of her angle to Linnea, appeared to be a hotel badge.

They still weren't sure that the color and style of the forged badge they'd brought from London were correct. Should she take the chance?

She said, "Excuse me, do you work at the Delfin Hotel?"

The woman lifted her head, the ambiance from the strung lights braising puffy, cold-rouged cheeks. She looked to be in her fifties. "Yes. Why do you ask?"

"Do you like it there? I was thinking of applying."

She turned to face Linnea, revealing the blue badge with a centered photo and a red stamp. "The Delfin is a proper hotel," said the woman. "They tolerate no nonsense. A good job for a young woman, *ja?*"

Demurely Linnea dipped her head.

"Is your family in the party?" said the woman.

It took Linnea a couple of seconds to make the connection. "My brother is a member."

"You will need a party recommendation. Perhaps your brother can obtain one. Put it in an envelope addressed to Herr Viklund and drop it at the front desk."

"Herr Viklund. Thank you."

At the safehouse, she boiled the vegetables she'd bought, edited the map she spread on the spindly table, and told Avry of her survey of the plaza, replaying her conversation with the maid.

He poured himself a drink from the half-bottle of <u>Brännvin that</u> Lars must have given him. "Care for a shot?"

"No, thanks." To imbibe in the safehouse struck her as unwise. She didn't like the stuff anyway.

He lit a cigarette. "I take it the woman meant the Nazi party."

"Yes."

"Your initiative was risky. The bit about your brother being in the party might have provoked questions you couldn't answer. We have to assume the Nazi buzzards all know each other. What if she spots you in the hotel? She'll ask how you got the job so bloody fast, won't she?"

"Wasn't it worth it, to confirm what the badge looks like?"

"Confirming it was Lars's job, not yours. Lars doesn't have to walk into the damn hotel."

His tone cut. She forced herself not to shun away. "Running into her seemed too serendipitous to pass up."

"This isn't training anymore; this is the game itself. The last thing you want is to let that fickle imp serendipity out of her box."

He tossed back his drink.

On the map, her reconnaissance paths traced like the petals of an open flower, the Delfin Plaza as its ovule. One of the loops swung her northeast to Östermalm along Karlavägen Street and past the building where she'd lived with her parents. She stopped to look at the place. The third floor pouted the dormered window of her room. It faced a strip of fir trees from which, under the weight of snow, a lovely bough had descended as if the tree were beckoning to her, and she'd fantasized she might traipse across to an enchanted principality.

Had *this* been her tree? Looked a bit scraggly.

Alongside the door, an inlaid brass plate vaunted the address. She remembered emerging here to climb into their grand motorcar, her father at the wheel. Later he shipped the car to Hamburg so he could swank about town.

Until he'd died.

Had she forgiven him? If nothing else, she comprehended him better. He'd been her chess opponent, and you can learn a lot about a person from his gameplay, as he can from yours. Always she insisted on playing black, maybe another mental artifact from the dreaded white gulls of Petrograd. In her girlhood, usually he won, overwhelming her with his quick moves, especially with his rooks he loved to maraud about, not fathoming how vulnerable they were out on their own. At age eleven and after, she beat him almost every game. His chess moves, like his life's, were too venturesome. To flaunt the image of success, he took on immense financial debt. To shine with the German moguls, he lied about his influence with the Swedish steel makers, his lying as cocksure as his chess play, and as insufficiently calculated. As the pressure on him mounted, the gregarious backslapper had put on an unruffled front, even to the day of his death. Brave of him, she had to admit.

No more forgivable.

Her infatuation with Stockholm, her desire to return to this street, did not match the venue. Joy should accompany the sight of the apartment building, the baked-in icon of her lost home. It didn't. On the sea voyage to America, the kids had hooted into air vents that pronged from the ship's deck like big question marks. The deeper in they leaned, the hollower their echoes.

She *was* Swedish, she told herself, and this was *her* street in the city where she belonged. Surely the identity was still there.

"*Linnea, jag tror inte mina ögon!*" Six feet away, her former neighbor Mrs. Grandahl stared with openmouthed incredulity, her round, friendly visage unchanged from Linnea's mental image across more than a decade. The woman had child-sat with Linnea when her parents went out. Always she'd brought along delicious pastries she'd baked. I can't believe my eyes, she was saying.

"Mrs. Grandahl, how lovely to see you."

"And I you, dear girl. You've returned to Stockholm. God be praised."

"I had no idea you were still here."

"Where would I go, dear? Look at you, grown up." She gave Linnea a hug, the crush of her arms and smell of her perfume the same as when they'd said goodbye. "I heard your father passed. So sad. A fine man. Please, come inside. I'll make *bakverk*, that's what I'll do, and we'll chat."

"I'm so sorry, I can't. I'm in town for just a few hours."

Mrs. Grandahl's face fell. "You'll return, surely?"

"Yes. I'm not sure when."

"Where are you staying? Is your mother with you?"

"I have to go. See you."

"Please pass my love to your mother," blatted the woman, flabbergasted, to Linnea's back.

To walk away was as awkward as anything she had ever done. No choice; staying would have summoned a thousand questions. What utter stupidity, to have dawdled in front of her old apartment building assuming no one would remember her.

She visited the fish market by the waterfront, bought fresh herring and potatoes, fried them at the safehouse, and divided them still steaming onto two plates. Now, facing Avry at the spindly table, bracing herself, she told him of her unexpected encounter in front of her old apartment building.

He stopped chewing. "What were you doing there?"

"I wanted to see my old street. I didn't think anyone would recognize me."

"Do you not apprehend how bloody delicate our situation is? You're supposed to be invisible."

"I know. I've scolded myself plenty."

"Your former neighbor's going to tell everyone she knows that she ran into you. What if she has a relative or friend in the interior ministry, and she asks them to look up your address in Sweden? They'll hit upon no record of your entry. This is wartime. People are suspicious. They'll start an inquiry."

"I made a mistake, I told you about it, and I apologized. What else do you want me to say?"

He shook his head. "That's twice you've tossed the dice on our security. Need I emphasize, you daren't flirt with a third?"

That evening they practiced the scripts. She regained her composure.

"You've mastered the role as thoroughly as is humanly possible, I'll vouch for it," he said, a little too elaborately, maybe his way of smoothing over his criticism earlier.

He showed her the letter he'd carried in the lining of his coat. To hold it, he donned gloves. "Leave no fingerprints. Handle only the envelope that you'll keep with you after our man takes the letter."

In handwritten German, it read:

Dearest Cousin,
Thank you for your generous gift to Helga. The doll house is lovely. She cherishes it more than any other of her possessions. When they see it, her friends marvel. She has arranged the furniture to imitate the parlor of your home, adding a teensy potted plant she crafted (all right, with some help from her father) and books she fashioned from folding papers into tiny rectangles. From a small box she turned on its side, she devised a fireplace with painted bricks and adorned with twists of foil that shimmer like flames when the light shines on. The candlesticks are toothpicks dipped in melted wax and posed upright, and the wall paintings are postage stamps clipped from letters. Every day she contrives another of these fantastic artistries she is eager to show to her favorite uncle.
With gratitude and love,
Sophia

Even for German, the prose was overwrought. "He'll be able to make sense of this?"

"It's written in the code he and Maria Toft used."

"What does it mean?"

"Instructions. Better you don't have the specifics."

"What if he asks me?"

"I doubt he will. If he does, it's credible the NKVD hasn't told you. They practice compartmentation, just as we do. Tell him it's in the old code he's quite familiar with."

Gingerly he restored the letter to the envelope.

As they'd done at the airfield shelter, they sundered the safehouse into dominions, hers the tiny bedroom, his the rearward half of the main room with the too-short bed. The kitchen and water closet were neutral ground. Prolonged silences descended; he'd run out of things to teach her, and he wasn't naturally chatty, least of all about his personal life.

That evening she asked, "Do you have a family?"

Seated on the half bed, his one eye tilted wider than the other, he said, "In Edinburgh, a wife and three daughters."

"How old are your daughters?"

"Eight, ten, and twelve, black-haired beauties all. I haven't seen them in a year."

"None of my business, but why not?"

"When I got back from France, my fingers were a mess from the nail pulling, and my mentality was just as bad. The brass decided I should go on furlough to restore my equilibrium. Three weeks I spent with my girls, and I grew accustomed to them, and they to me. When the time arrived to go back to the game, I told myself I was no worse off than other parents pitching themselves into the fray. The dread part was to shove my family to the back of my mind and keep them there. I almost couldn't. In this business, a man's concentration ranks preeminent. To lose it is deadly to him and the mission. The cost of staying alive, you might say."

Four and a half years the British had been at war.

At 11 p.m., she retired to the raspberry-walled room and pulled the bedcovers over. The delegation would arrive tomorrow. The approach was timed for midnight of the second night. In her head the script lines chased around like children in an overcrowded train car, not black-haired beauties either, but anxiety-racked wraiths. The jitteriness tightened her muscles, and she slept as if on a trampoline that let her sink only so deep before it bounced her awake.

The safehouse door opened and closed. Muted footsteps thudded on the stairs, and momentarily the gate creaked. Avry hadn't told her he was going out.

Like her mental images of the map of Stockholm and the blueprints of the Delfin Hotel, she had imprinted Avry's craggy mien as it flashed discernment, humor, rebuke. This evening, he'd drained the bottle of spirits, turning it upside down and shaking the last drops into his cup.

She shouldn't have asked him about his family.

It was past midnight. There must be nightspots that sold alcohol on the black market; the ones that did business legally would have closed by now, and he didn't have ration tickets in any event. What if he encountered the police? He knew only a handful of words in Swedish. His papers identified him as Norwegian, a language he couldn't speak very well either.

Talk about rolling the dice on their security.

– 33 –

Mid-February 1944

SD officer Helmut Gutermuth, second in command of the German embassy's military attaché's office, braved the ferocious Baltic winds slashing across the tarmac to greet the three men and one woman who deplaned from a three-engine Junker JU-52. The telegram of their impending arrival had given no hint of their mission, only that they would stay at the Delfin Hotel by the city-center waterfront and heavy steamer trunks would accompany them. He had been ordered to assist them.

Gutermuth had spent the past three years in Stockholm, and contentedly so. He had a comfortable apartment and special entitlements to rations, not bad for wartime, even if the Scandinavian cold so penetrated his fifty-two-year-old bones that on some days he pictured himself as made of ice. But the main reason was that nobody was shooting at him. Having fought as an infantryman in the First World War, he had no wish to relive the experience. Now he pressed his pince-nez eyeglasses on his nose, advanced, and smiled cordially at the middle-aged fellow he assumed to be the group's leader.

Glares from the four. He'd made a mistake.

The representative of a Nazi security organ, Gutermuth normally netted a measure of deference from those around. Not from everyone. His three years in diplomacy had exposed him to hubristic potentates—ambassadors, ministers, and other dignitaries—and their equally haughty wives and executive secretaries, women whose soft features could calcify to imperious scowls if they sensed themselves disrespected in some way. Bitches of this category must be given their due, he reminded himself, lest they complain to their husbands or bosses of the effrontery of an impertinent functionary. He would not be the one to upset the cart; a wise man abided by the rules.

What he had not encountered heretofore was the glower from the woman he now grasped was the team's leader and who seemed to bear decisive power in her own right. Women were not granted full membership in the Nazi party. That one might exert such wordless intimidation astonished him even more in that she was attractive, albeit in a feral way. Fear cramped his stomach, as happened sometimes when he consumed too much milk cream.

He helped them load the steamer trunks onto the small truck he had arranged, ushered the team into the embassy motorcar, and slipped behind the wheel. The woman rode in the front passenger seat. From time to time, he stole a glance at her, mulling the trivialities he might ply to lighten her mood. His stomach constricted anew. Better to keep his mouth shut unless she asked him a question.

While the team offloaded the trunks at the Delfin Hotel, she took him aside, leveling a half-threatening, half-disdainful stare. "I have read your file, Herr Gutermuth. It seems you enjoy a plum arrangement here."

Plum arrangement? Was she implying that his posting in Sweden made him a shirker? He worked tirelessly, sometimes twelve or more hours a day, accomplishing duties vital to German interests. On the verge of blurting his indignation, he thought twice. Already he'd made one misstep. Soberly he replied, "Madam, whatever impression you may have gleaned from the file, my duties are quite demanding."

"They are about to become more so. While I am in Stockholm, you will work for me. You will obey me and the members of my team in every detail. Do you understand?"

"Yes, madam."

"You will say nothing of our purpose here. No rumor-trading or pillow talk, and not a word to the Military Attaché or to the ambassador. Clear?"

"Yes, madam." Easy enough. He had no idea what her team's purpose was.

"Is this your phone number?" She showed him a notebook page with a number written.

"Yes."

"What is your number at home?"

He provided it.

She dictated the steps he must enact immediately. When he reached for his pocketed notebook, she said, "Don't write them down. Remember! Are you capable of that?"

"Yes, madam."

"Stay close to one of these phones in the event I call. You may go."

Trembling slightly, he motored off. He shouldn't worry, he reassured himself. Clearly the woman was dangerous, but her visit to Stockholm would last no more than a few days. Afterward his life would go back to normal. And yes, he should congratulate himself; he had discerned her nature quickly. He might have blundered worse.

All was well.

Elena handed a letter to the Delfin Hotel's security manager, Herr Bror Axelsson. The stationery bore the letterhead Reichminister des Auswärtigen—Reich Foreign Minister—typewritten, signed, and stamped, an official request to lend the bearer full assistance. The aegis was a fiction, the power behind it was not. The letter's request could be verified if he wished to phone the embassy. The instructions she'd given to Gutermuth had set up the mechanism.

Swedish and forty-six years old, Axelsson had the visage of a beaten-from-the-ring ex-boxer: The once-broken lower jaw resembled a discarded horseshoe; a three-centimeter, twig-shaped scar double-underscored his right eye, and shorn-to-the-scalp salt-and-pepper hair topped furry eyebrows that must have scurried out of the way of the trimmer. His brown suit's cuffs and collar showed stains he perhaps thought people didn't notice. What they couldn't miss were the Swastika pin decorating his lapel and the holstered pistol bulging under the jacket. Not long ago, he wouldn't have hesitated to poke the pistol in the face of an unwelcome intruder. Now such displays of force were wisely left to the police. Like a boat engine's propeller mired in seaweed, Axelsson and the Swedish Nazi Party he belonged to had lost much of their former bite.

Elena had read the files the SD kept on the Delfin Hotel, Axelsson's personal history, and the ebbing stature of the Swedish Nazis. Thus versed, she wasn't surprised when he lifted his overgrown eyebrows at her request for a master key to the rooms on the VIP floor. He wasn't stupid, this fellow. "The hotel tolerates no... alterations to its spaces," he said.

"I have no idea what you mean, Herr Axelsson." She plunked on his desk an open envelope bulging with Swedish kronor he seemed to have trouble peeling his eyes from. "Your helpfulness will reap recognition from the German government."

She was prepared to resort to intimidation. It proved unnecessary. He gave her the passkey.

"You should get yourself a new suit," she suggested.

The next day, he was wearing one.

Of the three men on her team, Henrik Durst was the oldest, age 43, a decade senior to her. He was the one to whom the obtuse SD attaché had tendered his greetings at the airfield, thinking he was in charge. Tall and gaunt, Durst sported eyebrows that were less two strips of hair than a Morse-code array of tufts. The face called to mind a tattered carpet runner badly discolored by spilled bleach, the right side below the cheekbone betraying a cavernous divot. No doubt he'd suffered burns and skin grafts, which perhaps explained why he hadn't risen higher in the SD; sunken, stippled faces were un-Aryan. But if he was resentful to serve under Elena's iron hand, he was smart enough not to show it.

The second member, Emil Zurcher, the technician, possessed the mien of a mischievous imp. Capable of staying awake for inhumanly long periods, he could sleep anywhere: in the back seat of an automobile, along stair steps, or like a cat in the rafters of an attic. If she required a wiretap or other technical surveillance, she always requested Zurcher, and she had no qualms about snatching him suddenly away from the projects of other sections. The section leaders brought their complaints to Rudolf Fenzl, who invariably ignored them.

The third, Brindtmann, nicknamed 'Brindt,' stood two meters tall and weighed over one hundred kilos. She had encountered him four years ago, a Gestapo thug whom his supervisors at the time regarded as *dumm wie Bohnenstroh*, dumb as a bean husk. She discovered that, if precisely instructed, he fulfilled his duties with a consummate literality, a rare trait and one she liked. She'd had him transferred to the SD, and under her command he typically performed such tasks as helping Zurcher with the equipment, driving a vehicle, and whatever else she told him to do. His size tended to attract notice, a disadvantage offset by his capacity to inflict violence without a flutter of reticence. He was the Doberman whose leash she held as tightly or loosely as the situation indicated. They were a symbiotic pair, she and Brindt, a formidable mind and a body to match. The image pleased her. No need to take it too far.

Into the night, Zurcher and Brindt labored to implant the listening devices in the VIP suite Admiral Diefenbach would occupy. Everyone had heard of bugs, so-called *Wanzen*, bedbugs. People assumed that the hidden microphones resembled insects that a painstaking search of a room or dwelling might uncover. In truth, nothing short of demolishing the walls and tearing up the floorboards stood any hope of revealing the infestation. The professionals were in no hurry to enlighten their prey, who, having peeked under the lamp shades and behind the wall hangings and discovered nothing, would succumb to self-delusion and speak openly.

What made Zurcher special when it came to such installations was his sublime meticulousness. To say his trait was German was to give too much credit to the Germans, the vast majority of whom could never hope to equal his artistry. The bug-installer's craft demanded a mastery of diverse techniques—drilling, plasterwork, painting, upholstery, wallpapering, acoustics, electrical circuits, masonry—whose difficulty a shortage of time invariably compounded. The suite's wallpaper was unmatchable. Steaming it would risk disfigurement, so he hid the microphones and wires behind the enameled base moldings that he and Brindt painstakingly dislodged. Upon replacing them, he repainted the seams with a fine-tipped brush, mixing the fast-drying paint to the identical shade of white (say *white* to Zurcher, and he would scoff; there were as many variations of white as the brush bristles he used to apply them). He pried up the carpet and several floorboards, and with a long-bitted hand drill he bored through to the room below that harbored the recording and monitoring equipment and fed the wires through. Fortunately, no one from the hotel's staff was around to witness the damage he wreaked upon the century-old castellation.

Their work finished, Zurcher and Brindt stood by on pins and needles while Elena inspected the suite. She sniffed for telltale paint fumes, kicked her toe at the carpet edges, and glided her fingers over surfaces, scrutinizing the tips for traces of plaster dust. To test the audio, she murmured, "I simply must have a warmer blanket," and went about whispering from various spots. "Parlor by the window, *eins, zwei, drei, vier.*" A pause. "Doorway to the bedroom…" *Und so weiter.* And so on. On the headphones in the room below, Durst confirmed there was no dead space where the devices wouldn't lend an attentive ear.

Before leaving Berlin, she had telexed the embassy in Stockholm the warning that British commandos were planning to attack the German delegation. Embassy officials questioned the report's veracity. *Mumpitz—* nonsense—*ja?* But dutiful Germans, they did as the telex instructed, alerting the Swedish authorities and requesting additional security measures. From her window, she looked down at the plaza where sawhorses blocked the two main entrances and the pedestrian gate, the manning policemen permitting only residents and workers whose names appeared on checklists to pass through. *Ausgezeichnet.* Excellent. The deployment was as professional as the SD itself could have done.

The delegation arrived. She introduced herself to the administrator, Wehrmacht Oberst Georg Wittermann, and issued him the order that no one from the delegation was to leave the hotel. Wittermann had lost a leg at Stalingrad more than a year ago, and from his pained expression, you would think the amputation had not properly healed. Braced stiffly on his wooden limb, he eyed her with an incredulity shading on rebellion. "Surely these orders don't apply to the delegation's negotiating sessions with the Swedish government."

"The meetings must take place at the hotel," she said.

"Impossible! We are a visiting delegation. The host country chooses the venues for official events."

She showed him the same document she had to Axelsson. "Not only possible, Oberst, but imperative. I assure you I have complete say in matters of security. The Swedish government has been notified of the threat and will understand."

"What threat?"

"British commandos plan to attack the delegation."

"That's absurd!"

"We are taking it very seriously nonetheless." Her tone wasn't harsh; some people you were better off treating with patience. If he refused to comply, she would threaten to relieve him from his duties, arrest him, and lock him in the hold of a German freighter. Behind her stood Brindt, whose bulk lent her a conspicuous gravitas.

Wittermann sighed. His experience on the eastern front perhaps had seasoned him to recognize when he was faced with someone who wouldn't back down. He said, "I will convey the restrictions to the delegation members. I assume they do not pertain to Admiral Diefenbach. He has been invited to a dinner tonight at the home of the Swedish Minister for Foreign Affairs."

"The restrictions encompass everyone. He shall demur."

Wittermann clicked his heels and bowed slightly. "You may expect a call from the admiral."

"By all means. He can reach me in room 318."

Elena's room was alongside the one housing Zurcher and Brindt. The first on shift, Zurcher sported the headphones like a favorite old hat, the crossbar cocked comfortably behind his head.

"Anything?" she said.

"Diefenbach just answered a call from Oberst Wittermann, who sounded agitated. He informed the admiral that the delegation is confined to the hotel."

He removed the headphones and held them up, and he and Elena leaned together as Wittermann's tinny voice seeped through. "What are your instructions, admiral?"

Diefenbach took an inordinately long time to answer, making Elena wonder if the microphones were working properly. At length, he said, "Notify the Swedes of the venue change, and that I regretfully cannot attend tonight's dinner."

Another pause. Wittermann said, "Anything else, sir?"

"Keep me informed."

In Germany, her teams had observed Diefenbach over many months. A disciplined spy conceals himself behind seeming normalcy, sometimes amid chaos, never in personal aberration. The watchers noted no suspicious behavior on the admiral's part; on the contrary, he appeared perfectly innocuous. No one achieved such mastery except through training, in this case surely from the NKVD. The honed dexterity now had allowed him to guess he was under surveillance, and his effected equanimity suggested he would practice restraint in his every word and deed. She doubted he would try to slip out of the hotel. If he did, the door guards she'd posted would stop him.

What worried her more was that the Soviets would try to get *in*.

– 34 –

Mid-February 1944

As the sun set on the day of the delegation's arrival, Linnea headed out on another reconnaissance. Gusts off the Riddarfjärden disheveled her hair and harassed the men who were trying to lower the flag outside the Riksdag House, and she was grateful for the shelter of the sidestreets she followed to the entrance to the Delfin Plaza. Here she halted. Red-and-white-striped sawhorses blocked the street. The two policemen manning them stamped their feet against the cold, their buckled rubber boots clinking as they checked their rosters and passed people through. A dozen queued. A cluster of others looked on, curious but uninvolved.

She peered past their shoulders. A woman in a coat, the blue hem of her maid's dress pooching out below, advanced to a policeman. He waved her through. Another woman stepped up. The policeman fingered through the multi-page roster on his clipboard and refused to pass her; apparently her name was not listed. She snapped a few unkind words at him, spun on her toe, and tromped off head down. As she veered by, Linnea said, "What was that all about?"

"German bigshots are staying at the hotel. The police have imposed special security. Every day for ten years I have passed through this plaza, and now I must detour around? For Nazis? Shameful!"

Along the connecting streets, Linnea made her way to the plaza's second entry. A tributary to the side permitted people to get to and from the grocery stalls without passing through the checkpoint. Evoking her mental map of the surroundings, she continued in a wide arc to a pedestrian path by the waterside. Here a policeman stood behind sawhorses that blocked the way. Anyone who approached, he shooed to the checkpoints.

She made her way back to the grocery stalls and pretended to examine vegetables while she assessed the activity in the adjacent plaza. At the hotel entrance stood a guard, his hands thrust in his pockets, his head swiveling alertly back and forth. When a woman walked up, the guard took out what seemed to be a roster, and she held out something Linnea guessed was a hotel badge. The guard checked the roster and passed her through. The same thing happened with the next entrant, and the next.

The police at the plaza's entry points were checking their rosters too, but with many prospective entrants, they didn't have to. The cops obviously recognized them as residents or workers here. One was a hotel maid, as Linnea could see from the woman's blue dress protruding under her coat. The few the cops didn't know—two apparent guests of the hotel showed up, foreigners, it appeared—were made to show their passports.

The door guard and police checkpoints, if they were still in place tomorrow night, could wreck the mission before she got anywhere near GALILEO.

At the safehouse, she recited her observations to Avry.

He said, "The guard at the hotel door examined the roster every time someone entered?"

"Yes."

"But the cops at the checkpoints were waving people along?"

"Looked like they knew most of them by sight."

"What about cars?"

"They weren't letting them through."

He began to pace, smoking and blowing out skeins that flurried like hyped-up sylphs let out of a jar. "Always when you think you've thought everything through to the last refinement, you bloody well haven't."

She didn't comment.

He said, "How many pages were the rosters?"

"Three or four."

"Does the grocery have a side exit?"

"A door leads to an alley where they bring in stocks. It doesn't open to the square."

"What about the apartment buildings that do?"

"I didn't try the back doors. I'm betting the police have ordered them locked."

At length he donned his coat and went out, no doubt to call Lars.

It was three in the morning when the scratch of the key in the lock awakened her. Avry looked drained, his face chafed red from the cold.

"I think we've devised a fix," he said. "Where's the map?"

She fetched it from the hiding place.

"Lars contacted a government man he trusts. The Germans claim there's a threat to the delegation, an attack plot of some kind. The Swedes have shifted the delegation's meetings to the hotel, and the police have cordoned off the plaza, as you saw."

"And?"

"He says the door guards at the hotel are Swedish Nazis who don't know the employees. And the one on the night shift will not have passed Hamfrid Matisson through previously, because she works the day shift."

"How is Lars so sure of that?"

"He knows his town and has good contacts."

A dicey assumption, it seemed to her.

He went on: "At the checkpoints, there's no way to be sure that whatever policemen are on duty won't know the real Matisson. She's been at the hotel for some years, and the local cops are very familiar with their beat and those who live and work around the plaza, as you saw. So you'll have to go around."

"How?"

He tapped his finger on a spot on the map between the hotel and the waterside road. "The government man will make certain the back entrance to the apartment building on the square's south side is open prior to midnight. You'll enter and pass through to the square and across to the hotel's entrance, circumventing the police checkpoints."

"What about the building's concierge?" She recalled their apartment house on Karlavägen, where the concierge annoyingly had patted her on the head every time she passed by.

"Goes to bed early, according to the government man."

"Did you meet him?"

"No."

"What's his ministry?"

"Lars wouldn't say."

She shook her head.

"The game is nothing if not rich in ambiguities," he added.

Was he joking?

He kicked his legs forward, lit another cigarette, drew deeply, and huffed out a lungful of smoke. "What counts is that Lars has confidence in him. We can either do likewise, or we can abort the mission."

She stared.

"Listen," said Avry, "Lars is as solid as a mountain. He wouldn't use someone who wasn't reliable. He's putting his own arse on the line, same as ours."

Having excoriated her for taking risks, Avry was betting the mission and their fates on a third party they knew nothing about.

"I'll decide after I have a walk by." What had she just said? *I'll decide.* As if it were her choice.

It was. If she balked, the mission was over.

She caught his eye. He knew it too.

"Get some rest," he said.

He poured himself a drink from the bottle he'd acquired somewhere.

From the street-facing window above Grosvenor Street, Verrick flicked a glance downward. It was mid-afternoon, and pedestrians were about, some with cloth bags of their slim purchases of rationed foodstuffs.

Casey as promised had arranged for an office for him. It turned out to be Donovan's. The secretary who delivered the reading folders looked at him funny. Who was he, and what was he doing at the General's desk? Over the interval since he'd returned from the Lodge, she'd brought him the daily reading boards, and he poured over the traffic from Washington and OSS stations in the neutral countries of Europe. OSS Stockholm's reporting, he noticed, tended to plow the same ground over and over, covering the arrivals and departures of German freighters, behind-the-scenes trade-policy deliberations, and snippets from soused German seamen overheard in a bar cursing Hitler and grumbling that their nation's morale had plummeted. The OSS evaluated intelligence information using several criteria, primarily the importance of the subject matter and the credibility of the sourcing. He deemed OSS Stockholm's reporting to be lackluster on both scales.

This afternoon's intel batch arrived somewhat later than usual. There was just one piece from Stockholm, to the effect that Swedish authorities had blocked access to Delfin Square to reinforce the security surrounding the visiting German delegation. The members were being sequestered at the hotel, their meetings with the Swedish officials having been shifted to a conference room on site. A comment at the end pointed out that such stringent security measures were extremely unusual in the Swedish capital.

Verrick fixated on the choice of words. Sometimes field comments conveyed pivotal insights, hinting at what the collectors deduced from the information. Here they seemed to imply that the Swedes were acting in coordination with the Germans, who for unexplained reasons were spooked.

He showed Casey the report. The younger officer didn't furrow his brows or steeple his fingers as some people did when they concentrated; it seemed he was thinking all the time. He said, "I can send a cable to Stockholm asking them to dig deeper. German activities in Sweden are the station's primary collection mission. All transmissions from our European stations pass through here on their way to Washington, so if we notice an intriguing piece, it's not unusual that we take the initiative and prepare follow-up questions."

Wentworth had insisted that the mission involve neither MI-6's nor OSS Stockholm's contingent. A request to amplify an incident OSS Stockholm already had reported would seem to fall outside the restriction. Verrick said, "Send the request. Make it sound just mildly curious."

At Donovan's desk, Verrick listed what the Brits had said about GALILEO:

-- German admiral, age 56, from a prominent industrial family.

-- Served as an attaché at the German embassy in Moscow. Speaks fluent Russian.

-- Secretly a communist. Spied for the Soviets.

-- In July of 1941, the Gestapo tracked down his contact, Maria Toft. About to be captured, she shot herself.

-- At her residence, the Gestapo found torn-up notebook pages in code. When deciphered, they pointed to the existence of four sub-agents, never identified.

-- Posted for two years to the naval base at Kiel.

-- Suspicions of him lifted, probably only partially.

-- Promoted six months ago to the General Staff.

-- Appointed to head the negotiation team to Stockholm.

In Verrick's head rang his conversation with Lieutenant Rahilly at Bletchley Park:

The revelation about the sub-agents must have sent the Nazis into a frenzy.

Indeed, sir. One that has lasted years.

What role had the sub-agents played? They might have fed GALILEO secrets, been his messengers or sentinels, or performed logistical or other chores. Each might or might not have known about the others or the significance of what he or she was doing; they may not even have comprehended they were engaged in espionage. Whereas devotion to communism drove GALILEO, their motives could have been altogether different: personal loyalty, money, love of adventure.

Germany was a police state. The internal security organs faced few impediments to whatever ruthless crusades they chose to implement. That they hadn't been able to unmask any of the four was mystifying. True, the sub-agents might have fled, but if they'd done so, presumably their sudden absence would have alerted the SD. The admiral *had* come under the spotlight, and the SD had investigated him and his associates. When asked why they backed off, Lieutenant Rahilly wasn't sure they had, not altogether; the SD was too tenacious. She posited that they lacked the hard proof needed to arrest a senior Nazi. Wentworth had made the same supposition. Bletchley Park's ISOS-ISK unit had a good feel for the SD and passed its counterintelligence discoveries to MI-6.

What was Verrick missing?

I'm afraid there are things I cannot discuss, at least at present.

Verrick watched as, from a gutter pipe twenty-five feet above Grosvenor Street, a squirrel bounded across a gap to a window ledge. A slip and the creature would fall to its death. Along it cavorted, leaping to the next sill, its audacious acrobatics incurring no break in stride. Not the way espionage worked, not at all. Soon after the advent of the COI-OSS, British instructors had visited New York to tutor the inductees in tradecraft, the basic course comprising 38 one-hour sessions interspersed with practical exercises. Describing risk-taking, Verrick's instructor, a wizened MI-6 veteran, had used a moth-eaten metaphor: "There are bold pilots and there are old pilots, and the possession of the former attribute generally precludes the attainment of the latter." The comparison was imperfect; spies were daring by definition. The point was, the game required forethought, canniness, and discretion. You never leapt before you agonized over the risks.

At Bletchley Park, Captain Pell had said they'd deciphered the SD's GALILEO file when they'd revisited old collections of intercepts, the revelations occurring *after* the agent had gone dormant. But might MI-6 have known about GALILEO *before* the Germans shut down the cell in the summer of 1941? Was it possible that, via their putative NKVD source, MI-6 had been pilfering the Nazi secrets GALILEO had been slipping to the Soviets?

In his attorney's role, Verrick had been able to bill his clients for the time he spent thinking about their cases. Thinking was not just ruminating or staring out the window at squirrels. It meant he had to have mentally structured something.

The simplest structure was a timeline.

The SD had raided Maria Toft's residence in July 1941, just a few weeks after the Wehrmacht attacked the Soviet Union. Giddy from their 1940 triumphs, their blitzkrieg tactics largely unchecked, the Nazis expected to roll over the Soviets the same as they had the Poles, the French, the Dutch, the Norwegians, and other European peoples. The British, despite having beaten the Germans back in the aerial contest called the Battle of Britain, were locked in a desperate struggle. Though the United States was not yet in the war, German-American relations were less than rosy. The two nations had withdrawn their respective ambassadors in 1938, leaving their representation to lesser-rank diplomats until both missions closed in late 1941. In the interval, the consuls and military attachés at the U.S. Embassy in Berlin collected intelligence that the Roosevelt administration read with surging disquietude. The COI, OSS's predecessor organization, was in its infancy, having come into existence that same year. OSS London's file room contained nothing on the Maria Toft incident; the earliest of the dossiers Verrick had read was dated December 1941.

If the U.S. Embassy in Berlin had picked up whiffs of the German roll-up of the GALILEO spy ring, presumably they reported the information to Washington. Copies would have reached the embassy in London, the hub of American diplomacy in Europe.

He headed to Casey's office. "Do you know anyone at the embassy who can give me access to their old telegram files without asking a lot of questions?"

"Might be tricky," replied Casey. "In 1940, the British arrested a U.S. embassy code clerk who'd been slipping classified telegrams to a group of British fascists in league with the Germans. The embassy managed to keep it from becoming public, but the files have stayed under tight lock and key ever since."

"I don't plan to have lunch with any fascists."

Half an hour later, Casey stopped by. "Archie Sanders is expecting you. He's in the embassy's political-affairs section. A friend."

To stroll to the American Embassy at 1 Grosvenor Square took Verrick less than five minutes. The U.S. diplomatic mission to London traced to 1785, when John Adams assumed the mantle as American ambassador, the lone representative of a fledgling nation. What would the founding father have thought of this elephantine, sandbagged edifice guarded by armed U.S. Marines?

Archie Sanders turned out to be a fit-looking, wavy-haired fellow in his mid-thirties who said he knew Casey from New York's pre-war legal scene. Verrick followed him down a stairwell to a half-lit basement corridor and a metal door with two deadbolt locks the diplomat opened with separate keys. Expecting a dank reliquary, Verrick stepped into a dry, brightly lit, windowless room with checkered black and green linoleum floor tiles and whitewashed walls along which the uneven stacks of file cartons seemed to trace panoramic silhouettes of the Manhattan skyline. Sanders said, "When the war began, the volume of dispatches swelled massively. This is our temporary repository. The documents are filed by site of origin and boxed by year. Which are you looking for?"

"1941, from our embassy in Berlin."

Sanders led him to chest-and neck-high stacks labeled 1941. "Might take you a while. I'll be at extension 4897. If anyone happens by, they'll ask who you are and what you're doing here. Refer them to me. Otherwise, call when you're done and I'll escort you out." He pointed to a phone on the adjacent wall. "Sorry I can't offer you a nicer reading venue, but Bill said to keep your presence here on the hush-hush."

"I'll be plenty comfortable," said Verrick.

The door clanged shut.

He sat on a carton and opened the others one at a time, extracting manila folders crammed with telegrams and memoranda. Whoever had sorted the 1941 contents might have done better to toss them into the air. He found messages from 1940 and 1942. Some were dog eared, coffee stained, or folded back on themselves. You might judge the importance of any document by the scribblings in the margins. Three of the misfiled 1940 pieces bore the jotted initials JPK, which Verrick assumed belonged to Joseph P. Kennedy, the U.S. Ambassador to the United Kingdom until late October of that year. Kennedy infamously had incensed both his British hosts and the Roosevelt administration with utterances construed as encouraging to the Germans.

The Berlin dispatches related historical developments: the speeches of Hitler, manifestations of virulent Nazi antisemitism, the German invasion of the Soviet Union, the effects of British RAF night bombing on Germany. Some recounted meetings with German officials and contacts, others summarized local newspapers. Many were purely administrative, for instance, weekly rosters of the embassy staff. Handling the papers stripped the oil from his fingers and imparted a gritty black residue. He came upon extraneous scraps: a call slip, someone's laundry receipt, a Christmas card, a restaurant menu. No matter how seemingly trivial the oddments, he restored them in the same order. The glare from the ceiling lights stung his eyes. He blinked and kept on.

A dispatch from late July 1941 described a late-summer-evening's social gathering of diplomats at the residence of the Spanish ambassador to Berlin. The German attendees ebulliently predicted that England, cowed by the shipping losses in the Atlantic, the siege at Tobruk in North Africa, and the

Nazi juggernaut across the Soviet Union, would sue for peace. Verrick skimmed the narrative long since overtaken by events. He was tempted to forego the remainder of the text. Lawyerly and intelligence experience had taught him to read documents to the final line. The penultimate paragraph related how a German officer, 'the more loquacious for drink,' rambled that 'the Russians were finished' and 'we closed down a nest of their spies.' The German added, 'One of them was a German Südwestafrikaner who shot herself.'

Verrick stared at the line. Maria Toft?

The timelines seemed to correspond.

Wentworth hadn't said Toft was a German Afrikaner.

At the turn of the century, the British fighting the Boer War built internment camps to house populations whose villages they had razed. So appalling were the conditions in the camps, the British suffered an international public relations disaster, stirring a fresh wave of anti-colonial sentiment worldwide. Later, during World War I, the by-then autonomous South African government, adhering to the Boer War example and with British administrative help, interned the inhabitants of the German colony of Southwest Africa, including women and children. American diplomats, representatives of a neutral government at the time, inspected the camps and reported on the conditions. These had improved from the Boer War days. The internees made do, adapting to the regimens their administrators imposed on them. Most of the Southwest African colonists ended up being deported to Germany. Verrick knew all this because, in the 1920s, as a lawyer in the U.S. Justice Department's Anti-Trust Division, he'd investigated South African diamond-market issues and come across the inspectors' findings.

If Maria Toft were the German Southwest Afrikaner alluded to in the telegram, she may have endured some period of internment during the First World War. She'd have come to the attention of the British officers who administered the camps. Like a prison, an internment camp offers a ready means of control, assessment, and inducement, thus it presents an ideal venue for recruiting informants. Assuming that the British secretly had conscribed her while she was still in a camp, she'd have been working for them for a quarter of a century by the time of her death in 1941.

The files harbored no further mention of the spy incident. The final Berlin embassy telegram announced the mission's closure. He restacked the cartons and phoned Sanders, who came down to escort him out.

"Find what you wanted?" said Sanders.

"I'm not sure."

The diplomat grinned. No doubt he was used to deflections from the spooks. Verrick reminded himself to be grateful for the forbearance of thick-skinned friends.

When he emerged onto Grosvenor Square, night had fallen. The cable of the barrage balloon tethered in the park's center stretched upward to vanish in the mist. The window curtains in the surrounding buildings were properly shut, and the cars, their blackout lanterns groping dimly through the umbra, seemed to meander about like lost spirits.

– 35 –

Mid-February 1944

Fear had its deepest roots in experience. After a while, though the fear might seem to go away, the roots remained.

In 1924, the Bolsheviks renamed the city of Linnea's birth Leningrad, and like the rest of Russia, they turned it upside down, forcing the family of three out of their elegant apartment into two small rooms in a building crowded with displaced people. Only her father's status as a foreign businessman, and that he had obtained dual Russian-Swedish nationality for his wife and daughter, afforded them the extravagance of a private room. There the family of three slept amid the few belongings they'd managed to rescue before the Bolsheviks confiscated their spacious apartment. The sudden pauperism reduced Linnea's clothes to a few day-to-day sets and two special dresses, one pink, the other white, and the matching shoes her mother had insisted they take.

"Don't worry, everything will be fine when we get to Sweden," said her father.

Still scheduled despite the chaos was a birthday party for one of Linnea's friends. She had to decide on the pink or the white dress. Her mother said, "My choice would be the white. You have to make up your own mind."

For the first time in her life, the notion of consequences weighed. One dress was newer, the matching shoes older. The second was like the dress she thought another girl would wear. The fabric of the pink was scratchy tulle, the white soft chiffon. Which would she be happier with?

Later her mother recounted tales of those days: the food lines, public beatings of alleged oppositionists, soldiers at checkpoints, the belongings of the bourgeoisie dumped into the street. Old Russia had been a contented land, she said. The Czar and his family loved the people and were loved in return. When she spoke of the Czar, it was as if he were still in power. "The Czar must be firm. Russians cannot be ruled except with a stern hand." She brushed her flinty fingertips across Linnea's cheek. "I wish the golden light of that time could have shone on you, dear daughter. What madness, to have cast it off so peasants could kick their landlords and murder the Czar and his family. Did they expect the peasants to grow wise? What did they become? Leninists! Villains!"

Though Linnea retained only fragments of her life at age five, one memory had stayed as sharp as a thorn: On her walk to the party, the other pedestrians hooted sneeringly at her extravagant outfit.

She'd chosen the vivid pink.

She lay on the bed in the raspberry room, her mind roaming over the treacherous path to GALILEO. What if the Brits had it wrong? What if he *wasn't* a spy? She pictured herself at gunpoint, conjured the image of her fingernails pulled out, the bloody platelets squeezed in pliers.

Stop! Think of useful things!

She had memorized the escape plan and its variations. If the mission went to hell and she found herself alone and on the run, she was to phone a certain number and ask to speak to Mister Lukas Sederstrom. Informed that Sederstrom had fallen ill, she would head to the Norrmalm district and to the northeast corner of Berzelii Park, holding a rolled-up newspaper in her left hand, and wait for Lars or Marcus to pick her up. If one of them failed to show within 40 minutes of her arrival, she'd walk east on adjacent Strandvägen or board the number 22 streetcar and ride approximately one and one-half kilometers. At the residence of Mr. Smythe of the British Passport Office, she would knock, and when the diplomat appeared she'd utter the codeword ENUMERATION. If all else failed, she'd approach the British Embassy and ask for Smythe by name. "Don't pitch up at the Embassy unless they're hard on your heels," Avry had emphasized. The implication was that he would be out of the picture by then, arrested, injured, or dead.

"The rolled-up newspaper's the safe signal?"

"An aid to recognition. The safe signals are two-way and built into the phone dialog. If you ask for anyone other than Mister Lukas Sederstrom by full name, your interlocutor will know you've been taken and forced to make the call. If your interlocutor doesn't say the fellow's ill, you'll know he's been grabbed. If this was a German-occupied country, we'd use more elaborate signals. Here, preferable to stay as simple as possible, so things don't get jumbled."

At daybreak, she was out again. Snow flurries blanched the cityscape, where among the head-bent Swedes she was just another umbrous bundle. She'd left Avry asleep in the safehouse, slumped sideways on the stunted bed. He wanted to press on, believing he and Lars had resolved the conundrum at the plaza. What they'd done was to introduce another: the government man. To have no information about him troubled her immensely. A counterbalance was her trust in Lars. She had met him, his sons, and his wife. The unmet government man was different. To her, trust was not a second-hand commodity.

Proceed, or balk?

Her route vectored her behind a blocky, five-story apartment house whose opposite side faced Delfin Square. The back was angled so the windows had a fair-weather view of the Riddarfjärden Strait. Here were not one but two doors, each roughly one third of the building's length from the left or right corner. Which was the correct door?

She guessed what Avry would say: the one that opens.

The government man would arrange it, according to Lars.

The game is nothing if not rich in ambiguities.

Each of the doors topped a small landing with three stairs. The door handles were angled metal. Simple light fixtures crowned the frames. Were they illuminated at night? No, said the blackout regulations. Stockholmers tended to forget them. If the door light was on, nothing would shield her from the scrutiny of people who might be staring down from any of the thirty or so windows. They might alert the concierge, who would call the police.

The wind was at her back, her footsteps steady, the streets sedate. Her mind was not. It howled questions. Was she prepared? How would she react if things went wrong?

On the ship to America, speaking not a word of English, she'd joined a gang of American kids and become one of them. Her self-possession had not failed her then. Why should it now? She fit in, she was Swedish. In the hotel she would turn into a Russian. No problem, she *was* Russian. The script lines danced in her head; her repertoire was honed. The hotel badge and letter were ready. She didn't know which door to enter. If she had to, she'd try both. She didn't comprehend the hidden message in the Sophia letter. GALILEO wouldn't expect her to. To compartment certain details was an NKVD trademark, Avry had assured her.

It was still early when she returned to the safehouse. She made them breakfast and ate her share, letting him sleep.

He sat up. "You reconnoitered?"

"I did."

"How does it look?"

"There are two doors on the building's back side."

His bloodshot eyes tipped up. "And?"

"I'll enter whichever one's open."

"Good girl."

"I want to go over the scripts again before tonight."

"Surely." He pushed to his feet, exuding the odors of sweat and alcohol. The apartment afforded no place to take a bath. Probably the building harbored a tub somewhere. Unwise to use it. The recourse? Wipe yourself down with a wet cloth.

He spotted the plate of fried eggs. "For me?"

"Yes."

While he ate, she perched on the sink counter's edge, her feet on the windowsill, and tried to calm her thudding heart. The ambient sounds washed over her: his fork clinking busily on the plate, a cawing crow, a woman outside speaking to a child as ice crunched under their footsteps. A garbage-can lid squeaked, its timbre distinct from the gate's telltale screech. Her Suveran wristwatch ticked.

Mid-February 1944

The Swedes, displaying a sterling noblesse, agreed to shift the negotiations to the Delfin Hotel, which meant to the hotel's conference parlor. Sized to accommodate proceedings of lesser magnitude, the room's table strained to fit the negotiators and proved woefully inadequate to seat the assistants and notetakers. The latter categories therefore had to stand, lining the surrounding wall like chagrined latecomers at a sold-out performance. The members of the German delegation asked themselves how Admiral Diefenbach could have acquiesced so blithely to the demands of the haughty woman who claimed to be from the Reich Foreign Ministry, but whom the two delegation members from the ministry had never heard of. Was she Gestapo? SD? And how could the admiral, or anyone for that matter, have taken seriously the alleged threat of an attack by British commandos in a neutral capital? The account was so implausible they were embarrassed to refer to it with the Swedes.

Toward Elena, Oberst Wittermann, the delegation's administrator, took on a stilted formality. He loathed her, obviously, but as long as the admiral remained disposed to go along with her outrageous security exigencies, Wittermann could only do likewise.

On the evening of the first day of the negotiations, Diefenbach and the Swedish senior negotiator shared a cordial dinner in the hotel's dining salon. Not until 9:30 p.m. did the admiral return to his room, where soon afterward Wittermann stopped by to show him the draft report to Berlin. Elena at her insistence had reviewed the message, which dealt purely with the negotiations and contained no complaints about the security restrictions.

In the room directly below, Zurcher and Brindt took shifts at the listening table. The audio wires were affixed to a recording device, an AEG Magnetophon they didn't bother to flip on during Wittermann's routine telephone calls. Durst was making one of his frequent rounds of the hotel, checking and rechecking the security measures, and Elena was in her room resting after a trying day. Earlier she'd endured an obligatory visit with the hotel's manager, Herr Viklund, its purpose to assuage an ego as overstuffed as the man's body. Viklund apparently delegated the minutiae of running the hotel to his subordinates, reserving his time for loftier business like dealing with VIPs. He possessed a literal shine; when he smiled, which was nearly always, the oil on his puffy cheekbones glinted. The Nazi lapel pin did too. It looked like real gold, no doubt bestowed for his years of service to the party. Like a punctilious student, he kept his hands folded in front. He knew how to keep them clean.

He smiled. "A drink, madame?"

"No, thank you."

"A cigarette then, perhaps?"

"Very kind of you, but no."

"I take it Herr Axelsson has implemented your wishes to your satisfaction?"

"He has."

"I have every confidence he will continue to do so, but if you feel otherwise at any time, don't hesitate to contact me directly."

Across the desk she slid an envelope containing five thousand Swedish kronor. "We very much appreciate your cooperation."

He didn't glance at the envelope. "I am appreciative also."

Quite ingratiating, this fellow. She wondered who else's payroll he was on.

Having concluded the insipid protocol with Herr Viklund, she made her own security inspection to verify that her instructions were being carried out just so. Door guards—Swedish Nazis known to Axelsson—stood front and rear. The guards had been shown photographs of Diefenbach and lectured not to allow him to leave the hotel. She validated their alertness by showing the photograph she carried of Diefenbach. The guards recognized the image and parroted the instructions. Good. A fire door embossed the building's right side. Initially, she had directed Zurcher to install an interior hasp and to padlock the door shut. When Axelsson heard about it, he raised such a fuss—apparently to seal these doors was a blatant violation of the municipal fire regulations—that instead she ordered a guard posted inside next to the door. She checked. The guard was present, and he correctly regurgitated his instructions.

On the assumption the Soviets might attempt to infiltrate someone into the hotel, she'd had Axelsson bring in more trusted Swedish Nazis happy to work for the pay. He posted them as monitors on each of the eight guest-room floors between the elevator and the stair exit, equipping each monitor with by-name lists of the room occupants and hotel employees so they could verify the identities of all those who passed by. The maintenance staff ran telephone lines to the little tables where the monitors sat. The hotel's supply of spare telephones proved insufficient; telephone sets were in high demand in Sweden, and to acquire more would be costly, according to Axelsson. "Buy them," she told him, handing him more cash. As a further precaution, she had him instruct the hotel's telephone operators to ask all callers whether from within the hotel or without for their names and to log them, the call times, and the rooms connected. Would the NKVD try to contact GALILEO by phone? Probably not, but involving the telephone operators in this intrusive way would discourage the Soviets from trying anything.

She counseled Axelsson to give special care to the monitors he assigned to the delegation's floor, the fourth. Only the most trustworthy and diligent individuals would do. He gave the day shift to his wife, the soundest of women, he attested, and the night shift to a blond-haired, twenty-year-old Swede named Kallgren. When she raised her eyebrows at the boy's age, Axelsson said, "I know him. He speaks good German. Very reliable."

In the security manager's office, Elena briefed young Kallgren. "You must not quit your post for any reason. If you have to go to the bathroom, you must call Herr Axelsson for a replacement in your absence. If someone not on the roster shows up or something else unusual occurs, you must telephone Herr Axelsson immediately."

"Ja, bestimmt," replied Kallgren, his blue eyes shining earnestly.

She contemplated providing him with a firearm but rejected the idea for the complications it would introduce.

She examined the list of the guests who had made reservations. Most were German business travelers who'd stayed at the hotel on previous occasions. Axelsson at her request made it a priority to speak to the first-time guests upon or soon after their arrival, to confirm they were who they claimed to be. All this was well and good. It didn't mean the security coverage was complete. There were phones in the conference room. Diefenbach was observed to take calls there, probably from Swedish officials contacting him to clarify points under discussion. To monitor the phone calls was impractical, her resources insufficient. Diefenbach of course didn't know this. Neither did the Russians. She had to trust her instincts that his phone discussions pertained purely to the delegation's business.

She happened to be in Axelsson's office when two plainclothes Swedish policemen appeared in the lobby. She assumed their unannounced visit stemmed from the threat the German embassy had passed to the authorities, producing the checkpoints in Delfin Plaza. She alerted Axelsson, who sauntered out, tugging at the lapels of his new suit. "Gentlemen, may I help you?"

The policemen sported fedoras they didn't bother to take off. One of them, the younger, flashed his identification. "We're just having a look around." His casual tone implied he wasn't asking for the security manager's permission. In Sweden, as elsewhere, police behaved like police.

"I will be happy to show you around."

The older of the policemen, picking a piece of lint from his coat sleeve, said, "Don't trouble yourself."

"Oh, it's no trouble, I assure you."

Axelsson subsequently related to Elena the plainclothesmen's tour of the hotel. They passed by the front and rear door guards and the hall monitors, paused to stare curiously at the guard at the side fire exit, visited the guest floors, the kitchen, the laundry, and—to Axelsson's mortification—opened the door of the conference room where the Swedish-German negotiations were underway. "I warned the policemen that eminent officials were inside. They paid no heed to me and went in and brazenly looked around. It is not my fault if they caused a stir."

She guessed the detectives couldn't have cared less if they caused a stir. "What was the purpose of their visit?"

"To verify we were safe, they said."

"That was all?"

"Yes. They didn't even thank me."

The policemen must have sized up Axelsson as quickly as she had. His new suit already was showing sweat stains at the armpits, and his face was reddening, no doubt from the burdens she was putting him under. He wasn't really cut out for intense security demands. Might he suffer a heart attack? *Ach*, the things she had to worry about.

Calm down. If her mission proceeded smoothly, the casual attention of the Swedish police meant nothing. Complications would develop only in the event she must take extraordinary measures, for instance, if she captured a Soviet intruder. An urgent field interrogation would be in order. At Elena's nod, Brindt would break fingers, arms, cheekbones, actions the Swedish police, were they to get wind of, would frown upon severely. The hotel, though it catered to Germans, enjoyed no diplomatic status. Screams might attract attention. The police would respond and ask questions; no one could stop them. She would be wise to shift a captive away from the hotel to a more secure setting. The German embassy presented an option, but going there meant involving the ambassador, who at a minimum would complicate her task, and he might not give her the latitude she needed, or any at all.

She had been prepared to threaten Oberst Wittermann with spending the rest of his stay in the hold of a German freighter. It happened that such a vessel, the *Odelia*, was docked along the Saltsjö channel east of Stockholm. She gave Durst a copy of the document she'd shown to Axelsson and to Oberst Wittermann. Durst was to visit the ship and coordinate with the captain for a discreet space in the event her team had to make use of it. The captain of a German merchant ship had no choice but to accede to an official Reich request. Swedish authorities wouldn't board a German-flagged vessel, she'd been assured.

Once aboard, her team would be free from intrusion and could take whatever measures were necessary.

– 37 –

Mid-February 1944

It had become Verrick's routine to eat a leisurely breakfast at the guest house and take his sweet time about heading to the OSS building. This morning was different. When Casey arrived today at 7 a.m., Verrick was waiting. He related the line he'd read yesterday in the late July 1941 dispatch that a Southwest Afrikaner woman spying for the Soviet Union had shot herself. He added his recollections from the inspection reports of the South African internment camps. "Most of the civilians in those camps were deported to Germany. The Brits would have been looking for candidates they could recruit as spies."

Casey said, "You're guessing they recruited Maria Toft, and later they remolded her into a double agent against the Soviets?"

"What better explanation for how the Brits came by so much information about GALILEO?"

Casey leaned back, crossed his fingers over his stomach. "Even if the drunken German had his facts straight, it's a leap to think she was working for the British."

"A reasonable one, in my view. Serving as GALILEO's cutout, she'd have learned everything about the spy there was to know."

"Didn't you say the Sovs handled GALILEO in Russian? Where would a South African have learned Russian?"

"Who knows? Maybe she spent time in the Soviet Union for training."

"Are you going to notify Donovan?"

"I'd like to ask Wentworth first."

"Why? You'll just be putting him in a position where he has to fend you off."

"If Maria Toft was their agent, she was working for them long before the Soviets entered the war. The British and the Soviets weren't allies at the time."

"Doesn't matter," said Casey. "If the Sovs find out she was a double agent, they'll go through the roof. Wentworth won't take the chance."

Hard to argue. Cold national interest prevailed.

Verrick said, "Did you send the follow-up request to Stockholm?"

"Yesterday. I made it sound as you said, mildly curious. Nothing's come back yet."

"All right."

"There's another SHAEF shindig tonight at seven, at the Navy Building."

"Thanks. I'll pass."

"All the same, when I signed up to attend, I took the liberty of adding your name, in case you change your mind."

At 5 p.m. he walked to the guest house and ate dinner in the small dining parlor. He'd been meaning to write to Grace. On the writing desk in his room he laid out the onion-skin paper he'd brought with him from New York, and in his best cursive he related his three hours with Matt, describing the diesel-belching Army truck at the Marble Arch, their meandering stroll, the colorful window planters, the Fleet Street restaurant, the salmon-flecked noodles, the blasé wine. A few days old, the imprints had become as precious to him as any in his life. He addressed the envelope and tucked the flap, not sealing it. Censors scanned personal letters for anything they deemed militarily sensitive, their razor blades excising words, sentences, sometimes whole paragraphs, leaving papers with holes like blocky Swiss cheese. He said nothing about his son's Army training, an account of which might not eke past the censors intact.

His watch read 7:15 p.m. Should he make an appearance at the SHAEF party? Unlike Casey, he had no practical reason to socialize with the military staffs here. On the other hand, there wasn't much going on at the guest house.

He'd attended too many social functions crowded with strangers to risk losing his raincoat, so he left it at the guest house and in his sportscoat walked the five minutes to the checkpoint at the entry to Grosvenor Square. The drizzle dampened his shoulders and hair as a military policeman verified that his name was on the guest roster and passed him through to the red-brick edifice at the northwest corner. The bash was in the foyer, where the staff had trotted out a phonograph player, a cash bar, and a table with a generous bowl of pretzels, which if made available to the snack-deprived citizens of London would have drawn a crowd. Among the amply fed SHAEF bash-goers, it went largely untouched. He paid ten cents for a glass of ginger ale, munched on a pretzel, and scanned the crowd of diverse uniforms, guessing Casey would be wearing his black naval officer's garb.

"Amazing how young they all are."

Alongside him, Archie Sanders, the diplomat who had helped him yesterday at the embassy, had sidled up cradling a drink, probably not ginger ale.

"I was thinking the same thing," Verrick said.

"How are you enjoying your visit to London?"

"I haven't been able to see very much of the place."

"Nobody sees much of it, not really. London is immense. The only ones who know it well are the cabbies and maybe the cops."

"How long have you been stationed here?"

"Almost six years. I arrived in the summer of 1938."

Verrick detected in Sanders's speech the slightest trace of an adopted British accent, probably inevitable after having been exposed for so long. "Were you here for Munich?"

"My first crisis. In the company of the ambassador, I met Prime Minister Neville Chamberlain, a heady experience for a newly arrived embassy hand. People disparage Chamberlain, say he appeased Hitler and abandoned Czechoslovakia. At the time, the popular sentiment in Britain was solidly on his side. Nobody wanted war. Memories of the first one were too raw."

"Have you met Churchill?"

"On several occasions, all while playing the ambassador's notetaker. With American envoys, Mr. Churchill puts on his most charming demeanor. Less so with his own staff. A bloody tyrant, they say."

Verrick was curious what Sanders thought of Joseph Kennedy. The former ambassador might be a sore subject. A more popular figure came to mind. "Does Eisenhower ever make an appearance at these parties?"

"Are you joking?"

"Not at all. I'm a neophyte at this kind of thing."

"I doubt that. But you'd have as much chance of seeing Ike here as you would the Pope."

"Have you met him? Ike, that is."

"No. I *have* met Beetle Smith. Speaking of tyrants. The SHAEF folks are terrified of him. Reportedly he even went after your boss."

Verrick recalled Donovan's account of his two sessions with Smith. The discussions had been extremely close hold; word of the contents shouldn't have leaked out. "Any details?"

"We should step out."

They shifted to the rain-damp sidewalk behind the perimeter sawhorses. Sanders fished out a cigarette and struck a match, the flame casting a saffron patina on his wavy hair. "I caught a snippet of a conversation between the ambassador and one of the ranking SHAEF men. He said Donovan had some kind of tussle with the Brits, in the course of which he visited Beetle at 6 a.m. two days in a row. The timing implies something big. In the interval between, Beetle sent an urgent cable to Washington, and Ike made a secure phone call to General Marshall."

"Were there any specifics on the cable or call?"

"Only that they had to do with the Donovan ballyhoo, whatever it was about. Actually, I thought you might know."

"I do my best to stay out of matters at that level." In the intelligence business, to dissemble was unavoidable. More troubling was the automaticity with which it sprang to his lips, no forethought required.

"I see," said Sanders.

Donovan had mentioned the cable but said nothing about the Ike-Marshall secure phone call, meaning he hadn't known about it; Smith must not have told him.

A lorry puttered past, the diesel exhaust blending with the cigarette smoke. Trying not to cough, Verrick changed the subject. "How is it you've been in London so long? Did they give you a choice?"

"Oh, I might have moved on. Everyone else has. They burn out working twelve hours a day, seven days a week, and braving the blitz when it was on. Me, the job energizes. I've made quite a few contacts I can call upon to assist the embassy in a variety of ways, and I've been around long enough to learn the ropes. The expression's from the days of sailing ships. The bigger the ship, the more rigging, and the embassy is a helluva big ship. I love the sense of mastery."

"Makes you the one folks run to for help."

"I don't mind."

"What's the most important rope you've learned?"

Sanders grinned. "To watch what I say, and to whom."

"Let's go back inside."

Verrick had another drink, a gin and tonic, though if the mixture contained gin, he couldn't taste it. The SHAEF barmen must be watering down the cocktails.

Sanders said, "I just saw a friend of mine. Do you mind if I peel off?"

"Thanks for the chat."

The crowd seemed to have thickened. He scanned for Casey again. Must be stuck at the office.

Someone tapped him lightly at the elbow. "Mr. Verrick?"

"That's right."

The speaker was an absurdly baby-faced Army colonel. He wasn't holding a drink. "Could you follow me, sir?"

On the way past the pretzels table, Verrick deposited his drink, and they wended through a doorway to a flight of stairs. The colonel veered at the top into a dim corridor smelling of floor wax, the walls lined with cartons stacked three high—a move was underway, apparently—and to an office where the lights still glared and the typewriters clacked. Not everyone was free to pop in at the bash. A master sergeant glanced up wordlessly from his desk. The colonel proceeded to a closed inner door, where he tapped twice.

"Come in."

"Go ahead, sir," said the colonel, who pushed open the door and pulled it shut behind Verrick, leaving him alone with Lieutenant General Beetle Smith.

"Someone told me you were in the building, Mr. Verrick." Smith gestured to a chair in front. "I hope you don't mind."

How did Smith know he'd be at the party, or even who he was?

Smith said, "You're the one General Donovan put in with MI-6 to observe this show of theirs?"

"I am." When blindsided, best to keep one's utterances to the minimum.

"Has it gone as expected?"

"I think so. The training took place. The British seemed satisfied. They notified me that the team reached the destination. Our own reports say the Swedes have thrown up extra security around the German delegation in Stockholm. Other than that, no word."

"How did she do in the training? The American woman."

"Superbly." Worth a mention, that he hadn't been able to follow the training conducted in foreign languages, i.e., pretty much all of it? A superfluous detail.

"Do you expect an update?"

"Eventually." He might have added that the Brits so far had remained maddeningly unavailable. Best not to say.

Smith's eyes narrowed. No doubt he was appraising the OSS man's candor. "All right. Thank you."

Verrick had his own query: When this affair started, General Eisenhower reportedly sent a cable and made a secure phone call to Washington. Why the call—was there a part of this matter too sensitive to consign to paper?

He said not a word. Only an idiot would pose such a question to Beetle Smith and expect him to answer.

Outside the door, the baby-faced colonel was waiting to escort him downstairs.

They cleaned the apartment. Avry poured the remaining Brännvin down the drain and ripped up the map, burning the fragments in the ashtray. They left the suitcases with their spare clothes in the front room for Lars to fetch later.

Last check: Matisson badge in her inner left pocket, Sophia letter in her right. In the side pocket of her coat, she carried Lindstrom's ration-ticket booklet in case the police stopped her somewhere away from the Delfin Plaza. *No woman leaves her ration tickets behind.*

Avry had relocated the phone to the floor so he could rest his feet on the ottoman. Now the little black hexahedron that had stayed silent these four days jingled, and they regarded it as if it were a long-tailed rat that had scuttled in. Phones were intrinsically dangerous; operators could listen to your conversation. This one was for emergencies only. When Avry had called Lars, he'd done so from pay phones.

She lifted the receiver. *"Hallå?"*

"Let me speak to the other," said Lars in English.

Avry took the receiver and listened but said nothing. He hung up. "Lars says the badge style is correct."

Which they already knew, from her interaction with the maid at the market.

"He confirms too that our man is in the VIP suite, room 420, on the northwest corner, far left as you head down the hall."

From her memorized blueprint, she identified the spacious, two-room suite, the hotel's best.

"There's a guard at the fire door from the basement. You won't be able to get out that way."

"Okay." She had no plans to exit via the basement.

"There are monitors in the guest corridors. Like the door guards, they're not hotel employees but Swedish Nazis. Each sits at a table by the elevator with a roster to ID-check those who pass by and a phone handy to call the security manager. When you go by, just tell him the guest in 420 called about a problem in the room. Very routine."

"Do the monitors work the same shifts as the door guards?"

"Lars didn't know."

"What if the monitor was on the day shift with the real Matisson and remembers her? I'll be deep inside the hotel. How the hell do I get out?"

"Talk your way."

She stared at him.

"You're overthinking it," he said. "The monitor will be on his last night. Nine chances out of ten, he'll be bored out of his mind and not even ask who you are."

His attitude was too dismissive.

"You've got a fallback, haven't you? If they grab you and Matisson's blown, revert to Lindstrom. You're a thief who stole Matisson's ID, and you're in the hotel to pilfer valuables. Safe bet the hotel will just toss you out."

"If they don't?"

He tilted his head. They'd discussed all this before. "They'll summon the police, who if they bother to hold you for any length of time—which is doubtful—we'll win you back. The Swedes are reasonable. They know very well the Allies are winning the war."

"And if the hotel tosses me to the Germans instead?"

"We'll still get you out. Cling to each cover for as long as you can, saving the Russian identity until last. If they roughen things up, try to buy time. They'll want to interrogate you properly, and they can't do it at the hotel, so they'll keep you alive."

"What does 'roughen things up' consist of?"

"Crude methods. Maybe they'll break a finger or two."

He made it sound trivial.

He gripped her shoulders. Maybe he thought his hands' pressure would lend weight to what he said. "This is the moment you've prepared for. If you're nervous, it just means you're thinking. You're as primed as you can be. In months we could make you stronger, quicker, more skilled in the craft. What really counts, we can't give you, the prowess, no matter that all is bedlam, to keep your wits. That trait's already yours. I have complete faith in you."

"I don't need a pep talk."

"We all do, now and then. But listen closely. Two things you must remember. First: Never cease taking stock of your situation. Adapt to what's in front of you. The strongest people, the ones who survive, are the most adaptable. If you let go of your mind, you surrender everything.

"Second: Under no circumstances admit you're an American or working with the British. If you do, the mission will be blown. If you're in the hands of the Nazis, they'll kill you."

He let go of her shoulders, stepped away, and lit another cigarette. Through the smoke he said, "Oh, and Lars said it's snowing like hell. Better to wear your boots and carry your shoes."

– 38 –

Mid-February 1944

Verrick awoke with a pounding headache. Last night, having descended from his brief interview with Beetle Smith, he'd stayed later than intended at the SHAEF party. Sanders had let it slip to an Army G-2 officer that Verrick was a top dog in the OSS, and soon there were half a dozen Army intelligence men who wanted to meet him. Unable to say anything of what he was doing in England, he related his service with Donovan in World War I and at the New York law firm. They regaled him with half-whispered tales of turmoil in the G-2. Eisenhower wanted to appoint a British general as SHAEF's chief of intelligence. The Pentagon was pushing back. Few topics were as stultifying to Verrick as military politics. He listened anyway. They kept shoving gin and tonic refills into his hand, obliterating his one-drink-a-day limit. Even watered down, the drinks sufficed to impose a hellish hangover. Not until 9 a.m. did he reach Casey's office.

Casey said, "I saw you last night in the middle of a bunch of Army G-2ers. You looked like the belle of the ball."

"I've got bells ringing in my head to prove it."

Casey slid a stapled document across the desk. "Get ready for more."

OSS Stockholm had answered Casey's follow-up request about the unusual security measures the Swedes had imposed at Delfin Square. According to an official police contact, the Germans had told the Swedes that British commandos were planning to attack the Nazi trade delegation. The Delfin Hotel had taken extraordinary precautions, posting monitors in the hallways and extra guards to keep vigil and inform the security manager of anything suspicious.

His head still splitting from last night, he reread the text. Hard to imagine either the Germans or the Swedes believing that the British would mount a commando raid in a neutral capital, least of all to attack a diplomatic delegation. Nonetheless the Stockholm police had imposed the cordon outside while the Swedish Nazis set up the monitors and guards within. Security authorities sometimes enacted defenses against preposterous threats for no better reason than they had nothing to refute them. Such might be the explanation here. The implications were no less onerous. How could Linnea slip into a hotel swarming with alert watchers, get to GALILEO, and get out, when her cover as a hotel employee would withstand no scrutiny?

The prudent course: Call the whole thing off.

"This report will be shared with the Brits, I presume."

"Of course."

He said, "I need to talk to Wentworth."

Casey dialed the number that rang at 54 Broadway, a nondescript building across from the St. James Park Underground, and asked for Pearlman. He listened and hung up. "He's not available. They can't say when he might be back."

"Let's call again in an hour or so."

Casey smiled. "Do you mind if I offer a piece of friendly advice?"

"Shoot."

"Wentworth will see the report, and he'll either update you on what's happening in Stockholm, or he won't. Let it play out."

True, what Wentworth chose to do was beyond their control.

"We'll call anyway," said Verrick.

At ten minutes past midnight, Linnea treaded toward the apartment building, her footsteps leaving obvious prints in the snow. No one happening along could fail to discern that a person had approached from the waterfront side. The falling snow eventually would shroud her tracks, how soon was anyone's guess.

She chose the door on the left. The lights above were off. The stairs and door remained in plain sight of the windows, and anyone looking down would have to wonder whom this woman was and why she was reaching for the rear door so late at night.

If she goes about as if she knows what she's doing, she's given the benefit of the doubt.

She turned the handle. The door yawned open. Inside, an illuminated low slash rescued the space from pitch darkness. As her eyes adjusted, the dim curves of wheels materialized, then the frames of bicycles; the residents must store them here. Gingerly she groped ahead for the handle, turned it. A stubby hallway led to the foyer. Ambience spilled from a window onto polished floor tiles. A vacant table, presumably the concierge's, hunched to the right. She pressed her back against the wall, quickly pulled off her boots and socks, donned her shoes over her silk-stockinged feet, and dropped the boots and socks in the bag she then slid behind the bicycles. Better to leave them here than in the hotel.

In the lobby, the vague scent of oil wafted. From the bicycles? No, it wouldn't emanate past the back room. She guessed that the government man had applied oil to the door hinges and lock mechanism so they wouldn't squeak. The maybe-just-oiled front door made no sound when she twisted the handle and pulled. Out she ventured into the plaza. She hadn't viewed it from this angle or so late at night. The market lights were off, the dolphin fountain a blurry smudge to the left. Under the windswept snow, the ground kept the patterns of the cobblestones like a gossamer net cast on a pale lake. The hotel entrance carved out a saffron rectangle ahead.

Step purposefully, not too fast. Don't gaze around, don't slip in the snow. *The inverse of the woman who knows what she's doing is the one who plainly doesn't. She garners scrutiny.* Thirty paces. Snowflakes alighted on her hair and neck, melted, dripped.

The guard was not the same one she had observed on her foray last evening. Her age or slightly older, he scanned the plaza, quickly fixing on her. The white circle of his red Nazi party armband leered like a baneful third eye.

Two paces off, she said, *"God kväll."*

He ticked his head at the apartment building her tracks receded toward. "You live in that place?"

"No, I stopped by to see a friend."

She brought out her hotel identification badge. If he'd come across the real Hamfrid Matisson and remembered her, she'd have to bolt. He examined his roster, his gaze roving downward, his expression flashing no recognition, the facial bones bumping out like rocks in a cloth sack. Sedentary, the carapace would have been unattractive. His was animated. Maybe the liveliness had given him a measure of success chatting up the ladies.

He seemed to be taking his time checking her ID.

She slipped off her gloves, displaying fingers absent a wedding ring. Avry had warned her about the flare of her eyes, how they were too memorable. Instinct now told her not to hide them. When he looked up from his roster, it was into her eyes. He extended the ID and fumbled it. The card fell to the snow. "Sorry," he said, retrieving it and tapping off the flakes.

"That's all right."

"You're on the day shift, according to this." He waved the list. Not a challenge. An opener.

"Supervisors work whenever they're needed. Didn't they tell you?" Half disinterested, half flirty. *Much for you to learn, my dear sentinel.*

"Your friend in the building there, a boyfriend?"

"Girlfriend."

He smiled. "Perhaps I'll see you again, Miss Matisson."

"Don't freeze out here."

"Oh, I won't." He pulled open one of the glass-inlaid double doors for her.

Many times she'd visualized the lobby. The real venue was shabbier. The floor mats drooled melted snow and grit from the bottoms of shoes. The chandelier looked a bit dusty, its lights currently extinguished, and a pole mounted from a balcony suspended a Nazi flag in whose folds the swastika parodied a dead insect. On the walls, thick rectangular pilasters alternated with panels of faded olive wallpaper, the oil paintings within depicting boats on spumy seas and heroic seamen shouting openmouthed against the squall. Nobody could hear them.

Past the mats, her heel strikes resounded like gunshots. According to Mrs. Johansson, only one employee, usually very junior, manned the desk late at night. The fellow's white shirt collar was too big for the neck that swiveled to follow her. If he asked who she was, she would have to explain. If he knew the real Matisson, she'd have to run. "Here's where confidence buys your passage," Avry had coached her. "Stride in like you own the place. The desk custodian will be reluctant to challenge you. You've passed the door guard's look-over, haven't you? You belong."

So it proved.

Hotel staff clipped their ID badges to their pockets or collars. "Keep your coat on through the lobby to cover the badge so an employee doesn't read Matisson's name."

The hotel's elevator was one of the modern variety equipped with buttons so the guests and staff could use it in the absence of the operator, who went off-duty at midnight. Few tried. "Maybe in New York people are used to automatic elevators," Avry had said. "In Europe nobody trusts them. And what happens if you get stuck in there? Take the stairs. It means you'll have to pass by four monitors instead of one. Keep your badge hidden on the way up, so they don't glimpse the name. If they do engage with you, avoid a conversation if you can, but play it through rather than appear secretive. Smile."

"What if an employee shows up on the fourth floor?"

"Improvise. Say you forgot something downstairs. Wait a few minutes and circle back."

"Won't it look odd, me carrying the coat?"

"Worse to stash it where it doesn't belong. Hotel workers notice things out of place."

She folded her coat over her arm, gripped her badge ready to clip on, and climbed the stairs. The morning runs at the Lodge had bolstered her stamina, and she wasn't even huffing when she reached the fourth. Quickly she attached the badge to her blouse pocket. Here was the hall monitor. He looked barely out of his teens. Vivid blond hair splayed over his forehead, and his lanky legs protruded beneath the little table. By his left hand lay two rosters—probably one listing guests, the other employees—a notebook, and a phone whose wire trailed along the floor beneath strips of tape. "Hello," he said. His blue eyes flicked to her identification badge. "Have I seen you before, Miss Matisson?"

"I don't think so. Normally I work days. This evening I stayed late. I was just about to leave when I got a call from a guest."

He checked the roster. No flirtations from this one. No Nazi party armband either. He was alert and self-possessed.

"Very well, Miss Matisson."

He jotted an entry in his notebook.

A hint of spring brushed over London, flaring through the rifts in clouds as if they were cracks in winter's dun eggshell. On his strolls in nearby Hyde Park, sometimes Verrick unbuttoned his overcoat to let the momentary warmth seep through his shirt.

From Wentworth, nothing. Phone calls to 54 Broadway invariably yielded, "I'm afraid Mr. Pearlman is not available." Sometimes an extended pause prefaced the reply. Never did the person offer to take a message.

He asked Casey, "Do they often act this way?"

"Most of the time they're more polite about fending us off. It may be that Wentworth really *is* away. Men like him travel, to Turkey, Egypt, India, you name it, and they might be gone weeks on end. Usually they designate someone to act for them. In this case, he didn't. Just the hand we were dealt."

Verrick didn't like the analogy, which made it sound like a game. In New York, his interactions with competing attorneys sometimes had featured psychological games meant to throw the opponent off balance or to notch up the frustration. He'd been the recipient of such rude tactics, never the instigator. The window faced a bare tree where two wrens clutched to a branch the wind tossed up and down, a better metaphor, he thought. "What do we know about false flags?"

"You mean the tradecraft?" Casey too had attended the 38-hour basic espionage course, or some evolution thereof. "Tricky to pull off. The party who makes contact must be convincing in the feigned nationality, and the classic target should either be too naïve or reluctant for his own reasons to press for bona fides. Once intelligence requirements are introduced, the facade doesn't hold up, the real flag becoming too obvious to ignore. The trick is to hook the target before then in some other way, usually with money."

"Does GALILEO strike you as naïve or disinclined to challenge anyone's bona fides? Or as someone who would knowingly work for the Brits for money?"

"No. They might try to blackmail him at that point."

"And not be able to trust a damn word he says." Outside the window, the wrens suddenly darted off. "Anyway, how can they possibly run him in Berlin? He's unapproachable there. Wentworth even said so."

"They must have a means of communication prepared," said Casey. "The letter from Sophia supplies instructions, presumably."

"GALILEO is a senior military officer. Wouldn't someone like him be the most important agent the Soviets could have in Germany?"

"Sure, theoretically."

"For two and a half years, they haven't communicated with him. Even if they had an agent handler in Germany, he or she couldn't get close to him, because he's been under surveillance by the SD."

"The Brits think they can pull it off."

"How?"

"Whatever they plan to do, surely they've thought it through."

"They told us they need GALILEO to improve the invasion's chances of success. Intelligence on German intentions. He's been on the General Staff for six months. If they had a way to get to him in Berlin, why did they wait until now?"

"It might have taken them this long to set up the arrangements. Who knows? Maybe they have a cutout, another Maria Toft. Or somebody in the telephone company who can install a secret phone line in his house."

"In *Berlin?*"

"It's possible."

"Not there it isn't."

Casey lifted his palms. "I give up. What are you trying to say?"

"We're missing something."

"When aren't we?"

Casey was right. What spymaster, or lawyer for that matter, ever had all the information he wanted?

At Donovan's desk, Verrick stared at the latest pile of reports, and to mind came the infinity of briefs, filings, and evidence he'd gone through in his legal career in pursuit of insights or leverage. Sometimes the sought-after nugget never surfaced. He guessed he could read every line of intelligence in the world and not hit upon what he was looking for.

To clear his head, he took a walk.

According to Avry, Linnea's training gave her the patina of an agent handler, the look she needed to withstand GALILEO's scrutiny. He'd been the Russians' agent for more than a decade. To put in front of him a minimally trained person posing as an NKVD officer seemed like a tremendous gamble.

Why not just slip an envelope under his door?

A human face makes all the difference.

Avry had compared agents to brat children. The association was obvious, but to call agents brats was like saying a lawyer's clients were brats. Some might be, others surely were not. If imbuing her with the persona of an agent controller was so essential, why trivialize the subject matter?

What did the Sophia letter say? Why had the Nazis raised all the fuss about the delegation's security when the threat was patent nonsense? Why would the otherwise impeccably courteous Wentworth have flown the coop without appointing a stand-in, lending the Americans the impression he'd left them in the dark? Why hadn't the SD been able to track down the four sub-agents, the Moons? The truth was not forthcoming, just as it wasn't when our ancient ancestors had stared up at the real moon and asked themselves what the hell it was, that scarred yellow orb in the sky. The ancients couldn't say, because they didn't have enough information.

As if to prove it, retracing the meandering route he and his son had walked, Verrick managed to get lost again.

One thing he did know: Winston Churchill would not have involved himself as he had in the project unless he fully grasped its purpose. Which didn't mean the idea was flawless. Some of Churchill's brilliant schemes had faltered infamously at the point of execution. In World War I, his Gallipoli plan deteriorated into one of the war's bloodiest failures and precipitated the statesman's loss of his cabinet post and self-exile to the trenches as a lieutenant colonel in the British Army. Anzio, another of Churchill's babies and a fiasco currently playing out on the west coast of Italy, had not harmed him politically because the Americans were in tactical command. Yet the gritty debacles in Churchill's career had seared him with the implacable determination that OVERLORD *must* succeed. He would stake everything to achieve it.

The fact remained: To run GALILEO in Berlin was impossible. Hitler's counterintelligence machinery was too rampant. The spy had come under suspicion and undoubtedly surveillance. Yes, MI-6 was the world's best espionage service, and there were agents who could slip in and out of the German capital. The OSS's chief in Bern, Allen Dulles, had met some of the members of the so-called German resistance who for various reasons could travel between Berlin and neutral Switzerland and claimed to have access to influential Nazi officials. MI-6 probably had its own such agents. Regardless, anyone who came anywhere near GALILEO was certain to reap the closest scrutiny from the SD, a competent and dangerous apparatus. Knowing this, would the spy trust the contact, especially one he'd received in a letter shoved in his face?

A human face makes all the difference.

GALILEO would be as suspicious of the one as he was of the other.

You might say OVERLORD made it all worth risking. A simplistic statement. You didn't mount a gambit as complex as the GALILEO operation unless you could win the play, whatever it was. To communicate with the agent in Berlin, perhaps the Brits had a technical means, like a clandestine radio, that could preclude the need for traditional contact. Brevity codes could shorten the duration of signals. To use them required specialized instruction. Could MI-6 train GALILEO in the techniques and maintain the false flag? Not to mention that the Nazis' radio-triangulation capabilities had advanced so far, it was hard to imagine a transmitter, no matter how cunningly wielded, surviving in the heart of darkness. Other methods, dead drops and brush passes—more tradecraft Verrick had learned from the Brits—might be plied to communicate via an agent they could infiltrate into Germany, perhaps a third-country national innocuous enough not to provoke suspicion. You could even embed secrets in letters between Germany and Switzerland, using disappearing ink to evade the mail monitors. But the more strident the hostile counterintelligence regime, the trickier it was to get away with impersonal communication methods.

How had Lieutenant Rahilly put it? *The SD aren't the types to let go, once they've sunk their teeth in.*

Clandestine radios, dead drops, brush passes, and secret writing, suitable for certain categories of agents, were untenable for anyone who'd come under professional surveillance, as GALILEO had. And in terms of pervasive internal security, Berlin reigned supreme.

Meaning the Brits could not run him there.

Back to square one.

– 39 –

Mid-February 1944

Along the hallway, the carpet absorbed her heel strikes. The closed doors of the guest rooms streamed by. *Don't ogle the numbers; the real Hamfrid Matisson wouldn't have to.* At the last door on the left, standing primly, her feet together—she was still Matisson until she got inside—she tapped.

The face of the man who opened barely resembled the photo of the officer at the social gathering. Crevices of age had supplanted the wry amusement. His gray hair was mussed, his hazel eyes bloodshot. In bare feet, he was not as tall as she'd expected, topping her by just three inches or so.

He regarded her detachedly. *"Ja?"*

She pushed in, her shoulder brushing against his. He took an involuntary step back. She batted the door shut and redonned the coat she'd been carrying. Lights off, curtains open, the room wore a faint illumination from the snowy plaza cast up through the window glass. The ambience sheened on his silvery silk bath robe trimmed with elegant gold piping.

"Bitte?" he exclaimed.

She spread her feet to shoulder width and instantly became Vena Nadovska of the NKVD, Russian, born outside of Petrograd. Like Stalin, she was made of steel. The words of the mother tongue tumbled effortlessly from her lips. *"Zdravstvuyte,* comrade. Listen carefully, our time is short."

He stared, his expression radiating a blend of horror, surprise, and recognition.

It was the latter that counted. *Don't let GALILEO fool you, he'll have expected this encounter for a very long time.*

"I am here to bring you back to the righteous fold, comrade. You must perform your sacred duty. The future depends on it."

She delivered her spiel in formal, native Russian. His wide-eyed glare declared that he understood every word.

In the room below, elbows on the stacked steamer trunks, the leather-padded headphones clasped on his ears, Emil Zurcher sucked on a French *Gitanes* cigarette. He would have to remember to empty the ashtray; Elena had scolded him about the unsightly mound of butts. He hoped the twelve packs he'd brought along would outlast his three and one-half days in Stockholm. While he listened to nothing happening in Diefenbach's room, he busied his mind with the calculation that he could smoke four cigarettes each hour, provided he slept at least four hours each night, and still have a few *kippen* left at the end. In these rationed times—beginning in late 1941, a Berliner legally could purchase only six per day, and now it was down to three—to smoke so much was profligate. Not that he cared. He obtained his cigarettes via the SD's rationing-exempt commissary. Nicotine was the elixir that switched him on, and deprived of it, he drooped.

He shouldn't worry. Even if Elena wouldn't let him go out—his constant presence was critical to the mission, she insisted—he could dispatch Brindt to buy cigarettes. They would be rationed here, as elsewhere in Europe, but surely available on the black market. The Swedes might have *Latakias,* one of his favorites, or maybe even American cigarettes. Expensive, undoubtedly. So what? He had no wife or family to spend his money on. He was more at home with prostitutes, the more raucous, the better.

If the cigarettes did not sharpen him sufficiently, he had a vial of Pervitin, or methamphetamine, a drug commonly distributed to German soldiers and pilots to keep them alert. When on his own time, to blunt his edginess, he indulged other substances too. He had frequented *Opiumhöhlen* until the seedy dens, easy enough to find in the decadent era of the Weimar Republic, ceased to exist under the Nazis. These days morphine was the substitute. He made his way to backrooms where the emaciated users lay on the floors, their eyes glazed. Given the choice of being wrecked by alcohol in a fancy club or by morphine in a hovel, most people would have taken the former. He went for the floor.

Years ago, he had studied electrical engineering at Berlin's Technische Hochschule. If he hadn't found his calling with the Sicherheitsdienst, no doubt he'd have ended up designing electrical harnesses for airplanes or plying his talents in some other stupefyingly sedate way. He was too high-strung for such occupations. The SD was the burrow where he could practice his craft and otherwise do as he pleased, as long as he performed his duties with the wizardry his masters expected. His greatest feat had been Salon Kitty, an elegant Berlin nightclub that hosted foreign diplomats, Reich dignitaries, and other fat cats who relaxed on the Moroccan-leather divans alongside the beguiling hostesses. Unbeknownst to them, the SD secretly owned the place. In the parlors, he installed hidden microphones that captured every word spoken. His colleagues from the Salon Kitty job, learning of his education, had bestowed on him the annoying moniker *Professor Elektriker*. Few called him by it these days, though Brindt, of all people, had picked it up somewhere.

A peculiar fellow, Brindt, not quite the oaf he appeared to be. You wouldn't call him a regular Hans either. He liked to brag about how he'd hurt people, in one case describing how he'd snapped a man's arm like a breadstick. Grotesque. Why Elena put up with him was anyone's guess.

Zurcher grinned. Could you imagine the poor soul who found himself married to that woman?

His ears perked. Someone had knocked at Diefenbach's door, followed by a click Zurcher recognized as the door-handle mechanism. Had someone entered?

Out of caution, he pressed the 'record' button.

There followed the admiral's soft *"Ja?"* and the thump of the door falling shut. A pause. *"Bitte?"* blurted Diefenbach, his tone strangely like indignation.

A woman's voice erupted. In Russian!

Zurcher jolted upright. *Nimm ab die Hosen!*—Drop your pants!—it was happening!

He slapped the size-48 bare foot of Brindt dozing on the bed. "Get Elena, now!"

"Where is she?"

"Try her room first!" Please, let her be there.

Nothing if not obedient, Brindt dashed out the door to the next, knocking so loudly the raps penetrated Zurcher's headphones. Less than thirty seconds later, Elena was alongside in stocking feet, otherwise fully dressed. He handed her the headphones, and they pressed their ears together to take in a woman's insistent, melodramatic-sounding voice in Russian.

Elena said, "You are recording?"

"*Selbstverständlich.*" Self-evident. The light touch of irony was as far as he dared go to express that she needn't have asked. He'd witnessed her reactions to people who second-guessed her authority, an example being that chucklehead from the embassy—what was his name?—Gutermuth.

To Brindt she barked, "Tell Durst to post himself at once at Diefenbach's door, and to bring his pistol. No one gets in or out of the room."

Off dashed Brindt, hopping as he pulled on shoes over his bare feet.

To Zurcher: "Has Diefenbach said anything to the woman?"

"Not since she first entered, and he said *ja* and *bitte.*"

"Keep recording until I say otherwise."

Another extraneous command. What else did she think he would do? He said nothing, of course.

She hurried to her room and back, pushing her feet into her shoes and squeezing her Walther PPK pistol into the waistband of her deep-blue skirt behind the jacket.

Brindt's bulky silhouette filled the doorway. "Durst is headed upstairs on the run!" he panted out.

"Good. Stay with me."

Suddenly the hotel's fire-alarm bells commenced the most God-awful clangor.

Over the three minutes of Linnea's opening spiel, GALILEO's expression had mutated from shock to disbelief to what resembled a wincing resignation. Though he said nothing, he showed not an instant's doubt that she spoke for the NKVD. His wordlessness would have disconcerted her had she not rehearsed variations of how he would react, among them his dismay at what was transpiring.

It was imperative, she went on, that he perform his duty to the proletariat. He had done so before. He must resume. Now was the time.

Victory was at stake. "I have something you must read." She extended the letter that poked from the side-cut envelope. "It is from Sophia. You will understand."

She hoped so. *Better you don't have the specifics.* The letter's cumbrous word choices—doll house, potted plant, tiny rectangles, twists of foil, favorite uncle—harbored hidden meanings he presumably would grasp.

He glared at the outstretched letter.

"Comrade!"

He stepped backward.

"You are to take this and do as it instructs!"

As she had practiced, she held out the envelope. His flicking eyes harbored a meaning she could not fathom. He hadn't said anything since *"Bitte?"*

"You must obey!" She jabbed the letter at him like a sword. Her confidence was melting. In the practice iterations with Avry, the agent always had taken the letter. What if he refused? Her worries about bad theatrics had come true. Her arm-out pose smacked of absurdity.

He snatched the paper out of the envelope.

Brimming with relief, she folded the empty sleeve into her inside coat pocket. "It is in the old code you are quite familiar with. Read it."

He didn't. He moved to the room's coffee table, picked up a lighter whose metal skin glinted in the tepid glow through the window, held up the letter, and set it on fire.

"Stop!" she shouted. "It is forbidden!"

She advanced to rescue the letter. He fended her away. In the ashtray, the flames reduced the sheet to an incandescent fist whose vermilion edges condensed to black. He tapped his fingers on the ashes, crumpling them. The stench of burnt paper wafted.

They hadn't rehearsed a scenario in which he destroyed the letter without reading it. She had no response. What response was possible?

The flames had imprinted a blotch on her retinas, and momentarily sight impaired, she didn't see him move, didn't see him at all until he snatched her by the upper left arm. To the door he wrenched her. "Get out quickly, if you can," he whispered in Russian, his lips a centimeter from her ear, in a voice so low she barely heard, "and hope you have not killed me."

He shoved her into the hallway and shut the door.

Now the fire alarm clattered.

What had happened? In the bell's cacophony, it was as if the turmoil in her mind had transmuted into sound. She had followed the scripts exactly as rehearsed, personifying a Soviet intelligence officer, prickly attitude and all, and put into Diefenbach's hands the letter from Sophia.

That he'd then burned without reading.

What might she have done differently? What might she do still?

Nothing. The mission had failed. *She* had failed. Legs unsteady, she braced herself against the wall.

Reacting to the fire bell, guests began to spill from their rooms. These were the hotel's VIPs, the delegation members and important businessmen and their wives. They exhibited annoyance and confusion that might soon burst into panic. That it wasn't yet probably could be explained by the fact nobody smelled smoke, nobody except Linnea, the whiff of the burning letter still in her nostrils. A nearby door flew open, and out limped a man in pajamas and bath robe. In his forties, his hair clipped short, he gripped a cane, discomfort contorting his facial muscles. A swishing gap above his socked right foot blinked the patina of varnished wood. Every few steps, he craned anxiously over his shoulder, and when he reached the stair exit, he paused to let the others pass.

Behind him, Linnea halted too. Against the outflow of people through the stairway door squeezed a tall figure. His elongated, burn-graft-blotchy face did nothing to reassure those who noticed. The limping man reacted differently. In German he said, "Herr Durst, I haven't seen the admiral!"

Durst scanned the bunched-up guests, his gaze glissading inertly over her. "Go," he said. "I will take care of him."

The limping man seemed undecided. "Yes, all right," he muttered at length.

The gaggle melted into the stairwell. Should she stay? Might she try to speak to GALILEO again?

Durst already was striding toward GALILEO's room.

The letter was in ashes, the mission unrecoverable.

She trailed the limping man into the cataract.

40

Mid-February 1944

Elena and Brindt had to plow against the descending guests, who in their coats or with blankets tossed over their shoulders thronged the stairway. To Brindt she snapped, "You go first." If she hadn't had his bulk as a shield, the herd would have trampled her. A hotel fire was nothing to joke about. Everyone had read about the grand structures gone up in flames with people trapped inside. Five years ago, the *Nouvelles Galeries* department store in Paris had burned, taking 73 lives. Brindt made slow but steady headway through the torrent, and she followed his sockless ankles that in the general disarray seemed normal.

Was there a fire? Her senses were sharp, her ability to detect odors especially. Yes, a hint of smoke tinged the air, yet so vaguely it was as if she imagined it.

At length they reached the fourth floor, tranquil compared to the stairwell. Two persons remained: Durst, posed like a praetorian outside the door at the far end of the hallway, and the young monitor, who apparently had taken to heart her exhortation to stay at his post. He held a pencil. She barked at him, "Write nothing down!"

He lowered it. "Yes, madam. Should I go?"

"Stay where you are!"

He blinked a few times.

Toward Durst she strode, and he toward her, meeting in the middle. Above the alarm's din, she shouted, "Has anyone come out?"

"No. I watched for the admiral on the stairs."

She advanced to the door, Durst and Brindt flanking her. "Pistols," she commanded. "Do not shoot unless he does."

They braced. She knocked. She would arrest Diefenbach and the Russian woman, spirit them downstairs to her room, and detain them, at least until she had the Magnetophon tapes translated. She must proceed cautiously. The admiral was assigned to the General Staff. Her authority stretched only so far.

What if the woman turned out to be a Russian-speaking whore who somehow had slipped into the hotel? In Berlin, sexual indiscretions by ranking Nazis were common and invariably shrugged off. If she interfered, she would face severe criticism. But the woman she'd heard on the earphones had not spoken like a prostitute, at least not in Elena's mental panoply of how a prostitute should sound. She had been issuing directives. Elena recognized the tone; she used it herself to speak to underlings. In any language, the inflections meant *listen to me!* The woman must be from Soviet intelligence. Someone at the German embassy would understand Russian. She would summon them to listen to the recording once she had the two in custody.

No response. She rapped again. The ringing alarm was preventing her from hearing movement inside. She tried the handle. Locked. From her pocket she fished the pass key Axelsson had given her and guided it into the door lock. Durst and Brindt steadied their pistols. She glanced along the hallway to the boy still standing stiffly beside his table, his visage paling at the sight of the firearms. Should she have allowed him to leave? No, he had seen the woman who'd entered Diefenbach's room. His ability to identify her might prove crucial. She raised her finger to her lips and pushed open the door.

The room lights were off, the sole illumination the snow-glow the plaza cast up through the windows, their curtains pulled back. She advanced through the sitting room to the bedroom. The bedcovers were down.

Nobody was here.

The fire alarm suddenly halted. Instead of silence, what filled her ears were agitated voices from the plaza below. The bedroom window gaped open. She edged over and peered down. Immediately she retreated. "You can stop recording," she said to Zurcher at the other end of the microphone wires. "Diefenbach is dead."

Durst stepped to the window curtain and glanced furtively around the edge. "*Scheisse,*" he muttered, and rightly so. A world of shit was coming.

She picked up the bedside phone receiver and dialed zero. "Connect me to Herr Axelsson at once."

The security manager was on the line in seconds.

"You must block the front door immediately," she said.

"How? People are exiting. The fire alarm…"

"Block the door! Any guests outside, usher them back in. Nobody must leave. Do it immediately!"

"All right," he said uncertainly.

She hung up. To Durst, she said, "Search the room, thoroughly but discreetly."

Along the corridor, Brindt hurried to keep pace with her to the boy. She said, "Your name is Kallgren, *ja?*"

"*Ja,* madam."

"Before the fire alarm went off, a woman entered the room at the end of the hall." She pointed. "Who was she?"

"Miss Matisson, a hotel supervisor."

"You know this how?"

"She had an employee badge. Her name is on the roster. I noted her arrival in my logbook."

"Had you seen her before?"

"No. She said she works the day shift but stayed late..."

"Where is she now?"

"She exited when the fire alarm sounded, with the guests."

The woman must have been in the deluge of people Elena had passed coming up. "Would you recognize her if you saw her again?"

"Certainly."

On the stairs, the surge from the floors above had abated. Voices rose from those still crowded below. To descend through them would take time.

"Come with me. Bring your notebook and the rosters." She pressed the button to summon the elevator.

"Should we not take the stairs?" said Kallgren. "The fire regulations..." On the wall alongside the elevator buttons was a fire warning sign.

"The fire is a hoax. Do as I tell you."

To exit the hotel seemed to be taking quite a while. On the stairs behind the man with the wooden leg, Linnea squeezed among the guests making their way down.

The alarm had been too coincidental. Had Avry or Lars pulled it to ease her escape? But how? They'd have had to have been inside the hotel.

One more floor to go.

Oh, the look that would cross Avry's face when she told him GALILEO had burned the letter without reading it. *Didn't you try to stop him?* He'd blame her. Everyone would. Blame attached to the premise: If she had played her role correctly, the agent would have acceded. He had reacted otherwise. Ergo, her fault.

She'd played Vena Nadovska exactly the way London wanted her to! Feeble.

At the last landing above the lobby, lost in her ruminations, she took a minute to apprehend that no one was moving. There must be too many guests crowding the hotel exit. In front of her, the man with the wooden leg leaned against the handrail, obviously in pain. He gazed around, his eyes settling on her.

"Was zum Teufel geht hier vor?" What the hell was going on? Though she'd taken off her badge and slipped it in her coat pocket, he must have guessed from her outfit she was on the hotel staff.

"Ich weiss nicht." She didn't know. The part of the lobby she could see was crammed. Perhaps a guest had collapsed in the doorway, clogging it. "Are you all right?"

"Yes. Just my damn leg."

"Upstairs, did I hear you ask about the admiral?"

"Did you see him come out of his room?"

"No. Who was that man you were speaking to?"

"Herr Durst, security." His eyes narrowed. "Why do you want to know?"

"Just checking, that's our job."

The reply seemed to satisfy him. "You speak good German."

"Danke schön."

Above the din of voices, the elevator door to the right of the stairwell clanked open. Signs prominently advised: ANVÄND EJ HISSEN VID BRAND! Do not use the elevator in case of fire! Someone had ignored the warning and ridden the elevator down, dauntlessly operating the buttons. Three people now appeared. One was the blond-haired monitor from the fourth floor, hardly the type to flout the fire regulations. He seemed to be following behind a dark-haired woman who, unlike most of the people in the lobby, was fully dressed, her sapphire-blue business skirt and jacket exuding purposefulness. She in turn trailed in the wake of a tall, bulky fellow who was barging bull-like through the crowd.

As politely as she could, Linnea eased past the halted guests to the edge of the marble stairway wall and craned around to survey the lobby. The front doors were shut. A line of young men, among them the chatty guard she'd encountered on her way in, physically barred anyone from leaving.

What the hell?

The bulky man arrived by the door. There segued a kind of huddle, the dark-haired woman doing all the talking. The blond-haired monitor began perusing the crowd as if in search of someone. Diefenbach? If so, why was the monitor the one looking? Others must know the admiral better.

Might the monitor be looking for *her*?

The boy commenced to meander through the crowd, swiveling his head from side to side, eyes roving. The burly fellow trailed him.

Linnea spun and bustled up the stairs through the startled guests.

41

Mid-February 1944

She exited the stairwell at the first floor above the lobby. The corridor was vacant, the monitor's desk unoccupied. The fire alarm had chased everyone out.

Never cease taking stock of your situation. Adapt to what's in front of you.

There wasn't much time.

At one end of the hall was a window. There she undid the latch and strained to budge the stiff side handle, the window probably not having been opened in months. At length it squeaked inward. Beneath ran a walkway roughly ten feet wide edging the brick wall of the building alongside. On the hotel wall roughly midway along was a door she guessed was the fire exit Lars had said was guarded from within. From the window's base, the drop to the snow-covered aisle looked to be about fifteen feet.

She buttoned her coat. Shoes or no shoes? Leave them on.

Out she climbed, her rear end to the void, face to the corridor, squirming so that her feet dangled and her belly balanced on the fulcrum of the stone ledge. Her movements brushed the snow off the flange, and she hooked her fingertips over its sharp edge and lowered her arms to their full extension. *Press your feet and legs together, knees bent and spongy, or you'll sprain them on impact.* It was still snowing. Maybe the couple of inches of snow on the walkway would cushion her landing.

She let go. As soon as she hit the pavement, she knew she'd hurt her ankle.

Could she walk? *Ouch!* If she went slowly... To the square or the back alley? The guards who blocked the hotel's front doors were facing inward at the moment. She had no idea what might be happening in back, perhaps more guards. Toward the square she limped, dusting the snow off the front of her coat, and where the walkway opened, she cut sharply left to distance herself from the hotel's entrance. Nothing she could do about her tracks in the snow, but at least she could keep to the tenebrous periphery where she was less likely to be spotted.

Ahead hulked a garbage bin. The Matisson badge was incriminating. She tried to tear it up. The damn thing wouldn't rip, the cellophane was too stiff. She dunked it, twisted but whole, into the bin.

Voices murmured. A glance rearward revealed people gathered around a figure on the ground close to the far corner of the hotel. The wind fluttered the edges of a blanket shrouding the form. Someone turned on a flashlight, the beam straying over bare feet and the sheen of gray silk. A bathrobe.

The elegant gold piping was unmistakable.

Get out quickly, if you can, and hope you have not killed me.

She forced her step. Or tried to. Her ankle screamed. The supine figure's image clutched her. Don't look! Had she killed him? Saddled him with so much anxiety he'd jumped from his window? The same gusts that lifted the blanket buffeted her. Avry had told her an agent's life weighed heavily on a controller's mind. She'd not expected the sentiment to take root in hers. It nonetheless had.

Think about where you're going! She needed to reach the apartment building and head through to the waterfront road and to a side street half a kilometer away, where Lars waited in his truck.

...and hope you have not killed me.

Footfalls tapped urgently behind. She guessed whoever made them would race past her, maybe a runner in search of a doctor...

Viciously a hand gripped her hair and yanked her backwards. She thumped to the ground. Someone began dragging her.

"Diese Frau?" said a man in German. This woman?

"Ich weiss nicht. Zu dunkel ist," muttered another. I don't know. It's too dark.

They peered down as if at a reindeer shot in the woods. One was the blond-haired monitor from the fourth floor, the other the burly fellow from the lobby, his bare ankles protruding from shoes. The shoes pumped as he tugged her by the hair. The close-in brickwork of the neighboring building slid by like the walls of a train tunnel.

"Ahhhh!" she gritted.

"Stille!" snapped the big one. Quiet!

"Hjälp! Hjälp!" she yelped in Swedish. From ground level, her calls went nowhere.

Maybe he thought letting go of her hair would shut her up. He adjusted his grip, clenching his fist around the collar of her coat.

…your best chance is to get away from your opponent as swiftly as possible. Most importantly, avoid falling down.

She was already down. Her feet scraped the ground. Her shoes fell off. As if by courtesy, the blond boy collected them while the giant tugged her toward the passageway's midway door.

She fingered open her coat buttons, threw her arms back. The coat slipped away. Sideways she rolled to her feet and broke into a limping run. Faster! *Keep in mind, your first goal always is to get away. Don't hesitate; you mightn't have to run far, but you must be quick!*

She'd nearly made it to the plaza when the boy, the damned boy with his heron's legs, wrapped his arms around her from behind and lifted her off her feet. She pedaled air. Her shoes dangled from his fingers at her chest. *Best to strike him with a heavy object…* None availed, so she plucked a shoe from his grip, wriggled around, and swatted him in the eye with the heel, once, twice. He cried out and let go. She gained her balance and staggered toward the plaza. Her ankle shrieked. *Ignore the pain!*

The burly one had maneuvered around to block her. She darted to flank him. He shifted with more agility than his bulk said was possible. She jinked left, went right. He mirrored. She flailed at him with the shoe. Like a playful cat, he parried, until with an effortless snap he punched her in the left cheek.

Everything went blank.

Verrick dreamt of New York City. True to the venue, the dream frothed stress. A deadline pressed him to accomplish something he hadn't prepared for, and he'd frittered away his time to the last minute. Now he had to face the music, which came, oddly, with drums.

Someone was rapping at his door.

He groped, tugging the cord on the bedside lamp. The wind-up alarm clock said 4:45 a.m. "What?" he grunted.

"Sir, you're needed at headquarters. I have a car waiting outside."

A car to drive him a distance he could walk in three minutes? Must be important.

"I'll be right there."

Blinking away sleep, he brushed his teeth, staring at his scruffy face and bleary eyes in the mirror. Outside he climbed into the sedan that puffed white exhaust into the chilly night, and barely a minute later he climbed out at 70 Grosvenor and took the steps to the foyer two at a time. The duty officer said, "Sir, Lieutenant Casey's in his office."

The time was 4:56 a.m. What had happened? In Washington, the time was earlier, four minutes before midnight. Donovan must have transmitted an urgent message to OSS London. The contents could refer to anything in the world.

Upstairs, the only light seeped from the slit at the base of Casey's door. He tapped and entered. Casey looked altogether too wide awake. His eyeglass lenses facsimiled the lamp's green-shaded top. He held out a dispatch. "You're not going to like this."

It wasn't from Washington but from Stockholm, an intelligence report of immediate precedence titled APPARENT SUICIDE IN STOCKHOLM OF NAZI DELEGATION HEAD ADMIRAL DIEFENBACH. The source line read, 'An official of the Swedish government.' At approximately twenty-five minutes past midnight Stockholm time, German Admiral Constantine Diefenbach, garbed in a bathrobe and pajamas, had leapt or fallen from his fourth-floor window at the Delfin Hotel and plunged to the plaza below. The body bore no apparent signs of foul play. Swedish authorities had taken possession of the remains, which German embassy representatives were petitioning to have returned immediately. Tonight was to have been the delegation's last in Stockholm, the members scheduled to travel back to Berlin in the afternoon. In the report's ultimate line, the Swedish government official remarked that the German embassy's attitude was unhelpful and might preclude an autopsy.

"Our station got the report out fast," Casey said. "It's not daylight yet in Stockholm."

Linnea had said the approach would transpire between midnight and 1 a.m. on one of the nights of the delegation's stay, probably the last, the timing based on the circumstances extant. The hour of Diefenbach's suicide aligned.

Verrick said, "Let's send follow-up questions to Stockholm. What else have the Swedish police learned? Were there witnesses? Are they detaining anyone? Was anything found on the body?"

"Sure, right away."

Verrick picked up the phone on Casey's desk and dialed the familiar number that rang at 54 Broadway. The line was answered with a frigid "Hello?"

"I'd like to leave a message for Mr. Pearlman, to have him call me on an urgent basis."

A pause. Papers ruffled. The respondent, probably the overnight duty man, said, "I'm afraid he's not available to receive a message."

Tempting, to ask for someone who *was* available. He couldn't; knowledge of the mission was too restricted. He hung up.

Casey said, "Same as before?"

"The same."

"Do you think the false-flag attempt precipitated Diefenbach's death?"

"We have to assume so, don't you agree?"

"Too early to assume anything, in my view."

"Who at MI-6 other than Wentworth would have access to the GALILEO mission?"

"Menzies, certainly. And probably Claude Dansey, the main deputy. I'd stay away from Dansey. He's not a fan of ours."

"Can we contact Menzies?"

"Not without Donovan's say so."

"Let's ask."

So it was that two cables went out from 70 Grosvenor Street early that morning, the first to Washington, eyes only to Donovan referencing the report on Diefenbach's death, the second to OSS Stockholm with the follow-up questions. Casey typed both, passed the drafts to Verrick to review, and delivered them to the window of the communications office manned round the clock. Casey said, "We'll probably not hear anything back for a while. You might as well return to the guest house and grab some sleep."

"I'll stay."

"Suit yourself. I'm going home."

In Donovan's office, Verrick closed the door, hung his coat, and slumped at the desk, his head on folded arms. At the Hornchurch Lodge, he had perused the photos of the Delfin Hotel and the fronting plaza. The working assumption had been that the admiral would occupy one of the posh rooms on the fourth floor. What a scene it must have been: Diefenbach's broken corpse on the cobblestones outside, the police keeping people away.

He recalled Wentworth's iteration of the possibilities for how the admiral might react to the approach. Jumping out the window to his death had not been one of them.

Had Linnea been present when it happened?

At 7:10 a.m., the duty officer rapped on the door. He had a folded cable. "From Washington, sir."

Verrick opened it.

```
EYES ONLY VERRICK / CASEY
REQUEST TO CONTACT HEAD MI-6 DISAPPROVED.  AWAIT
MISSION READOUT.
DONOVAN
```

In other words, let it play out.

Inwardly he rebelled.

Outwardly he did as he'd been instructed.

Nothing.

42

Mid-February 1944

More from a compulsion to follow procedures than out of hope it might do any good, Elena sent Brindt and the boy Kallgren to rove the hotel in search of the Russian woman. She herself headed to the security office, where Axelsson threw what amounted to a minor fit. He could explain blocking the front door to prevent guests from leaving—a man had fallen to his death and lay outside—but in no way could he justify the guard at the side exit. The fire authorities would notice, and he would be held responsible.

"Very well, remove the guard," she said. The Russian bitch surely had fled the premises by now anyway.

Already the firemen had arrived and commenced to investigate. What had triggered the alarm? In a basement storage room, they located a metal bucket full of the scorched remnants of rags that appeared to have been soaked in cooking oil. None of the hotel staff who worked in the basement had been present so late. The fire captain theorized that someone had smelled the smoke from the short-lived but lively conflagration and yanked the fire alarm. Might the same person have set the fire? Naturally no one came forward to admit anything. After pondering the matter, the fire captain explained that, under certain conditions, oily rags could combust spontaneously.

Equal in probability, thought Elena, to the ghosts of ancient Vikings having slipped in and torched the rags.

From the doorway of Axelsson's office, she watched the lobby clear. Word of the suicide had spread, unsettling the guests. Some were so distraught that members of the hotel staff had to accompany them back to their rooms. Everything was under control, the staff reassured the guests.

Elena they could not console. Diefenbach was dead. The Russian woman who had visited him had escaped. The Soviets had set the sham fire and triggered the alarm, creating the bedlam needed to cover her exit. Rarely had Elena lost control of a situation. Tonight, it was impossible to conclude she hadn't.

The lobby steamed from the trampled snowmelt. Under her jacket, sweat from her armpits saturated her blouse. The juices in her stomach roiled. It was a hazard of the counterintelligence profession that a practitioner bore the reproach for uncaught spies. The same stress that motivated her to relentless efforts could make her sick, it had happened before, and now she was on the verge. In Berlin she would have to explain her actions to Fenzl and probably to SD Director Schellenberg. More worrisome was the grilling in store from RSHA head Kaltenbrunner, a scar-faced fanatic whose breath perpetually reeked of alcohol. Diefenbach had served on the General Staff, and she'd probably have to face them too, silver-hatted snobs of the mentality that a woman's claimed expertise in counterintelligence—or any complex field, for that matter—wasn't to be taken seriously. How would she defend herself? Everything depended on the recording. Translated, it might allay what otherwise would be judged a gross failure. Provided, of course, that no further catastrophe struck between now and then.

The Swedish police would investigate Diefenbach's death. They would locate the fourth-floor monitor and obtain his account of the mysterious woman and the arrival of Durst, Elena, and Brindt. The police might read the hallway monitor's notes of the woman's entrance to Diefenbach's room and the telephone operator's log entry of Elena's call from the room to Axelsson's office. They would examine Diefenbach's suite. Might they detect the listening devices? Probably not. Zurcher's work had been as immaculate as always. The possibility nonetheless worried her. Never could she live down the embarrassment, should the authorities of this paltry nation expose her team's activities.

She instructed Axelsson to have the operators immediately discontinue their call logging. As soon as he did so, from his desk phone, she dialed Gutermuth's home number and ordered him to locate a trusted Russian speaker and to escort him or her quickly to the hotel. Disconcerting, to put her fortunes in the hands of the maladroit SD attaché. On the positive side, he immediately recognized her voice on the phone, and having once incurred her displeasure, he seemed to know better than to protest that it was the middle of the night.

Across the lobby now clumped Brindt, still in his sockless shoes, *wet* shoes that were leaving tracks. And he seemed to be panting, his chest rising and falling. As useful as he could be, sometimes it embarrassed her to be seen in his company. No doubt he would report that the Russian woman was gone without a trace.

"We have her," he heaved out. "The one from Diefenbach's room."

She blinked. Brindt, the one the Gestapo had called *stumpfsinnig*, a simpleton, had done his job to perfection! She was so pleased she might have hugged him, were she the kind who hugged people. She wasn't. "Where?"

"Behind the boiler room. The firemen have finished their inspection. It is safe. The boy is guarding her."

Her eyebrows ticked up.

"It is all right," he said. "He helped me catch her. She is unconscious. We have her tied to a chair."

"Lead the way."

She tagged after him to the stairwell and down. Along the way he explained how he and the monitor from the fourth floor had emerged from the side door to the alley, where they observed footprints in the snow. The tracks originated not from the door but from a trampled spot below an open window where a person must have exited. They followed the tracks to the woman and captured her after a brief scuffle.

"Were you observed by anyone?"

"*Niemand.*" Nobody.

In the basement corridor lingered the faint odor of smoke from the bucket fire. Brindt had stashed the woman in a secluded pipe room behind the boiler, the overhanging pipes silent but for their occasional shy cavitations against their brackets. Neither the fire authorities nor the police would have cause to enter this nook. She was in her mid-twenties and faun haired. Hemp cord lashed her to a rough wooden chair, her forearms to its arms. The knot of the blindfolding handkerchief sprouted like the wings of a butterfly that had landed on her slumped-forward head.

On the room's opposite side, seemingly as far away from the bound figure as he could get, young Kallgren dawdled anxiously. A bruise reddened the brow above his left eye. "What will happen to her?" he quavered.

A delicate situation. Had this been Germany or one of the countries the Germans occupied, his squeamishness wouldn't have mattered. In Sweden, it augured complications. Elena adopted her pleasantest tone. "You must compose yourself, boy."

He seemed to tense even more.

"You helped seize this woman. Bravo."

"Will you harm her?"

"Of course not. We simply must ask her a few questions."

His trepidation appeared to subside. Axelsson had stationed him on the fourth floor for his trustworthiness. Was he so? Was he even a Nazi?

"Is this the woman you spoke of, who identified herself as Hamfrid Matisson and entered Admiral Diefenbach's room, number 420?"

"Yes."

"You are certain?"

"I am."

She advanced toward him. Involuntarily he stepped back. "Don't worry," she said soothingly, guiding him gently by the arm. "You have done your duty. You should be proud of yourself. You will be rewarded, I promise you."

"I don't care about that."

"Well, I care, and I shall see that you receive what you have earned. Go to Herr Axelsson's office and send him to me. Make sure you speak to no one else about what happened tonight, not to the police, the firemen, or your family. Play dumb. Can you do that?"

He nodded.

"Stay inside the security office until I tell you otherwise."

"Yes, madam."

"Go."

She weighed whether to have him killed.

She examined the items Brindt had collected from the woman: a coat, a pair of shoes, a man's Suveran wristwatch, a Swedish ration booklet in the name of Thorgun Lindstrom, and an empty envelope sleeve cut open diagonally at the side. No handbag, wallet, money, keys, or papers. Here too was an item he'd fetched from a trash bin, a blue Hotel Delfin employee badge in the name of Hamfrid Matisson. She'd discarded it there, he said. Encased in bent and twisted cellophane, the badge featured the woman's photo. Identifications in separate names didn't prove the woman was NKVD, but they pointed that way.

Axelsson arrived. She met him by the softly hissing boiler. His expression evinced unease; the building's mechanical substructure was unfamiliar territory to him, it seemed. He proceeded to douse Elena with more complaints. "The hotel has become a madhouse. A dead guest in front, a fire alarm, a possible case of arson. The police have questioned me. The newspapers have phoned, they even called Herr Viklund at his home. It is too much. Too much."

One weakling after another, she thought. Yet she still needed him. The night was racing ahead, and the challenges she faced were complex. Before daylight, she must discern the captive's true identity and either dispose of her or get her out of the hotel and to the freighter. "It will be over soon," she told him in the same pacifying tone she'd used with the boy. "In less than twenty-four hours, the delegation will depart, and I and my team as well. You will receive another payment, a generous one."

"What do you want me to do?"

"Collect up the monitors' notebooks and the operators' logs. Deliver them to my room. If the police ask, say you have given the records to a German official. Understand?"

"Yes."

"Then you may send the monitors away, except for the boy from the fourth floor. Keep him in your office."

"His eye is badly bruised. The police will notice and ask him what happened. I should go back there."

"You must tell me something first. Come here." She stepped into the pipe room, revealing the unconscious woman blindfolded and tied to the chair. "Who is she?"

Until now, he hadn't been aware of the woman's presence. He registered her mussed hair, the swollen cheek below the left eye, her shoeless feet in scuffed-up silk stockings on the cement floor. "I have no idea."

"You haven't seen her before?"

"Never."

"She claimed to be Hamfrid Matisson, a hotel employee."

"Hamfrid is our housekeeping supervisor. This woman doesn't look remotely like her."

She handed him the photo badge Brindt had fished out of the trash bin.

His untrimmed eyebrows arched up and down like racing caterpillars. "A forgery. It even has my faked signature on the back! Who would devise such a thing?"

She retrieved the badge. "Return to your office. Tell no one about this."

"Shouldn't I notify Hamfrid…"

"Not a word. Is that clear?"

"Yes." No doubt cringing inwardly, he flicked a last glance at the woman in the chair.

Jellyfish.

A more reliable figure appeared. In Diefenbach's hotel chamber, Durst had made a discovery. He handed her a folded letter. The text was in German, handwritten, and signed by somebody named Sophia. Strangely worded, it evoked a code. She slid it into the diagonally cut envelope sleeve. A perfect fit.

"Where?"

"On the desk, in plain sight. I checked it for secret writing. No indications." He meant he'd subjected the paper to the portable infrared light they had brought along in one of their trunks. The method was rudimentary; some formulas of secret writing did not fluoresce under infrared. Conclusive testing required elaborate chemical applications. But whether it harbored secret writing, or the text itself embodied a code, she was confident the SD's cryptologists in Berlin could unravel it.

She tucked the letter in her pocket.

The photograph on the Matisson card reminded her she needed proper photos of the woman. Fingerprints too. She sent Durst to fetch the camera and fingerprint kit. Minutes later he was snapping photos, straight-on and in profile, of the woman with the blindfold removed, Brindt to the side leveling her head like a trophy as the flashbulbs went off. Then they inked her fingers, rolling the tips on a standard card. Fastidiously Durst wiped the ink off her skin afterward.

"Carry the film and fingerprint card on your person. This too." She handed Durst the forged ID. "Head to the rooms and begin packing. Leave the Magnetophon out."

She gripped the woman's chin and bobbed the head a few times. "Wake up, *Dornröschen.*" Sleeping beauty.

A groan.

Elena said, "Look at me!"

The eyelids lifted, and Elena regarded the woman's eyes, their intensity remarkable.

"Whoever you are," Elena said, "you are no housekeeper."

43

Mid-February 1944

Yellow and red steam pipes gridded the concrete ceiling, the wheels of valves blossoming out, stains probably from piled coal blackening the brick walls. She expected to smell coal dust; she smelled sweat. Someone crudely but firmly had tied her to a bare-wood chair. Her face hurt. The dark-haired woman she'd spotted in the lobby stared down like a stern schoolteacher whose lesson she had neglected to complete. The woman was saying something in German. "What is your name? You understand me, I am certain."

Any Swede, whether he or she spoke German or not, would know that *'Wie heisst du?'* meant *'Vad heter du?'* in Swedish. "Hamfrid Matisson," she muttered.

"You are lying. I have confirmed you are not Hamfrid Matisson. Who are you?"

Confirmed? The woman must have located someone who knew the real Matisson. The tussle in the alley gushed back, the big German's fist slamming into her head. Which also explained the ache. She guessed she was in the hotel's basement.

The woman slapped her across the face. Ouch!

And if they toss me to the Germans instead?

We'll still get you out. Cling to your covers for as long as you can.

Another slap.

If they roughen things up, try to buy time.

How much did she have?

Yet another affliction accompanied the counterintelligence profession. In moderation, paranoia could be beneficial, dispelling the complacency ordinary people naively indulged. A larger dose was toxic. Elena had seen colleagues succumb, the gears in their minds run amok with the suspicion that everyone they encountered could be an enemy agent. The problem lay in the ever-widening permutations. As in a game of chess, the more moves one contemplated, the more they multiplied toward the infinite. Elena's mind was beginning to spin in that direction. Who had set the fire? The assumption that the Soviets were responsible meant at least one additional collaborator lurked in the hotel. Surely the NKVD would have adjudged the hotel with its connections to Germany to be a priority intelligence target, and they would have tried to recruit people inside. Whom had they gotten to? A member of the staff? One of the monitors? Axelsson? Viklund? At any minute, Soviet agents might barge in with pistols and turn the pipe room into an abattoir.

It was then that Gutermuth, the SD attaché, showed up. His presence in the outer boiler room sired the same distasteful expression on him as it had on Axelsson, the austere setting apparently offending his cultured tastes. On his nose perched a pince nez he perhaps thought made him look distinguished. Trailing came a thin fellow with albino-blond hair rising toward the front like the spritely crest of a sea wave. She met them by the boiler, out of sight and earshot of the woman in the chair.

Gutermuth said, "Madam, I regret to report that Admiral Diefenbach's death has created a serious controversy. By morning, it will be the topic of discussion all across Sweden."

Her patience slipped another notch. Did he think she wasn't mindful she had a crisis on her hands? Beneath his veneer of deference, she detected smugness. No doubt his title at the embassy had inflated his self-importance. She wanted to crush him. Now was not the time. She flicked her head at the pale man. "The Russian speaker?"

Gutermuth introduced the interpreter, whose name was Schlosser.

"Go to room 320," she told Schlosser. "A man named Zurcher is waiting there. He has a recording of a woman speaking in Russian. Listen to it and return here with a transcript in German as soon as you can."

Gutermuth attempted to follow in Schlosser's wake. Clearly to be in her presence discomfited him. "You stay," she snapped. "How well do you speak Swedish?"

"I am certified as fluent."

Certified. What a strutting peacock. "Come with me."

As with Axelsson, the sight of the disheveled woman tied to the chair disconcerted the attaché. His breathing quickened. An officer of the SD should be inured to such things. Her low opinion of him plunged to a new depth.

"Tell her in Swedish we are certain she is not Hamfrid Matisson."

He translated in a tone almost apologetic, or so it sounded to Elena, using words like *Vänligen* that she'd heard in the hotel, taking it to be a form of *bitte*, or please, and *flicka*, meaning *Mädchen*, pointless, time-consuming courtesies.

The woman replied in Swedish. Gutermuth said, "She says we should let her go. We are not the police; we have no authority to detain anyone. She is a Swedish citizen and has legal rights. Which is correct."

"Don't tell me what is correct. She must *prove* her nationality."

"Plainly she is Swedish. Her accent is of Stockholm."

"Ask her where are her papers?"

"The Swedes don't carry papers."

Infuriating. "Ask her anyway!"

The woman responded to the effect that she would be happy to explain everything to the police, who should be summoned, otherwise she should be released immediately.

The antics were devouring precious time. To Brindt, Elena said, "Cut her finger off."

Gutermuth's eyes widened. "You cannot be serious."

"No? Watch."

Nothing lent her command more credibility than Brindt, already in motion and unfolding a pocketknife. When he seized the woman's left hand, she blurted something out.

Gutermuth hurriedly translated. "She says to wait, she will explain."

Elena ticked her head to suspend her order. At once Brindt retreated. "Inform her I have no patience for lies," she said. "She had better admit her true identity at once."

An exchange ensued. "She says her real name is Thorgun Lindstrom," said Gutermuth. "She acquired Matisson's identity card from a man who sells stolen and forged documents. Tonight she entered the hotel intending to visit the rooms of guests and pilfer whatever treasures she could. People commonly leave jewels or money lying about, and if they glance away, she snatches them." Gutermuth tipped his head at the tied-up woman as if her revelation satisfied him.

Profound, the man's stupidity.

Elena said, "Where are the things she stole from the rooms she visited?"

"She says the fire alarm disrupted her plans, and she had to leave without taking anything."

A fallback tale. The bitch was stalling. In four hours, dawn would arrive. Crucial to get her to the merchant vessel *Odelia* before then.

In German, Gutermuth said, "Madam, may I speak to you in private?"

Through years of strife and humiliation, Gutermuth had served his country. As an infantryman in World War I, he breathed in chlorine gas, scarring his lungs. After the war, he endured the effects of the cruelly punitive Versailles Treaty and the diminution of the German military. Reduced to the lowest rank, he guarded buildings while communist agitators threw rocks at him, a chaotic scene not uncommon in the decade of chaos that helped precipitate Hitler's ascension to power. The National Socialist leader grew popular promising to right the wrongs done to the Fatherland and ranting about the back-stabbing Jews and communists. In such times, the German people historically had looked to a great champion like Charlemagne or Frederick the Great. Might Hitler be such a savior, as the Nazis claimed him to be? Giving them the benefit of the doubt, Gutermuth joined the party and made his way to the SD.

At the debut of Germany's next war, he expected his life to become tumultuous again. SD officers were being plucked out of Berlin and posted close to the fighting. When a vacancy appeared for attaché duty in Stockholm—his mother was Swedish and had steeped him in the language— he submitted his application with no real hope it would win approval; he boasted no special connections. Luck smiled, the stars aligned, say what you will, somehow he got the job. He arrived in Stockholm in the Spring of 1940, in the wake of the Nazi invasion of Denmark and Norway, to witness the

Swedes acquiesce to German demands that Wehrmacht troops be permitted to routinely transit Sweden overland to and from Norway. Heady, the days when all of Europe shuddered at German power. To be a Reich emissary was to bask in the luster. Proudly he ambled into the lobby of the Grand Hotel, his sharp heels tapping on the porcelain-tiled floor, his fingers gliding on the polished mahogany rail of the double staircase. In the dining room, under the eight-meter-high ceiling, the waiters had fawned over him.

Almost four years later, he was still here, basking less. The war was not going well for Germany; the balance of power had swung in favor of the Allies. Among his duties, he culled the daily Swedish newspapers, reading the embarrassingly straightforward accounts of German setbacks. He did not read all the newspapers, there were too many. To cover the field, he relied on a team of Swedish local hires, and his daily interactions with them had attuned his ear to the local accents and sharpened his insights into the nation's mentality. When objectionable articles appeared, for instance slanderous and unfounded allegations of Nazi atrocities in eastern Europe, he prepared indignant-sounding diplomatic notes he delivered to the Swedish government. The notes used to have an intimidating effect. These days, the minute he walked away from handing over his huffily worded *bouts de papier* to the Swedish Foreign Ministry, he guessed the recipients casually flipped them in the trash.

Unaltered was the most significant aspect of his presence in Sweden: Nobody was shooting at him. To remain here until the war's end was his ambition. Why shouldn't it be? Had he not endured his life's share of hardships?

Having dutifully followed the instructions to put himself at the disposal of the SD team from Berlin, it was outrageous that he should have to cower under the thumb of this menacing woman who comported herself as if she were in a German-occupied country. Even in this hotel the Nazis controlled, her actions were irregular, to say the least. But to threaten to mutilate a Swedish citizen? Pure madness. People would find out. Stockholm was a cauldron of whispers.

They adjourned to the boiler room where, his stature formal, heels together, he said, "Madam, to detain this woman poses an enormous risk to German relations with Sweden. She appears to be a petty thief, of no importance, yet dangerous indeed if kept in our custody. We cannot hold a

Swedish citizen against her will. Certainly we must not harm her. There was a time when the Swedes were wary of offending us. To this day, they caution their newspapers not to print troublesome stories about Germany. Yet Sweden is a democracy, and increasingly the press shrugs off the restraints. As I told you, the admiral's death will attract scrutiny. If word of this woman's detention leaks, it will create a scandal of the first order."

"And how would it leak? Through you?"

"Certainly not! My concern is the welfare of German-Swedish relations."

"You speak as if such things are more important than German security. Are you a traitor, Gutermuth?"

"Madam…"

"I should have you arrested and remanded to the Fatherland. To do so is within my authority." She regarded him with a sneer, reminding him of the cat that has sunk her claws mortally into her prey and licks them to savor the clinging blood. How could he have been so foolhardy as to argue with her? To wrench him from his sanctuary was not only within her power, she would relish it.

He clenched his jaw to still the quivering. "Madam, I regret if I have given offense. I didn't…"

"Shut up. I have no time. Are you prepared to carry out my orders or not?"

"I am."

"You are to complete three tasks. Arrange for an automobile with diplomatic license plates to be brought to the rear of the hotel. Deliver the keys to my hand within the hour."

"Yes, madam."

"Take our trunks from room 320 and transport them to the embassy. Keep them under lock and key for the time being, then move them to planeside for the delegation's flight to Berlin this afternoon. I and my team shall travel with them."

"Yes, madam."

"And I shall require a vial of sodium pentothal and a syringe. Bring these at the same time as the automobile keys."

Sodium pentothal was a common drug used in anesthesia. His contacts probably could obtain a small quantity during the business day. To phone them in the middle of the night would stir curiosity, and the Swedish authorities very well might hear of it.

To acquire the chemical within the hour?

Impossible.

"I will do my utmost, madam," he said.

"You had better."

– 44 –

Mid-February 1944

The attaché, Elena guessed, would bring the car and arrange for the movement of the trunks. He would fail to deliver the sodium pentothal. He knew it and was afraid to say. A coward and a traitor. She should destroy him.

Trivial. A task for another day. To deal with the woman in the chair required her complete concentration.

The Russian speaker Schlosser returned, breathless as if he had run. Elena liked when people overexerted themselves on her behalf, and to hear him pant amid the boiler's hiss lifted her mood. "What have you found?" she said.

He handed her four sheets of handwritten transcript, some words crossed out, others inserted. "The woman speaks in native Russian," he wheezed, his voice scratchy, as if he had a throat cold, "with what sounds like a Leningrad accent. I listened twice, still I am not completely certain of the accent. You said to get the transcript to you quickly."

Elena read. The woman had done almost all the speaking. After his startled *"bitte?"* Diefenbach said nothing. The woman addressed him as 'comrade,' exhorting him to do his duty and alluding to his past accomplishments. Now he must do more. She had brought him instructions from Sophia.

Sophia—the name on the letter Durst had found in the admiral's room.

'You are to take this,' the transcript went on, no doubt referring to the letter. 'It is in the old code you are quite familiar with. Read it.'

So Diefenbach *was* GALILEO. The recording and the letter furnished the irrefutable evidence that justified her years of effort on the case. Rare, to be able to use the word *proof;* so much in the field of counterintelligence hovered eternally out of grasp. Here was a triumph! Those who had quipped behind her back of her endless hunt for the 'thousand-year spy' would fall silent.

The final line: 'Stop! It is forbidden!' Schlosser had annotated in German, *keine weiteren Ausdrücke.* No further expressions.

She frowned. *What* was forbidden? Had the woman blurted this in reaction to Diefenbach throwing himself from the window? And why had the admiral said nothing after *bitte*? Or had he spoken, and the microphones not picked it up?

She folded the transcript sheets and slipped them in her pocket alongside the letter.

Zurcher entered, lugging, oddly, the bulky Magnetophon in its case. He rested it on the floor, undid the cover hinges, turned to Elena, and said, "You must listen to the recording."

"Later. I have no time now."

"Please, it is important." Unusual, Zurcher's insistence. He knew better than to argue with her. Trusting his instincts, she nodded. He plugged in the headphone jack and gently clasped the phones around her ears. The device had an internal battery adequate for brief use. Leaning in so he could listen too, he pressed the ANLAUF button.

Diefenbach's *'bitte?'* introduced the woman's dictate-like exhortations in Russian. These went on for a time, the voice sounding the same as the captive's. The flow of words grew syncopated and ended in an agitated outburst Elena guessed meant Stop! It is forbidden! There followed what might have been a whisper, a creak—the door opening?—and the jangling of the fire alarm.

She lifted her gaze to Zurcher, whose expression signaled to keep listening.

A more prominent thud penetrated the ringing alarm, then some rustles, another interval of silence, and distinct knocks. Momentarily the alarm racket halted. There were muted, distressed voices in the background. Finally, she heard her own: "You can stop recording. Diefenbach is dead."

He clicked off the replay and said, "I analyzed the noises. I think she killed him. Perhaps he tried to attack her. It's why she said, 'Stop! It is forbidden!' She must have struck him to disable him. The creak was when she opened the window, the rustles when she dragged him across the floor and threw him out. It must have been her. No one else was in there."

Zurcher was clever, ingenious really, but he seemed to have taken his analysis too far. Why would Diefenbach have attacked the woman? To have done so suggested he was innocent, a notion wholly at odds with the rest. To have lost emotional control ran contrary to the behavior the SD's surveillants long had observed in him. And why would she have thrown him from the window? How could she have? She'd have had to shove him when he was off balance, or else somehow incapacitate him and muscle his dead weight through the opening. If the NKVD had intended such truculent handiwork, they'd have sent a man. Far more plausible was that Diefenbach killed *himself,* either in the woman's company or upon her exit. He must have guessed his suite was bugged and German security had listened to her statements. He foresaw his imminent arrest, transport to Germany, and interrogation. It made perfect sense that he would kill himself, as his cutout Maria Toft had done, putting himself beyond the clutch of the counterintelligence apparatus and safeguarding his four sub-agents, the Moons. The SD hadn't uncovered any of them.

She removed the headphones and handed them to Zurcher. "Say nothing whatsoever of this theory of yours. Forget about it. Do you understand?"

"*Natürlich.* "

"The tape is vitally important. Make sure it is securely packed and the case locked."

"I need a few more minutes to sever the wires to the *Wanzen.* "

"Do so. Then stand by to depart by car."

Zurcher left. She turned to Schlosser. "Listen carefully. This is what I want you to say to the woman in Russian."

The latest entrant bore a likeness to Christopher, his wavy hair as sallow as vanilla ice cream, his chin pointy. Linnea half expected a plagiarism to spout from his lips.

"What is your name?" he said in Russian. His voice didn't sound like Christopher's, rather as a skeleton's would, raspy with bone dust. The accent said he was German. Her fallback to the Swedish thief Thorgun Lindstrom seemed to have placated the civilized, Swedish-speaking older fellow with the pince nez. More trouble than it was worth, to detain a petty criminal. Wiser to let her go.

To have introduced this Russian speaker meant the dark-haired German woman, the one who'd told the brute to cut off her finger, wasn't buying it.

"*Jag förstår dig inte,*" she said in Swedish. I don't understand you.

"Oh, but you do." Christopher-hair must speak Swedish, too.

"I don't understand you," she repeated.

"You are Russian, from Leningrad."

How could he know that? Keep your face impassive. Show no reaction. You don't comprehend a word.

"Soviet intelligence sent you to direct Admiral Diefenbach to resume his spying. You gave him a letter from Sophia."

How did he know the name? Was GALILEO *alive?* A blanket had covered his body on the plaza. Might he have survived long enough to gasp something out?

"What does it mean, 'Stop! It is forbidden!'? What were you telling him not to do?"

My God, had they been *listening* to her spiel? How else could they have known the line? Yes, they must have been, and GALILEO had been aware. It explained why he'd been so averse.

"What is the doll house?" He said doll house in German, as it had been written in the letter: *das Puppenhaus.*

The blood drained from her face. The doll house had not been spoken aloud. GALILEO had not read the letter; she'd watched him burn it to ashes. Like a rowboat in a rough sea, her stomach tossed. She leaned to the side and threw up. Vomit spattered the cement floor.

"You understand me perfectly," said Christopher-hair.

Nothing was more obvious to Elena, either. The bitch was a Soviet. She must be interrogated in depth. But even if the coward Gutermuth acquired a vial of sodium pentothal, Elena doubted that the interrogation could be accomplished here; there wasn't sufficient time. The woman must be transported to Germany, where over as prolonged a period as necessary, with patience and the application of the correct tools, she would break. Perhaps she knew something about the Moons. The slightest revelation might at last allow Elena to identify them.

The woman had turned deathly pale, her aspect forlorn. She must comprehend that they wouldn't let her go. Handle her cautiously, thought Elena. Avoid any chance she would emulate Maria Toft and kill herself. It was imperative to get her to the *Odelia*. Craven though he was, Gutermuth was correct on one point: the admiral's death would shine a spotlight on the hotel. The police would dig for explanations. The defeats on the eastern front had weakened Germany's image and diluted the loyalty of the Swedish Nazis. Two Swedes, Axelsson and the boy Kallgren, were witting of the woman's presence. Would they hold up when the authorities questioned them? Also, the Soviet collaborator who'd set the fire and pulled the fire alarm must be cognizant that the woman was being detained on the premises. The collaborator would notify the NKVD, infamous for its ruthlessness.

Ruthless or not, the Russians weren't foolhardy. They needed time to prepare a plan, and Elena was still ahead of them. The car should be here soon enough, and she'd move the woman.

There was still time to ask questions.

She had ordered Brindt to cut off the woman's finger as a threat to provoke a reaction. It had worked. But more was required, and quickly.

To Schlosser, she snapped, "Ask her again who she is!"

From a hundred rabbits you can't make a horse.

A horse wouldn't have vomited on the floor. No doubt about it, she was a rabbit. Her weak stomach had betrayed her. Damn the fear that caused her to lose control of herself.

In Russian, Christopher-hair said, "Who are you? What is your name?"

She said nothing.

He shouted in her face, "You are a Soviet! Your purpose was to reactivate the admiral!"

She ignored him. He was a functionary who simply repeated what the dark-haired woman told him to say. The woman's demeanor exuded authority. Something else too. Stress. Linnea recognized the manifestations from her mother, who, forced to sell their possessions to escape the debts, yanking her daughter by the hand through the unfriendly streets of Manhattan looking for a place to stay, had verged on a breakdown.

Why was the German woman so pressured? Because, though she might rule this room and these men, beyond were things she couldn't deal with, and they were coming at her, and she was running out of time.

Linnea's thief cover was weak. The Germans weren't biting. Even so, she might burn off more time.

Christopher hair said, "Who set the fire?"

"Let me go," she said in Swedish. "You have no legal right to detain me."

He translated the statement.

The woman said, "Cut off her finger."

The big fellow opened his folding knife. This time he proceeded, slashing the hemp cord restraining her forearm, snatching her left hand, straightening her little finger, and severing it as if it were a carrot. Snipped off, the pinky fell on the floor.

Where had she heard the sound before? Not from her own lips. Perhaps in a nightmare from her gull-tormented childhood. Shock flooded. Like a phonograph record stuck in the same groove, she keened and sobbed. If she hadn't thrown up already, she would have now.

Christopher-hair looked like he might throw up too. In German he said, "Madam, is this necessary?"

"Ask her again!"

"Who are you? Please, answer. We know you are a Soviet."

The dark-haired woman bellowed, *"Schneide sie noch einmal!"* Cut her again!

The brute yanked her left hand from where she clutched it against her chest and repeated the pitiless surgery, this time on her ring finger. No wedding ring ever would decorate her left hand, not on the finger that plopped down beside its severed sister.

"Madam, please," said the translator.

"She will answer, or I will cut off the rest of her fingers and proceed with her toes!"

He bent close to Linnea's ear. "I implore you," he said in Russian. "She says she will keep cutting. She means it. Please, tell us who you are."

Linnea's hand dripped blood. From a hundred rabbits, you cannot make a horse, undeniable, just as the poor are always with us, and people lie to themselves, and pain and suffering are inevitable. You had to face facts. She lifted her head, and seething in pain and rage, shrilled in Russian, "Tell that bitch I am Vena Nadovska of the NKVD, and she can go to hell!"

Christopher-hair translated. No translation was necessary. The woman stared at the fierce visage confronting her. Linnea could almost hear her thoughts: The dangerous animal was uncovered. What was she to do with it? Would cutting off more fingers achieve anything?

"Ask her who are Diefenbach's sub-agents," said the woman.

Linnea exploded in German, "*Idiotin!* Do you think they would tell me such a thing?"

The woman's posture shifted as she digested the response. She turned to the brute, and Linnea braced for more savagery. *Under no circumstances admit you're an American or working with the British. If you do, the mission will be blown. If you're in the hands of the Nazis, they'll kill you.*

The man she had seen on the fourth floor, whom the limping fellow had said was Herr Durst, security, appeared in the doorway and said, "The car is here."

Elena thought of an alarming possibility. Though the car had diplomatic plates, the Swedish police might nonetheless stop it on the way to the ship. She and her team carried diplomatic passports and enjoyed immunity. The woman would present an obvious exception. If the police spoke to her, she would claim to be a Swede and blurt that the Germans were detaining her illegally.

Plainly she is Swedish. Her accent is of Stockholm.

The police would believe her, and they'd remove her from the car.

The Moons' identities would be lost.

She pulled Durst into the boiler room. "Did Gutermuth deliver anything else? A vial of liquid?"

"No. He is upstairs now, taking away the steamer trunks. Should I send him down?"

She'd already decided that she would pull the attaché out of Sweden; a posting to the Dnieper line in the Ukraine would cure his smugness. The one exploit that might have saved him was to have acquired the sodium pentothal, but of course he'd failed, as whining milksops like him invariably did.

The drug would have been useful. Not only did sodium pentothal function as a truth serum, a sufficient dose would have rendered the woman incoherent, unable to sob out her predicament to any policeman who might stop the car enroute to the ship. But something else might work. "Tell Zurcher to bring me the morphine and syringe from the medical kit, before Gutermuth takes it away."

Very little happened in Berlin that didn't come to the attention of the SD. Some of what did required delicate handling, for instance the depravities of certain senior Reich officials. A category equally sensitive concerned the transgressions of members of the SD. For some time, she had been aware of Zurcher's visits to seedy morphine dens, information that in other hands might have destroyed his career or even provoked his arrest. Morphine addict or not, he was skilled, loyal, and not easily replaceable, so the reports had stopped with her. She hadn't even raised the topic with him.

He arrived momentarily with the syringe kit and the morphine.

She said, "I need the woman alive but unable to speak. Do you know how to administer morphine in the right amount?"

His features flashed wariness, but to his credit, he didn't playact innocence. "The effect will be temporary," he said. "Forty minutes or so."

Forty minutes was enough. "Do it."

– 45 –

Mid-February 1944

Whatever clear-headedness might have survived the amputations, the injection finished off. Odd, the fellow who wielded the needle. Of modest height, his eyes bulged like those of a gremlin in a storybook illustration, his lips levering a cigarette so naturally he might have been born with a proboscis.

"Jetzt wirst du schweben." Now you will float. His voice was high pitched, almost feminine.

The sensation came on quickly, and she seemed to be watching from a distance as the sockless brute splashed a dark liquid on her bleeding stubs and wrapped them with gauze whose ends he knotted together. He untied her from the chair and half-supported, half-carried her along the basement corridor, which, from her inscribed mental imprint of the hotel's floor drawings, she knew led to the rear alley.

Never cease taking stock of your situation. Adapt to what's in front of you. The strongest people, the ones who survive, are the most adaptable.

Where were they taking her? Either to some hideout the Nazis controlled in Sweden, or to Germany by ship or plane. Her first two covers had collapsed. She had bought time clinging to them. So far, the third held.

How long would she last under interrogation?

She needed to escape *now.*

Not a chance. In the brute's grip, she might as well have been the lamb in the jaws of the fox she'd pictured in the clouds. Even if she could break loose, how far could she get? Her left arm was useless, her ankle sprained and maybe broken. Mentally she was indeed afloat, and more so by the minute. If he hadn't been holding her up, she'd have crumpled to the floor.

If you let go of your mind, you surrender everything. Sorry, Avry. Why hadn't they given her an L-pill? Something about risking that she'd be sorted out as a professional. Too late, they had her pegged. They would resume cutting off her fingers, or do something worse, and she would tell them she was an

American working with the British. She would reveal Lars and his sons, and the Nazis would kill them.

Then they'd kill her.

Why the hell had she put herself here? Verrick always had been uneasy with the mission, she'd sensed it, and she'd not for a minute believed Avry's reassurances they'd get her out if captured. She wouldn't see her mother again. Tears gushed.

Stop! Vena Nadovska of the NKVD didn't cry!

Her knees buckled. The brute hooked his arm around and lifted her. With each step his hip bumped hers, fluttering her stockinged feet *entrechat* over the cement floor to the rear exit. Amid the snow flurries squatted an automobile puffing white exhaust like a hulking dragon. Alongside posed the dark-haired woman flanked by two men, a trio in descending order of height. On the left, the tallest, was blotch-faced Durst, to the right, the shortest, the gremlin, who through his cigarette smoke seemed to regard Linnea with faint amusement.

The flankers scattered to open the back doors. Linnea's bulky escort passed her to Durst, who stuffed her in, the smoking gremlin sliding in from the far side, sandwiching her between. The German woman took the front passenger seat, the sockless brute the wheel. The doors slammed.

Her head rolled like a ball on a ship's deck.

They set off. Two minutes along, the woman twisted rearward. "Is she conscious?"

Durst jostled her injured side. The pain soared. On the other, the gremlin lifted her head by the chin, his fingers stinking of cigarettes.

She mumbled, *"Nimm deine Hand weg, du dreckiges Schwein."* Get your hand off me, you filthy pig.

"A live wire we have here, Elena," the gremlin said. He pressed his lips close to Linnea's ear. "You know, I am very accustomed to handling live wires."

The brute in the driver's seat laughed and said, *"Ja, Professor Elektriker!"*

"Halte dein Mund!" snarled the gremlin. Shut your mouth.

What a bizarre exchange. The drug was scattering her thoughts; no longer could she shepherd them. Visions assailed her. She was a child in Petrograd, and passers-by jeered at her pink dress. A stern woman commissar bellowed. The seagulls swooped, and she couldn't lift her hand to protect her head. She was Vena, and she thrust her hands into the mud for turnips. She pulled out a chess piece, a white rook. Her hands were caked with dirt. She scrubbed. The dirt wouldn't come off. She was Linnea again, naked and alabaster on a slab, her sightless eyes frozen open.

She begged her mind to shut down, and it obliged her.

The automobile was a 1939 Mercedes Benz 770, oversized and ostentatious, nonetheless equipped with diplomatic plates and blackout lights. They passed unimpeded through the police checkpoint at the exit to the Delfin Plaza, and Elena estimated the chances were excellent that, if they encountered another checkpoint, the police would perfunctorily wave them through. The more distance they gained from the city center, the safer they would be. She told Brindt to keep the speed down, so the car wouldn't attract attention. The ambiance from the snow-dusted streets made the blackout lights extraneous. Along the thoroughfare, extinguished pole lamps paraded like ghostly marchers at a funeral procession. The car ascended into a hilly district of four and five-story residential buildings.

What if the Russians were following them?

She barked, "Turn here!"

Brindt veered. No matter how sudden or contradictory her commands, he never questioned them. She guided him through the silent, snow-dabbed neighborhoods, along stretches hairbreadth or capacious, past parked pull carts and automobiles, up rises, down slopes, and on one of the latter she had him halt in the middle of the lane to watch for a tailing vehicle that might crest the ridge behind. There was none. "Put us back on the main road."

The snow flurries thickened. The captive appeared to have passed out. Elena pressed her fingers against the forehead. Hot. Blood soaked the gauze around the mutilated hand. Aboard the freighter, they would bandage it properly. She'd assign one of her team to accompany the woman on the sea journey. Not difficult to keep her alive, Durst could manage. On second thought, the task was too vital to risk. Zurcher should go too. Once they and the woman were secured in the special quarters the captain had promised,

Elena and Brindt would return to the city, retrieve the steamer trunks, and head to the airport to catch the delegation's flight to Berlin.

The *Odelia* would not reach Hamburg for at least twenty-four hours. Merchant ships left their anchorages only at night to evade Soviet submarines prowling the Baltic Sea. To bring the captive along on the plane would have been so much more efficient, but the bound and bleeding woman would reap too many questions from the diplomat passengers. Earlier in the war, Elena might have requested a separate aircraft to retrieve them. Now, with aviation fuel in such dire supply, to summon one on short notice was impossible. With the interlude in mind, she would be prudent to send a message to Fenzl advising him she had collected vital evidence. The Russian woman embodied it. The Magnetophon recording and the coded letter from Sophia—with luck, the SD's cryptologists could break it quickly—could bridge the gap until the ship arrived.

What other treasures could she bring? To Zurcher, she said, "Can you rouse her?"

He gyrated the woman's head as if it were a glass globe with a miniature castle and fake snow inside. Her eyes fluttered open.

Elena shouted, "Who are Diefenbach's contacts in Germany?"

The woman moaned.

"Diefenbach's contacts. A name!"

The eyes rolled. She muttered something.

Elena asked Zurcher, "Did you hear what she said?"

"Sounded like 'Galileo.'"

Elena almost gasped. How could this be? Never was the spy's codename used outside German counterintelligence channels. The woman's possession of it could only mean the Soviets had penetrated her organization.

The Moons were inside the SD!

She seized the captive's hair. "How do you know that name? Speak!"

"Elena!" burst Brindt.

They had descended from the residential neighborhoods to a road fringing the dockyards. A line of sawhorses blocked the lane. A laborer in a canvas jacket and scruffy newsboy cap, his face leathery and unshaven, waved a flashlight.

Brindt lowered the window. *"Was zum Teufel passiert?"* What the hell was going on?

"Omväg." The man waved the flashlight rightward. *"Konstruktion."*

"What did you say?"

"Construction detour," said Zurcher from behind. "He wants us to follow it."

The roadman indicated tire tracks that appeared to plummet off the main artery into lowlands.

"Dort?" said Brindt, incredulous. There?

The oaf flailed the flashlight.

"Is he drunk?" said Durst.

"I don't see any construction," said Zurcher.

To Elena, the roadman's gestures were strangely reassuring. Police checkpoints worried her; inebriated simpletons did not. To argue with him might draw the scrutiny of someone savvier. "Turn," she said.

Brindt's thick-muscled arms tugged the steering wheel laboriously to the right. Ahead they crept, the auto's nose dipping down a rough track into a misty field, the tires crunching on the snow.

"Are you certain you're on the path?" said Zurcher.

When Brindt failed to reply, Elena said, "Go slow."

They mashed over snow-tufted reeds, passing forlorn trees. Hunched forward, Brindt squinted past the Mercedes hood ornament and eased his bulky torso to the left or right as the way curved. The long hood imitated the bow of a ship over a whitecapped ocean.

To take the detour may have been unwise, mused Elena. Too isolated. What if the car got stuck? She was about to order Brindt to stop and turn around when a glow materialized ahead. Thirty meters in front shone a light. It must be the detour terminus. As they neared, a beam flared directly at the car. Irritating. She raised her forearm to shield her eyes. Behind the corona, a figure held up a gloved palm, the universal signal to stop. Brindt complied. Another gesture indicated the car's blackout lights.

"Cut them," said Elena. He did so.

"There is a car coming up from behind," said Durst.

Through the rear window, the twin blackout lights of a vehicle neared. Elena's heartbeat accelerated. Ahead, the hand-beam's effulgence divided in two, the first vectoring toward the driver's side, spotlighting Brindt, the second to Elena's door. At the driver's window, a disembodied arm made a circular motion, meaning roll down the glass. Brindt obeyed.

She could make out nothing of the persons holding the lights. *"Dies ist ein Diplomatenauto!"* she shouted. This was a diplomat's car. "Let us pass at once!"

The light on the driver's side hovered half a meter from Brindt's scrunched face. Something was wrong. Detour workmen did not behave this way. Brindt knew it too; he visibly tensed.

The voice, when it came, was in German and incongruously matter of fact: "So you are the one who likes to hurt women."

Brindt reached for his gun.

"Nein!" screeched Elena.

The gunshot blew Brindt's brains through a hole that had been his right ear, the gore spattering Elena, who suspended her hands in front of her face as if she were holding up an imaginary cabbage to inspect. What was left of Brindt's head flopped against the steering wheel. She half saw, half sensed the gun barrel swivel toward her.

"Offen!" boomed the holder. Open.

She lifted the lock. The door flew wide, and a hand gripped her by the collar, yanked her out, and flung her to the ground.

"Legst du hin!" Lay there.

She lay perfectly still, facing upwards, squinting against the beam that shone in her face. On the margins of her vision, lights gamboled like mammoth fireflies. Obscure figures moved about. Alongside her thudded Durst and Zurcher. The ground was watery beneath the snow, and the briny wetness began to seep through her clothes, the stems of marsh grass jabbing at her neck. Now the light in her face descended to within centimeters. Hands groped roughly all over her, rummaging through her pockets. They snatched away her pistol. Doors opened. The NKVD were reclaiming their girl. They had slaughtered Brindt, the driver of a German diplomatic car. What was to stop them from killing her, Durst, and Zurcher?

"This is a neutral country!" Elena shouted.

Two large shoes materialized centimeters from her head. She closed her eyes, expecting a bullet. A liquid rained. Urine. The swine was pissing on her! "Gaaah," she foamed through closed lips.

Gunshots crescendoed, the telltale staccato of a submachine gun. Brass casings tumbled, glass shattered, metal clanged. The stink of cordite suffused the mist. They were shooting the car!

"Stay on the ground, or I kill you," said a voice in Russian-accented German.

Car engines growled; not hers, it was shot to pieces. The last of the lights extinguished. The noises receded. In the fresh darkness, she sat up, urine dripping fetidly from her hair.

"Zurcher?"

"Yes, madam."

"Are you injured?"

"I don't think so."

"Durst?"

"I am unhurt."

"Do you have the woman's badge and the film? The fingerprint card?"

The sounds of rustling. "They took them, along with my passport and weapon."

She fished in her coat. The Russian's crude search had found her pistol and passport but missed the Sophia letter and the transcript, still nestled together in her pocket.

"The Magnetophon tape?"

"Safe at the embassy," said Durst, "consigned for the flight to Germany."

– 46 –

Late February 1944

Linnea's head hurt. When she tried to sit up in the bed, it was as if she were straining against ropes.

She looked. The ropes were only in her mind.

The room was windowless, the walls unadorned and absent the scrapes and dings of normal habitation. A hospital room, or a cell? Either way, it came with a nurse, a thick-bodied woman in a plain gray dress who said nothing as she replaced the dressing on Linnea's left hand and the damp rag on her forehead and administered an injection of a milky white fluid. During the change of bandages, Linnea observed the stumps of her two fingers sewn with black thread.

At night, humming to herself a tune that sounded hazily familiar, the woman switched off the lamp, leaving the room in blackness except for a razor slash of yellow light under the door. The disembodied line became Linnea's roadway to sleep. She dreamt of Ivett's fingerless mittens wrapped around the stovepipe. Knee to knee on the ship's voyage to America, Eudoxia taught her strange words: doll house, cover story, enumeration. A letter burned, a fire bell clanged, a blanket-shrouded figure lay on the ground. Her hair was gripped from behind. Yanked backwards, she lost her shoes. Barefoot she ran, two men pounding at her heels. She made it to an apartment building, seized a bicycle on the way through, and furiously pedaled. She wasn't speeding up, her legs were too thin. She gazed down at spider legs. She was a spider, and they had clipped off two of her appendages, leaving her with six. Such was the pathos of her dreams.

What *had* happened? The truth was like the speck in milky coffee that eludes spooning out. She revivified the capering lights, the claps of gunshots, muted voices in Russian, and the nebulous imprint of having told the Germans the name GALILEO.

The hours served up more questions. Where was she? Who had her? The NKVD? The Swedes? What should she say when they interrogated her? Tell them she was Hamfrid Matisson or Thorgun Lindstrom? Neither would work. Matisson was someone else, and Lindstrom did not exist. Better not to say anything.

The nurse hummed. Wordlessly Linnea accepted the ministrations. Much of the time she slept.

I am Vena Nadovska of the NKVD, and GALILEO is my agent.

The reality backwashed: Her agent was dead.

Who were the men who'd pulled her from the car? The voices in Russian sounded like someone offstage in a theatrical drama. If her rescue had been a performance, why not this? Was the nurse playacting? Was Linnea still in the hands of the Germans? The idea bothered her until she recognized the tune the woman hummed, one of the Swedish folk songs her father used to sing. But did humming the tune prove the nurse was a Swede and not a clever Nazi?

Too much thinking—stop! She couldn't. Perilously she treaded into memory, to the pipe room and the cruel woman with the dark hair. How could the Germans have learned about *das Puppenhaus?* The term had appeared only in the letter GALILEO burned to ashes; neither he nor she had spoken it aloud. The more she strained at the mystery, the more it slithered off the spoon.

Her mind steadied. The throbbing in her hand tapered. She slept less. The passing time slowed to a languorous crawl, and lacking anything else to do, she counted to 3,600, each count a second, equaling an hour. Prisoners must count their hours this way, each vacant and meaningless. Desperately she wanted to speak to Verrick. Could she ask for him? No, she shouldn't use a language before it was spoken to her.

Impractical. She had to ask the nurse in Swedish to go to the toilet. Escorted across a hallway to a bathroom, she stepped gingerly. The pain wasn't so bad; she must not have broken her ankle. Inside was a mirror. The right side of her face looked normal. The left was purple and gray, reminding her of the woods at the first hint of spring when the redbud blossoms began to shade the bare trees.

She guessed thirty-six hours had gone by when the woman brought clothes, not the blood-stained garments she'd been wearing, but a heavy wool skirt, a silk blouse, underclothes, and boots, everything apparently new. With her one hand, she pulled on the wool socks and ankle boots. She expected her left hand to hurt when she pushed it through the blouse sleeve. The bandages slid smoothly.

The nurse gestured. Linnea followed. At the hallway's end, a door opened to a landing above snowy woods. Morning sunbeams slanted through tall firs, dabbing the blond pinewood boards of the cabin they exited. They descended steps to a path that curved to an older, stouter building, the siding gray and weathered. The nurse opened the door and signaled that Linnea should enter. The nurse herself did not. The door fell shut.

Here waited Sebastian Wentworth.

She'd only ever seen him in his three-piece suit and tie. Today, as if mimicking a hayseed out for a stroll in the woods, he sported rubber-bottomed lace-up boots, brown corduroy trousers, and a dark green shirt of rough wool. Gently he gripped her by the shoulders. "My dear girl, so good to see you safe."

The sound of spoken English sent her head spinning. Perceiving her wooziness, he led her to a chair. "I'm dreadfully sorry about what those savages did to you."

"I'm okay, sir. Happy to be alive." How husky her voice sounded.

"They tell me you haven't spoken. Wise of you. Your hosts couldn't have told you much."

"Who are they?"

"Helpers. Swedes."

"Were they the ones…"

"I'd rather not say. Confidences, you know."

"What happened to…"

"Our man, yes. Unfortunate. The plan had risks. You did all we asked, as well as anyone could have."

"I doubt that."

"You shouldn't. We're all proud of you."

Sounded like fluff. "Where is Avry?"

"I'm afraid he had other duties."

"Am I interned here?"

"Goodness no. We'll get you back to England shortly. The Mosquito makes weekly dispatch runs in support of our legation. The flights can carry a passenger or two, discreetly, an arrangement we have with the Swedes."

326

She recalled the night-fighter Mosquitos she'd glimpsed on her first evening at the Lodge. *Fastest kites in the sky.*

"In the meantime, I'll ask you to relate what happened on the night you entered the hotel. Please tell me everything, in the greatest detail you can remember."

OSS Stockholm took two days to turn out their update on the events surrounding the death of Admiral Diefenbach. The report was sourced to official Swedish authorities. Although the Swedes had been reluctant to speak on the topic, they revealed that the firemen investigating the cause of the alarm at the Delfin Hotel had found a bucket of burned rags in the basement. Whether the rags had been set on fire by accident or mischief, the authorities couldn't say. Diefenbach's remains, not autopsied, were returned to the Germans, whose delegation departed Sweden by air later that same day, taking the body along. The extra security at Delfin Square was discontinued. A grim cloud of blame hovered, but because nobody could point to negligence or fault, it dissipated.

A motorcycle courier delivered to 70 Grosvenor Street an envelope addressed to Verrick. In Casey's presence, he tore it open and read the handwritten note:

> *Please destroy this after reading.*
> *She is safe, if a bit damaged, and will be returned to St. Andrews on Tuesday at about 8 a.m. You are welcome to meet her there.*
> *Please preserve all details strictly within the current circle.*
> *Pearlman*

Verrick's surging relief that Linnea was safe crashed against 'if a bit damaged.' What the hell did that mean? He handed the note to Casey.

"Good news, all things considered," said the younger man.

"Where is St. Andrews?"

"East coast of Scotland. Easy to get there by train. Under the circumstances, an automobile might be advisable. It's about a nine-hour drive."

Today was Sunday. Plenty of time. "Can you schedule a car?"

"Of course."

They notified Donovan by telegram. That evening, a reply arrived from Washington.

```
EYES ONLY VERRICK / CASEY
REF UPDATE ACKNOWLEDGED.
MI-6 NOTIFIED THAT CASEY ADDED TO MISSION CIRCLE.
VERRICK TO TRAVEL TO WASHINGTON IMMEDIATELY BY AIR.
NEW TASK AWAITS. USE MILITARY AUTHORIZATION CODE 62A.
DONOVAN
```

'MI-6 notified' implied that Donovan was in separate touch with someone in the British Secret Service regarding the mission. Authorization code 62A apparently empowered Verrick to bump other passengers. Stunned, he reread the message. Kept here weeks, why couldn't he stay a few more days? What was so important to require him urgently in Washington? He should ask Donovan to delay his return, so he could meet Linnea when she landed. Then again, Casey could meet her.

"Damn it."

Casey said, "Listen, I'll pick her up, debrief her, and send you and Donovan the readout."

Verrick thought of the questions he would have asked Linnea. It struck him how much he had been anticipating their reunion. The strength of the emotion surprised him.

Already he'd mailed Linnea's outgoing letter to her mother. He had two additional letters Casey had culled from her postal box and given him. "Remind me to give you back her mother's letters," Verrick said.

It was past dusk when they reached the airfield. They exited the car and walked toward the graceful outline of the Mosquito. Frigid winds screeched across the tarmac, and she pulled up the fur-lined hood of the parka Wentworth had given her.

The debriefing had lasted hours. She had told him everything.

He'd told her nothing.

He stopped five paces off the plane's nose. "Wonderful chaps, the crew. I'm afraid I'll have to ask you not to speak to them. The security of the mission precludes their knowing you're an American."

He'd said something like that before, in the sedan when she first encountered him. *Hello. My name is Sebastian. You shouldn't say anything for the time being.*

"What about in England?"

"The mission remains strictly bigoted. Read in on your side are Mr. Verrick and Lieutenant Casey."

Who was Lieutenant Casey? She supposed she'd find out.

"Someone from Grosvenor Street will meet you upon landing. Bon voyage."

She hoped Verrick would be the one to meet her. She wanted to be in the company of someone she trusted and could speak to freely.

By the plane waited two shadowy figures. One of them said, "You must be our special parcel? Oops, almost forgot, you aren't allowed to talk back." Like Graham from the Heinkel, the airman sounded like a cheeky teenager. "I'm Donald, your pilot. Jimmy here's the navigator. We'll have you on board, then."

They led her to a ladder. The two wing-mounted engines prodded beyond the nose, the rounded propeller cones stretching like friendly arms to greet her. Someone must have informed Donald and Jimmy that her left hand was injured, for they went to pains to brace her climbing the narrow ladder. She popped up in what mimicked a little greenhouse. Donald's red-filtered flashlight rouged a squeezed nook behind the two slightly out-of-echelon seats. Arranged under a radio console were blankets, a bucket, and a metal thermos, all bookended by two sealed canvas sacks she guessed bundled the diplomatic mail. A neatly S-folded canvas seatbelt in front imitated the bow on a present.

Donald said, "We usually tuck passengers in the bomb bay. Dismal down there. You, being injured as you are, get to fly up top with us. There's hot soup, if you like. Blankets too. The DeHavilland Mosquito's made of spruce, keeps us a bit warmer than the metal-skinned kites. Flying iceboxes, those are. The bucket's to pee in, if you have to. Won't peek, I promise."

Great.

"I'm supposed to insist you buckle yourself in. You can, or not. The flight duration is three hours. Oh, here are some earplugs. The voice of Beelzebub himself, the Merlins have."

The engines, he must mean.

The flashlight's red glow swung to a setup on the fuselage wall. "Your oxygen mask, the on-off switch, self- explanatory. We fly above thirty thousand feet. I'll signal you when it's time to don the mask. If you hear booms, don't worry, Jerry flak, pot shots, really. We'll be far above their range."

She wanted to ask about the pot shots. Couldn't.

The pilots took their seats. The Merlins ignited, their roar indeed fearsome. She stuffed in the rubber earplugs. The sound muted; the vibration stayed. She knelt up to watch through the cupola as the Mosquito rolled and accelerated, the runway lights rushing past. The wheels lifted and the nose angled toward the vertical, and like the bullets they resembled, the Merlins shot heavenward. She was tugged backward, not by the hair, by the laws of physics. With the five fingers of her right hand and the three of her left, she clung to the seatbacks.

They climbed to a lofty height, and she lost the terrain until the serrated edge of the Skagerrak slid into view. No flak. She settled under the blankets, affixing the safety strap awkwardly. The cabin temperature plummeted. Her shivering worsened to convulsions. Might oxygen starvation be the problem? The pilot hadn't signaled her; maybe he'd forgotten or thought she was asleep. She strapped on the mask, flipped the switch. The hearty gas warmed her, and she dropped off. If she dreamed, she didn't remember.

Jimmy prodded her. "Coast of Scotland."

So it was they landed at RAF Leuchars, and with the crew's help she climbed down to the tarmac. They pointed her in the direction she should proceed. Not permitted to say thanks, she waved goodbye with her good hand. The sunrise torched the horizon, pinkening the rounded hangars and the roof of a sedan, people alongside. She recognized the woman driver who'd picked her up at Factory House on the first night and the bespectacled American who'd given her the forms to sign. He said, "Welcome back,

Linnea. I'm Bill Casey. We've met." He flashed the perfunctory smile of a bureaucrat dispatched to fetch her.

"Where is Mr. Verrick?"

"Summoned home. He wished he could have been here. Unfortunately, it wasn't possible."

Will I see you when I get back?

Count on it.

Casey said, "Have you eaten?"

"No."

"Let's get you fed."

"I'd prefer not to, just yet."

"Are you sure? Long drive to London."

"Only some water, please," she said.

– 47 –

Late February 1944

Committed, capable, loyal. That was Verrick to a T. An organization man. An honorable man. Nonetheless he possessed a contrarian streak that meshed untidily with his other attributes. In the late 1930s, he'd handled the case of a famous actor suing the studio he was contracted to. Verrick built a strong case. The studio's team of lawyers offered a settlement he considered inadequate. He advised the actor to decline and to press ahead with the lawsuit. The actor agreed. Or appeared to.

Donovan called him in. "Gabe, your client wants to settle."

"I told him what the studio offered. He said to keep fighting."

"At your urging."

"That's right. We'll win."

"He respects you too much to argue. The fact remains."

"We'll *beat* the studio."

"I have no doubt you would. It's not the smart move."

Verrick guessed his telegram from London asking for permission to speak to MI-6 head Stewart Menzies had so alarmed Donovan that, fearing a resurgence of his subordinate's pugnacity, he'd yanked him out.

The hunch proved false. At OSS Headquarters in Washington, a sullenness pervaded. The interval he'd been gone had seen several of the top OSS men second-guess Donovan's organizational construct. The outfit was too complex, they argued, resembling a kind of Rube Goldberg machine. They wanted to restructure it to streamline some functions and jettison others, especially paramilitary activities they thought should be left to the Army. They penned memoranda, effecting a minor rebellion. Verrick, having played no role in or even been aware of the bureaucratic kerfuffle, shook his head in disbelief. He'd been hailed back from London for the sole reason he was the one who calmed people down.

Unequivocally he backed Donovan. He spoke to the others. The heresy subsided.

His next task was to represent the boss at a meeting with FBI Director J. Edgar Hoover. OSS-FBI contretemps were not unusual, and to prepare he studied the issue that had to do with the Bureau's primacy in cases involving Latin America. He rode a taxi to the Justice Department building, where he hobnobbed with the Bureau men awaiting their boss's arrival. Hoover entered, halted, and staring coldly across the table apprehended that Donovan had sent a stand-in. The FBI director thereupon walked out, and wordlessly the other Bureau officials followed, abandoning Verrick to the secretary who ushered him onto Pennsylvania Avenue.

For Pete's sake!

Friday evening, he trained home to Manhattan. Grace hugged him at the door. "Tell me about Matt," she said, and he'd not even taken off his coat before he was going on about their son's confident command of his truck-borne paratroopers in London. Three days he stayed in New York. He helped her to prepare dinner Saturday evening. Shortages kept the fare light, mostly vegetables, the desserts not as sugary as they would have been pre-war. The friends she invited were more hers than his, holdovers from their first apartment building in Manhattan. They assumed he was still at the law firm and asked him about his work, and he concocted a story of a corporate case so mundane their eyelids sagged. Grace, aware he was dissembling, changed the subject.

She'd acquired seats to a Broadway performance of Shakespeare's *Richard III*, and good seats they were, a few rows off the proscenium. The goal of entertainment was to transport the audience. With Grace, the play succeeded. Him, no. His thoughts roiling, he had difficulty paying attention.

In Washington Tuesday, the staff handed him a sealed envelope. Inside were two brief cables from Casey, eyes only to him and Donovan. The first reported that Linnea had returned to London and was in fair condition, considering that she'd been captured by the Germans. In interrogating her, they had severed the ring and little fingers of her left hand. Her ankle was sprained, her left cheekbone broken. Her upper arms showed livid purple bruises, the left from GALILEO's grip, the right from a brutish Nazi's.

Verrick's mouth fell open.

A full readout of her debriefing was forthcoming, the cable promised.

People got hurt in war, he told himself. Some died. Linnea had survived. Be grateful. Casey was there and would handle things in his competent, cool-headed way. He would level no recriminations at the Brits. Outrage accomplished nothing.

The second cable said the Soviets had bombed Stockholm. What? On the evening of 22 February, a flight of aircraft penetrated Swedish air defenses, striking the capital and a suburb. Miraculously no one had been killed. An examination of the bomb remnants proved Soviet culpability, though Moscow denied it. Swedish authorities publicly speculated that the Soviet aircraft had become lost and bombed the wrong country.

The timing, just four days after the death of GALILEO, howled otherwise.

The Swedes thereupon released a Soviet spy they had arrested some months prior.

Strange indeed.

Casey's debriefing readout arrived in ten pages of single-spaced narrative. Here at last was the grist to explain what the mission had been about. Linnea recounted the infiltration and her sojourn with a Swedish family. She depicted the safehouse, her reconnaissance outings, and her discovery that the police had sealed off Delfin Plaza. Casey had inserted references to the prior intelligence reports on the plaza's closure and the stated rationale. By some sleight of hand, the contact who'd met them upon infiltration, whose name supposedly was Lars Johansson, arranged for a mysterious Swedish government contact to unlock the back door of an apartment house on the square. What kind of civil servant could perform such a feat on short notice? It meant Lars was part of a network. Avry seemed to trust the connection, implying he'd been aware of it beforehand.

Who was the government man?

Who, for that matter, was Lars?

Linnea thought the Johansson surname was an alias. Index traces might pull it up. Had this been a regular case, Verrick would have requested them, but Donovan had promised Wentworth not to initiate mission-relevant inquiries in the OSS system. Verrick would have to go to Donovan for permission to go back on the commitment. Not worth it. He continued reading. The government man fulfilled the request, and Linnea circumvented the police checkpoints and reached the hotel. She made her way to the fourth floor and to the hall monitor, one of the reinforcements Lars had said were Swedish Nazis but not hotel employees. She went into some detail about the monitor, his youth, blond hair, and diligent demeanor.

In GALILEO's suite she delivered her much-rehearsed spiel and the letter. Casey asked her about the letter's contents, and she regurgitated what she recalled, perhaps half the text, she estimated; she'd only read it once. Signed by 'Sophia,' the text was rife with apparent codewords—doll house, potted plant, painted bricks, twists of foil, toothpicks dipped in melted wax, fantastic artistrics—Avry had said would mean something to GALILEO. Her account of the agent's reaction made Verrick wince. Nothing was clearer than that the admiral *was* GALILEO, nonetheless he balked at taking the letter, and she had to all but force it into his hands. Then, without reading the contents, he burned it and crumpled the ashes. He seized her by the upper arm, whispered in her ear, 'Get out quickly, if you can, and hope you have not killed me,' and shoved her into the corridor. Immediately upon her emergence, the fire bell erupted.

Coincidence? She imparted her suspicion that the Brits had set off the fire alarm to aid her escape. Casey asked, how could they have timed to the second when she exited the room? She had no idea. Joining the people spilling from the guest rooms, she descended to the lobby, where she caught sight of the blond-haired monitor from the fourth floor in the company of a bulky man and an urgently moving, dark-haired woman. They seemed to be looking for someone, and she guessed that someone was her. To the upper floor she scampered, dropped out the window, hurt her ankle on impact, and tried to limp off. The sight of GALILEO dead on the plaza stunned her. He must have thrown himself from his window. Ever since, she'd been asking herself if she had provoked his death and what she might have done differently.

The bulky fellow was the one who grabbed her from behind and dragged her by the hair. When he let go in favor of her coat collar, she managed to slip out of the garment. The blond Swedish boy—him again—impeded her escape. She struggled, struck him in the eye with her shoe, broke free, and tried to run. The German blocked her. When she tried to dodge around, he punched her unconscious. Casey's narrative said nothing of whether the tale had traumatized her to relate. Verrick assumed it had.

Why did I talk you into it, Linnea dear?

He almost couldn't get through the account of the interrogation. She had the vague impression she'd been photographed and fingerprinted. She ran through the characters present: the dark-haired German woman named Elena, the big brute who'd hit her, an older dandy who spoke Swedish, a willowy, blond-haired German who spoke Russian and Swedish, and a middle-aged, blotchy-skinned man named Durst. Clearly Elena was their leader. Verrick harked to Lieutenant Rahilly's vignette of the SD's 'foxhound' Elena Rolke. Might the dark-haired woman have been her? The Germans asked Linnea about Sophia and the doll house and the meaning of 'Stop! It is forbidden!' The questions implied that not only had they been listening to what had transpired in GALILEO's room, they somehow had gleaned the contents of the letter. How was that possible, when he'd burned it to a crisp?

At Elena's command, the brute cut off two of her fingers.

Verrick had to put down the cable. He cleaned his eyeglasses, breathing slowly to calm himself. Yes, better that Casey had done the debriefing. Casey did not lose control of his emotions.

He resumed. She'd gritted out her Soviet identity, Vena Nadovska of the NKVD. Did they believe her? Yes, she was certain they did; it was the answer they wanted. A new figure she described as 'gremlin-like' arrived to inject her with some substance, then the brute, the same one who'd hit her and cut off her fingers, bandaged them. By the time he'd manhandled her to the car, she was slipping in and out of awareness. In the back seat of a sedan, squeezed between Durst and the gremlin, she fell into a fragmented oblivion. Suddenly Elena was barking questions, and Linnea muttered the name GALILEO, or so she fuzzily seemed to recall. Whether her captors understood, she couldn't say. The rest of her recollections were sketchy. Disembodied orbs frolicked in the twilight. Voices echoed in Russian and German. She thought someone shot the brute, but she wasn't sure. What happened to the other Germans? She didn't know.

Adroitly Casey shifted the focus to her debriefing session with Wentworth: What questions had the MI-6 man asked? Which had he pursued in depth? Oddly, Wentworth didn't seem at all interested in the government man Lars had enlisted to slip her through to the square. Neither did he pose questions about her rescue or her gaffe in blurting out GALILEO. He took her through the sequences like a tutor who already knew all the answers. Her questions to him—had Avry or Lars triggered the fire alarm, and how could the Germans possibly have extrapolated the contents of the Sophia letter?—yielded responses like 'Seems a bit improbable, doesn't it?'

At the conclusion of the debriefing, Casey asked if she had anything she wished to add. She replied that she'd lost her agent, the mission had failed, and she couldn't help but believe that she'd failed too.

The tale drained Verrick to read. What had it cost her to relate?

He restored the document to its envelope. In London, he'd reached the conclusion that the Brits couldn't run GALILEO in Berlin, therefore their objective in approaching him must have been different from the one they declared. They instilled in Linnea the premise she was GALILEO's controller, yet they scripted her entire presentation. What an agent might say, and how the controller should respond, entailed an infinity of variations impossible to commit to rote, yet Avry took her through her lines like an actress rehearsing a role.

In the Germans' custody, she revealed the codename GALILEO. Even if no blame attached—she was drugged at the time—the ramifications were alarming. The Brits had acquired the codename from decrypted Enigma messages. Hearing it from the mouth of a captured enemy, the Germans could only construe an internal breach. What if they surmised that their unbreakable cipher system had been broken? Wentworth should have explored it in more detail. The same reasoning begged the question of why the Brits had told Linnea the codename in the first place. The principle was sacrosanct: An intelligence officer inserted into an enemy-held zone must harbor no knowledge of separate, critical projects. Wentworth had said it himself. True, neutral Sweden was safer than the Nazi-occupied countries, nonetheless her mission was to walk into a building the Nazis controlled. Careless, or deliberate? The former was troubling, the latter incomprehensible. It implied that the Brits had been willing to compromise their awareness of the codename.

Seems a bit improbable, doesn't it?

Some people when they encounter mental walls hurl their energy at them like wrecking balls. They pace, scrawl memos to themselves, plow their fingers through their hair. Though walking might on occasion help to clear his mind, nervous exertions accomplished nothing. Scores of legal cases had taught him that deep thinking possessed no physical component. When the time came to fiercely concentrate, he could do so anywhere. And that time was when the facts reached their anticipated crest.

He had all he was ever likely to have.

– 48 –

Early March 1944

As usual, Willie Mauer dressed quietly so as not to wake Jana. In the parlor he lifted the window and caught the chirps of birds. The air felt mild. He sniffed, and so subtle was the scent of blossoms, he might be imagining it. Had the long winter broken at last? Perhaps he could leave behind his overcoat.

Spring or not, today promised to be dismal. Himmler's takeover of the Abwehr had come to pass. In Istanbul, a defection by a senior Abwehr officer had so outraged Hitler that he'd sacked Admiral Canaris and shuffled him off with some trumped-up title, pending retirement. The rumors even had it that Canaris was under house arrest. And though the dreaded realignment seemed to be taking grip slowly—thus far, Mauer's section and its functions remained untouched—it was only a matter of time before Himmler and his cronies reduced the once-respected military intelligence service to a mockery.

Mauer blotted the ugly situation from his mind. So much more important was that Jana should leave Berlin. He would insist, bang the table if he had to. Spring meant better weather and more bombs falling on the city. She *must* go.

First, he had to get through today. Outside he whiffed the air again, reaping only the dust from bombed-out buildings. Perhaps the floral fragrance had been a trick of the mind.

Not imaginary were the men trailing him. He spotted them almost immediately, two pairs, tracking both sides of the street behind. Had he intruded on a surveillance schema that involved someone else? The solution was to put himself out of the way. At the intersection with Wormserstrasse, he slued to the right. When was the last time he'd been on this street? Years ago, Jana and he had owned a dog—perhaps the animal comforted the childless couple—and sometimes they walked him along here. Midway down lived a family of Jews who on pleasant evenings would sit on the stoop of their house, and they bade cheerful greetings to Jana and him as they passed by. The family was gone now, of course, along with all the other Jews of Berlin. It seemed like ages since he'd thought of them.

The surveillants had turned behind him onto Wormserstrasse. It seemed he was their target.

Why not confront them?

These days in Germany, nobody did anything before thinking twice. Had he been careless? Over the years, he'd made derogatory quips about Hitler, never, he believed, within earshot of anyone other than Jana or Gels. But what if one of the Gestapo's ubiquitous informants had overheard him? He thought of his apartment building's Portierfrau, Mrs. Emmit. Some snitches, having nothing genuine to report, invented enticing tidbits they fed to their masters. You had to assume the Gestapo was aware of such chicanery and capable of sifting truth from fabrication.

Perhaps these men simply were going the same way as he, a coincidence.

He had nothing to fear, he told himself. He was Kommodore Wilhelm Mauer of the Kriegsmarine, accomplished, dutiful, and loyal. He'd done nothing wrong. Moreover he'd shown undeniable brilliance. Maybe that was why they were tailing him, as a protective escort. With Canaris out of the picture, was it so outlandish an idea that he would be elevated to lead the Abwehr?

A sedan skewed to the curb, its backseat window rolled down. Within, a woman with dark hair, her face the type you saw on certain marble statues, the lines hard, the eyes recessed, said, "Mauer, *ja?*"

"Yes. What is it?"

"Get in."

"Why?"

"I will not ask again. Surely you don't wish to create a public commotion."

He'd taken a step toward the car when one of the men who had been trailing shoved him against the side and began to frisk him.

"What are you doing?" said Mauer. "I'm a German officer!"

"Where is your service pistol?"

"I don't carry it."

The frisker relented and opened the back door. Mauer climbed in. "What is the meaning of this?" he said.

The dark-haired woman regarded him. "Are you familiar with Admiral Constantine Diefenbach?"

A mystifying question. "I've heard the name, and that he died recently in Sweden. I never met him."

"What do you know of his circle?"

"His *circle?* Nothing."

"You're lying."

"Certainly not. Why would I?"

"We will see."

"This is absurd. I am leaving." He reached for the door handle.

"You are under arrest."

"Why?"

No answer. Please, leave Jana out of it. He dared not say so. This woman might hear it as an implication.

He blustered, "I demand an answer!"

"You demand nothing. Stretch out your arms."

Reluctantly he did. The man in the front passenger seat clipped handcuffs on, snatched the hat from his head, and fitted a black hood over.

Berlin went dark.

– 49 –

April to November 1944

Verrick's duties morphed. The projects of the OSS encompassed North Africa, Burma, East Asia, and other places. He didn't travel there. Donovan did, in fact so often that the OSS Director was rarely in Washington.

In early June, Verrick learned just hours in advance that the invasion would fall in Normandy. Later he heard that Donovan had requested permission to accompany the armada. No, replied SHAEF. Donovan went anyway, talking his way aboard the U.S. cruiser *Tuscaloosa*. Landing on the French coast, he proceeded ashore, venturing far enough inland to draw enemy machine-gun fire. Complaints thundered. What the hell was Donovan doing, he who carried in his head America's and Britain's most guarded secrets, exposing himself to capture?

Verrick and Grace read of the parachute jumps by the U.S. 101st and 82nd Airborne Divisions into the flooded marshes of the Cotentin Peninsula. Anxiously they awaited news their son was alive, but not until early July did a letter from him arrive, the muddy edges saying as much as the handwriting within. That same day, they saw in the paper that the 101st had returned to England to prepare for future missions.

Through the summer and fall, Verrick split his time between Washington and New York. At work he read the intelligence, and on the train journeys he digested two or three newspapers he brought along. To keep pace with all the news was impossible. Late July delivered the stunning report of an assassination attempt against Hitler. The plotters had set off a bomb at the Führer's *Wolfsschanze* headquarters near Rastenburg, East Prussia. The explosion might have killed the bastard and ended the war. He lived and it went on. The Gestapo rounded up thousands for any association, no matter how ancillary, with the plotters. The Allies broke out of the Normandy beachhead and sprinted across France. They liberated Paris. The newsreels reechoed the carillon of Notre Dame's bells and the roar of the hundreds of thousands of Parisians who joyfully deluged the boulevards.

He followed too the latest developments from OSS Stockholm, watching for anything relevant to the GALILEO case. The tightrope-walking Swedish government, though inching closer to the Allies, was still authorizing exports of ball bearings and other war-purposeful materials to Germany. The station reported that the Nazis were funding the shipments with looted gold. In September, a strange account surfaced. According to a Swedish government spokesman, the AS had rounded up a ring of Swedish-Nazi assassins for hire. Their most recent victim, the killers confessed, had been Bror Axelsson, the security manager at the Delfin Hotel. The thugs had no idea why he merited his fate; they simply killed whomever they were paid to kill. They accepted more blood money to do away with a twenty-year-old, blond-haired Swedish boy, but their inquiries all over Stockholm produced no trace of him. The government spokesman didn't provide the name of the intended second victim. Verrick recalled Linnea's description of the young monitor.

In view of the unseemly goings-on at the Delfin Hotel, the spokesman added, the Swedish authorities had closed the establishment, sealing the doors with rugged chains and hardened-steel padlocks.

As if they were the gates to hell, mused Verrick.

In November, Donovan ordered Verrick to London again, this time for a conference with MI-6 over the modalities for infiltrating agents into Germany. Allied forces had hit the Siegfried Line, or West Wall, at the German frontier, and they urgently needed agents inside the Nazi homeland who could provide intelligence on how the Wehrmacht was mounting its defenses and a host of related requirements. In fact, the two services already had reached informal agreement based on proposals that Bill Casey had authored in London. The conference merely would formalize matters.

Verrick packed two suits of winter-weight wool, five pressed shirts, and three neckties. He added a pair of dress shoes for the conference, setting aside a much-worn, comfortable pair for the interminable plane ride and on the off-chance he might have time to stroll around London.

The day before he headed off, he went to see Donovan, who for once was at headquarters and not on some jaunt halfway around the world. The director's inner office featured maps pinned with the latest military progressions. Beside the desk, a stand-mounted globe fitted with an electric bulb inside glowed like a crystal ball.

The OSS Director looked up. "Gabe, how are you? Here to talk about your upcoming London conference?"

"No. I need your permission to ask Sebastian Wentworth about GALILEO."

Donovan frowned. "Why?"

"I want to know what really happened."

"Ancient history. Not worth your time."

"I think it is."

The director put down his pen and swiveled his chair to face the window. Co-located with the National Institute of Health, the OSS headquarters occupied a rise along the Potomac shore. The autumn leaves blocked the view of the river, yet Donovan gazed as if he could see through. "Why dredge up finished business? It annoys people."

"My role was to do just that, if I recall."

"All the same, the answer is no. Leave it alone."

In three words, Donovan had released Verrick from responsibility. He could walk away.

You didn't lie to her.

No, he hadn't. He'd let the Brits do it. He hadn't been sure what they were up to, but he'd known that the purpose they'd put forward was distinct from their true intent. He talked her into staying against her inclination and ushered her into their spider's web, letting her think she was being trained as an agent controller, the manipulator, when she was the one being manipulated.

He'd done his job. The OSS was not the Salvation Army. Nonetheless he had incurred an obligation. A moral man could not doubt it. Over the months since he had seen her last, he'd strained to divine what it entailed. The answer eluded him.

The obligation stayed.

He said, "Do *you* know what happened?"

"Gabe, let it go."

"I have a right to hear."

"Nonsense. No such right exists."

"I promised her I'd try to find out what was behind all this."

"Linnea Thorsell?"

"That's right."

"You had no business making a promise like that."

"It served a purpose at the time. The Brits were plying their cute artifice on her. She hates falsehood, and she wanted to quit. I talked her out of it. To build trust, I had to mean what I said. If I hadn't, she'd have known."

Donovan's blue eyes always had appeared cold. Now they were ice. He stood up and stepped to the globe. "What's the attachment between you and this woman less than half your age?"

"There is no attachment."

"Pure as the driven snow." Donovan's glare fixed on him, meaning *level with me.*

"There is no attachment," Verrick repeated. He had asked himself if his dealings with Linnea had induced some subconscious preterition in him. People said the subconscious was like the forest where the tree falls and nobody hears it. Who cared what they said. He didn't believe it.

Donovan's frown deepened. Their longstanding friendship bought a lot. It didn't buy everything. Learning from past wars, the American military had imposed on its upper ranks a ruthless standard: Fuck up, and you were out. The OSS had not embraced the mindset. It hadn't entirely escaped it, either. Donovan's indulgence stretched only so thin. He must be thinking it was time to sever the discussion and dismiss Verrick from the office, maybe dismiss him altogether.

"There's a second bigot list," Donovan said. "Elevated, they call it. The seal is absolute."

It took Verrick a minute to react. "Who is read in?"

"The Americans? The president, Marshall, Eisenhower, and me. The Brits didn't wish to include me at first. They found it impractical not to."

"Tell them to add me to the list."

"Inappropriate. Even if I did, and they were to agree, it wouldn't answer all your questions."

"Like why did they bring us into the damned thing to begin with? To dump the blame on us in case the Russians found out?"

"Why knock at a door that will never be opened? The select few who possess the full story won't breathe a word of it, not to you, me, or anyone."

Verrick might have taken the statement as his cue to leave. He stood where he was. *Go ahead, throw me out.* Donovan faced him. It seemed he did not want to throw his old friend out. They had reached an impasse. It helped that both were seasoned attorneys. The difference between an experienced and an inexperienced attorney was that the former tended to know how a given situation would unfold, and it lent efficiency to how he or she proceeded. Thus, two competing lawyers, having been around the block and in the absence of clients who expected all sorts of razzle-dazzle grandiloquence, table thumping, and fist shaking, could achieve accordance quickly.

Verrick said, "Let me ask Wentworth to add me to the list. If he says no, I'll walk away."

"No histrionics?" said Donovan.

"No histrionics."

He didn't have to add that he was giving his word. It went without saying.

The war had nourished select bureaucracies, and though the world was changing, the bureaucrats clung ferociously to the powers they had amassed, or thought they had. MI-6 was such a fiefdom. In this, the autumn of the war in western Europe, the United States overwhelmingly provisioned the resources and combat brawn, and a logic prevailed among many Americans that the lopsidedness should buy them a measure of influence, if not hegemony, in fields Britain heretofore had dominated. The British fought back with every punctilio and codicil at their disposal, wielding the resource of the island under their feet. American intelligence activities mounted from British soil could proceed only with MI-6's detailed review and concurrence. The Americans raged that the Brits were intrusive as hell, vetoing perfectly sound proposals for trivial reasons and imposing a stultifying oversight. The former colonial masters held their ground. If an American dared to mention that British intelligence officers in the United States blithely disregarded the limitations levied on them, they swept aside the point as irrelevant. Keep to the topic at hand, man.

It was this disputatious *mise-en-scène* that Casey's brilliant plans had cut through. Formalizing them nonetheless proved grueling. The British were their usual polished selves, quoting established agreements verbatim and lending weight to the finest nuances of the 'form of words' that the accords might take. Hours rolled by as the discussions stalled on the turn of a phrase or the tense of a verb. Casey's presence might have sped things along, but it turned out that the young spymaster was currently in France helping to prepare OSS agents soon to be infiltrated into Germany.

At the lunch break, he asked the British head man to pass along that he wished to meet personally with Sebastian Wentworth. The fellow simply nodded. Two days went by with no reply, and Verrick surmised that Wentworth had demurred. On the third day, to his astonishment, a folded slip of vellum came sliding across the table.

Gabriel,
To your request, meet me at Speakers' Corner, Hyde Park, at 8 p.m. tonight.
Pearlman

– 50 –

Late November 1944

From the OSS guest house, twelve minutes at a medium pace put Verrick at the famous corner Parliament had set aside for people to speak freely, provided they kept to certain rules. Was it a coincidence that Wentworth had chosen this spot, or another example of the MI-6 man's subtlety?

In the distance hulked the Marble Arch, where Verrick had met up with his son in February. Whether Matt currently was in England or somewhere on the Continent was anyone's guess. Not long ago, regiments of the 101st Airborne Division had participated in Operation Market Garden, a plan British Field Marshall Bernard Montgomery had avouched would open a corridor between the Allied lines east of Antwerp and the Rhine River at Arnhem, Holland. The audacious thrust had failed, costing many soldiers their lives. Only when Matt's letter arrived did Verrick and Grace know their son had survived. Naturally it said nothing about his current whereabouts.

From the south strode a figure in a black raincoat. Wentworth moved with an easy athleticism that suggested he'd have been as happy to run. He stretched out his hand. "Gabriel, so good to see you again. How goes the conference?"

"Fair progress. We'll probably need another day to iron things out and prepare the final agreement."

"An important and necessary endeavor. I don't envy you the work. Is there a point I can help with?"

"On the conference, no. I wanted to ask you about GALILEO."

"I see." Indeed he saw. That they were meeting at this odd spot was testament. "Behind us, isn't it? Please don't tell me you're one of those people."

Verrick had heard the expression on the lips of Englishmen before, the identities of 'those people' never specified. You had to suppose there were various types, none of them good. Wentworth must be referring to those who obstinately insisted on reviving matters already decided, embarrassing themselves and wasting everyone's time.

"I don't think so."

"Is this your own inquiry, or are you speaking officially?"

"Mine, though I obtained permission to ask."

They began to walk. Verrick, primed by the conference's wrangles over language, chose his words with care. "I'm told there's an elevated version of the GALILEO bigot list."

"Who informed you of this?"

"Donovan. He said nothing else about it."

"And you'd like to be added on."

"I would."

"Over my head, I'm afraid."

That might be true, but Wentworth had the power to recommend. He was saying he wouldn't.

"Might I try something else, then?" said Verrick. "A kind of game. I'll tell you what I *think* happened, and you say if I'm off the mark. Of course, you don't have to say anything, if you don't want to." *No histrionics.*

Wentworth seemed to ruminate. Deep in the park they were, no one around. Surely one inner voice advised him to decline, that to go along with the overture was unnecessary. A second adjuration must have reminded him he was an intelligence officer, and to listen, all that Verrick was asking him to do, was generally wise. There was a third whisper too, from the visionary who calculated that America's fledgling days in the intelligence field, and Britain's supremacy, were ending. What would follow? Perhaps William Donovan would not remain at the forefront when the Americans came into their own. Others would ascend. Verrick might be among them. Would it be judicious to turn him down?

Also, the sportsman in Wentworth liked games.

"I'll hear you out, within limits."

The limits, Verrick apprehended, equaled any accusation or tone Wentworth objected to, whereupon he would sever the discussion. The limits were as big as the world, and the line Verrick had to traverse as delicate as a taut thread.

"When you learned that Admiral Diefenbach would head the delegation to Sweden," Verrick began, "one of your first steps was to circulate a piece of disinformation to the effect that British commandos planned to attack the Germans in Stockholm. At first, I didn't grasp why you would spread a story that seemed both preposterous and counterproductive. Why invite security attention to the very target you were moving against?"

Wentworth said nothing.

"As you'd hoped, the SD seized on the report, not because they believed it, rather so they could use it to button up the man they suspected of being the elusive spy GALILEO. Maybe they thought the Soviets would try to spirit him out to stage a propaganda coup. The Soviets were *your* problem too; their involvement would have compounded things beyond measure. You had to keep them out.

"You needed a native Swedish speaker, someone who could gain entry to the Delfin Hotel. For the longest time, I couldn't get my head around why you needed a person who spoke native *Russian* too. Linnea's role was to deliver a message, one whose contents were in a coded letter written in *German* she was to hand to GALILEO. Anyone could have done that. Nonetheless, you took care to select a native-born Russian, so she could perfectly utter the lines you had scripted. Why? Because her recital wasn't meant to convince GALILEO of anything. It was for the benefit of those who were listening to and probably recording every word spoken. You knew GALILEO would be surveilled. How incompetent would the SD be, if they didn't have his hotel room covered? Your plan wasn't to praise Caesar. It was to burn him."

The Shakespeare paraphrase raised a subtle hint of amusement on the Englishman's countenance. He enjoyed wordplay. "Go on," he said.

"From among your clandestine Swedish allies, you put together a formidable team, not only Lars and his family, but your friends in the Swedish security services. They'd been watching the Delfin Hotel for a long time, and they'd recruited informants within. Who were the informants? The hotel's security manager? The Germans must have thought so; they had him killed. They went after the young kid too, the one who monitored the fourth floor. Why they suspected him, I'm not sure. He helped them capture Linnea.

"At your request, your Swedish friends took control of the room adjacent to the hotel's VIP suite and surreptitiously equipped it with some very special features: viewing portals and a hidden door. When the Nazi security team emplaced their listening devices around the suite, your friends were watching. They observed too as Linnea entered GALILEO's room and delivered her spiel. As soon as he ejected her, they entered via the hidden door, subdued him, opened the window, and hurled him out. Simultaneously, someone lit a bucket of rags in the basement and pulled the fire alarm. It created pandemonium. Was the alarm to help Linnea escape, or—and here I venture onto thin ice—was it to slow her down?"

"I object most vehemently to the insinuation," said Wentworth.

"As I said, I speculate."

"Do you honestly think these things play out according to some immaculate plan? Fieldwork amounts to ninety percent improvisation and responses taken on the fly as the situation develops."

"May I continue?"

Wentworth flicked a warning glance. "Yes."

"Do I believe you aimed for Linnea to be captured? I don't. Were you ready if she were? Certainly. It would be tricky, once she got in, to get out of that hotel full of Nazis. Her covers were designed to fail in cascade, first to the thief Thorgun Lindstrom, and secondly to the NKVD officer Vena Nadovska. You knew that if the Nazis captured her, they'd try to get her to Germany for a professional interrogation, and that they'd head either to the airfield or to a German freighter in port. They chose the latter. You had studied the possible routes, and you intercepted them on the way, your agents making quite the show of speaking Russian. What was it you said about responses taken on the fly as the situation develops? This one was not like that. It was choreographed in advance and as honed as a scalpel."

Wentworth might have objected to the pronouncement. He didn't. Perhaps he liked to hear his brilliance applauded, even if applause wasn't what Verrick had in mind.

"Everything hinged on putting that letter into GALILEO's hands, and by extension, the SD's. That he burned the original made no difference to you; your men had a copy, and they left it in the room where it was certain to be found. What was in the letter? I assume it had something to do with the so-called Galilean Moons, the sub-agents.

"Maria Toft was your double agent, a German Afrikaner. At some point in the course of her long service, you dangled her to the Soviets. She ended up as the NKVD's cutout to GALILEO, and she learned chapter and verse about him and reported it to you. Soon after Germany invaded the Soviet

Union, the SD commenced a fierce spy hunt. Her life was at risk. You planned to get her out of Berlin, but you had to proceed with caution; the Soviets were your new allies, and they hadn't granted her the permission to flee. One of the last things she did at your behest was to conceal in her apartment some torn up notes whose contents you'd devised. They pointed to the existence of four sub-agents. You hoped that soon after she was gone, the Nazis would find, reassemble, and decrypt the scraps. Though Maria never made it out, the SD did as you'd envisioned. They named the sub-agents after the Galilean Moons, inaptly, as it turns out. The moons of Jupiter exist, you can see them with a telescope. These other Moons, you can't, because they aren't real. What better stratagem in war, than to waste the time of your enemy?

"Maria's death vexed the SD. Bletchley Park deciphered their communications, and you read about how well you'd done. For nearly three years they chased after the elusive Moons, never getting any closer. Their fixation gave you a card to play, but like all cards it was only as good as the timing of its use and the hand it fit. You needed just the right moment, and you waited."

In the weak light, he caught the tightness of Wentworth's expression.

Verrick said, "Now I've gone as far as I can go. I don't know why you played it the way you did. What in God's name was worth all this?"

There were people ahead, and to avoid them the MI-6 man veered onto one of the diverging paths. They walked along, the only sound their footfalls. The tree branches scythed overhead. It seemed that no reply would be forthcoming. Verrick was one of those people after all. He had wasted everyone's time.

Wentworth said, "He saved her life."

"Who did?"

"The Swedish boy, the one you referred to. He spent some minutes in the big ruffian's company listening to his tales of bloodlust. If the boy hadn't seized her, the German would have shot her in the back."

Verrick digested this. "So I'm right."

"To whom else have you related this theory of yours?"

"No one."

"Not even to your friend Casey?"

"No. I haven't talked to him in months."

"I need something from you: Your irrevocable word of honor you shall repeat nothing of what you just told me or what I'm about to say, neither to Casey nor Linnea nor anyone else. You will write nothing down, transmit nothing."

"What about to Donovan?"

"He's already witting. I daresay he would regard it as water under the bridge. I ask you to give me your unconditional promise."

"She thinks she's failed, and she'll go on thinking so unless she's told the truth."

"I doubt it haunts her. If it does, she'll get by. There's a war on, if you recall."

Verrick almost couldn't agree. The implications were too heavy. Long had the notion tumbled in his head that he would keep his promise to Linnea and relate what had been at the heart of the mission. Reassure her she hadn't failed. If he gave his word, he could tell her nothing meaningful. In fact, he'd have to lie to her.

Or he could decline, and the truth about GALILEO would elude him. It would elude her, too.

Either way, she lost.

"You have my word," he said.

Wentworth cleared his throat.

"At the beginning of this year, a regrettable incident occurred. If it had involved anyone else, we would have called it a tragic embarrassment. With the officer in question, it was nothing short of a catastrophe. A Royal Navy Lieutenant, Benedict Callahan by name, working on the OVERLORD naval plans, on some misguided whim decided to take a joyride over France with an RAF friend of his. The mission was photo reconnaissance, not so chancy as it would have been in the past, we had air superiority by then, and the pilot had flown dozens of recons. But what was quotidian to the pilot was to his friend Callahan the thrill of a lifetime, and so our naval officer who knew the locus of the invasion, information that could lose the war if divulged to the enemy, donned a flight suit, jammed himself into the tight cockpit of a

Spitfire Mk 16 where you wouldn't think two could fit—rail thin, these chaps must have been—and off they went. The pilot flew low on the photo run. So fast and maneuverable is the Spit, it doesn't often fall prey to flak. By a one-in-a-thousand chance, a German 88 unit in the vicinity scored a hit on the plane's engine. The aircraft plowed into a French farm field, the pilot dead probably before they hit the ground. Callahan was injured, we're not certain how severely.

"The Germans who captured him immediately were curious why this single-seat aircraft had carried two men. Clearly the survivor was not air crew. He must be something else, perhaps a spy to be parachuted into France. They turned him over to the SS, who evoked Hitler's so-called Commando Order mandating the execution of commandos and spies, after questioning, if needed.

"Here was where our otherwise unforgivably irresponsible fellow did the unexpected, you might say the exceptional. He held out. Refused to answer their questions. The SS resorted to drugs and torture. Had they been experts in their craft, they'd probably have broken him. As it was, they killed him. Injuries from the crash may have sped his demise. What they extracted was no more than a jumble of words, many unintelligible. Bletchley Park intercepted the interrogation report. Believe me, it makes for dreadful reading, essentially incoherent, just page upon page of seemingly random words and nine numbers rounded to the tens. We gave it to our own savants to try to make sense of. They couldn't. Meaningless blather, they concluded. A damned lucky turn.

"The SS team sent their transcript to the Gestapo headquarters in Berlin. Perhaps because there was nothing else the Gestapo could do with it, they delivered it to the Abwehr, the military intelligence service, to a career naval officer named Wilhelm Mauer. We had heard of him. An uncannily gifted chap, Mauer. He was the one who, as a member of an investigatory commission in 1941, contended that the German Enigma formula might have been broken. Thank God no one else on the commission accepted his theory. Nonetheless, the German Navy, as a precaution based on his independent appraisal that Admiral Canaris forwarded to them, strengthened their encryption machinery for U-Boat communications. Caused us a world of trouble."

"What did Mauer do with the interrogation report?"

Wentworth halted, reached in his coat, and extracted a small notebook. He spent a minute drawing something with his fountain pen and held the page out. "What do you see?"

In the crepuscular light, Verrick had to squint to make out a pattern of semi-vertical lines, parallel at the bottom, diverging at the top, tracing what resembled an art-deco Y. "No idea," he said.

"Can you imagine a smokestack, a stylized one?"

"If you say so."

"In the interrogation report's hodgepodge of ostensibly random utterances, some appeared more than once. 'Smokestack' showed up four times. Mauer concentrated on the word. He examined the numbers, which were rounded to the tens, ranging between 30 and 170. Generalized numbers did not accord with a proper military plan, and there were not nearly enough of them to fill in the many sea lanes an invasion would entail. He visualized the smokestack as a kind of planning template, and he applied the numbers to give it scale. He assigned the larger numbers to the upper, wider extensions of the smoke, the shorter ones at the lower stack as parallels, hypothesizing they must point to somewhere along the north coast of France. Where, he asked himself, could a figure of such dimensions fit? It happens that, due to the peculiar geography of the English Channel, only one location works. The smoke and stack converge at roughly 50 degrees north latitude. Mauer's concept was simplistic compared to the actual NEPTUNE plan that labeled the confluence as Area Z, an oval the planners informally nicknamed Piccadilly Circus. His fundamental deduction nonetheless held, predicting that the invasion would happen at the Bay of the Seine, Normandy."

"Jesus."

"From the Bletchley Park intercepts, we saw that the Germans were intrigued. They showed Mauer's paper to Hitler. The obliquity of the logic fascinated the Führer. All he had to do was to shift two additional Panzer divisions to the Normandy coast, as General Rommel was urging him to do, and the Wehrmacht would have had the combat power at hand to wreak havoc on the landings. It seemed we would have to rethink the invasion plans. That's when we remembered the card you referred to."

"You used the Sophia letter to discredit Mauer."

"Precisely. When deciphered, it branded him as one of the Moons, a sub-agent who had worked for GALILEO. By extension, his theory had to be disinformation. The Nazis thereupon tossed it in the rubbish. Hitler tilted toward General von Rundstedt's view that the Pas de Calais would be the invasion site, and he withheld the additional Panzer divisions Rommel wanted moved to the Normandy coast. Only after the invasion were these units given their march orders, and ravaged by air attacks, they took days to close the distance. By then, it was too late. The Allied beachhead was irreversibly established."

"What happened to Mauer?"

"Arrested. His wife, too. *Sippenhaft*, they call it when they blame a person for the crimes of a relative. Or perhaps they suspected she was another of the Moons. The two were questioned but confessed to nothing. They might have survived; the invasion occurred just where Mauer had foretold. But the assassination attempt against Hitler in July doomed everyone in any way tainted with disloyalty, proven or unproven. Mauer and his wife were executed at Plötzensee Prison."

Verrick was struck silent. A man destroyed because he was good at his work. The sheer ruthlessness of it.

What would have happened to his son, he thought, had those additional Panzer divisions been waiting when he parachuted into Normandy? What would have happened to all those men?

Wentworth went on: "You may ask, why should we strive to keep our achievement a high secret? The answer is threefold. First, we don't wish to advertise how the negligence of a British officer almost cost us OVERLORD, there's national pride at stake, no trivial matter in time of war. Second, the Soviets would be very discontented to learn of our meddling with their agent, not to mention the outrage of the Swedish government that we infringed on their neutral soil. Third, our insights could not have come about except through the codebreaking marvels of Bletchley Park. These will remain of tantamount importance far into the future and must not be exposed. You grasp the implications, surely."

They had looped around to Speakers' Corner, where the mist had thickened; Verrick could not see the Marble Arch anymore. "Congratulations, Sebastian. Your service has lived up to its reputation."

"Thank you. Keep in mind that GALILEO wasn't the only deception undertaken on behalf of the invasion. Others fed false information to the Germans to make them think the landings, once they happened, were a feint.

Yet I believe that our contribution in Stockholm remains second to none, and the more so it was, the less we can talk about it, in fact, not at all."

Wentworth did not have to speak the words that shouted in Verrick's head: *And neither can you.*

– 51 –

Late February to Late November 1944

For two weeks following Linnea's return to Britain, the OSS kept her at the familiar safehouse, where she underwent a debriefing by Bill Casey, regained her health, and ate altogether too sumptuously. She occupied the same room where she'd been locked in, only now she had the key and came and went as she pleased, taking long walks to burn off the calories from the rich meals. On the day she finally returned to Factory House, she asked herself, how could six weeks have changed a place so much? A rufous-haired, stuffy British Army major now led the section, replacing Alistair Bird, promoted to a higher echelon. And several of the section's analysts had been transferred elsewhere, among them her friend Ivett, and Dodgy Dray as well.

In Linnea's absence, the Eastern Europe portfolio had gone to another analyst. Linnea got Italy, the same Italy she knew next to nothing about. Fresh people arrived. One was a limping, dire-countenanced British lieutenant named Charles—no one dared call him Charlie or Chuck—who'd lost half his right foot in North Africa from treading on a land mine. Sickly thin he was, diffident and handsome too, with a hidden mischievous side. He helped her to devise tricks, some too elaborate to be enacted but delightful to think about. He paid no attention to her maimed hand, and she none to his foot. They became conspirators and friends.

By chance she caught wind of a report from weeks ago, to the effect that the Soviets on 22 February had bombed Stockholm. She looked the incident up. The Swedes seemed to have shrugged it off as a mishap of war. Yet how could a bombing within days of GALILEO's death have been a coincidence? The Soviets had blamed the wrong people, she thought. *I killed him.*

The long-awaited invasion struck the Normandy coast, succeeding without the help of the agent the British had tried to snare on the German General Staff. She read of the beach landings, the parachute jumps behind enemy lines, soot-faced men leaping out of planes into the flak-streaked night. Verrick had told her his son was in the 101st Airborne Division. She prayed the boy was safe. She skimmed a transcript of German propaganda that called U.S. paratroopers *übelste Untermenschentum amerikascher slums:* the most abject sub-humanity of American slums. Well, at least one of them was the son of a well-off New York attorney who lived in a posh upper-west-side apartment. So there.

As the summer ensued, the damned buzz bombs—Hitler's so-called *Vergeltungswaffen,* revenge weapons—began to wreak havoc all over London. Then came the V2 rockets that hit with no warning whatsoever. Once more, thousands fled the capital.

In late July, the Allies commenced their breakout from Normandy. General Bradley's forces, Patton's Third Army in the lead, surged across France. Exhilarating, to follow their fantastic progress. Paris liberated! The Soviet front advanced to within 330 miles of Berlin. A massive tragedy unfolded in Warsaw, where the Polish underground launched an uprising against the Germans, who after initial reversals reinforced their ranks and destroyed the capital, killing 200,000. The Red Army, just 12 miles to the east, did nothing to help the outgunned Poles. Stalin even refused permission for the western Allies to use airfields in Soviet-controlled territory to resupply the partisans. The prognostication in the report MI-6 had spiked had come true.

Linnea mastered the Italy account. The liberation of Rome multiplied her workload, her eight fingers typing the assessments keeping fervent pace. The typing slowed. Having butted against the Gothic Line in Italy's mountainous north, the Allies set their priority to pin down the German forces rather than to seize terrain. The autumn rains guttered the campaign into a grim stalemate in which little changed from day to day. She took the opportunity to pitch her idea for a paper on European post-war prospects to the new section head, Major Cary.

He fingered his bristly red mustache. "Aren't you a bit *junior* to take on such a far-seeing piece?"

"I think I'm up to it. The emphasis will be on Eastern Europe. I'm well acquainted."

He grunted and promised to mull it over. In their spare minutes, she and Charles schemed pranks to play on him.

The autumn brought hopes for the war's imminent end. Even the prudent U.S. Army Chief of Staff, General George Marshall, predicted it would be over by Christmas. The weather faded. So did the hopes. Not only did the Nazis refuse to collapse, facing the Allied forces in Holland during Operation Market Garden, the German Army fought tenaciously. To an analytical mind, it made no sense that a regime would choose to prolong its people's suffering and inflict the same upon the world, when it was plain they'd already lost. How could the Germans remain loyal to Hitler, a madman? The conflict raged on, a slap in the face to human decency and rationality.

London turned chilly. She tacked up her **Сибирь** sign pointing from her map of the Italian boot to her desk, her right hand bunching the edges of the woolen shawl at her neck, while with the three fingers of her left she flipped the pages of the daily traffic. An analyst's life was to read and read. Sometimes packets of clipped-together administrative bulletins made the rounds. Habitually she glanced at the subject lines and skipped the rest; almost never did they say anything she cared about. In mid-November, she came upon a classified circular blandly announcing that a capacious meeting room in Whitehall would not be available on such-and-such dates because of a scheduled Anglo-American intelligence conference. The bulletin named the leaders of the respective delegations. Heading the American side would be Mr. Gabriel Verrick.

She almost leapt up from her desk. He was coming to London, the one person she could speak to openly about what had happened!

She calmed herself. It was important she convey her suspicions cogently, without emotion. She would leave nothing out, she'd even show Verrick her mutilated hand, she wouldn't be embarrassed, not with him. Why did she regard him so? He wasn't her personal confessor. Nonetheless she could hardly wait. She had to think he wanted to speak to her as well.

Will I see you when I get back?

Count on it.

She pondered whether to reach out to him, perhaps to leave a message for him at OSS London. But no, she was a junior officer, and for her to ask to see him would raise eyebrows. Far easier, she thought, that he should contact her. During the given dates, she awaited the summons, the notification she had a phone call or that a car was waiting outside. At lunchtime when she walked back from the dining hall with Charles—she had to slow her pace to match his—she scanned the street for the sedan pulling to the curb, the back door falling open, beckoning her. Verrick must know she longed to speak to him, to tell him of her suspicions, especially the one that had evolved in her mind since her return, that the real mission hadn't been to gain control of GALILEO but rather to compromise him to the Nazis. But why had the Brits gone about it *this* way? Maybe, their heads together, she and Verrick could sift out the truth.

It didn't happen. November eclipsed. He was gone.

He hadn't wished to see her because she'd failed.

There it was. She didn't often dwell on it. A tough business, war. In the end, doing your best wasn't what counted. Winning was, and she hadn't won.

He hadn't even called. Perhaps it wouldn't have mattered so much to her, had she not chosen to trust him.

Her instincts about him had been wrong.

Her evening meal finished, she strode alone toward her barracks. The weather mirrored her inner rawness, the wind off the Thames blasting discourteously in her face. She leaned into it. If she'd wanted to, she could have taken the bus. She preferred to walk, though whether for exercise or out of a kind of penance she couldn't say.

Five paces ahead, a black sedan veered to the curb. The passenger-side door fell open, and out stepped not Verrick, but raven-haired, better-that-you-don't-say-anything Sebastian Wentworth. He said, "Brisk one tonight, eh?"

He had re-donned his three-piece suit, and the sight whisked her to a Saturday evening she'd spent with Charles not long ago, a few private hours stolen together to celebrate Martinmas. Nothing wrong with that, they were friends. Did she trust him? Not entirely, her cuts from misplaced trust ran too deep. She harked for the lie, the hint he was trying to manipulate her. He had not done so yet. Maybe he wouldn't. She kept vigil.

Didn't mean she couldn't enjoy his company.

Somehow the topic of their voice-muted, somewhat gin-soaked conversation spun to English school neckties that Charles was able to recognize by their striping. She tested him, describing Wentworth's, of black, or perhaps it was deep blue, with pale blue stripes, not a sound test because she didn't know the answer herself. She revealed nothing else about the wearer, neither his name nor the circumstances in which she had encountered him.

Charles said, "Was there a touch of green in the pale blue?"

"Maybe a subtle shading."

"Well then, I'd give odds it's an Eton tie, and an Eton man beneath. Was he finely dressed, the gent?"

She rested her head on his shoulder, conjuring Wentworth. "Very."

"Splendidly cut?"

"The man or the suit?"

"Both."

"I suppose. The suit was elegant, the man confident and distinctive."

"Sounds like one accustomed to strutting the venerable halls of power." Disapproval pierced his remark. He was from a modest Fens family whose outlook he classified as 'bred-in-the-bones Labour Party,' and mellowed from the flask he had brought along, his words became a lyric. "Many are the ways to distinguish a man such as he: the bespoke garments, the superior bearing, the air of unflappability, his every word the most fitting. He conforms to the lofty social stratum he occupies, and it to him, hand in glove. What really defines him, if you look closely, is the column of ghosts who trail in his wake. They're the ones who've given their all so he can be the man he is."

"You're joking."

"Not something I'd joke about. I've seen too many like him."

He was a little drunk, and she was happy for him, poor, wispy soul. Yet his appraisal of Wentworth was unkind. Too cynical. Then again, maybe it was true. She had barely escaped becoming one of those ghosts herself.

She took a minute to regain her composure. "How are you, sir?"

Wentworth smiled. "Well, thank you. Do you mind if I walk with you? I'll give you a lift to your barracks after."

"All right."

They leaned into the wind, and when they were well away from the car, he said, "You may be aware that Verrick visited London recently."

"I am."

"Did you speak to him?"

"No. I had hoped to. He didn't call."

"Unfortunate. My doing, really."

"Oh?"

"I put him under a stern oath to say nothing to you about the mission. I suppose he thought it better not to contact you, than to do so and not be able to say a word relevant. Or else to lie. I don't think he could. Not to you."

"What would he have to lie about?"

"He was worried you'd feel you had failed. How could he inform you otherwise? It set me to thinking, better to tell you than not."

"Tell me what?"

"You didn't fail. You succeeded by every measure. Please take it to heart. It's true, though I cannot reveal how."

They pressed into the wind. The car, she noticed, was creeping along at a distance behind. She said, "Thank you. The fact is, I try not to think about it anymore."

"So much the better. Soon the war will end, and we'll move on, all of us. These matters will fade into the past."

"Is Avry well?"

"He is."

Should she ask Wentworth if what she suspected was true, that Avry and Lars and maybe the mysterious government man had thrown GALILEO from the hotel window? That they'd pulled the fire alarm? And the meanest of all, the one that haunted her: had they intended her to be captured?

No point asking. He wouldn't say.

She took the ride, at whose end she shook his hand and exited at the compound's gate. The car chuntered off. Good, he was gone. What had been the purpose of his brief stop-by? Had he revealed anything, or was this another meaningless pat on the back? It was as if, in the guise of kindness, he was checking up to make sure she was keeping mum. Yes, that was probably the reason.

He'd given her something, nonetheless.

I suppose he thought it better not to contact you, than to do so and not be able to say a word relevant. Or else to lie. I don't think he could. Not to you.

The wind buffeted her. She didn't notice. In her mind, she was in the lush meadow, the one from her dream the night before the boxing training. Her bare feet brushed through the cool grass, and she chased her friends among the soft loam trees swishing like dogs' tails under an indigo sky, and for an instant there came the rapturous serenity only children can feel.

She stopped at the post office and from her box collected a letter from her mother. She'd not informed her she'd lost two of her fingers. How would she explain? Maybe tell the same tale she had to Charles and her other colleagues at Factory House, that she'd accidentally slammed her fingers in a car door. Oh, how her mom would fuss. Cup her face and sob, my poor, poor darling.

Then she'd accept it.

Jeff Wallace lives with his family in southwestern Virginia. His prior historical-suspense novels are *The Man Who Walked Out of the Jungle* and *Rapidan*.

www.ingramcontent.com/pod-product-compliance
Lightning Source LLC
Chambersburg PA
CBHW050535260626
47157CB00002B/307